Paris Noir

ALSO EDITED BY MAXIM JAKUBOWSKI FROM CLIPPER LARGE PRINT

London Noir

Paris Noir

Capital Crime Fiction

Edited by

Maxim Jakubowski

W F HOWES LTD

This large print edition published in 2008 by
W F Howes Ltd
Unit 4, Rearsby Business Park, Gaddesby Lane,
Rearsby, Leicester LE7 4YH

1 3 5 7 9 10 8 6 4 2

First published in the United Kingdom in 2007
by Serpent's Tail

A CIP catalogue record for this book is available
from the British Library

ISBN 978 1 40742 489 7

Typeset by Palimpsest Book Production Limited,
Grangemouth, Stirlingshire
Printed and bound in Great Britain
by MPG Books Ltd, Bodmin, Cornwall

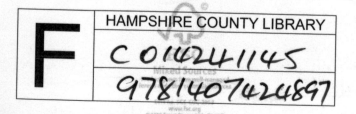

CONTENTS

INTRODUCTION

MAXIM JAKUBOWSKI

By a twist of fate, my parents moved to France when I was only three years old and my first encounter with the dark side of Paris was when, a year or so later, I was parachuted into the *école maternelle* and, little British boy that I happened to be (albeit with a Polish name of sorts), was quickly bullied and mildly beaten up by all the other kids because, a long-lasting grievance in France, the British had once burned Joan of Arc!

Needless to say, becoming fluent in French became a personal priority, and I promptly made certain my true nationality was soon forgotten as well as finding out that Joan of Arc's fiery demise was actually at the hands of her French compatriots . . .

To cut a long story short, I went on to live in Paris until my mid-twenties and have since cultivated a curious relationship with France and the French. But my love of Paris has never changed, a city of delights and contradictions which still manages to fascinate, surprise and unsettle me on every visit to old and new haunts. Much better commentators than me have waxed rhapsodic over the centuries about this city of light, its culture, its geography, its soul, its uniqueness, but being a foreigner in Paris, a spy beneath my bilingual cloak, has also allowed me different insights into the character of the city, its rainbow assortment of people and quirks. Indeed, Paris has proven a magnet for decades to generations of foreign writers, artists, more than just tourists, and this head-on clash of visions has generated some truly wonderful books, films and art.

When I decided to follow up my *London Noir* volume of crime and dark stories of over ten years ago, it became quickly obvious to me that I should tackle Paris, if only to compare my own vision of the city with that of others with different backgrounds, tastes and idiosyncrasies. I knew that many crime and mystery writers of my acquaintance had also spent time there or, in some cases, still made regular visits, and it made sense to invite a rather prestigious assortment of authors each to interpret the theme of Paris Noir in their own inimitable way. I think the results speak for themselves and offer a rich and varied panorama of Paris today, a psycho-history through the lens of noir fiction.

The writers and friends who climbed on board hail from the UK, the USA, Canada and also France, and all confess to an ambiguous relationship with the French capital. Some stories embrace history and politics, others examine crime and social ills, yet others even skirt fantasy, but all display a strong sense of place and take the reader on a thrilling ride through familiar and unfamiliar streets and *quartiers*, which even the literary tourist knows little about.

Tighten your seat belts, *Mesdames et Messieurs*.

MINOR KEY

JOHN HARVEY

It used to be there under *Birthdays*, some years at least. The daily listing in the paper, the *Guardian*, occasionally *The Times*. 18 September. Valentine Collins, jazz musician. And then his age: 27, 35, 39. Not 40. Val never reached 40.

He'd always look, Val, after the first time he was mentioned, made a point of it, checking to see if his name was there. 'Never know,' he'd say, with that soft smile of his – 'Never know if I'm meant to be alive or dead.'

There were times when we all wondered; wondered what it was going to be. Times when he seemed to be chasing death so hard, he had to catch up. Times when he didn't care.

Jimmy rang me this morning, not long after I'd got back from the shops. Bread, milk, eggs – the paper – gives me something to do, a little walk, reason to stretch my legs.

'You all right?' he says.

'Of course I'm all right.'

'You know what day it is?'

I hold my breath; there's no point in shouting,

losing my temper. 'Yes, Jimmy, I know what day it is.'

There's a silence and I can sense him reaching for the words, the thing to say – 'You don't fancy meeting up later? A drink, maybe? Nice to have a chat. It's been a while.'

'OK, then, Anna,' he says instead, and then he hangs up.

There was a time when we were inseparable, Jimmy, Val, Patrick and myself. Studio 51, the Downbeat Club, all-nighters at the Flamingo, coffee at the Bar Italia, spaghetti at the Amalfi. That place on Wardour Street where Patrick swore the cheese omelettes were the best he'd ever tasted and Val would always punch the same two buttons on the jukebox, B19 and 20, both sides of Ella Fitzgerald's single, 'Manhattan' and 'Every Time We Say Goodbye'.

Val loved that song, especially.

He knew about goodbyes, Val.

Later, anyway.

Back then it was just another sad song, something to still the laughter. Which is what I remember most from those years, the laughter. The four of us marching arm in arm through the middle of Soho, carefree, laughing.

What do they call them? The fifties? The years of austerity? That's not how I remember them, '56, '57, '58. Dancing, music and fun, that's what they were to me. But then, maybe I was too young, too unobservant, too – God! it seems impossible to believe or say – but, yes, too innocent to know what was already there, beneath the surface. Too stupid to read the signs.

Patrick, for instance, turning away from the rest of us to have quick, intense conversations in corners with strangers, men in sharp suits and sharp hair-cuts, Crombie overcoats. The time Patrick himself suddenly arrived one evening in a spanking new three-piece suit from Cecil Gee, white shirt with a rolled Mr B collar, soft Italian shoes, and when we asked him where the cash came from for all that, only winking and tapping the side of his nose with his index finger – mind yours.

Val, those moments when he'd go quiet and stare off into nowhere and you knew, without anyone saying, that you couldn't speak to him, couldn't touch him, just had to leave him be until he'd turn, almost shyly, and smile with his eyes.

And Jimmy, the way he'd look at me when he thought no one else was noticing; how he couldn't bring himself to say the right words to me, even then.

And if I had seen them, the signs of our future, would it have made any difference, I wonder? Or would it all have turned out the same? Sometimes you only see what you want to until something presses your face so fast up against it there's nothing else you can do.

But in the beginning it was the boys and myself and none of us with a care in the world. Patrick and Jimmy had known one another since they were little kids at primary school, altar boys together at St Pat's; Val had met up with them later, the second year of the grammar school – and me, I'd been lucky enough to live in the same street, catch the same bus in the morning, lucky enough that Jimmy's mother and mine should be friends. The boys were into jazz, jazz and football – though for Patrick it was the Arsenal and for Jimmy, Spurs, and the rows they had about that down the years. Val now, in truth I don't think Val ever cared too much about the football, just went along, White Hart Lane or Highbury, he didn't mind.

When it came to jazz, though, it was Val who took the lead, and where the others would have been happy enough to listen to anything as long as it had rhythm, excitement, as long as it had swing, Val was the one who sat them down and made them listen to Gerry Mulligan with Chet Baker, Desmond with Brubeck, Charlie Parker, Lester Young.

With a few other kids they knew, they made themselves into a band: Patrick on trumpet, Jimmy on drums, Val with an ageing alto saxophone that had belonged to his dad. After the first couple of rehearsals it became clear Val was the only one who could really play. I mean really play: the kind of sound that gives you goose bumps on the arms and makes the muscles of your stomach tighten hard.

It wasn't long before Patrick had seen the writing on the wall and turned in his trumpet in favour of becoming agent and manager rolled into one; about the first thing he did was sack Jimmy from the band, Val's was the career to foster and Jimmy was just holding him back.

A couple of years later, Val had moved on from sitting in with Jackie Sharpe and Tubby Hayes at the Manor House, and depping with Oscar Rabin's band at the Lyceum, to fronting a quartet that slipped into the lower reaches of the *Melody Maker* small group poll. Val was burning the proverbial candle, going on from his regular gig to some club where he'd play till the early hours, and taking more Bennies than was prudent to keep himself awake. The result was, more than once, he showed up late for an engagement; occasionally, he didn't show up at all. Patrick gave him warning after warning. Val, in return, made promises he couldn't keep; in the end, Patrick delivered an ultimatum, and finally walked away.

Within months the quartet broke up and, needing ready cash, Val took a job with Lou Preager's orchestra at the Lyceum: a musical diet that didn't stretch far beyond playing for dancers, the occasional novelty number and the hits of the day. At least when he'd been with Rabin there'd been a few other jazzers in the band – and Oscar had allowed them one number a night to stretch out and do their thing. But this – the boredom, the routine were killing him, and Val, I realised later, had moved swiftly on from chewing the insides of Benzedrine inhalers and smoking cannabis to injecting heroin. When the police raided a club in Old Compton Street in the small hours, there was Val in a back room with a needle in his arm.

Somehow, Patrick knew one of the detectives at West End Central well enough to call in a grudging favour. Grudging, but a favour all the same.

When Val stumbled out on to the pavement, twenty-four hours later and still wearing the clothes he'd puked up on, Patrick pushed him into a cab and took him to the place where I was living in Kilburn.

I made tea, poured Patrick the last of a half bottle of whisky, and ran a bath for Val, who was sitting on the side of my bed in his vest and under-pants, shivering.

'You're a stupid bastard. You know that, don't you?' Patrick told him.

Val said nothing.

'He's a musician, I told the copper,' Patrick said. 'A good one. And you know what he said to me? All he is, is another black junkie out of his fucking head on smack. Send him back where he fucking came from.'

A shadow of pain passed across Val's face and I looked away, ashamed, not knowing what to say. Val's father was West Indian, his mother Irish, his skin the colour of palest chocolate.

'Can you imagine?' Patrick said, turning to me. 'All those years and I never noticed.' Reaching out, he took hold of Val's jaw and twisted his face upwards towards the light. 'Look at that. Black as the ace of fucking spades. Not one of us at all.'

'Stop it,' I said. 'Stop it, for God's sake. What's the matter with you?'

Patrick loosed his hold and stepped away. 'Trying to shake some sense into him. Make him realise, way he's going, what'll happen if he carries on.'

He moved closer to Val and spoke softly. 'They've got your number now, you know that, don't you? Next time they catch you as much as smelling of reefer they're going to have you inside so fast your feet won't touch the ground. And you won't like it inside, believe me.'

Val closed his eyes.

'What you need is to put a little space between you and them, give them time to forget.' Patrick stepped back. 'Give me a couple of days, I'll sort something. Even if it's the Isle of Man.'

In the event, it was Paris. A two-week engagement at Le Chat Qui Pêche with an option to extend it by three more.

'You better go with him, Anna. Hold his hand, keep him out of trouble.' And slipping an envelope fat with French francs and two sets of tickets into my hand, he kissed me on the cheek. 'Just his hand, mind.'

The club was on the rue de la Huchette, close to the Seine, a black metal cat perched above a silver-grey fish on the sign outside; downstairs a small, smoky cellar bar with a stage barely big enough for piano, bass and drums, and, for seating, perhaps the most uncomfortable stools I've ever known. Instruments of torture, someone called them and, by the end of the first week, I knew exactly what he meant.

Not surprisingly, the French trio with whom Val was due to work were suspicious of him at first. His reputation in England may have been on the rise, but across the Channel he was scarcely known. And when you're used to visitors of the calibre of Miles Davis, Bud Powell, Charlie Parker, what gave Val Collins the idea he'd be welcome? Didn't the French have saxophone players of their own?

Both the bassist and the drummer wore white shirts that first evening, I remember, ties loosened, top buttons undone, very cool; the pianist's dark jacket was rucked up at the back, its collar arched awkwardly against his neck, a cigarette smouldering, half-forgotten, at the piano's edge.

Val and I accepted a glass of wine from the proprietor and sat listening, the club not yet half full, Val's foot moving to the rhythm and his fingers flexing over imaginary keys. At the intermission, we were introduced to the band, who shook hands politely, looked at Val with cursory interest and excused themselves to stretch their legs outside, breathe in a little night air.

'Nice guys,' Val said with a slight edge as they left.

12

'You'll be fine,' I said and squeezed his arm.

When the trio returned, Val was already on stage, re-angling the mike, adjusting his reed. 'Blues in F,' he said quietly, counting in the tempo, medium-fast. After a single chorus from the piano, he announced himself with a squawk and then a skittering run and they were away. Ten minutes later, when Val stepped back from the microphone, layered in sweat, the drummer gave a little triumphant roll on his snare, the pianist turned and held out his hand and the bass player loosened another button on his shirt and grinned.

'*Et maintenant,*' Val announced, testing his tender vocabulary to the full, '*nous jouons une ballade par* Ira Gershwin *et* Vernon Duke, 'I Can't Get Started'. Merci.'

And the crowd, accepting him, applauded.

What could go wrong?

At first, nothing it seemed. We both slept late most days at the hotel on the rue Maître-Albert where we stayed; adjacent rooms that held a bed, a small wardrobe and little else, but with views across towards Notre Dame. After coffee and croissants – we were in Paris, after all – we would wander around the city, the streets of Saint-Germain-des-Prés at first, but then, gradually, we found our way around Montparnasse and up through Montmartre to Sacré Coeur. Sometimes we would take in a late afternoon movie, and Val would have a nap at the hotel before a leisurely dinner and on to the club for that evening's session, which would continue until the early hours.

Six nights a week and on the seventh, rest?

There were other clubs to visit, other musicians to hear. The Caveau de la Huchette was just across the street, the Club Saint-Germain-des-Prés and the Trois Mailletz both a short walk away. Others, like the Tabou and the Blue Note, were a little further afield. I couldn't keep up.

'Go back to the hotel,' Val said, reading the tiredness in my eyes. 'Get a good night's sleep, a proper rest.' Then, with the beginnings of a smile, 'You don't have to play nursemaid all the time, you know.'

'Is that what I'm doing?'

Coming into the club late one evening, I saw him in the company of an American drummer we'd met a few nights before and a couple of broad-shouldered French types, wearing those belted trench coats which made them look like cops or gangsters or maybe both. As soon as he spotted me, Val made a quick show of shaking hands and turning away, but not before I saw a small package pass from hand to hand and into the inside pocket of his suit.

'Don't look so disapproving,' he said, when I walked over. 'Just a few pills to keep me awake.'

'And that's all?'

'Of course.' He had a lovely, disarming smile.

'No smack?'

'No smack.'

I could have asked him to show me his arms, but I chose to believe him instead. It would have made little difference if I had; by then I think he was injecting himself in the leg.

The next day Val was up before eleven, dressed and ready, stirring me from sleep.

'What's happening?' I asked. 'What's wrong?'

'Nothing. Just a shame to waste a beautiful day.'

The winter sun reflected from the stonework of the bridge as we walked across to the Ile St-Louis arm in arm. Val had taken to affecting a beret, which he wore slanting extravagantly to one side. On the cobbles close to where we sat, drinking coffee, sparrows splashed in the shallow puddles left by last night's rain.

'Why did you do it?' Val asked me.

'Do it?'

'This. All of this. Throwing up your job—'

'It wasn't a real job.'

'It was work.'

'It was temping in a lousy office for a lousy boss.'

'And this is better?'

'Of course this is better.'

'I still don't understand why?'

'Why come here with you?'

Val nodded.

'Because he asked me.'

'Patrick.'

'Yes, Patrick.'

'You do everything he asks you?'

I shook my head. 'No. No, I don't.'

'You will,' he said. 'You will.' I couldn't see his eyes; I didn't want to see his eyes.

A foursome of tourists, Scandinavian I think, possibly German, came and sat noisily at a table nearby. When the waiter walked past, Val asked for a cognac, which he poured into what was left of his coffee and downed at a single gulp.

'What I meant,' he said, 'would you have come if it had been anyone else but me?'

'I know what you meant,' I said. 'And, no. No, I don't think I would.'

'Jimmy, perhaps?'

'Yes,' I acknowledged. 'Perhaps Jimmy. Maybe.'

Seeing Val's rueful smile, I reached across and took hold of his hand, but when, a few moments later, he gently squeezed my fingers, I took my hand away.

Patrick was waiting for us at the hotel when we returned.

'Well,' he said, rising from the lobby's solitary chair. 'The lovebirds at last.'

'Bollocks,' Val said, but with a grin.

Patrick kissed the side of my mouth and I could smell tobacco and Scotch and expensive after-shave; he put his arms round Val and gave him a quick hug.

'Been out for lunch?'

'Breakfast,' Val said.

'Fine. Then let's have lunch.'

Over our protests he led us to a small restaurant in the Latin Quarter, where he ordered in a combination of enthusiastic gestures and sixth-form French.

'I went along to the club earlier,' Patrick said, once the waiter had set a basket of bread on the table and poured our wine. 'Sounds as if it's going well. They want to hold you over for three weeks more. Assuming you're agreeable?'

Val nodded. 'Sure.'

'Anna?'

'I can't stay that long,' I said.

'Why ever not?' Patrick looked surprised, aggrieved.

'I've got a life to live.'

'You've got a bedsit in Kilburn and precious little else.'

Blood rushed to my cheeks. 'All the more reason, then, for not wasting my time here.'

Patrick laughed. 'You hear that, Val? Wasting her time.'

'Let her be,' Val said, forcefully.

Patrick laughed again. 'Found yourself a champion,' he said, looking at me.

Val's knife struck the edge of his plate. 'For fuck's sake! When are you going to stop organising our lives?'

Patrick took his time in answering. 'When I think you can do it for yourselves.'

In his first set that evening, Val was a little below pat, nothing most of the audience seemed to notice or be bothered by, but there was less drive than usual to his playing and several of his solos

17

seemed to peter out aimlessly before handing over to the piano. I could sense the tension building in Patrick beside me, and after the third number he steered me outside; there was a faint rain misting. 'He's using again,' Patrick said. 'You know that, don't you?'

I shook my head. 'I don't think so.'

'Anna, come on—'

'I asked him.'

'You asked him and he said no?'

'Yes.'

'Scout's honour, cross my heart and hope to die. That kind of no?'

I pulled away from him. 'Don't do that.'

'Do what?'

'Treat me as though I'm some child.'

'Then open your eyes.'

'They are open.'

Patrick sighed and I saw the grey of his breath dissipating into the night air.

'I'm not his jailer, Patrick,' I said. 'I'm not his wife, his lover. I can't watch him twenty-four hours of the day.'

'I know.'

He kissed me on the forehead, the sort of kiss you might give to a young girl, his lips cold and quick. A long, low boat passed slowly beneath the bridge.

'I'm opening a club,' he said. 'Soho. Broadwick Street.'

'You?'

'Some friends I know, they're putting up the

money. I thought if Val were interested it would be somewhere for him to play.'

'What about the police? Isn't that a risk still?'

Patrick smiled. 'Don't worry about that. It's all squared away.'

How many times would I hear him say that over the years? All squared away. How much cash was shelled out, usually in small denominations, unmarked notes slipped into side pockets or left in grubby holdalls in the left luggage lockers of suburban railway stations? I never knew the half of it, the paybacks and backhanders and all the false accounting, not even during those years later when we lived together – another story, waiting, one day, to be told.

'Come on,' he said, taking my arm. 'We'll miss the second set.'

When we got back to the club, Val and the American drummer were in animated conversation at the far end of the bar. Seeing us approach, the drummer ducked his head towards Val, spoke quickly and stepped away. 'It's not me you have to worry about, you fucker, remember that.' And then he was pushing his way through the crowd.

'What was all that about?' Patrick asked.

Val shrugged. 'Nothing. Why?'

'He seemed pretty angry.'

'It doesn't mean anything. That's just the way he is.'

'How much do you owe?'

'What?'

'That bastard, how much do you owe?'

'Look—'

'No, you look.' Patrick had hold of him by the lapels of his coat. 'I know him. He was busted in London last year, thrown out of Italy before that, jailed in Berlin. He's a user and a dealer, the worst kind of pimp there is.'

'He's OK—'

Patrick pushed Val back against the bar. 'He's not fucking OK. You hear me. Keep away from him. Unless you want to end up the same way.'

On the small stage, the pianist was sounding a few chords, trying out a few runs. 'I've got to go,' Val said, and Patrick released his grip.

All of Val's anger came out on stage, channelled first through a blistering 'Cherokee', then a biting up-tempo blues that seemed as if it might never end.

Patrick left Paris the next day, but not before he'd set up a recording date for Val and the trio at the Pathé-Magellan studio. The producer's idea was to cut an album of standards, none of the takes too long and with Val sticking close to the melody, so that, with any luck, some might be issued as singles for the many jukeboxes around. Val always claimed to be less than happy with the results, feeling restricted by the set-up and the selection of tunes. Easy listening, I suppose it might be called nowadays, dinner jazz, but it's always been one of my favourites, even now.

It was when we were leaving the studio after the last session that the pianist invited us to go along later with him and his girlfriend to hear Lester Young. Val was evasive. Maybe *oui*, maybe *non*. The one night off from Le Chat, he might just crash, catch up on some sleep.

'I thought he was one of your favourites,' I said, as we were heading for the Métro. 'How come you didn't want to go?'

Val gave a quick shake of the head. 'I hear he's not playing too well.'

Young, I found out later, had already been in Paris for several weeks, playing at the Blue Note on the rue d'Artois and living at the Hotel La Louisiane. A room on the second floor he rarely if ever left except to go to work.

Val had brought a few records with him from England, one of them an LP with a tattered cover and a scratch across one side: Lester Young, some fifteen years earlier, in his prime.

Val sat cross-legged on his bed, listening to the same tracks again and again. I poured what remained of a bottle of wine and took my glass across to a chair opposite the door; traffic noise rose and faded through the partly opened shutters, the occasional voice raised in anger or surprise; the sound of the saxophone lithe and muscular in the room.

When the stylus reached the run-off groove for the umpteenth time, Val reached over and set his glass on the floor. 'OK,' he said. 'Let's take a chance.'

As we entered the club and walked past the long bar towards the stage, a tune I failed to recognise came to an end and Young, caught in the spotlight, stared out, startled, as the applause riffled out above the continuing conversation. Up close, he looked gaunt and ill, dark suit hanging ragged from his shrunken frame, pain all too visible behind his eyes.

I took hold of Val's hand and squeezed it hard.

The drummer kicked off the next number at a brisk clip, playing quick patterns on the hi-hat cymbals with his sticks before moving to the snare, a signal for Young, saxophone tilted at an angle away from his body, to begin. Within the first bars, he had dragged the tempo down, slurring his notes across the tune, the same stumbling phrases repeated and then left hanging as he stepped back and caught his breath, the spaces between his playing wider and wider until finally he turned away and stood, head bowed, leaving the guitarist to take over.

'I Can't Get Started' was played at a funereal pace, the sound coarse and almost ugly: 'Tea for Two', one of the tunes Val had been listening to back in the hotel, started promisingly before teetering alarmingly off course; only a measured 'There Will Never Be Another You' rose from its foggy, thick-breathed beginning to become something that had moments of beauty between the self-doubt and misfingerings.

'If I ever get into that state, poor bastard,' Val

said, once we were back outside, 'promise you'll take me out and shoot me.'

Yet in the succeeding weeks he went back again, not once but several times, fascinated despite himself, watching one of his idols unravel before his eyes. Then there was the time he went along and Young was no longer there; he'd cancelled his engagement suddenly and returned to the States. Two weeks later he was dead.

The evening he heard the news Val played 'There Will Never Be Another You', just the one chorus, unaccompanied, at the beginning of each set. The next day I walked into his room in the middle of the afternoon, and saw him sitting, half-naked on the bed, needle in hand, searching for a vein.

'Oh, Christ, Val,' I said.

He looked at me with tears in his eyes then slapped the inside of his thigh again.

I slammed the door shut, grabbed my coat and purse and ran out on to the streets. For hours I just walked, ending up who knows where. At a corner bar I drank two brandies in quick succession followed by a crème de menthe and was promptly sick. I wanted to go back to the hotel, pack my bag and leave. What the hell was I doing there? What game? What stupid dream? There was vomit on the hem of my dress and on my shoes.

When finally I got to the club it was late and Val was nowhere to be seen, just his saxophone, mouthpiece covered, on its stand. In answer to my unspoken question, the pianist just shrugged and, still playing, gestured with his head towards the street.

I heard Val's shouts, muffled, coming from the alley that ran from close alongside the club down towards the quai Saint-Michel. Val lay curled in on himself, arms cradling his head, while two men took it in turns to kick him in the back, the chest, the legs, anywhere they could, a third looking on.

The sound of police sirens was too indistinct, too far away.

When someone helped me to my feet and I walked, unsteadily, to where Val still lay, unmoving, I thought that they had killed him. I thought he was dead.

For three days I sat by his bed in the hospital and held his hand. At night, I slept in the corridor outside, legs drawn up, on a chair. One of several broken ribs had come close to puncturing a lung. A week later I held his hand again as we walked in the hospital garden, with its bare earth and the stems of roses that had been cut back against the frost.

'How are you feeling?' I asked him.

'Fine,' he said, wincing as he smiled. 'I feel fine.'

After that there were always dull headaches that prevented him from sleeping and sudden surges of pain, sharp as a needle slipped beneath the skull. Despite the months and years of osteopathy, his back never sat right again, nagging at him each time he played.

★   ★   ★

Valentine Collins, jazz musician. Born, 18 September, 1937. Died, 13 April, 1976. Thirty years ago. No need any longer to take the ferry to Calais and then the long, slow journey by train, and not caring to fly, I treated myself to Eurostar, first class. A slightly better than aeroplane meal and free champagne. The centre of Paris in less than three hours. Autumn. The bluest of blue skies but cold enough for scarf and gloves. I feel the cold.

The Métro from Gare du Nord to Saint-Michel is crowded with so many races, so many colours, Val's face would not have stood out at all. Not one of us, Patrick had said, and it was true, though not in the way he meant.

The rue de la Huchette is now a rat-run of kebab houses and crêperies and bars, so crowded, here and there I have to walk along the centre of the narrow street.

Le Chat Qui Pêche is now a restaurant and the sign has been taken down. For a while I think I might go inside and have a meal, reminisce a little with the waiter, if he has a little English to complement my meagre French. But it is enough to stand here at the pavement's edge with people spilling round me, wondering, some of them, perhaps, what this old woman is doing, just standing there, staring at nothing in particular, none of them hearing what I hear, the sound of Val's alto saxophone, a ballad, astringent, keening, 'Every Time We Say Goodbye'.

BAR FIGHT

JASON STARR

If Omar wasn't drinking way too much it probably wouldn't have happened. But that night he'd been drinking Gwenroc for over three hours straight at a bar on rue Oberkampf, and when the skinny man bumped into him, spilling some of his drink on his shoulder, he turned and snapped, 'Hey, watch where you're going.'

The man looked around, like he thought Omar must have been talking to somebody else. But it was after midnight on a Tuesday and there were only a few other people in the bar.

'Excuse me?' the man said.

'You spilled your drink on me,' Omar said, wiping the liquid off his jacket. 'You should watch what you're doing, be more careful.'

The man's blue eyes narrowed into slits. 'Drink? You mean this?' he said, and poured the rest of the drink onto Omar's head.

Omar stood up and faced the man. The man looked around – Omar wondered if he was looking for a friend who might be in the bar to help – then said, 'How about we settle this outside, you dirty Muslim bastard.'

Omar wanted to punch him in the face right there, but before he could react Frederic, the bartender, said quickly, 'Not in the bat.'

The man held out his arm, as if to say 'After you,' but Omar wasn't going to leave first. He knew that as soon as he turned his back the man would try to sucker punch him. When the man headed towards the door, Omar left thirty euros on the bar to cover his tab, and carrying his jacket over his shoulder, followed the man outside.

Until he had stood up and started walking, Omar didn't realise how drunk he was. He hadn't had anything to eat since a ham sandwich for lunch, and he'd had only booze since.

It had been raining all day and it was raining even harder now. The man was waiting on the sidewalk in front of the bar. Omar was about to put down his jacket and get ready to fight when the man said, 'Not here – around the corner.'

The man started to walk up the block and Omar followed, staying a few metres behind. The man was walking unsteadily and seemed drunker than Omar. It was raining even harder now, the big drops splattering against the pavement.

They went around the corner, on to a darker, narrower street. After every couple of steps the guy kept looking back over his shoulder, like he thought Omar might try to jump him, but Omar was walking at the same pace, keeping the same distance between them. The street was dark and empty. About a third of the way down the block, the guy stopped and raised his fists like a boxer.

'Where's your head scarf, mujahadeen?' he asked.

Omar responded, 'I don't wear a head scarf.'

'Yeah, sure you don't. All you dirty bastards do, even in the summer. Come on, what're you waiting for, let's go. I'll make you sorry you ever left Iraq.'

Figuring it would be best to make the first move. Omar lunged forward, dropping low at the last second, tackling him by his legs. Then the guy surprised him, turning him around, so he had his back on the sidewalk and the guy was on top. This was exactly what Omar wanted – a wrestling match. He was taller and stronger than the man and he knew he would have an advantage. Using his legs, Omar flipped the guy over and he was back in control again. He pinned him down, then starred to beat him in the face. Left-right, right-left, he kept it up as fast and as hard as he could. Blood was dripping out of the guy's mouth and nose, but it was hard to tell how much he was bleeding because the rain was splashing against his face.

'Fucking Muslim bastards,' the guy managed to get out. 'Screwing up our country, rioting, coming over from Clichy-sous-Bois, no respect for the law, stealing money from our children, screwing our women . . .'

Omar kept beating the babbling racist in the face

until his arms were exhausted. Then he stood up, pulling the guy up with him. He pushed him against a wall, gave him a few hard punches to the stomach, making the man gag, then he gave him the knockout punch, catching him right between the eyes. The guy's head snapped back, banging against the brick. Omar held the guy up for a few more seconds, then let go, letting his limp body collapse onto the concrete.

Omar felt like he'd just run a marathon. He was gasping so hard his lungs hurt. The rain was coming down in sheets. He looked around, but there was still no one in sight. He kneeled down over the body. The man was unconscious, but still breathing. Omar reached down and slid his hand into the man's back pocket, removing his wallet. There was a bunch of credit cards and banking cards – the guy's name was Michel Perreaux – and there were sixty-four euros. He pocketed the racist bastard's cash, then slid the wallet back. He was about to get up when he noticed a smaller bulge in the man's right front pocket. Hoping it was more money, Omar removed a thin leather case and opened it. Only after staring at the badge for several seconds did the words register: Préfecture de Police. He stuffed the badge and the wallet back into Michel's pocket. Michel was starting to wake up, squirming, moaning something. Omar lifted Michel's head and then banged it against the concrete, knocking him unconscious again. Then he stood up, put on his jacket, and started walking back towards Oberkampf.

When Omar arrived at his small, two-room flat in Montparnasse, he gulped some Whisky de Bretagne straight from the bottle, then took a long shower. When he got out, he took another gulp of booze, then leaned close to the mirror on the medicine chest and examined his face. Although he had pains in his jaw and cheeks, he didn't look like he'd been in a fight. He didn't have any cuts or swelling or black-and-blue marks. His knuckles on both hands were a little sore, but that was about it.

If Omar had known the guy was a police officer, there was no way he would've started anything, despite the slurs and everything else. He would've just finished his drink and gone home. But now he knew he was in big trouble. The police would probably come looking for him later tonight, if they weren't looking already. Although Omar's parents had been born in Paris and he wasn't very religious, he knew the police would treat him like any other Muslim. He'd have to lie low for a few days, spend as little time as possible in the 11th Arrondissement, and the entire Right Bank.

But Omar knew he'd have no chance if the cop was dead.

The police would never give up trying to find a cop killer, especially a Muslim cop killer. Omar wasn't sure how hard he'd banged the guy's head against the concrete, but it could've been hard enough to kill him.

Omar watched some TV, but he was just staring at the set. He wanted to call his ex-girlfriend, Rania, just to talk to her, or maybe even convince her to let him come over to her place and hide out for a few days. But it was too late and, besides, she didn't want anything to do with him any more. She was looking for a rich, successful French guy – a white French guy – who didn't drink and stayed out of trouble and who could take care of her and be a good father. That sure as hell wasn't Omar.

Omar brushed his teeth, swallowed a few painkillers, and went to bed.

He barely slept. Drinking all of that whisky on a half-empty stomach had been a bad idea and it didn't help, having to worry all night about getting arrested for murder. After he got ready for work, he looked online, but there was nothing about a cop getting beaten up or killed. Omar wondered if the cop could still be lying there. Bums often slept in the street in Paris and people always walked right by them.

At about 8.15, Omar headed towards the Métro. He wondered if there was a description of him going around already. If there wasn't there would be soon. Even if the cop was dead, Frederic the bartender, or someone else at the bar, would tell the cops all about the fight. Omar couldn't believe he'd got himself into this situation. He always went about his own business, never looked for any trouble. But trouble always seemed to find him. It wasn't the first time he'd got into a bar fight. Over the last year alone he'd been in several fights. He had to give up drinking, was what he had to do. Rania was right about that. If he wasn't a drunk he certainly wouldn't be in the situation he was in right now.

Omar worked in customer services for an insurance company. During a break, he went into the hallway and called Rania on his mobile. He said he had to see her again, that she had to give him another chance. She told him to stop calling her and hung up on him. When he called back he kept getting her voice mail.

For the rest of the day, Omar couldn't stop thinking about Rania. He had to convince her to take him back somehow.

At five o'clock, he left the office. As he headed towards the Métro, someone grabbed him from behind, forced him against the side of the building, and cuffed him.

'Hey, what's going—'

'Shut up,' a voice said.

Officer Michel Perreaux turned Omar around to face him. Perreaux was wearing dark sunglasses, but Omar could see the cuts and purple bruises all over his face. Another cop was next to him – probably his partner.

Omar was thrilled that Perreaux was alive. At least it meant that he wasn't going to spend the rest of his life in jail.

'Look, I'm sorry about last night,' Omar said. 'It was a very big misunderstanding. I was drinking too much, way too much and—'

'Get in the car.'

Omar didn't move so Perreaux pushed him ahead towards the squad car. The cops stuffed Omar into the back, then they got into the front.

'I didn't do anything,' Omar said. 'This is bullshit. What did I do?'

'You assaulted a police officer,' Perreaux said.

'You started it, not me. You spilled your drink on my head. It was your idea to go outside and fight, not mine.'

'Was it my idea for you to steal my money?'

'I didn't steal from you. I have no idea what you're talking about.'

'Then what happened to my money? Did it just vanish?'

'Somebody else must've robbed you while you were passed out.'

'And then he resisted arrest,' Perreaux said to his partner. 'Didn't he, Georges?'

'He shouldn't've tried to take your gun away from you like that,' Georges said. 'He's lucky he didn't kill somebody.'

As the car headed down Batiste, Omar realised that the cops must've found out where he worked from Frederic the bartender. Omar remembered having a conversation with Frederic about his job a few weeks ago.

They drove somewhere to the outskirts of the

city. It definitely didn't seem like they were heading to a police station.

Finally, in an industrial area that Omar didn't recognise, the car pulled up by an abandoned building. For the first time in years, Omar prayed to Allah. If Allah got him out of this Omar would go to the local mosque every Friday, read the Koran regularly, and he'd stop drinking so much. He'd become the type of man Rania wanted him to be.

Perreaux came around and opened the back door and said, 'Get the hell out.'

'Where are you taking me?' Omar asked, terrified.

'I said get the hell out of the car or I'll shoot you with the handcuffs on.'

Omar got out of the car slowly and then the two cops pushed him along towards an alley.

Perreaux said, 'Come on, walk, you goddamn mujahadeen bastard – pick up those lazy feet and walk.'

Omar tried to kick Perreaux, but he couldn't get any strength into it. The other cop grabbed his arms and then Perreaux started punching him. It felt like he was using brass knuckles and the pain in his jaw was like nothing he'd ever experienced. Omar knew his nose was broken too, and probably a few other bones in his face. Everything was a daze and Omar hoped he'd just pass out and wake up in a hospital bed somewhere. Well, the first part of his wish came true, but when he opened his eyes both cops were still beating him mercilessly. He was propped against a wall and he felt sharp pains in his stomach and face. He tasted warm salty blood.

'Muslim bastard. Maybe this'll teach you not to steal. You're supposed to be religious people, meanwhile you're all fucking thieves.'

'Hey, Michel, I think I broke one of his teeth.'

'The dirty mujahadeen won't be eating for a while, huh?'

Omar heard more cursing and laughing, then he blacked out again. When he woke up, he was lying on the ground and every part of his body was in pain. It was quiet for a while, then he heard voices.

'Michel, what're you doing?'

'Shut up.'

'Come on, don't do that. Let's just get out of here.'

'I said shut up.'

'Come on, Michel. You got even, let's just—'

'I said shut up.'

It was quiet again. Omar opened his eyes slightly, but he wished he'd kept them shut. Perreaux pulled his pants down and began peeing on Omar's face.

When it was over Georges said to Perreaux, 'Come on, let's get out of here.'

Laughing, Perreaux said, 'It's a good thing I had all that wine during lunch today, huh?'

The cops left, laughing. Omar wiped at his face

with his sleeve a couple of times, trying to get the blood and piss off his lips, but then he was too exhausted to move his hand any more and he just lay there.

Then, as his eyes started to close again, he thought he was imagining it. But no, it was definitely there, attached to the side of the building, maybe twenty metres away, pointed in his direction. It was working too, because it was shifting slowly back and forth.

Looking up at the surveillance camera, Omar managed a wide smile.

THE LOOKOUT

MARC VILLARD

LYDIE

I pull away from the pavement, dropping two Rastas in front of La Cigale. There's a Gladiators comeback show on tonight. Then my taxi cruises into Square Anvers, picking up a scared blonde. She says she lives at La Madeleine. Midnight.

In thirty minutes we'll be alone among the taxis and motorbikes, speeding down the city's streets. I take the wide boulevards, avoiding drunken louts staggering onto the tarmac, cans of beer in hand, and sleepy couples, cyclists without lights.

I'll never forget Paris, all the cities I've driven through. Stockholm's powdery snow. The strangled guitars of Barcelona's Rambla del Raval. The shouts of restless rockers in Camden. The youngsters streaming with sweat in the port of Naples, about to sail for Ischia. The drizzle darkening Amsterdam's windows. And I was forgetting Berlin: Berlin, its smell of warm beer in the nightclubs, leather gear and Lobotomie playing punk rock. All slip by under the wheels of my Citröen, between my fingers fiddling with my twenty-third Camel. The girl behind me moans on, talking about health and the environment, but I don't give a shit. My cab's my kingdom. I slam the brakes.

'Get out, bitch.'

She gets out, shouting, while I tune in to Radio Nova: Solomon Burke pounds out 'Don't give up on me'. I can see him from here, Stetson glued to his head, in his regal attire, slumped on his king's throne. I change into second, go back up to Barbès where the lights are smothered by kebab smells.

Glance in the rear-view mirror: a forty-five-year-old woman's there, bags under her eyes, hair tumbling over her black biker's jacket. The night is vast, the wind picks up under the elevated section of the Métro. Neon explodes in the dark. I park the Citröen round the corner from Virgin and go into Mekloufi's bar.

SUGAR

I've got Roger in front of me and I already know what he's going to say. A tirade about how I've got him by the balls on my walkie-talkie. Lomshi, next to me, thinks the same thing.

'Right guys, I'll give it to you straight: my balls are attached to your walkie-talkies. The deal's going down in Square Saint-Bernard. Sugar, you're covering rue Myrha and you, Lomshi, rue Stephenson. Is that clear?'

'Got you, Roger.'

'The slightest thing, you call me, that's it. You're the only ones on that frequency.'

'How much are you dropping?'

'Five hundred grams of coke. OK, get to your positions.'

I scarper to my bit of terrace on the fifth floor, just round the corner from the mosque on me Myrha. Then my imperial eye sweeps the street. Nobody. So I take out my Colombian, my papers and my matches. And roll myself the spliff of the century. If Marley could see me with my Rasta hat, he'd be proud of me. I light it, inhaling the sweet smell. Vague glance down the street. I zone out, thinking about the cock fight the night before in the Sernam warehouses. I'd bet on a little runt with a gold comb the breeder called Chico. He was fighting a creature that was raised easy in the dust of the cock-fighting pit. After three minutes both of them were pissing blood and my breeder'd lost his beast who deserved a fortnight's holiday in the country. But he was dead, doped with brandy, his neck broken by a country hick.

I must have dropped off as I found my joint singeing my jeans, which cost me a fortune at Diesel.

Shit, it's coming back to me, the deal. I risk a glance over the concrete parapet and see five cops, two in plain clothes, who are shoving Roger against a wall and laughing, swinging the coke at arm's length.

Fuck. The shame of it.

I crawl across the terrace like a road, tumble down the staircase and hurtle down the five flights, sick to the stomach with fear. As I reach the lobby, I see Roger whispering something to Lomshi, who's just arrived. Lomshi's my age, fifteen, he's the lookout for all the Barbès dealers. Then he runs off towards the corner of rue Myrha and rue des Poissonniers. Running to tell all the drug barons hiding out at the Les Becs Salès bar.

The cops cuff Roger and bundle him into a car marked 'Police'.

The fear of it.

Lookouts aren't allowed to doze off. The walkie-talkie crackles in my right hand. I stash it in the fuse box in the hallway. Then leg it to the bottom of the street. I run down the street behind Saint-Bernard, think about doing a tour of Barbès, choosing the darkest, seediest streets. It's not hard.

The cannabis slows me down.

I think of my sister, on the Tarterets estate.

Of my brother, Mamadou, working like a bastard at the post office, feeding the whole family.

I hear a Capelton reggae number, it's doing my head in.

I think of the pile of money we made from the deal and deposited at the BNP.

And most of all, I clock the two guys running after me. A dark patch and I cut into rue Polonceau and jump over the fence around the square. Ten or so babes surround a rabble of boys playing football and swapping panini in the half-light. I crouch behind a bench and close my eyes. I don't want to die.

LYDIE

The guy playing guitar at Mekloufi's is known as Mimine and he knows three songs: 'Black Eyes', 'Minor Swing' and 'Clouds'. When he's finished those three, he turns to his accompanist, another guitarist, and they improvise. I still don't get why they've got gypsies playing a Moroccan bar but who cares: the beer costs two curos, the music isn't bad if you like Django Reinhardt and the boss cooks couscous for the regulars. Perfect.

The promotional clock tells us it's 9 p.m. Through the cafèwindows, I check out the immigrants rushing back to their tiny freezing rooms, women in African robes and baggy-jeaned rappers jangling their two-carat bling.

I'm working till midnight tonight because Alex, the second driver, only picks the car up at 6 a.m. tomorrow morning. I throw ten euros on the table and stick my nose outside, just as a fine drizzle begins to fall. A young Senegalese woman decked out like a Christmas tree rushes towards me, waving her tresses.

'Are you the taxi?'

I nod.

'I'll take it. I'm going to rue Polonceau.'

'You're kidding. Rue Polonceau's three hundred

metres away on foot, that works out a lot per hundred metres.'

'I know, but I'm going to a birthday party and I don't want to get my hair wet. Shall we go.'

I get into the cab, turn on the meter and tune into TSF which is playing 'Paris Blues', an old Terry Callier number that brings tears to my eyes. In five twists of the steering wheel I'm back up La Goutte J'Or, turning into rue Polonceau. The girl gets out at number 14. A bit further on, a whole group of mothers and kids leaving the square with old newspapers shielding their heads. I put the meter back to zero when a son of Jah – a teenager – throws himself on to the back seat, bent double.

'Come on, grandma, get going!'

I half turn round and give him a professional slap. Little shit.

'Hey, what was that for? Get a move on, I'm in a hurry.'

'I'm not your servant, kiddo.'

'OK, OK.'

Then I spot three black guys, dressed hip-hop style, making their way towards us. And swivel to look at the kid, who's turning green.

Trembling, he holds out a twenty-euro note.

'Go, lady, please.'

I move into first, but as I pass the black guys, they throw themselves on my bonnet, stopping me. Shit, it's not the day for it.

I open the glove box and pull out the Beretta,

putting on the safety catch. Then, pretty tense, I push the door open, waving my gun.

'Touch the taxi and you get shot.'

'Hey grandma, stay cool, we just want to pick up our friend in the back.'

'He's not your friend. Get back all three of you.'

SUGAR

I know those guys: three of the Barbès drugs boss's henchmen. Look like rappers but they've got chickpeas for brains. I hear them whining to the taxi woman: they're scared of her gun. I yank open the door and shout to the old girl:

'Lady, it's best to just go.'

She turns towards me and at the same time I get a knife in the shoulder. Shit, it burns. I quickly get back in, shouting, while the taxi woman shoots a few bullets into the air to frighten off the scum.

She gets behind the wheel.

'It's bleeding.'

'Shut it, trouble.'

She throws the taxi into reverse, backs down La Goutte d'Or and we reach boulevard Barbès in the rain. And I think I'm dying.

'A hospital . . .'

'I know. Let me think.'

It's not my day. My district's a no-go area and my only chance is to get back to Tarterets to lie low and wait for them to forget me.

She's turned on the radio and I recognise something by Dr Dre.

I see her eyes in the mirror.

'Shit, it hurts.'

'Don't pull on the blade, it's stopping the blood flow. I know Hôtel-Dieu well, we'll go straight there. When we get there, you say nothing about my gun. You got knifed by some crazies in the street and I picked you up afterwards. Understood?'

'You haven't got a licence.'

'I have but I don't want any hassle. Who are those guys? And who are you?'

'None of your business.'

She slams on the brakes. We're at the corner of boulevard Saint Martin. Everything's blurry under the rain which mists up the glass.

She walks round the cab and opens my door. She's already soaked.

'Get out, you moron.'

'But why?'

'I like to know who I'm dealing with.'

'OK, I'll tell you, but get a move on, I don't want to die in a taxi.'

At last she starts up again. This woman's stressing me out. With all the hassle I've got, I didn't need this too.

'Right, explain.'

So I describe my glamorous life in the square. Of course I don't give names. I say I went into a diabetic coma on the terrace in rue Myrha. Rashid my neighbour's got diabetes.

'You don't look like a diabetic. You were smoking dope and off your head, I reckon.'

'I was not. I can control my drugs.'

'Oh yeah, you're in control. And now you've got all the dealers in Barbès on your arse, wanting to avenge their friend.'

I don't answer but she's right. We reach A&E, there are lights flashing, ambulances drive to and fro in front of the taxi. The knife digs into my shoulder when I move. Taxi woman turns to me and pushes back the blonde hair hanging over her eyes.

'What's his name, this dealer you didn't warn?'

'Why?'

'Just curious.'

'Roger.'

'Roger who?'

'Solal. You know him?'

She turns back to her steering wheel, leans back on her seat and says in a thin voice:

'He's my son. I knew it.'

Shit, what luck. I don't know what to say. The shame of it.

Roger's mother.

'Get out, now.'

'Uh, I'm . . .'

'Get out!'

I quickly get out of the car, bent over like an old man, and walk slowly towards A&E, so as not to dislodge the knife.

LYDIE

Looking to pick up, I'm back on boulevard Sébastopol. And I realise: I never took the kid's money. Roger's face appears on my windscreen. A man. now. But it's the child I still see. The child who cried at the physio's, wheezing with broncheolitis. The child who held his breath, pretending to drown, leaving me gasping on the edge of swimming pools in the Essonne. Roger, going under a lorry with his bike, hiding his lacerated, stitched face from me. Roger at the Marley concert shouting 'No woman no cry,' mouthing the words in English, eyes shining with joy.

And now, Roger in a cell in La Goutte d'Or, destined for Fleury-Mérogis. I go back up towards Barbès Métro station: Mekloufi's is still open. I park the car twenty metres away and go in.

Mimine is settling into an impro, picking up the melody from place de Brouckère. He's learning new tunes, that's good. I sit myself at the bar and ask for a Kronenbourg. Thinking of my boy. A few minutes later, I go down to the phone booth in the basement and call Patrick, my ex's, number.

'It's me, I'm calling from Barbès.'

'Lydie. D'you know what time it is? What's going on?'

'It's not good. I picked up a young black kid and we were held up. He was knifed and Roger's been busted with a load of coke on rue Myrha.'

'Good God, Lydie, I live in Nice, remember?'

'I know.'

'He's my kid, but he chose you. He chose Paris. Listen, I'm not saying it's your fault.'

'It's always the parents' fault.'

'I quit the drugs squad in Nice. They offered me organised crime, it's more hands on. You want me to put a call in for Roger?'

'I haven't seen him in six months. But yeah, I think we've got to do all we can. He's at La Goutte d'Or, d'you know anyone there?'

'The captain, Delpierre; I'll call him, he owes me one.'

'Thanks. I'll finish my beer and go and find my darling boy. It's good to hear your voice.'

'And yours. Keep me in touch. *Ciao* Lydie.'

Now I'm walking towards the dark, narrow Goutte d'Or. Yes, I'm walking towards Roger – a man, it's true. The kind of guy I'd have hated at twenty. I think of Patrick, cosy and warm on the coast, of the years I've spent in city streets, of the bad smells in the early morning, the bad food, the bad fucks. Of the guys I ditched, of life's irony which made me save Roger's lookout's arse. The dozy police station is 200 metres away when suddenly I see two black guys in Tacchini tracksuits coming towards me. And I recognise them.

'So, grandma, gonna show us your gun? We didn't have time to see the make.'

I step out of the way to avoid them. We're alone. As I walk faster, the bigger one's hand stops me.

His body's glued to mine and the bastard hisses in my ear:

'You, you're just pretending, but I'm for real.'

And he sinks a knife in my back. Christ, my legs give way, my head hits the edge of the pavement. I hear their steps retreating. I try to shout but there's some kind of bubble between my lips. I think of all the things I haven't done, the froth on a beer, triumphant jazz, the cops I'll never see again. That's the good news. My body shrinks. I say 'Roger'.

And then.

And then I say nothing.

Translation © Lulu Norman and Ros Schwartz

NEW SHOES

JOHN WILLIAMS

Sometimes when it's late and you've been listening to Lucinda Williams and you have a bottle of Gigondas empty beside you and the noise from the drinkers in the rue Mouffetard down below won't let you sleep, a line from an old song gets lodged in your brain, *And I can never, never, never go home again*, and you can't help but remember, remember how you got here.

In the spring of 1981 there were only three places in Paris to busk. The first and easily the best, probably the best place in all of Europe, was outside the Beaubourg. Can I start to explain how fabulous the Beaubourg was back then? This building with its primary-coloured plumbing on the outside, with its giant Perspex escalator clambering across the front. I can hardly credit it myself – twenty-five years of living in this city has allowed familiarity to do its job of breeding contempt – but really back then it seemed to represent a whole world of possibilities, a future in which anything could happen. We'd lost sight of that you see, in those the first years of Thatcher, living in a city, Cardiff, that was closing down around us.

But back to the point. There were three places to busk in Paris that spring, and the big open space in front of the Beaubourg, always full of tourists and locals marvelling at this new wonder, was by far the best of them. The others were the Métro and the rue St André des Arts, but each of those had its problems, as we discovered.

Who were we? We were seven, no eight, refugees from the punk-rock experience, boys and girls hoping to shift our lives from black and white into technicolor. We'd pooled our dole money and student grants and wages from the anarchist print shop and crammed into the back of my old Transit van and headed to Paris to busk. Our act, such as it was, consisted of playing hits of the day – David Bowie, Adam and the Ants, Robert Wyatt, whatever – in ragged vocal-harmony style backed only by percussion and kazoos. At the time, and mostly because we were young, and in some cases even cute, it went over OK. I won't bother you with all our names, since you'll only forget them and anyway there was only one that really mattered. If any of the others play a part along the way I'll name them then.

The one that mattered, matters even, was called Beth and the week before we left she had her hair restyled in a Louise Brooks bob. Actually I thought she looked more like Anna Karina in *Vivre Sa Vie* impersonating Louise Brooks than Brooks herself, if you see what I mean. Either way it's obvious I was smitten. As for the rest of how she looked, well, I'm sorry, but I don't feel inclined to go past her hair. Let memory fall lightly on what follows.

We'd been there, I suppose, for a week, long enough at least to have found some kind of routine. A lot depended on the weather. If it was fine we did well, two hour-long sessions in front of the Beaubourg and we were made for the day; we could eat and drink and some of us could even stay at the gypsy's hotel. If it rained things were harder. No one wants to stand and watch buskers in the rain, not even in front of the finest new building in the western world, so the only option was to go down into the Métro.

There were good things about that, the sound you get singing in the tunnels is beautiful, it's a cathedral for drifters, for losers, for *loubards*, for my people, and we sounded like angels down there. The bad side was the cops. Those French cops back then were bastards. Thank our lucky stars we were all white, or almost all, and Yaz was a girl so she was OK, but anytime they'd run out of black kids to persecute they were on our case, moving us on, checking our IDs, threatening us with all kinds of shit. One time, the first time, Don talked back to them. We didn't make that mistake twice. They threw him up against the wall and practically ripped his arm off his shoulder as they searched him for drugs. They had no luck there, of course, as even on a good day our budget didn't stretch any further than plastic bottles of *vin rouge*.

Rainy days we stayed in the *forêt*, out in St Germainen-Laye, right on the western fringe of the city. It was my idea. I'd been there the year before, when I'd stayed with an anarchist called Ifor. This time, though, Ifor's house had been shuttered and locked. The neighbours said he'd gone to Mexico. But it was right by the *forêt*, so we'd parked the van and some of us slept inside and the rest took tents and camped. And in the morning we'd jump the barrier into the RER, just like the local kids, and go to work.

As I say the weather made all the difference and this day, the point where we'll start, was fine. More than fine, it was unequivocally the best day of my life so far. Scratch that, let's make it ever. It's not as if I'm going to be revisiting that happy innocence again.

Anyway, right from the start everything was running right, I knew it from the moment I clambered out of the van, where I'd slept stretched out across the front seats. I'd seen Beth emerge from the tent she was sharing with Yaz, just that same instant. We'd walked down to the stream together, washed our faces and cleaned our teeth, not saying a word, just suddenly at ease with each other, at ease with what we both knew was coming. There had been no rush. That was the strangeness of it, just a week of slowly falling, of singing and dancing in the street.

Later that morning we arrived at the Beaubourg. Our favourite pitch, the one right dead centre, was occupied by some circus guys, so we moved off to one side and started to set up. We shrugged off our coats and showed off our Oxfam finery, pulled out our kazoos and drum-sticks.

There was already quite a crowd gathered around our rival buskers, so I walked over to have a look. They were a bunch of travelling circus types: there was a bed of nails laid out on the ground waiting for action, and next to it there was a guy stripped to the waist, jet black ponytail and tattoos, breathing fire.

These guys were good. I would have happily stayed and watched them, but strangely, as we set up and started clanging our way into 'Sound and Vision' – 'blue, blue electric blue' – the crowd started drifting towards us. By the time we launched into 'Heartbreak Hotel' we were out-drawing the fire eater and his posse by four to one. I introduced the band in bad French and took the cap round, making sure to make eye contact with each and every one. This, by the way, is the true secret of busking success, not being a virtuoso flautist or hard enough to lie on a bed of broken glass, but having someone go round and collect the money with a smile and a wink and a smattering of bad French.

When we took a breather at the end of our first set, the fire eater came over to warn us off. 'You are not permitted,' he said, and we looked at each other.

'Is our place,' he added. I was not about to argue with a man who breathes fire, and his friend who lay on a bed of broken glass, and I was about to apologise and say we'd come back later, when Don stepped forward and faced up to the fire eater and the fakir.

'No,' he said, all but jabbing his finger in the fire eater's face, 'it's not your place. You go back over there, do your thing. We're staying here.'

Christ. I looked round and saw Beth's eyes on me. Was I going to back Don up in his foolhardiness? I certainly didn't want to. In the end I did nothing, didn't advance to stand shoulder to shoulder with Don or back off, just stood there in no man's land watching the fire eater stare at Don. I wondered what came next – the punch, the butt, the suddenly present knife? What was Don's problem? Why couldn't he let it go, didn't he realise we were little more than kids? But then the fire eater just shook his head, spat on the ground and backed off, barking something in a language I didn't even begin to recognise.

We clamoured around Don then, all of us angry and relieved at his bravery. And it struck me that Don was actually a big guy and his Mohican, with its three giant spikes, was distinctly unusual, and evidently menacing, for people who hadn't spent the last few years in the punk-rock micro-climate.

Our next set was a riot, our good humour infectious enough to bring the sun out, and by early afternoon we had enough money not just for food and drink but for lodging too.

We ate lunch by the Seine, as you do when you're young and you've never been to Paris before, back in a time when baguettes and pâté and red wine were still exotic fare, unavailable at home.

What did we do next? It's all something of a haze, but I'm sure we went back to the Beaubourg and took the escalators up to the top, took pictures of each other against the skyline. And a bubble started to form around Beth and me. Things were said you can't remember, but serve to signify that your heartbeats are converging, coming closer and closer still.

Towards evening we crossed over the river at Pont Neuf and went to Renée the gypsy's hotel. We asked if she had room for us. She smiled, sat there huge in her robes in the front room. 'Yes darlings,' she said, 'I have three rooms. Five beds. You will be OK, I think.'

We thought so too. We didn't assign the beds just yet. It was not only Beth and I who were caught up in anticipation of what developments the night might bring.

On a roll now, we decided to go out and sing some more. The only place to busk after dark was the rue St André des Arts, a tourist-packed, café-lined walkway though the busiest part of the Left Bank, from St Michel to the rue Bonaparte. Halfway along, the road suddenly widened outside a school. It was the perfect place to set up and play: the night was fine and warm and the tourists were out in force, their generosity levels raised by drink. Beth sang her featured number, '24 Hours From Tulsa', with all the sweetness and charming flatness of a young Françoise Hardy. My cap was filling up not just with the usual francs and centimes, but actual folding money.

Emboldened by our success, I actually started asking for requests, when a window opened in an apartment four stories up and across the road from us. A man leaned out, yelled something, disappeared, then reappeared with a bucket of water, which he threw down at us, splashing a couple of tourists but doing little harm.

'When he does that he always calls the police afterwards,' said a passing local.

'Oh, right,' I said, 'so how long do the police take to arrive?'

'Ten minutes,' said the local.

'OK,' I said to the crowd, 'the police are coming in ten minutes, that means we have five minutes to play a request, what would you like?'

An American smartarse called out for some Captain Beefheart. We looked at each other, Don gave me a thumbs up and whipped up a mighty percussive burst from which we launched into something that bore a very faint resemblance to 'Big-Eyed Beans from Venus'. I'm sure to those watching it was just a cacophony, but, as I say, we were young and we were cute and they must have felt something of our own intoxication, because they laughed and cheered and put more money into the cap, then we saluted and promised to be back same time, same place tomorrow, and hotfooted it down the street just as the police came barrelling along in the opposite direction.

We were heading for the buskers' café. It probably had some other name, maybe it was the Café St André des Arts or something entirely forgettable like that, but everyone knew it as the buskers' café. It was full of 1970s hangovers, French guys with long hair and battered acoustics exchanging tips on how to play Neil Young songs. Up to now we'd held each other in amiable mutual contempt: they thought we were idiot punk rockers who couldn't play an instrument, we thought they were ridiculous old hippies in Gauloise-reeking velvet jackets.

This time though, as we approached, I could see a whole bunch of these guys, five or six of them, mostly with guitars out, sitting at the big table in the window. They were banging their way through 'Hey Jude', which was not unusual, except for the fact that they were all joining in and two of them were playing the spoons on the table, and in the instrumental break one of them pulled out a kazoo. We stood there open-mouthed. The hippie bastards were stealing our act.

It would have been too embarrassing to go in there now. So, as usual, everyone looked to me to come up with an alternative. I for the anarchist had taken me to a bar around here, I was sure. Could I remember where it was? Of course I could. I led the way unerringly, and soon we were sitting around the front table of a real locals bar, counting our takings and drinking the cheapest *vin rouge* yet, while watching a Chinese kid, maybe ten years old, score several million on the pinball machine.

For a while we were all one, high on the adventure, but as the evening wore on Beth and I went back into our bubble and drifted towards the back of the bar. I walked over to the counter to order more drinks. There was a guy leaning there, a real classic French boho in his late thirties, looked like Jean-Pierre Leaud's dodgy older brother. He looked at me, then looked at Beth and said something to the *patronne*, and she laughed and reached up for one of the good bottles of wine and poured off three glasses. Jean-Pierre smiled and handed two glasses to me, then raised his glass. '*Salut*.'

'*Salut*,' I said back, and Jean-Pierre motioned us towards the bar stools next to him, and told us his name was Laurent, and I talked to him in bad French and translated everything for Beth, and I could see in Laurent's eyes just how fine he thought Beth was, and I was not worried, just proud, because I knew our heartbeats were just casing themselves together, ready to beat fast.

Soon we were sitting at a booth together and Laurent was talking about shoes. He had stared at Beth's shoes as we'd moved from bar to booth and shaken his head and said that 'a *très belle fille* like you needs better shoes than those'. Those being a pair of deliberately old-fashioned schoolgirl sandals. 'I have some wonderful shoes at my apartment,' he said. 'You must come and see. I will give you some.'

I translated for Beth and she smiled and said '*Oui, merci.*'

'You like to come now. Is not far.'

We looked at each other and laughed, shook our heads.

'No problem,' said Laurent, 'I will see you again,' and he returned to his perch at the bar and we went back to the others, who must have been waiting for us, as they stood up as one and we headed out into the street.

I knew then, as the night air hit, that I was drunk. I picked out the route back to the gypsy's hotel without thinking, almost without looking. As we passed the school on St Andre des Arts I turned to Beth, the self-same second she turned to me, and our kiss started there, lasted all the way home and up the four flights of stairs and into a room that was instantly ours and I'll spare you the details, spare me the details.

In the morning we staggered down to breakfast late, sat in Renée's parlour, eating croissants and drinking coffee from bowls. The bubble around us seemed positively hermetic and it was only when we were finally dressed and standing outside with the others, looking like a band of gypsies, that I realised it was raining, not just a shower but the implacable stuff that's booked in to stay.

We did our best, tried a few bedraggled songs outside the Beaubourg, went down into the maze of Châtelet Métro, but nothing was right. The public hurried past us and the sense that we were a team had been destabilised by Beth and me. By mid-afternoon we'd barely earned enough for food, let alone another night at the gypsy's. Don had had enough.

'Fuck this for a game of soldiers,' he said, as we huddled outside a patisserie awning. 'Let's go back out to the *forêt*, go to the sports centre there, have a swim.'

The others grunted agreement. I wasn't ready to give up, wasn't prepared to cede defeat to the bloody weather, but Don was implacable and the rain kept on, so I opted for a partial surrender.

'Fine,' I said, then turned to Beth. 'You fancy going to see a gallery first?' She nodded and stared at her feet, embarrassed to be marked out like this as part of a couple, apart from her friends, but still clear in her choice, choosing me.

That settled, we said we'd see the others later, out at the *forêt*. They headed off to the RER and we took the Métro up to Notre Dame de Lorette and soon found ourselves the only people in the Musée Gustave Moreau, all princesses and serpents and opium, beloved of any young aesthete who's read Huysman's *Against Nature*, and yes, of course, I was that soldier. But its emptiness was really the thing, drifting through this grand house full of weird paintings midway between kitsch and powerful, in our bubble, sealed in our bubble. Did we kiss in front of . . . Did we . . . No, too much recall.

Afterwards we drifted south, walked down St Denis and goggled at the whores, found some little second-hand shops at the southern end and bought a '50s shirt we both liked. Skirting Les Halles, not going anywhere in particular, just putting off our return to the *forêt*, I took us into Parallèles, an anarchist bookshop Ifor had shown me one time. And there, reading a copy of *Actuel*, was Laurent.

'Hey,' he said, '*mes amis*.'

'Hey,' we said right back and we got to talking. We went to the bar a few doors down and Laurent bought the drinks and we talked some more, then he asked what our plans were.

'Not much,' I said, 'we have to go out to St Germainen-Laye.'

Laurent looked disgusted. 'But why? There's nothing there, it is just . . . bourgeois.'

I explained that we were camping in the *forêt* and he laughed at that and said, 'OK, but go later tonight. I'll take you some places that are not so . . . bourgeois.'

Beth and I looked at each other, and I mumbled something about money and our lack of any, but Laurent brushed it aside. 'I have money, don't be so bourgeois.'

Well, neither of us wanted to be bourgeois, that

was for sure, so we looked at each other again and smiled and said, 'OK, *merci.*'

It was full dark by the time we left the bar. Time to eat, said Laurent and led the way up to Chartiers, off the rue Montmartre, a big old Toulouse-Lautrec place with mirrors and moustachioed waiters and cheap decent food. It's a bit of a tourist classic, of course, I know that now, but right in that moment it was wonderful.

We sat down and looked at the menu, and I translated what I could. Beth wrinkled her nose up and said, 'Don't they have anything for vegetarians?'

Laurent heard her, laughed and said, 'You are in Paris now. We do not have this vegetarian shit.' And then he ordered snails and entrecôtes and red wine for all of us.

Beth looked at me and said 'Oh God, please don't tell Yaz.' And then her foot found mine under the table, and when the steak came she ate it with all the relish of a pale girl who hadn't seen red meat in a year.

Did we go to La Tartine next, to drink the black wine of Cahors, sitting on the same banquette once perched on by Lenin? My memory wants to say yes, but common sense says that must have been the next night, because the club was in the other direction from Chartiers. Whatever, we went somewhere and drank a *verre* and Laurent asked if we would like to go dancing, and we both said 'yes'; then, 'What about the time, we must get to the *forêt*,' and Laurent gave us the look that said we were in danger of becoming bourgeois again and sighed and said, 'Maybe you have time to catch your train. If not you stay with me, *pas de problème.*'

So we went dancing. I never found the place again. By day I suspect it looked like a hundred other restaurants along the boulevard Sébastopol, one of central Paris's least charming thorough-fares. By night, though, it was African. We were amazed. This was before world music was invented, you understand. Reggae was as exotic as things got, as far as we knew. Yet now we were in Africa.

Up till then we – well I at least – had barely registered the city's African population, and now we were surrounded by them: fresh-faced young guys in suits, women in smart dresses. I felt shabby and pale, but I didn't care, I was too busy trying to take in the music. There was a band playing, I'd like to think it was someone legendary, Dr Nico perhaps. Whoever they were they were great, the circling guitars and the ease of the bass and drums. I was intoxicated three times over: by the music, by Beth next to me, her feet starting to measure out the beat, and by way too much red wine.

Things blurred a little. We sat down for a while then we tried to dance. An African guy came up, laughed at us, then offered his hand to Beth. She smiled at him and took his hand and he moved her round the floor. I sat back down next to Laurent.

'You look tired, my friend,' he said, 'maybe you'd like something to pick you up?'

'Sure,' I said, for a moment thinking he meant a black coffee, but not demurring when he slipped a wrap into my hand and suggested I make the acquaintance of M. Cocaine.

It would be nice to blame everything on that old cocaine. Certainly it didn't help, but just as *in vino veritas* is basically true – you may say things you regret but the reason for the regret is their truth – so cocaine may turn you into an asshole, but that asshole is your own inner asshole.

And let's not forget it's also really good fun. I took a toot in the toilet and the blurring went away and later on, on a nod from Laurent, I introduced Beth to my new friend, and she liked him pretty well too, and the night wore on the way you can most likely predict. And yes, of course we did, and not in the toilets but in some kind of pantry off the deserted kitchen, her elbows resting on a marble shelf.

It was lucky we had taken our chance when we did though, as Laurent's place turned out to be no more than a one-room eyrie on the Ile de la Cité, fabulous views but no privacy, and no bed either. Laurent was no gentleman, he took the big dark wood sleigh bed and we took the blankets on the floor, holding each other at first for warmth, then pulling apart, lost in our own private battles for equilibrium as the chemicals fled our systems.

Next morning was awkward and sore-headed as you might expect. We fled around eleven leaving Laurent still in bed, a vague promise to meet in the bar by Parallèles that evening.

We found the others outside the Beaubourg. They looked a sorry crew without us. Em had taken my role as leader and her fitness for the job can be gauged by the fact that this is the first time I've mentioned her; a nice girl but dull. They were pleased to see us at first, relieved I suppose, then angry at our thoughtlessness. We tried to slot back into our roles, and succeeded more or less. It was OK, the sun peeked out in between shows, we made lunch money then dinner money, but the harmony was off, and later on I raised the status of meeting Laurent to an obligation.

'You coming back to the *forêt later on!' asked Don.*

'Maybe,' I said, 'expect so, but if not we'll see you here. Usual time, usual place, yeah?'

'Fine,' said Don, 'see you then,' and we fled, relieved, back into our new Parisian life.

That night Laurent took things up a notch. We exchanged Chartiers for Bofinger, still, then and now, the best of the big old brasseries. You could, if you wanted, find me there from time to time even now, maybe on a Sunday evening late, but you might, I must confess, regret it.

That first time it was sublime. Laurent ran into

friends there; beautiful people, film people. They'd been working on a Rohmer movie earlier in the day. Was one of them the lost girl of French film herself, Pascale Ogier, soon to be dead of a heart attack at twenty-five? Part of me would like to think so, to think that I was not the only one whose stars were so far out of alignment. I read once what her mother wrote after Pascale died. It trumps my own self pity every time.

En ce moment, je joue au théâtre avec des acteurs très jeunes, qui ne l' ont pas connue. Et tous les soirs, je salue. Quatre fois, cing fois, six fois. All bout de la sixième fois, je regarde les visages, dans la salle. Parmi ces visages, il y en a toujours un, un peu pâle, entouré de cheveux noirs, qui sourit. Une jeune fille. Il y en a toujours me. Et pendant un court instant, je pense: 'Tiens, Pascale est venue, ce soir. Elle aurait pu me prévenir.' C'est très bref.

Jesus.

I'm delaying things now as you can see, reluctant to move forward. Tiens indeed. After dinner we – Beth and me, Laurent and his friends – walked through the Marais till we came to Les Bains Douches. It looked from the outside like what it was, an old swimming pool. Except there was a man on the door checking names and a gaggle of beautiful people offering themselves up for his approval. We had no problem, the guy on the door even favoured Beth with a small bow and a *Bonsoir Mam'selle*.

It was a vision of the very near future. Inside a year there would be places like this in London, New York, Berlin, but right then there was nowhere cooler on earth than Les Bains Douches, nowhere where the new worlds of fashion and music and film were more inseparably intertwined, creating what . . . 'The Eighties', I suppose, with all their flash and filigree.

I loved it. I was in raptures. I could see everything ahead of me. I was talking to a friend of Laurent's, he said he was sure he could find work for a cool guy like me, making music for films. I wanted it all, to swallow it whole. I wanted to live here forever and I was so grateful to Laurent, so in awe of his command of this world, and so coked off my face that, later that night, when we were sat there on a banquette, watching Beth dance to Grace Jones, and Laurent leaned over and said, 'You mind if we share?', I didn't even hesitate, just nodded like I'd known all along that this was the price on the ticket.

I mean, I should say I knew she liked him, and it wasn't as if I forced her. It's only that when she looked at me, like she was asking if I was sure this was OK, I just smiled again, a smile I hope to Christ has never passed my face again.

It was simply managed. They left together. I stayed on for an hour or so, maybe more, you know how time flies when you're with M. Cocaine, and I had my new friends to talk to, my new career to plot. Then I came back to the Ile de la Cité. Rang the bell and went up and straight away Beth left the big sleigh bed and joined me on the floor. In the morning Laurent went to work, and Beth cried in my arms and said not a word.

That was the end of us. It wasn't the real end, of course, there was a coda, a tailing off, the same old sad decline, but that was the end. Of course.

And I did at least receive my rewards. A month later I had a job as musical director for the first ever French punk-rock movie, and I was living in an attic flat of my own, on the rue de la Roquette. I saw Laurent from time to time. Once at the Palace he leaned over to me, said, 'You still see that girl? You know she really liked you, man. She told me I could only fuck her in the ass, said the other place was strictly for love.'

There are things, you know, you prefer not to hear. More than that there are lessons you prefer not to learn. Like this one: that some things, when they break, they stay broken.

That's enough. I have, as I mentioned, been drinking, and if I stay in any longer I will become maudlin, listen to more records I shouldn't. Instead I shall go out, take a *petite tournée* around the bars. I'll see if there's a girl who would like some new shoes.

THE REDHEAD

CARA BLACK

'We must never let the new generations forget what happened here during the Occupation, in their own neighbourhood, the horrors, the deportations,' Monique, the lycée teacher, said, her eyes sombre. 'Your presentation on the Resistance will be so welcome . . . Your work is so important.'

Lucien had just handed the young brunette their Resistance Association pamphlet and smiled. 'We're proud to speak with your students,' he said. 'That's our mission here.'

They stood in the small Association office overlooking Canal Saint Martin, with the carved woodwork ceiling, a non-working marble fireplace, and second-hand file cabinets. Mina, a widowed great-grandmother, sat at the worn metal desk affixing address labels on envelopes. Lucien combed back his white hair with his fingers, then gestured to her. 'Mina and I do what we can. We're the old-timers and have been doing this work for years. Call and we'll arrange it.'

Lucien showed the teacher out, opened *Le Parisien* and sat down. Outside the window, bicycles sped along the cobbled Canal Saint Martin *quai*; an arched metal bridge spanned the dark green strip of water framed by the blue-washed sky.

'*Tant pis!*' Lucien's age-sported finger stabbed at an article on the newspaper's second page. 'The redhead's publishing her "Resistance memoirs".'

'Her lies, you mean,' said Mina, shaking her grey-haired head. 'As if she'd admit being a Jew who slept with a German soldier!'

'According to this,' Lucien said, 'she implies we killed him.'

Mina dropped the volunteer labels on the desk. 'But how can . . . ?' The words caught in Mina's throat as she remembered that rainy July night in 1943. The Wehrmacht's marching jackboots echoing on the street, below in the damp, dripping cellar, bricking the soldier's body in the wall by sputtering candlelight. The image of his pink cheeks, the blond hair flashed in front of her.

'Eh? I don't believe it, Lucien.' Mina pulled the sweater tighter around her thin frame.

Jews hid in the *quartier* to avoid deportation; in coal bins, in attics, in cellars. And in this one cellar, bad luck had it, Lucien's mother, then the concierge, had hidden their Hebrew school teacher. But La Rouquine, their comrade who lived upstairs, hadn't known. She'd arranged a rendezvous in the cellar with her lover. Her jackbooted soldier in Feldgrau, the green-grey hue that still sickened Mina.

'Read that, Mina.'

Mina adjusted her glasses and read 'nicknamed La Rouquine for her red hair, the author, widow of the former Interior Minister, reveals her exploits with the Resistance on Canal Saint Martin and new theories about her father's wartime disappearance connected to the suspected murder of a Wehrmacht sergeant . . .'

Mina stifled the fear welling inside her. 'Our names aren't there, Lucien. Relax. That happened in wartime, more than sixty years ago. He was the enemy. What does a dead Nazi matter now?'

'Keep reading.'

'La Rouquine insists on setting the record straight concerning a Wehrmacht sergeant who, she claims, allowed Jews to escape and was murdered by Resistants ignorant of his true sympathies.' Mina's voice wavered. 'La Rouquine will show the press Resistance hideouts in a network of cellars including the murder site, in her words, of "a noble" German, following her book launch on Friday.'

Mina crumpled the newspaper.

'As if he were a Resistance sympathiser!' she snorted. 'He was her lover. It's a publicity stunt, this web of lies. She can't accuse us . . . mon Dieu, Lucien, she slept with him!'

'Her word against ours. And she's respected, reputed to receive the Légion d'Honneur. No one will believe us.' He shook his gnarled fist. 'The Association will be ruined, a scandal . . . prison, your grandchildren will know . . .'

71

'Prison? We're old. It was wartime. You make no sense.'

'La Rouquine suspects we killed him. She's made him out to be a hero, she'll accuse us.'

'He was her lover,' Mina said. 'And why after all this time? She knew where to find us, to confront us.'

'Don't you see? She's planned this for years. Strikes out on the offensive, as usual, to bolster the grand illusion she's a Resistance heroine,' Lucien said. 'Her politician husband died, no one's left to protect her or her lies. She figures we'd never dare accuse her since . . .'

Mina stared at him. '*Tiens*! A German soldier bricked up in a basement wall during wartime poses no threat to us. Let him keep mouldering.'

'But you killed him, Mina,' Lucien said.

Mina trembled. Why did he bring that up?

'Or have you forgotten murdering the soldier like everything else that happened that night, Mina?'

As if she could forget.

'But h . . . he attacked. It was him or me, Lucien!'

She'd tried to push it away after all these years. The real reason, the haunting past. Mina thought of their years of work supported by donations now at risk. But La Rouquine wouldn't pursue this, she wouldn't dare unless . . . something else incriminating lay in that cellar.

The telephone drilled. Lucien sat up startled. 'The *flics* already! Questions . . .'

72

She had to act calm.

'They won't necessarily link this to us,' Mina said. 'Let me handle it.'

She picked up the receiver of the old black rotary dial phone, the tattooed numbers on her arm visible.

'Resistance Association, *bonjour*.' She listened. 'A murdered *Feldwebel* . . . Sergeant?' Mina's wrinkled face sagged. 'Sadly, many of our members who could provide insight have passed . . . concerning this memoir? Monsieur, the war spawned countless stories and rumours . . . I have no idea . . . an interview? We're very busy . . . next week . . . call back and we'll make an appointment.'

'Who was that?'

'A reporter sniffing a story,' she said. 'We'll leave it alone, he'll go away.'

'La Rouquine won't let it go away. You can't bury your head in the sand now.'

Mina noticed Lucien's stricken face. Once he'd been young, the ringleader of their Resistance youth group, and wore wooden-soled Occupation-made clogs like the rest of them. At the beginning, their meetings were innocent, Mina remembered. Politically ripe, they met with their friends after Hebrew lessons at Saturday-*shut*, collecting money for the Spanish Civil War, for the children in Madrid, determined to open people's eyes. Lucien and the others came from families living in one room like hers. One bag of coal a month for heat. Always the smell of leather seeping from the factory on the heels of the cold. The one metal courtyard spigot, the only source of water for the five-storied building, carried up worn winding stairways. The toilet on the *palier*, in between floors, the buckets rimmed with ice on January mornings.

Now he was a frightened old man afraid of secrets. More afraid than she was.

She stared at him. 'What aren't you telling me, Lucien?'

'They'll find them.'

His tone sent a shiver up Mina's spine.

'Them? What do you mean?' A quiver of unease ran through her.

'Him. That's what I mean, Mina. We have to check the cellar, make sure there's no trace of him,' he said, his thin mouth set in a determined line.

She shook her head. Her arthritis had kicked in, she was on blood pressure medication. No way would she budge.

'You're panicking over nothing,' she said. 'I need to go home, cook for my great-grandaughter's bat mitzvah party.'

'So you want to take the chance when La Rouquine shows up with the press . . . ?'

'*Non* . . . I don't know.'

Fearful and confused, she had no answer. With a sinking feeling she knew the past had come back to haunt them. But then, had it ever gone away?

74

Lucien dialled a number on the phone. Mina stared out the window at the budding plane trees lining the *quai*. Could anyone ever get away from the past?

He slammed down the phone, interrupting her thoughts.

'Get your bag,' he said. 'According to the concierge's daughter they're doing electrical work in the cellar. It could mean they're opening the walls.'

Mina's shoulders twitched. She dreaded the five-minute walk she'd avoided with painstaking care all these years, the street full of memories. Now it looked like she had no choice.

Out on the *quai* Mina's misgivings ballooned as they turned the corner into rue du Faubourg Saint Martin. Her hands trembled seeing the wrought-iron balconied sand-stone apartment building, like all the others except for the deeper blackened patina of soot. Next door stood the old Lévitan warehouse. Now a remodelled publicity firm but during the Occupation, the German warehouse storing looted goods from Jewish deportees' apartments.

They stood in the now deepening twilight in front of a crowded café. On the boulevard's pavement around them Indian men clustered in conversation, an African woman in a bright yellow headdress pushed a stroller. The new immigrants of the tenth arrondissement, but in their day it had been Russians, Poles and Lithuanians.

'There's people everywhere,' she said.

'We have to check, Mina,' he said.

'And if we find something, what would we do?' She pulled his arm. 'Let's leave, Lucien. We'll deny everything.'

But he hit the numbers on the digicode and the door buzzed open.

'Ah, Monsieur Lucien, long time no see,' said a young woman with a baby on her hip standing at the concierge's door. 'Maman's shopping, *desolé*.'

Startled, he stepped back then recovered.

'*Ça va*, Delphine,' he said, greeting her with kisses on both cheeks. 'Just getting things from storage. Don't worry, I remember the way, we'll see ourselves out.'

'Careful on the stairs, one of the lights went out,' she said, nodding to Mina. 'They're steep.'

She meant for old people like you. Mina thought. *'Merci.'*

He led the way past the wirecage elevator. In the back. Mina saw the rear cobbled courtyard with green garbage containers by planter boxes of delphiniums and pots of geraniums.

Lucien opened the cellar door, leaned on his cane, took one step down.

Mina stopped. 'But this is ridiculous! My back's gone. I won't go down there again. I can't.'

'You came this far, Mina! Don't make it so difficult.'

Lucien clutched his cane, staring at her.

'This feels wrong,' Mina said.

'It's simple,' said Lucien. 'It was always the plan. We made a pact.' He switched on the cellar light.

'A pact . . . what do you mean?' asked Mina.

Lucien ignored her. 'Ready?'

She stood, not budging. 'What pact?'

He leaned forward, lowered his voice. 'Years ago our group made a pact never to reveal what happened. Or to let anyone find the body.'

'But everyone's gone except us.'

'That's why I must keep my word.'

She'd never heard about this pact . . . what did it mean? Dread filled her but before she could ask more he'd gone ahead. She clutched the railing as Lucien proceeded down the narrow stone stairs. Dampness and the smell of mildew and rotting wood assailed her nostrils. And it took her back to that time so long ago but still vivid today.

Sixteen years old, her hands browned with shoe polish and sore from stitching leather uppers on wooden-sole shoes – doing the piece work her parents took in to survive and put food on the table. She walked in public always anxious an official would demand her papers and discover she'd folded her jacket lapel over her yellow star.

Lucien shone the flashlight over the arched stone walls branching into tunnels under the building. Flaking stucco powdered the beaten earth floor. Electrical wires and tools were set to the side. Lining the walls were caged storage areas for each apartment, holding plastic bins, children's bikes, chairs behind the wooden enclosures.

'It didn't look like this before,' Lucien said in alarm. 'That's all new.'

'When did you last come here?' Mina asked.

'Years ago,' he said. 'It's Maman's old storage. I rent it. They never ask questions.' Lucien shuffled ahead. A bare electric bulb cast stark light over their faces.

'Number 38, that's it.' Lucien reached under the enclosure, rooted in the dirt, pulled out a key and unlocked the padlock. He opened the door of a warped wooden shed to a musty smell.

Mina saw the cobwebbed foot-pedal sewing machine in the corner. 'You kept that, Lucien . . . here?'

His father had been a skilled tailor. 'Eh. I had no room in my place. When I came back from the camp, that's all that was left.' He shrugged but Mina caught the wistful look on his face. Lucien's family had been deported and he was the only one who returned.

Lucien pushed aside boxes and shone the flashlight on the bricked-up stone wall.

'I remembered wrong.' Lucien shook his head. 'See, the bricked-up part goes further all along the wall. Which part was it?'

The absurdity of the venture struck Mina. '*Zut alors*! If we can't find it, how can any one else? Let's go.'

He'd gone to the side of the locker, shone the beam and stepped back. '*Mon Dieu!*'

The toes of faded black leather boots stuck

through a hole in the crumbling mortared brick. The blood drained from Mina's face. She turned to run and his cane landed across her arm.

'No you don't,' he said. 'It's too late.' Lucien blinked in fear. 'They'll find him. I didn't live all these years to be arrested for murder,' he said, his voice now edged with steel. 'I promised the others.'

'You're crazy!'

'So Mina, you'll let her get away with lies . . . again?'

'But what can we do?'

'We can manage part of it,' said Lucien. 'Call your grandson, tell him there's old furniture and we need his help. Get him to bring his butcher's van. But first . . .'

He took a pick, then handed Mina a garden hoe from the locker.

'You expect me to use this?' Mina asked.

Lucien spread sheets of plastic from the locker over the dirt. 'There's no way to cover this up, we've got to get him out.'

He was right.

While they worked, a slow process, footsteps rumbled from the floor above. Lucien switched on an old transistor radio, the static and bad reception drowning out the noise of the chipping and scraping. The wartime-grade mortar chipped away and crumbled. Mina knelt on the ground removing the bricks, piling them one by one. After half an hour, scraps of the wool Feldgrau soldier's uniform showed.

Mina wiped the sweat from her brow and sniffed.

A dry must-filled odour and sixty-year-old air emanated from the wall. The air of decay. Her mind went back to that night, this cavern lit by sputtering candles; they'd arranged for their Hebrew teacher to escape on a waiting canal barge and Mina had been early, the first of the group to arrive.

But instead of Lucien and their teacher, she'd found the blond, well-fed Wehrmacht soldier, the perfect Aryan. The young, handsome soldier from the warehouse next door who'd turned a blind eye to her yellow star and given her food. Not once but several times. She'd never told the others or her parents where the food came from. Or about the warm touch of his hands when he held hers. Now the soldier held a bottle in his hand, beer fumes emanated from his breath. 'I waited for you, thought you like this,' he said. 'Now why does Hansi think that?' He squinted his eyes as if in thought. 'Hansi thinks you're nice. A nice girl.' He slurred his words in broken French. Drunk, he was drunk.

'You've been drinking.'

'For courage.' A fragment of a smile shone on his handsome rosy-cheeked face. 'My Kommandant wouldn't like me to share this.'

She felt a wave of dizziness and looked down at her feet. Bread, cheese and slices of ham lay on a blanket on the floor. She'd only eaten a bowl of grey potatoes that day.

'Hansi won't tell about your friends.'

'My friends?' She backed up, tripping on the pile of stones on the dirt floor. 'Who told you?'

He grinned, his blue eyes glazed. 'The redhead.' He staggered against the wall. Young, only eighteen, two years older than her. 'Hansi wants his girl.'

So La Rouquine informed on them, she realised with a start, and the escape plan. And Hansi wanted La Rouquine. Now there'd be no more food. An irrational bolt of jealousy shot through her. No more of his kindness or the smile that lit up his eyes when he saw her.

She stiffened.

Waving his arm, he gestured to the food. 'Eat. Then Hansi will teach you card game.'

'No, you have to go . . .'

She heard the creaking of the floorboards overhead, the cellar's door opening. And she panicked. How could she explain this to the others, to her Hebrew teacher in hiding from the Germans?

But she knew how it would look finding her with a German soldier, taking his food. They'd accuse her of collaborating when all she'd been was hungry and keen to feel the kindness he'd shown her.

'I think you are playing. You like Hansi.'

'I do . . . I mean I don't . . . can't.'

He smiled. A light lit in his eyes. 'In the *vaterland* at school Hansi writes poetry. Now you inspire Hansi.'

And La Rouquine, did she inspire him, too?

81

'You have to go. Now.'

Footsteps sounded on the stairs. She grabbed his hands, his warm hands, and pulled. If he didn't leave the others would think she had betrayed their Resistance cell, sabotaged the tutor's escape.

'They're coming, they can't know . . . find you . . . please.'

He shook his blond head, folded his arms across his uniformed chest unbudging. '*Nein*. Hansi stay.'

This was going horribly wrong.

'The redhead . . .'

That's when she'd found the stone and smashed his head. Stupefied, he stumbled. She'd pounded his head again and again. Until his blood pooled in a puddle in the dirt, glinting in the candlelight.

'Watch out.' Lucien's pick struck with a hard thud, then the bricks crumbled in a whoosh of billowing grey dust, revealing a hollow. Inside a mummified figure in the fragments of a Wehrmacht uniform leered with brown leathered lips, the dried-up hollow eye sockets open above pinched-in cheeks. The desiccated brown-skinned hands twisted as if clutching the wall.

Mina gasped in horror. Hansi, once handsome, was now a grotesque mummy.

'Well preserved, eh?' Lucien said. He reached for the gold swastika signet ring on Hansi's pinkie. He pulled, and the finger came away with his ring.

The bile rose in Mina's stomach.

'Help me before he disintegrates more.'

Lucien lifted and together, with effort, they pulled the corpse out. Awkward, like holding a store dummy, and quite light except for the heavy boots and mouldering wool uniform disintegrating at their touch. Hansi's stiff hands like claws poking out. 'See a sergeant's stripes,' Lucien said. He and Mina pulled the garbage bag over it. The black jackboots protruded. Before they could put another garbage bag over them footsteps sounded.

'Lucien?' said a voice.

His red rheumy eyes batted in terror. 'The concierge.'

Mina pushed him forward. 'Get her back upstairs.'

An aproned woman in support hose, clogs and hair in a bun smiled. 'Aaah, your friend . . .'

Lucien walked forward, blocking her view. 'Jeanine . . .'

'Good thing you came, your other friend came looking for you,' she said, peering over his shoulder.

'That's strange, I haven't lived here in years, Jeanine. Who?'

She shook her head. 'A bourgeois matron, well dressed, red hair. But I didn't give your address, I told her I'd tell you first.'

Mina's heart pounded. La Rouquine! Her pills, she'd taken her blood pressure pills at breakfast but didn't know if her heart would hold out.

'Jeanine, I'll meet you upstairs,' Lucien said, 'and settle what I owe for the locker.'

Lucien waited until her footsteps receded. 'She's curious. Put him back in.'

'And have La Rouquine find him, she's been here already!' said Mina. 'We'll fit him in the bag, take it out the courtyard door to the trash.'

'He's too stiff, he won't fit.'

'Then break his legs, Lucien,' she said, in exasperation.

Mina turned away at the sight of Lucien leaning on the corpse's shoulders, the brittle sounds of breaking bones. She shone the flashlight in the gaping hole. She saw what looked like old blankets and fished around with the flashlight. A black spider skittered across a man's old-fashioned brown shoe with a raised heel. She pulled the rotting blanket apart, saw a trousered leg inside. And she screamed.

'Shut up.'

'Who else did you kill, Lucien?'

Lucien's shoulders shook. And a single tear slid down his cheek. He pulled the blanket aside. Black hair drooped over a desiccated brown face, a hunched figure in brown rags.

'But I don't understand,' Mina said, bewildered. 'I helped you brick up the wall . . .'

'La Rouquine said she slept with the German to save her family,' Lucien said. 'She lied. Never did it.'

'What? But I thought . . .'

'Everyone did. She was protecting her club-footed

84

father, who worked next door in the Germans' warehouse. He took deportees' jewellery and sold it on the black market.'

Her heart thudded at the revelation. She'd got it all wrong. Mina swallowed hard. 'You mean . . .'

'You took our teacher to the canal barge and we finished bricking him up,' Lucien interrupted. 'But La Rouquine showed up, made excuses and beat a quick exit. Later her father came down to his locker, he saw the blood.'

'And then?' Mina stared at the corpse's twisted foot.

'Her father threatened first to turn us in to the Kommandantur, then to blackmail us.'

'Never. He was a Jew!'

Lucien shook his head, venom in his eyes. '*Non*, only her poor mother. He had a club foot, that's the trouble. Too easy to identify.'

'You killed her father and bricked him up, too?'

'Like you said, either him or us,' he said.

Her shoulders crumpled in shame. She averted her eyes, regret filling her. But she couldn't tell Lucien the truth.

'Mina, you remember the Wehrmacht patrols on the street,' Lucien said. 'What choice did we have?'

She struggled, pulling more bricks away. 'Hurry, before the busybody comes back.'

'I lied to her mother, to everyone in the building.' Lucien kicked the dirt. 'I looked them in the face every day! And I'm still lying. Now La Rouquine's going to find him. It's prison!'

'Be quiet,' Mina said, now determined. 'Get him in the bag, then keep the concierge busy, then it's out in the courtyard. I'm calling my grandson.'

Lucien refused and collapsed against the wall, staring with a vacant look. She stood by the staircase and punched in her grandson's number. Only his answering machine. Why didn't these young ones ever answer their cell phones?

In the end Mina manoeuvred the stiff hunched figure of the father into the bag, wrapped it with duct tape. Her breathing grew laboured, coming in short gasps. The air was a miasma of dense dampness, the odour of desiccated corpses and rotting wool.

Lucien, immobile on the floor, clutched his knees, mumbling.

'Lucien, we have to get them upstairs,' she said, shaking his shoulders. 'Get up, I can't do this alone.'

His eyes batted in terror. 'The diamonds . . . prison . . .'

Mina twisted her hands; the more the past unravelled, the worse it grew. 'I don't want to know.'

'We funded the Association by selling the diamonds her father stole.'

Mina recoiled in horror. 'All these years and you never told me.'

'How do you think we kept the Association

going?' Lucien gave a short laugh. 'All blood money.'

She thought of all their work, the effort. 'But if he stole from Jews, it's helped Jews for years.'

Lucien shook his head. 'And I took some to open my shop.'

Shocked, she looked around. 'Quit living in the past. It's over. Look, we've got to get them out of here. Now!'

Lucien looked at her with unseeing eyes.

Mina needed to think, but with the bodies and Lucien, and the tainted air, each breath was an effort. Somehow she had to carry the man she had killed upstairs.

Back by the soldier's corpse, Lucien was crawling and crying on the floor.

'Help me, Lucien,' she said, 'get his boots.'

'The Wehrmacht's coming,' Lucien said. 'I saw them.'

Terror clutched her. He was back in the past. Gone.

'That's why you have to help, Lucein, or they'll find him . . . right?'

He nodded, his eyes now bright, almost crazed.

'Good, take his boots, lift, that's right, now through the tunnel, up the stairs.'

Somehow they managed. The soldier's brittle hands scraped the wall like he didn't want to go, a last effort to stay. Sickened, she forced herself to mount the steps with the burden of his mummified corpse.

At the landing, Lucien peered out. The sound of a violin came from above, the cry of a child, but no one stood in the hallway.

With one hand, he opened the door to the courtyard, and the black jackboot emerged from the garbage bag, They'd forgotten to duct tape it. She shoved it back inside.

'Hurry, Lucien,' she said, panting.

'In the shadowed courtyard, near pots of geraniums, they stuffed the soldier's corpse into an empty garbage container. Mina emptied the contents of another bin over it.

'One more, Lucien,' she whispered, 'before the Wehrmacht come. You all right?'

He waved Mina away, shuffled ahead, leaning on his cane.

Back in the cellar, the duct-taped garbage bag sat by the crumbled mortar, bricks and gaping hole. 'Lucien, you take this bag, I'll cover the hole.'

For a moment, Lucien looked bewildered, then a brief flash of pain crossed his face.

'Can you manage?'

He nodded with a glazed look

'Put it in the same place, you understand, before the . . .'

'*Oui*, before the Wehrmacht,' he interrupted. He pulled the bag and shuffled across the packed dirt floor.

Mina set the bricks back but it looked so obvious, any-one would be able to tell. And with the mortar gone, holes still remained. She didn't know how long she kept working, trying to fit bricks in the empty spaces. What could she do? Frantic, she searched the locker. She found an old dresser on wheels, and straining, lugged it to cover the hole. For now it would do.

Footsteps and shouts sounded from the stairway.

'Madame?' the concierge said. 'Madame, you must come now!'

Mina dragged the hoe, shovel and pickaxe back into the locker, shut the gate and put the padlock back on.

'The medics . . . *quelle horreur*!' The concierge appeared, nervously rubbing her hands.

'What . . . what's happened?' Mina tried to catch her breath.

Mina's eye caught on the brown *Soldbuch* fallen in the dirt. The *Ausweisepapier* passport-sized book that doubled as identification and pay book for German soldiers. She stepped on it before the concierge could advance further.

'Monsieur Lucien's had an attack,' she said.

Horrified, she tried to cover it with her foot. 'I'm coming.'

The concierge turned and Mina bent down to grab it. A Wehrmacht ID card with the name Hans Gruber; inside, a piece of paper. She froze, then made herself move, stuffing it inside her pocket with trembling hands.

A medic leaned over Lucien, who lay sprawled on the tiles with an oxygen mask over his pale face. Another medic's crossed hands pumped Lucien's chest in measured thrusts.

'Heart attack, 85 rue du Faubourg Saint Martin,' he said, into the microphone clipped on his collar. 'Send a second team.'

A woman with her hair in curlers stood watching on the staircase. Mina's mind snapped back into gear. She saw the garbage bag beyond Lucien's body.

'Lucien did too much, I told him,' the concierge said. 'I said I'll carry the garbage out. But,' she tugged Mina's sleeve and stared at her, 'he said the Germans were coming. He's gone a little funny, *non*?'

Mina said nothing, her feet rooted to the floor.

'I knew his mother, she never came back from the camp,' the concierge said, tugging Mina's sleeve harder, 'but I heard things when I took over. They hid Jews down there.'

Static erupted from the medic's microphone. 'We're out front, give us a status report.'

'No response,' said the medic.

Mina put her hand to her mouth. The medic thrust harder but Lucien's eyes had rolled up into his head.

'Make way, *s'il vous plaît*.' Stretcher bearers bumped the wall in the narrow hall.

'Too late.' The medic shook his head. The other medic stood and picked up Lucien's cane.

'Lucien?' Mina said. But he'd gone.

She choked back a sob. Her eyes settled on the

garbage bag. Now it rested on her. The medic looked around. 'His possessions, Madame?'

The concierge shook her head.

'*Non*, the poor man was taking things to the garbage. Let me take that, Monsieur.'

Mina stepped forward in alarm. Lucien's white face gleamed in the ball light. The medic stood blocking the courtyard door.

'*Non*, I'll do it,' she said.

'But Lucien said . . .'

Mina ignored her, grabbed the bag and, praying the concierge wouldn't stop her, dragged it past them. She had to get the bag out of here. In the courtyard, she paused, looked around to make sure they weren't watching, then heaved the bag. But she couldn't lift it high enough to reach into the bin. Exhausted, she leaned against the wall. Took deep breaths until the pounding pressure in her brain stopped. Lucien . . . she couldn't think about that now.

She hefted the bag again with all her strength, heard the crackling of brittle bones, and this time it landed in the bin. From inside came the squealing of rats disturbed by the noise.

Now she'd taken care of the proof. But she couldn't rest. Back in the hallway, she made herself walk past Lucien who was being lifted onto the stretcher. Past the curious look of the concierge.

Out on the street, yellow sodium streetlights shone on bystanders. Were they watching her? She kept going, trying to ignore the catch in her heart, that racing of her blood. The doctor warned her if that happened she had to stop and rest. Stop whatever she was doing. But she couldn't stop. Not just yet. A few more steps and she'd reach the bus stop.

Her pulse slower now, she scanned the street. Just ahead on her left the Number 47 bus approached the stop. She'd take the bus, get away. Keep the secrets. She took another step.

The bus driver never saw the old woman stumbling in the darkness into the street. His bus jolted at the thud and he heard the scream. He braked to a halt and jumped out.

'Madame, I didn't see you,' he said, kneeling by the old woman. '*Mon Dieu* . . . speak.'

Mina tried to open her mouth. Little white lights danced in front of her and she saw it all so clearly now. The Feldgrau uniform and the diamonds scattered in the blood they hadn't bothered to hide. She clutched her pocket and the little lights faded.

Passers-by paused on the pavement. Someone pointed. A *flic*, one of the passers-by, stopped and ran towards the old woman sprawled on the cobbled street. The *flic* knelt down and saw the woman's twisted broken neck. He felt for her pulse. Nothing. Clutched in her hand was an odd brown book. On the opened page he saw faded old-fashioned German script – Hans Gruber, *Blut-Gruppe O*, *Feldwehel*, and a sepia photo of a young man stamped over with an eagle clutching a wreath surrounding a swastika. And creased in the fold a yellowed paper with what looked like a German poem and the words *Mina je t'aime*.

PARIS CALLING

JEAN-HUGUES OPPEL

'Paris is calling for help, gentlemen . . .'
The suits with matching ties and pocket handkerchiefs sit around three sides of the boardroom table, stony faced. The only woman present (suit-blouse-neckscarf – not matching, for ultimate chic) greets the opening remark addressed solely to the men with a resigned shrug. She's more than used to the all-but-automatic boorishness of her peers, whatever their position in the social or political – above all political – hierarchy.

The speaker seems to notice his omission. By way of excusing himself, he grimaces vaguely in the woman's direction before going on, his torso bending forward slightly as he rests his fists on the table below him like pillars under a viaduct.

His sharp gaze took in his audience, face by face, before he uttered his first words, a way of quickly making acquaintance to avoid the tiresome ritual of introductions. No one avoided his eye. Someone coughed slightly, breaking the graveyard silence that had prevailed until then in the boardroom of a sumptuous building in the ministerial district.

No minister is present. They are all represented by their chiefs of staff or their deputies. The woman with the offbeat scarf hails from Foreign Affairs.

The speaker has the unmistakeable air of a secret service mole. Yes, Paris is calling for help, he repeats, enunciating each syllable, adding, after a short pause for breath, that as he speaks, right here, right now, it's no longer a question of deciding if the capital's terrible cry is justified or not, but of understanding why we remain deaf to it still today.

The woman with the scarf discreetly admires the speaker's subtle rhetoric, which somehow makes 'we' sound like 'you'. With a jerk of the chin, the speaker indicates the file handed to each person before they entered the room, a file whose contents will perhaps help unblock a few ears in high places. This hardbound file contains: a thick pamphlet of spiral-bound A4 pages, in small print to save paper; a series of colour and black-and-white photographs, numbered in the chronological order in which they were taken; a CD-ROM containing the report and photographs in current software formats for computer nerds incapable of reading anything – words or figures – unless it's on a screen.

The speaker reminds anyone who might not know that a study's been requested from his serv . . . from the organisation he works for. The slip draws a few ironic smiles from the assembled audience. Next the speaker announces that the summary of this study can be found in the written report which details all the sociological issues. The photographs are there to illustrate certain aspects of the phenomenon, the better to capture the imaginations of superiors whose minds are sometimes on other things; with a decent budget, they might have had animated images and stereo sound too.

In several shots, a casual observer might nonetheless note at first glance that a burning car in the night is a beautiful thing.

There were hundreds of them in the streets and in residential car parks in the autumn of last year, and in all four corners of the country. The fire had started at the gateways to the capital, following the umpteenth tragic news report of suburban youths pitted against police officers. The fire in the city had lasted a month.

A month of riots.

Riots that were predictable. The speaker would go even further, weighing his words: they were so predictable they should never have happened at all.

'Business good, Momo?'

'Well yeah, I s'pose, sir, but shit, it's been better! Hash doesn't pay like it used to, and I'm not even talking about the stuff that falls off the back of a van, hi-fis and TVs . . . Prices are rock bottom! Lucky there's still mobiles to make a bit of profit on, otherwise business would be a total disaster!'

'So it's lucky I turn up from time to time, huh?'

'Don't I know it, sir. You pay well but times are hard and I'm the family bread-winner, so you've got to understand I'm putting up prices for information . . .'

'You're on the ball, aren't you! Life's tough, especially for the poor, or didn't you know? People have got no money now, Momo, so they're going back to basics; first things first and the small stuff goes out the window, see?'

'I don't see anything when you start talking like the class brainbox!'

'Because you went to school, I suppose? It's true you can count . . .'

'Of course!'

'People are skint so they haven't got the money to buy your junk any more. D'you get it now, Momo?'

'Yes sir, I get it. But it stinks, if you ask me, because if that's true and it goes on like this any longer, things'll stay in the shit and we'll have to find ways out of it so we can put food on the table, see?

'If not, I'm telling you, all hell's going to break loose on the estates.

'The shit's really going to hit the fan, sir.'

The Prime Minister's chief of staff is disconcerted by the speaker's last assertion, delivered as if it were gospel truth: was he accusing the government of incompetence? Or worse, laxity? The Minister of the Interior's right-hand man immediately weighs in, fearing a dirty trick by opponents hidden even among those loyal to the majority party.

The speaker raises a conciliatory hand. He's accusing no one in particular. He's merely making an observation.

An observation that someone, anyone, should have made ages ago: the accumulation of social problems and architectural aberrations, the increased poverty resulting from the continued rise in unemployment and the growing precariousness of remaining jobs, of deliberately badly controlled illegal immigration and thus of more-or-less latent racism, which will eventually lead to the ghettoisation that automatically acts as a breeding ground for religious fanaticism, and . . . Need he go on? This has been the state of affairs for a good half century, deteriorating almost daily, depending on which party's in power, so we shouldn't pretend we just discovered the scale of the disaster upon opening our eyes this morning.

Undisguised anxiety is painted on most of the faces around the long table. Some of the speaker's words were unpleasant to hear, but more than that, they've prompted enormous doubts as to the reality on the ground. Several hands go up, requesting permission to speak.

The first question asked, relating to the allegedly 'badly controlled' illegal immigration, in fact sums up almost all the rest.

The speaker could have bet on it.

He restricts himself to reminding everyone that if there were available jobs elsewhere, no one would willingly leave their country and their family to come and sweat blood and tears in France. And if these jobs were properly remunerated, unemployed nationals would snap them up, but since the pay offered is worse than laughable, they're reserved for a docile workforce that's easily replaceable and thus exploitable because it's outside the law. Illegal workers fulfil these criteria perfectly.

Californians don't risk their lives swimming across the Rio Grande to go and work their fingers to the bone as illegal slaves in Mexico.

The speaker makes this point with a broad mocking smile.

His humour doesn't raise a laugh in the boardroom. The smile fades into a carnivorous scowl; the speaker chews his words like a predator that's captured its prey after three months of enforced starvation.

Once they've established that the massive presence of foreigners on their soil is artificial, but definitely never presented as such, it's easy to understand why racism rages on and why emphasis on minority issues is fast becoming prevalent. By humiliating the other without giving him a say in the matter, a painful feeling of powerlessness develops within him, and powerlessness leads to violence if over-enthusiastic souls fan the flames of revolt. The religious fanatic is a fine example of this bellows effect. One only needs to observe the growing number of veiled women and girls within a Muslim community adrift in Christian lands to measure the quasi-exponential expansion of a religion whose stranglehold tightens a little more each year around bewildered populations attempting to shelter behind the barriers of tradition.

The Ministry of Foreign Affairs delegate points out in passing that the veiling of women and girls in fact has very little to do with religion, fanatical or not, and a great deal to do with oppression by men who consider it's always less tiring to eat couscous than to make it.

The men around the table and the speaker feebly concur, looking away.

'Pissed off, Momo? Your girlfriend ditch you?'

'Her? Her father and brothers are giving me dirty looks, yeah, they're morons, but no it's not that.'

'What then?'

'Haven't you seen the neighbourhood, sir? It's enough to piss you off, isn't it? It's not a neighbourhood any more. There are so many cops on the street, day and night, it's a fucking pigsty! It wasn't exactly fun and games before, but now a guy can't work!'

'Is the deal breaking down again, Momo? My condolences! Well, you shouldn't have gone overboard with the Molotov cocktails ... It looked good on TV, but the President wasn't exactly thrilled, you know.'

'The President can go fuck himself! Is he going to put food on my table? Can he strip a truck with his eyes closed, the fat bastard? Cut good Colombian with the right dose of flour? Respray stolen cars? My arse.'

'That I don't know, but apparently he has other, hidden, talents. Tell me, little Momo, did I hear you right? There are still cars to steal? That's news! You didn't burn them all last month?'

'Don't take the piss, sir, I swear, life's no joke right now. If I'm broke, I can't pay the rent and my family will be evicted, the mayor said so, the bastard!'

The speaker draws himself up, an incantatory finger pointing to the ceiling. More serious, according to him, is the vanishing social mix in the capital.

A lot more serious because it has implications for the near future, so near it's already around the corner.

Does anyone here know the price per square metre in Paris? the speaker hammers it out to the beat of a requiem. Of the lowest possible rent, if you can find someone willing to let you even a crummy studio on the top floor with no lift? Who, among the Parisian middle classes, can still afford to live in the centre of Paris these days? The last remnants of accessible working-class districts are disappearing one by one under so-called joint urban rehabilitation programmes, which don't even bother to hide their true nature – lucrative property speculation – any more.

The Finance Minister's chief of staff looks at the speaker askance. He can't quite place this young upstart who makes remarks that a hardened left-winger wouldn't disagree with, and, making no bones about it, decides to ask him where he lives. Unfazed, the speaker replies that he lives in the outer suburbs but for security reasons he's not authorised to discuss that here. He won't, however, insult anyone by asking for private addresses at such a fine gathering of senior ministerial officials, who ought to be aware of how many of their subordinates really can easily afford to live less than twenty minutes away from their workplace.

Never lost for words when the opportunity presents itself, the only woman in the room points out that it's become commonplace at international level: what mid-income household can still afford to live in the centre of London, for instance? The big cities are emptying themselves of their poor, one after the other. The exodus speeds up when a hurricane has the bright idea of ravaging the metropolitan coastline. Having said that, the rich don't all cling to their town houses but prefer a life of luxury in the country or the privacy of good company in five-star apartment complexes with a pool and private militia, sifting visitors at the entrance.

The speaker doesn't disagree, but his concern is Paris, Paris whose well-off inhabitants are not only deaf to the complaints of suburbanites but also blind to the urgency of their situation since they don't realise the ghetto's been reversed. The speaker's tone suddenly turns bitter, the words fall one by one like bombs.

It's time to stop feeling sorry for ourselves. Urgent full-scale measures must be taken, unless we want to see the isolated city plundered, invaded by new, ravenous beggars who will cross the orbital road – on horseback if necessary, if they haven't eaten their horses first. Their kids with wolf-like fangs are no longer content with fine words when it's become impossible even to make a dishonest living. The speaker knows them. The speaker's seen them. The speaker no longer sees those who were once his best informants on the ground.

Yesterday, they stole. Today, they have guns.

Barbaric hordes are surrounding the capital. It will only take a spark for the city to be besieged, while awaiting the final assault which will have the last privileged few taking refuge on the Ile Saint Louis or the Ile de la Cité, in the middle of the Seine, blowing up the bridges behind them. In the glow of the fires that will devour the nights, the city of fire and blood will plunge into the chaos of a future with no tomorrow. So yes, again yes, Paris smells danger and sends out an alarm signal. Paris is calling. Paris is calling with all the strength it has left. Paris is calling for other cities to help before it's too late.

'You were meant to call me, Momo. Did you forget?'

'No, sir, but I couldn't. I was busy, I couldn't find the time, you'll have to forgive me . . .'

'Oh, so you found a job? An honest job, I mean?'

'Don't swear, sir!'

'Ha, that's a good one, well done! I knew you were a good grass and now I see you can be witty too. So tell me, am I going to have to do without your services, Momo?'

'Well, sir, it won't be like before, sir, yeah, I'm sorry but . . .'

'But you've found someone who pays better than me, that's all. I get it, I'm not stupid, I only hope you're not barking up the wrong tree. They're saying second-hand Kalashnikovs bring in more than dope these days, Momo?'

'I don't know, sir. Seems so, yeah. But then some people would say anything to get attention.'

'Momo, you disappoint me, you know that?'

'I'm not a grass any more, sir!'

Alone and last to leave the boardroom, the woman with the scarf slowly closes the open file in front of her as if sealing a tomb. The speaker's lyrical flights have scared her. His last words are still ringing in her ears, like a haunting refrain: Paris is calling for help . . .

But who will hear?

Translation © Lulu Norman and Ros Schwartz

THE FLÂNEUR OF LES ARCADES DE L'OPÉRA

Featuring Begg and Lapointe,
Metatemporal Detectives

MICHAEL MOORCOCK

THE FIRST CHAPTER:
IN THE LUXEMBOURG GARDENS

In all the many cases investigated by Sir Seaton Begg of the Home Office Metatemporal Investigative Agency, one of the most curious concerned his co-operation with his opposite number, Commissaire Lapointe of the Sureté du Temps Perdu, involving not only the albino gentleman connected to a royal house whom we call 'Monsieur Zenith', but also members of an infamous terrorist gang, a long-dead enemy of Begg's German cousins and the well-known adventuress, Mrs Una Persson. As Begg's friend, the pathologist Dr 'Taffy' Sinclair, remarked, 'For a while it seemed that Chaos, in all its unchained wildness, had been let loose through every region of our vast and complex multiverse, so that even now we cannot be certain whether it was contained or whether we are merely experiencing a moment of relative harmony in a howling cacophony . . .'

'I cannot tell you, my old friend, how delighted I am that you should come over at such short notice.'

Lapointe, his assistant Bardot, Taffy and Begg were wandering through the pale gold autumn light of the Luxembourg Gardens. The chestnut trees were shedding dark reds and yellows and the flower beds were full of beauty on the verge of succumbing to winter. Lapointe had thought it expedient for them to talk in the open air where there was less chance of being overheard.

'The train? Was it comfortable?'

In his light tweed sports jacket, white shirt and well-pressed flannels, Lapointe had a bulky, stiff-necked, slightly professorial air, with a great wave of grey hair untidily arranged over his pale fore-head. His deep green eyes, angular features and heavy body gave him the air of a large amiable dinosaur. Begg knew his opposite number had one of the sharpest minds on the Continent. Single-handedly Lapointe had captured the ex-police inspector turned crook: George Marsden Plummer (alias 'Maigret' in France) who had once been Lapointe's chief. Lapointe had also been the one to bring 'Fantomas' to book at last. Together he and Begg had tracked down 'Jock Collyn', other-wise known as The Master Mummer, and been instrumental in his lingering to this day on Devil's

Island. Inspector Bardot, on the other hand, had no spectacular record, but was much admired at the Quai des Orfèvres for his methodology and his coolness under pressure. Small, dark, he seemed permanently and privately amused. He wore a buttoned three-piece grey suit and what was evidently an English school tie.

The two Home Office men had come from London via the recently opened Subchannel Excavation, whose roads and railway lines now connected the two nations, a material addition to the decades-old Entente Cordiale, an alliance which had been cemented by the signing of a European-wide Mutual Co-operation Pact, which, with the Universal Civil Rights Act, united all the Great Powers, including the Confederated Forty-Seven States of America, in one mighty alliance, sharing common laws and goals.

'Perfectly, thank you,' said Begg, speaking excellent French. Lapointe had put the STP's private express at his disposal. The journey had taken less than an hour and a half from London to Paris. 'I must say, Lapointe, that you French chaps have your priorities well in hand – rapid and comfortable transport and excellent food among them. We had a superb lunch en route.'

The French detective acknowledged this compliment with a small self-deprecating shrug.

Taffy, taller than the others, murmured his own discreet appreciation.

'I gather, Dr Sinclair, that you are recently back

from the Republic of Texas?' Lapointe courteously acknowledged the pathologist, whose expertise was internationally famous.

'Indeed.' Sinclair removed his wide panama and wiped his glistening head with a large Voysey-patterned Liberty's handkerchief, which seemed an uncharacteristic part of his otherwise muted wardrobe. Save for his taste in haberdashery, nobody would have guessed that during his time at Oxford he had been a leading light in the post-Pre-Raphaelite revival and that women had swooned over his massive head of hair and melancholy features almost as much as over his poetry. Like his friend and colleague, he wore a cream-coloured linen suit, but whereas Begg's tie was a rather flamboyant bow, Sinclair's neck was adorned by his old school colours. Indeed, his tie was identical to Bardot's. The two had been contemporaries at Blackfriars School and later had attended the Sorbonne before Bardot, eldest son of a somewhat infamous Aquilonian house, entered the service of the Quai d'Orsay and Sinclair, after a spell in the army, decided to follow his father into medicine and the civil service.

'You are familiar with the shopping arcades which radiate off the Place de L'Opéra?' murmured Lapointe once they were strolling down a broad avenue of chestnut trees towards the Gardens' rue Guynemer entrance. 'And you are aware, I am sure, of the reputation the area has at night, where assignations of the heart are pursued and men and women of a certain inclination are said to come together.'

'I have read something of the place,' said Begg, while Taffy nodded gravely.

'These arcades are the most complex in Paris, of course, and extend into and beneath the surrounding buildings, in turn becoming a warren of corridors and suites of chambers connected to the catacombs. They have never been fully mapped. It is said that some poor devils have been lost there for eternity, cursed to wander forever beneath the city.'

Begg smiled. 'I am familiar with Smith's Kitchen in London, which is similarly configured. I know the stories of the Arcades, yes. How fanciful they are, I have yet to judge. I know, too, that they were spared destruction by Haussmann, when he was building the boulevards of Paris for Louis Napoleon, because the Emperor himself wished to preserve his own somewhat lavish pied-à-terre where he maintained the notorious Comtesse de Gavray.'

'Exactly, my friend. Whose favours he was said to share with Balzac the Younger. I gather there was some scandal. Didn't Balzac denounce her as a German spy?'

'In 1876. Yes. It was the end of her career. She fled to Berlin and ended her days in penury. Strangely, this present case has echoes of that one.'

As he reached the little glass and wrought-iron

café across from the Théâtre des Marionettes, Lapointe paused. 'The coffee here isn't too bad and I see there is a table just over there where we are unlikely to be disturbed.'

With the acquiescence of the others, Lapointe let them seat themselves at the dark-green metal table and signalled for a *serviteur*, who came immediately, recognising a regular customer. A brief exchange followed. Typically, the Englishmen ordered café crème and the Frenchmen took theirs espresso. They sat in silence for a little while, admiring the merry-go-round, with its vividly painted horses rising and falling in comforting regularity, circling to the tune of a complex steam-driven fairground calliope, as excited little boys and girls waved to waiting parents. The puppet theatre was yet to open and many of the children, Begg knew, would disappear into its darkness soon enough to witness the traditional bloody escapades of Guignol which had entertained French children for the past century or more.

It delighted Begg to see that the same diversions which he had enjoyed as a boy were equally pleasing to this, the first generation of the new century. He was always grateful that his father's diplomatic work had allowed him to make a home in the French capital. For him London and Paris made a natural marriage, if not exactly of opposites, then of complementary personalities. Both had powerful public images and a thousand secrets, not all of them by any means sinister.

Commissioner Lapointe leaned forward so that his voice could only be heard by the other three men at the table. 'You have no doubt already reached the conclusion, my friends, that this business concerns the ongoing problems we have in Germany. While the insurgency is generally under control, Hitler's terrorists continue to trouble the German government and our friends in the Reichstag have asked us for help. In the main we have done our best to remain uninvolved with internal German politics. After defeating Hitler and driving him out of Poland, we were quickly able to support a new democratic government and withdraw our troops to this side of the Rhine. However—' Lapointe shrugged, slowly stirring his coffee.

'Röhm and his Freikorps?' murmured Begg.

'Precisely. They are relatively few, of course. But Röhm's insurgents continue to do considerable damage. They have attacked Wehrmacht barracks, civilian institutions and even targets outside the country. They have set off bombs in public places and continue to violate synagogues and Jewish cemeteries. While Hitler remains at large, insurgent morale remains high and their plans ambitious. Disaffected petite bourgeoisie for the most part, who had hoped to succeed in war where they had failed in peace. Well, gentlemen, we have reason to believe they are planning an ambitious attack outside Germany's borders. This attack, we think, is aimed at creating a large number of civilian casualties, probably Jewish. And we are fairly certain that it will occur in France, probably in Paris.'

'And how can we be of assistance?' asked Begg, clearly puzzled by their being asked to engage in what, on the surface, appeared to be primarily an internal matter for the French government.

'In two words, my old friend—' Lapointe glanced around before dropping his voice even lower. '*Monsieur Zenith* . . .'

Now the British investigator understood. He sat back in his chair, his face suddenly grave. From his pocket he took his ancient briar and a tobacco pouch. He began to fill the pipe with dark shag. Taffy Sinclair, too, was frowning. A profound silence surrounded the four men. At last Inspector Bardot spoke. 'He is known to be in Paris. Indeed, he has been here for some time. A familiar figure in the Opéra arcades. He has exposed himself quite openly, yet, whenever our people attempted to apprehend him, pouf! He is gone like smoke.'

'Eventually, it became clear to us that we would be better engaged in keeping watch on him,' continued Lapointe. 'For some months he has continued the same habits. Every morning between eleven and one he appears in the passage D'lappe, always wearing perfect morning dress. He takes his coffee at L'Albertine. He reads his newspaper: *Le Figaro*, usually, but sometimes the *New York Herald Tribune*. He strolls. He makes a small purchase or two. He enters a bookshop and inspects a few volumes. He has even been known to visit Larnier's Waxworks. Occasionally, he buys a book – usually a classic of some kind. Then, at lunchtime, he will either stroll towards the Quartier Latin, taking the Pont St-Michel, where he will eat lunch at Lipp's or he will enter one of the more shadowy branches of the arcades and – vanish! Sometimes he will be seen again in the afternoon, making his way to the Louvre, where he will inspect a different exhibit, though he seems to favour Da Vinci's *Portrait of a Young Jew in Female Dress*. Then he will return to the arcades and, yes, he will disappear again.'

'He speaks to no one?'

'Oh, he will pass the time of day with any number of persons. He is politeness itself, especially where a lady is concerned. He has conversed with more than one of our own people, usually realising immediately who they are. He is the very model of a gentlemanly *flâneur*, whiling away his hours in what some would call a desultory way. He buys his cigarettes at Sullivan's, his newspaper from the same kiosk at the south-eastern corner of the arcades. He carries a cane in ebony and silver. His gloves are always that perfect shade of lavender, matching his cravat, his coat cut just so, his hat at just such an angle, his buttonhole always the same, a crimson rosebud emphasising those blood-red eyes of his. Women, of course, are fascinated by him. Yet, with a recent exception, he keeps no regular engagements with anyone, though he will enjoy a little flirtation over an aperitif, perhaps. He tips well and is much liked by the staff wherever he takes refreshment. Sometimes, a Lagonda limousine calls for him at the north-west entrance and he enters it. We have been able to trace the car to the general area of Clichy but all we know is that it is driven by a Japanese chauffeur and is garaged in rue Clément, in the name of a Monsieur Amano. There its batteries are recharged. Everything is in order. The Lagonda has not left Paris since we have been observing it.'

'And as far as you know neither has Monsieur Zenith?'

'Exactly.'

'Where does he go at night?' Dr Sinclair wanted to know.

'That's the thing, old man,' said Bardot in English, 'we simply can't find out!'

'It is as if he becomes invisible from the evening hours until mid-morning,' added Lapointe. 'Then, suddenly, he appears in the Opéra Arcades, perfectly dressed and poised, as ever. Even if we had a cause to arrest him, which we have not, he would still evade us. Indeed, if he had not been seen in the company of a suspected Nazi agent, we would not devote so much interest to him. He is a decorated war hero, after all, leading a Polish electric cavalry brigade during the recent conflict. But sadly his actions suggest that he is helping organise whatever Nazi plot is about to be unleashed on honest civilians. His name has come up more than once, in various coded messages we have intercepted. Sometimes he is merely Monsieur Z, sometimes 'Zenith' and sometimes 'Zodiac'. All versions of his own given name, of course. There is no doubt at all that he is Count Rudolf Zoltan von Beck, descendant of the infamous 'Crimson Eyes' who terrorised the people of Mirenburg and London in the course of the last century. He renounced his title as hereditary ruler of Wäldenstein. But as for the suggestion that Hitler intended to restore him as pupper monarch there, had his plans for the conquest of Europe been successful, that is surely nonsense!'

'Especially since he voluntarily gave up his title,' mused Sir Seaton. From his mouth now issued alarming quantities of dark smoke as he fired up his old pipe. 'I am still curious as to why he moved his base from London to Paris. He was even rumoured to have been seen recently in Berlin. It is as if he were fascinated by our friend Herr Hitler. This is not the first time he and that gentleman have been linked, in various incarnations across the multiverse.'

'Perhaps he agrees with Hitler's ideas?' ventured Lapointe. But Begg shook his head.

'They are scarcely 'ideas'. They are the opinions of a beerhall braggart of the kind commonly found throughout the world. They emerge to fill a vacuum. They might appeal to an uneducated and unemployed labourer, a dispossessed shopkeeper or some disenchanted professional soldier like Röhm – even some brainless and inbred titled fool. But Zenith is none of those things. Indeed, he is both well educated and of superior intelligence. His only weakness is his thirst for danger, for the thrill which fills the veins with pounding blood and which takes one's mind off the dullness of the day-to-day.' It was as if Begg knew exactly what moved his old adversary. The expression on Dr Sinclair's face suggested that he thought the metatemporal investigator's remark might well have been a self-description. 'And he would only ally himself with such a creature if it somehow suited his own schemes. Years ago, after he was rescued from secret police head-quarters in Belgrade, where he had been imprisoned and tortured for his resistance to the dictator, he gave me his solemn promise that he was renouncing his old ways and from then on would only steal from the thieves, as it were, and contribute most of his gains to excellent causes, some of which would founder completely if he didn't help. And the Polish military will tell you how he equipped that electric tank division from his own funds!'

'So you think he is planning a job in Paris?' asked the commissioner. He allowed a small smile to flicker across his face. 'After all, we are not short of the undeserving rich . . .'

'Perhaps. Or he could be diverting himself here while all the time what he is doing at night is the important thing. Eh?' From under his lowering, sardonic brow. Sir Seaton returned Lapointe's smile. 'Might he be making himself so public that all our attention is drawn to his flaneurism and we ignore his true activities?'

'What do you suggest? We need to know details of Hitler's plans soon, Sir Seaton. We must anticipate and counter whatever terror the Nazi insurgents intend to unleash.'

'Naturally you must. What else can you tell me?'

'Only that the adventuress Mrs Una Persson recently took rooms above the Arcades, shortly after I contacted you. For the last three days she has been seen in the gardens walking her two cats, a grey and a black Oriental shorthair. She is a known associate of Monsieur Zenith, is she not?'

'Of him and others,' agreed Begg, his eyes narrowing in an expression of reminisence. 'And does she have a female companion, perhaps? A Miss Cornelius?'

'Not as far as we know.'

Sinclair seemed surprised. His eyes darted from Lapointe to Begg and then to Bardot, who shrugged.

'Mrs Persson has been seen talking to Zenith,' Bardot offered. 'Yesterday she had lunch with him at L'Albertine. We had a lip reader eating at a nearby table. Zenith mentioned Hitler and Rohm. He might have spoken of an explosive charge in Paris. Unfortunately we did not learn where. She said that she had investigated a site where a bomb would create the most damage. So certain of those among our superiors are now convinced they are working together for the Nazi insurgents.'

Lapointe interrupted rapidly. 'Of course, I find that impossible to believe.' He shrugged. 'But I have, as we all have, certain bosses, owing their jobs more to their connections than to their native abilities, who insist on believing Zenith and Mrs Persson are in league with Hitler and his underground army. It could be, perhaps, that they are both working for themselves and that they have plans which Hitler's activities will facilitate. My guess is that some treasure is involved, for it is not Zenith's habit to dabble in civilian politics. At least, as far as I know. Not so, of course, Mrs Persson. Is there some way you could find out any more, Sir Seaton? Something I could take to my superiors which will let me get on with the real business Zenith has in Paris? Whatever that may be.'

Sir Seaton finished his café créme, smiling out at a group of little boys and girls running with fixed attention towards the pleasure of the carousel.

'I could ask him,' he said.

THE SECOND CHAPTER:
A CONVERSATION AT L'ALBERTINE

Inevitably, Seaton Begg met his albino cousin close to the noon hour in the Arcades de L'Opéra where eight galleries branched off a central court, containing a paved piazza and an elaborate fountain. He appeared almost by magic, smiling courteously and lifting his hat in greeting. Impeccably well-mannered, Zenith, of course, was incapable of ignoring him.

'*Bonjour, cher cousin*!' The albino raised his own tall grey hat. 'What a great pleasure to come upon you like this! We have a great deal to talk about since our last meeting. Perhaps you would be good enough to take a cup of coffee with me at L'Albertine?'

After they had dispensed with their hats and ordered, Count Zenith leaned back in his chair and moved his ebony cane in an elegant, economic gesture in the direction of a beautiful young woman wearing a long, military-style black coat, and with a helmet of raven-black hair, walking two cats, one a grey Oriental, the other a black, in the sunny gardens at the centre of the arcades. He gave no indication that he was already acquainted with the woman who was, of course, Mrs Una Persson, the famous European adventuress. 'Has anyone, I wonder, ever really tried to imagine what it must be like to have the mind of a beast, even a domesticated beast like one of those exquisite cats? I think to enter such a brain, however small, would be utterly to go mad, don't you, Sir Seaton?'

'Quite.' The Englishman smiled up at a pretty waitress (for which L'Albertine in the morning was famous) and thanked her as she laid out the coffee things. 'I have heard of certain experiments, in which a beast's brain has been exchanged with that of a human being, but I don't believe they have ever been successful. Though,' and in this he was far more direct than was his usual habit, 'some say that Adolf Hitler, the deposed Chancellor of Germany, had succeeded and that he did indeed go quite mad as a result. Certainly his insolent folly at attacking three great empires at once would indicate the theory has some substance!'

Only by the slight movement of an eyebrow did Zenith indicate his surprise at Begg's raising this subject. He said nothing for a moment before murmuring something about the Russo-Polish empire being already at the point of collapse. His own Romanian seat remained part of that sphere of influence, as Begg knew, and the fact was considered a source of some distress to the albino.

'As one who showed such courage on their side during the war, you cannot be one of those who thinks Hitler should have been encouraged to attack the "alliance of eagles"?' Begg offered. 'The other Great Powers have since made an oath to protect the Slavic empire. Perhaps you feel that we have not been more resolute in tracking down the Hitler gang? I cannot believe you share their views.'

'My dear Begg, the deposed Chancellor was a beerhall braggart supported by a frustrated military bully, a plump bore with aristocratic pretension and a third-rate broadcasting journalist!' References to Röhm, to Göring and to Goebbels, whose popular radio programme was thought to have helped Hitler to power. 'It was a matter of duty for anyone of taste to frustrate his ambitions. He was warned often enough by the Duma, the Assembly and your Parliament. His refusal to sign the articles of confederation were the last straw. He should have been stopped then, before he was ever allowed to marshal his land leviathans and aerial battleships. As it was, it should have taken three days, not a year, to defeat him. And now we have the current situation, where he and his riff-raff remain at large, doubtless somewhere in Bavaria, and far too many of our armed forces, as well as those of Germany herself, are engaged in putting a stop to his so-called Freikorps activities. I understand that it's believed by some fools in the French foreign service that I yearn to 'free' my ancestral lands from the Pan-Slavic yoke, but believe me, I have no such dream. If I were to deceive myself that the people were free under the reign of my own family, I would deserve the contempt of every realist on the planet. And if there are, indeed, certain self-esteeming coxcombs on the Quai d'Orsay who believe I would ally myself with such degenerate opportunists, I shall soon discover their names and, in my own time, seek them out and challenge them to repeat their presumptions.'

Begg permitted himself a small smile of acquiescence. It was as he thought. He had needed only this statement by his cousin to confirm his understanding. But what was Zenith doing here

122

in Paris, keeping such a strange, yet regular schedule? He knew that there was little chance of the albino offering him an explanation. All he had done was rule out the theory, as his French opposite number had hoped, of certain under-admired civil servants at the Quai d'Orsay. He regretted that he was not on terms of such intimacy with Mrs Persson. Although it was unlikely, she could be allying herself with the Hitler gang to further her own schemes.

Of course, Zenith had said nothing of any collaboration, though it was probably not the first time he and the Englishwoman had worked together, she for her political purposes, he for financial gain. Zenith required a great deal of money with which to maintain his lifestyle and finance the causes he favoured. It was known that he employed at least six Japanese servants of uncommon loyalty and proficiency and maintained several houses in the major cities of Europe as well as on the Côte d'Azur. For all that he had received an amnesty after the war, he remained wanted by the police of some Western countries, especially America, yet lived elegantly in such insouciant openness that he had rarely been captured. The opposite numbers of Begg and Lapointe preferred always to wait and watch rather than place him under arrest.

It was the secret of Zenith's great success that he understood the psychology of his opponents marginally better than they understood his: thus his penchant for openness and his willingness to depend entirely on his own quick wits should he ever be in danger. One day, Begg hoped, that cool intelligence would be employed entirely on the side of the law. Meanwhile, he remained convinced of Zenith's highly developed sense of honour, which meant he never lied to those he himself respected. Moreover, Zenith was as hated and feared by the criminal classes almost as much as he was sought by the police. That ebony stick of his hid a slender sword remarkable in that it, too, was black, and into it had been carved certain peculiar scarlet markings which a trick of the sword-smith's art gave the appearance of seeming to move whenever the blade was unsheathed.

Begg had pursued the man across the multiverse more than once and knew that sometimes that sword became an altogether larger weapon, usually carried in an instrument case of some kind. Zenith was a skilled musician, as expert on the classical cello as he was with the popular guitar. Begg knew, also, that more than once Zenith's opponents had been found dead, drained in some terrible way not of blood but of their very life force. Underworld legend had it that Zenith was a kind of vampire, drawing his considerable physical power from the very souls of his enemies.

At that moment, no casual customer of the salon would have seen anything but one elegant man of the world in amiable conversation with another. An observer might have noted that both seemed to be taking an admiring interest in the tall woman walking, *à la* Colette, her two Oriental shorthair cats in the noon sunlight, passing through the sparkling waters of the central fountain, with its classical marble merfolk doing homage to Neptune, whose trident was green with verdigris. The spraying water formed a blur of rainbow colour giving the woman an almost unearthly appearance as she entered it and stood for a while staring thoughtfully into the middle distance, seemingly utterly oblivious of the two men.

Begg smiled to himself, well aware that this was Mrs Persson's characteristic way of taking stock of those she believed were watching her. It had the effect of disconcerting any observer and causing them to turn their gaze away. Even though she aroused no such response in Begg or Zenith, whom she recognised, nonetheless it seemed even to them that somehow she stepped through the shimmering wash of colour and, with her cars, disappeared.

'You are acquainted, I know, with Mrs Persson,' murmured Begg. 'The Quai d'Orsay, if not the Quai des Orfèvres, are convinced that she is working for the German insurgency. I would be surprised if it's true, for I thought her nature too romantic to let her fall in with such a gang.'

'Mrs Persson is not usually in the habit of confiding in me.' Monsieur Zenith raised his hand as a signal for the waiter to bring him a drink. 'Will you join me, Begg? Is it too early for an Armagnac?'

When the detective acquiesced, Zenith raised a second finger and made a small gesture. The waiter nodded. Almost immediately Zenith was watching with approval as the *serviteur* mixed his absinthe and placed two specially formed pieces of sugar in the saucer, while Begg received a generous measure of St-Aubin. It was rarely his habit to drink his favourite Special Reserve before lunch, but he was more than usually anxious to remain on agreeable terms with his old opponent. Zenith appeared to live chiefly on Turkish ovals and absinthe.

'Would you permit me, cousin, to ask you a rather direct question?' he asked after a couple of appreciative sips.

'How could I refuse?' A smile, almost a grin, appeared on Zenith's handsome lips. Clearly, this unusual approach amused him. And Begg knew he desired amusement almost as much as he needed action to relieve his ennui.

'I have to assume that your business in Paris has some association with the present situation in Germany. I am also curious to know what Mrs Persson's association with the Germans might mean.'

'I fear that any confidence Mrs Persson chooses to share with me must remain just that.' Zenith's voice sharpened a little. 'Naturally the British and French are in haste to conclude their present business with Colonel Hitler, but, while I wish them well, you must know—'

'Of course.' Begg regretted his directness. He believed he had offended his cousin, whose sense of decorum was if anything somewhat exaggerated. There was no retreat now. 'I suppose I am asking your help. There is some suggestion that many innocent lives are at stake.'

'My dear Begg, why should you and I care if a few bourgeois more or less are gone from central Paris by next Sunday?' Monsieur Zenith finished his absinthe. He removed a large, crisp note from his slender case, laying it on the table and standing up. 'And now, if you will forgive me, I have some business which cannot wait.'

Begg rose, trying to frame some kind of apology or even protestation, but for once he was at a loss. With his usual litheness and speed, Zenith slipped his hat from the shelf and, with a perfunctory bow, strolled towards the exit.

Cursing himself for his uncharacteristic impatience, Begg watched his relation depart.

Only as he took up his own broad-brimmed hat did a small smile suddenly appear on his face and under his breath he murmured a heartfelt '*Merci beaucoup*'.

THE THIRD CHAPTER:
INTO THE LABYRINTH

Of course, Commissaire Lapointe had set his men in waiting for Monsieur Zenith and the albino was followed, once again. Once again, as his old colleague was bound to admit to Begg, they had lost him. Mrs Persson, too, was gone. The four metatemporal detectives met that afternoon in Lapointe's rather grand offices overlooking the Seine.

'She was last seen visiting Caron's print shop, in that section of the arcades known as La Galerie de l'Horloge. Three men, their faces obscured by wide-brimmed hats and turned-up collars, followed her in about ten minutes later. But she was never seen emerging. Two of our fellows entered on a pretext just as old Caron was closing for lunch. The shop is small. It has long been suspected as a place of illegal assignations concerning the Bourse and the arms trade. There is an even smaller room behind it. Neither Mrs Persson nor the trio of men were to be found. My chaps did, however, discover a good excuse for our making a further visit to Caron's. He also specialises, it appears, in a particularly unsavoury form of pornography, in which Nazi insurgents are portrayed in acts of torture or worse with their victims. The photographs are almost certainly authentic. Caron made an error. He omitted to hide the photographs in his office when our men entered. So, although they pretended to notice nothing, it will be possible for us to stage a raid, ostensibly by that of the regular vice department, to see what else we can discover. Would you and Dr Sinclair care to accompany us?'

'I would be unable to resist such an invitation,'

said Begg, while Sinclair assented by lowering his magnificent head.

'I think you are right, old friend, in your interpretation of Monsieur Zenith's communication,' added Lapointe. 'Not only will Hitler's plot be realised in a crowded part of Paris, it will occur before next Sunday.'

'So he suggested. But whether Mrs Persson is party to this plot, we still do not know. The sooner we can question her, I think, the better.'

'Precisely!' Lapointe inspected his watch. 'Come, gentlemen, there is a powerful car awaiting us! Her batteries are charged and ready!'

So it was that the four men, accompanied by two uniformed sergeants, arrived at the Galerie de I'Horloge with its magnificent glass and wrought-iron roofs and ornate gas lamps, its rows of small shops on either side, and crowded into M. Caron's little establishment carrying a search warrant, on the excuse that he was known to be selling forbidden material.

Begg felt almost sorry for the little plump, grey-haired print-seller, who visibly shivered in terror at the understanding he was threatened with arrest. When, however, the material which was the excuse for the raid was revealed, Begg's sympathy disappeared. These were almost certainly pictures taken from the infamous Stadelheim fortress, where prisoners had been tortured, humiliated and subjected to unmentionable sexual horrors. Caron swore that he was not responsible for the material being in his office. 'It was the woman, I assure you, gentlemen. The Englishwoman. She knows . . . she . . .' And the little man broke down, weeping.

It did not take long to elicit from the print-shop proprietor the secret of Mrs Persson's ability to vanish. Behind a large cabinet of prints, he revealed another door, with steps leading down into dank darkness which echoed as if into the infinite cosmos. 'She . . . she insisted, Messieurs. She knew my shop had once been a gate into the labyrinth. It is by no means the only one leading from the arcades. As I am sure you are aware, the labyrinth has long served as a sanctuary for those who do not wish to be apprehended, for a variety of reasons. I wanted nothing to do with it, thus the cabinet pushed against the wall, but the Englishwoman – she knew what was hidden. She demanded to be shown the gate.' Again he began to weep. 'She knew about my – little business. She threatened to expose me. The photographs . . . I was greedy. I should have known not to trust such degenerates.'

Commissaire Lapointe was counting the large denomination banknotes he had discovered in the old man's safe. 'Degencrates who were apparently helping to make you rich, m'sieu! We also know about your arms brokering.' He replaced the money in the safe and locked it pocketing the key. 'Have you told us everything? Have the passages been used by members of the German so-called "underground"? Is it they who gave you the photographs? In exchange for guns?'

'I don't know who they were. They appeared in this room one day, having pushed aside the cabinet. It's true they had come to know of me through my interest in perfectly legal discontinued ordnance. They gave me the photographs in return for using the door occasionally. They were foreign civilians, they assured me. They spoke poor French, but I could not recognise the accents. As for the woman, she came and went only by day. She never asked to use my premises out of normal hours. I never saw her with anyone else. She was never gone very long. This is, I promise you, the longest she has ever been d-down there . . .' With a shudder he turned his back on the mysterious doorway.

'Well,' Lapointe decided, 'we shall have to wait for her, I think. For the moment you will be charged with distributing pornography. Take him away.'

After the proprietor had been led off, still snivelling, the metatemporal detectives settled down to await Mrs Persson's return, having replaced the door and cabinet exactly as they had discovered it. But the afternoon turned to evening, long after the print-seller would have closed up, and still she made no appearance.

Eventually, Bardot was dispatched to Mrs Persson's apartments and soon returned to report that her apartment was unoccupied, save for two

131

somewhat hungry and outraged Siamese cats. 'I fed them and changed their litter, of course, but . . .' He shrugged.

This news brought a frown to Begg's aquiline features. 'I think I know Mrs Persson pretty well. She would not desert her cats, especially without making arrangements to feed them. She has not only broken her usual habits, but probably did not do so willingly.'

'My God, Begg! Do you mean she has been captured by whoever it was she has been seeing behind that cabinet? Murdered? By Zenith, perhaps? Could he be playing a double game?'

'Possibly, old man . . . Instinct tells me that, if she is not found soon, she will be in no condition to help us with our enquiries.'

'Her paymasters? They have turned against her? Or did Zenith betray her?' Lapointe drew a deep breath.

'Monsieur le commissaire, time is in all likelihood running out for Mrs Persson, if she still lives. We could be further away than we thought from discovering which public place is under threat. And we have, if Monsieur Zenith told me what I think he did, only three more days at most before they strike! Come on, gentlemen! Help me shift his cabinet.'

The doorway again revealed, Begg took a small but powerful electric lantern from his overcoat pocket and, a serviceable Webley .45 revolver in his other hand, led the way down into the echoing darkness. The two sergeants were left behind to guard the entrance.

From somewhere below there came a slow, rhythmic, almost tuneful booming as if of some great clock. It was a sound familiar to three of the detectives and there was not one in whom it did not cause a thrill of horror. For a second Begg hesitated, and then continued down the long flight of stone steps which revealed, by the marks in the mould which grew inches thick upon them, signs of recent usage.

Only Bardot had not heard the sound before. 'What on earth is it?' he enquired of Sinclair.

The pathologist frowned, clearly wondering if he should reply. Then he made up his mind, speaking rapidly and quietly: 'Well, firstly, old man, it is not exactly of our earth. We believe it is a regulator of sorts. It is what we, who have travelled frequently between the worlds, sometimes refer to as the Cosmic Regulator. Others know it as the Grand Balance. I have heard it more than once, but never seen it. There are many conflicting descriptions. I have wondered if every person who has seen it has imposed their own image upon it. The Regulator is said to lie at the very centre of the multiverse, if the multiverse can be said to possess a centre.'

'Have you ever known anyone who has seen it?' whispered Bardot, wiping cold sweat from his brow. He had only recently been transferred to the STP.

Sinclair nodded. 'I believe Begg has set eyes on

it, and perhaps Lapointe. But even they, articulate as they are, have never described it. It is often represented in mythological iconography as a kind of scale, with one side representing Chaos and the other Law, but nobody knows its true form, if it has one at all.'

'Law and Chaos? Are those not Zoroastrian conceptions? The forces which war for control of the world?'

'So far nobody has ever managed to gain power over the Balance, but should someone eventually succeed, it will mean the end of Time but not of consciousness. If Chaos or Law controls existence, we shall *continue to live at the exact moment before the extinction of everything*. For eternity! Or so the theory goes. But there will always be madmen to challenge that conception, to believe that by controlling the Cosmic Balance they can exert their own desired reality upon the multiverse. Heaven help us if Hitler and his lunatics are close to making such an attempt!'

Only half-comprehending this idea, Bardot firmed his shoulders and continued to follow Begg's thin ray of light down into the sonorous darkness.

THE FOURTH CHAPTER:
THE ROADS BETWEEN THE WORLDS

As they reached the bottom of the steps, they found themselves on uneven flagstones, peering through a series of vaults supported by ancient pillars.

'No doubt,' suggested Sinclair, 'these are your famous Parisian catacombs?'

'Possibly. I am not familiar with every aspect of them.' Bardot peered into the rustling darkness.

The strange, distant booming continued. Whether the noise was mechanical or natural, it was impossible to determine. Lapointe and Begg both cocked their heads to listen. The echoes resounding through the vaults made it almost impossible to determine their source. At one moment Sinclair thought it might be water, at another some sort of engine. He was of a disposition to discount his own metaphysical speculation.

The vaults seemed endless and their darkness sucked the light from Begg's lantern, yet the detective continued to lead the way as if he had some idea where the labyrinth offered an exit.

'The arcades above us are a maze,' remarked Lapointe, 'which to some degree trace this other maze below.'

'Remarkable,' murmured Begg. 'I had some idea of what to expect, but had no idea we were so close to the Regulator. This is not the first time I have used such a gate myself to move between one reality and another. But I have never before felt so near the centre. What about you, Lapointe?'

'I must admit I have never heard it except as a very distant echo,' replied the Frenchman. 'Until now I have used mechanical means to negotiate the spaces between realities. We are issued with Roburian speedshells by the department. Naturally, old friend, I knew that you had not always taken advantage of such vehicles . . .'

'One learns,' the detective muttered, almost to himself. 'One learns.' His progress seemed almost erratic and without logic as he moved backwards and forwards, then side to side, keeping the mysterious sound constantly at a certain distance, treading a trail which only he could sense.

Now they made out a silvery light ahead.

'Can it be possible that the Arcades de l'Opéra lead directly to the roads between the worlds?'

Hearing this, Sinclair gave an involuntary shudder.

Above them the great arches grew taller and taller until they were impossibly high, no longer structures of human architecture, but part of a natural vault which had become part of the night itself. And then all four men gasped, pausing in their tracks as Begg's lantern revealed a long, twisting pathway which seemed to vanish into infinity. Above them, as well as below them, were other paths, all of them crossing and re-crossing. And on some could be distinguished tiny figures, not all of them human shapes, walking back and forth along these causeways.

When Sir Seaton Begg turned to address his fellow detectives his eyes might have been glistening with tears.

'Gentlemen,' he whispered, dousing the lantern, 'I believe we have discovered the roads between the worlds!'

And now their eyes became used to the light which emanated from the moonbeam roads themselves. They stretched in every possible direction, both above and below. The legendary trails which led to all possible planes of the multiverse.

'I have dreamed of this discovery,' said Begg. 'On occasions I have glimpsed these roads as I passed from one aspect of reality to another, but I never suspected I would ever discover access to them by accident. To think, the gateway to them has existed in Paris, presumably since the beginning of time, their patterns perhaps unconsciously imitated by the architect who designed the galleries above. Our mythologies and folktales have hinted, of course. There have been sensational tales. Yet they hardly prepare one for the reality. Is this Zenith's and Mrs Persson's secret, do you think?'

'And is it also Hitler's?' asked Lapointe grimly. 'Are his ambitions greater than we ever expected?'

Dwarfed by the vast network of moonbeam roads, the detectives were frozen in their uncertainty. There were no maps, no evident routes to follow. They had discovered an extraordinary, mysterious reality!

'At least it is no longer a mystery as to how Zenith was able to evade our men. And Mrs

Persson also. How long have they known of this route?' Bardot wondered.

Begg shook his head slowly. 'I believe Mrs Persson has probably been using these roads for a very long time. Yet it is my guess that she did not come this far voluntarily.'

'How on earth can you make that supposition, Begg?' enquired Lapointe.

'Her cats,' said Begg. 'I know she would never have left her cats unattended. She would have brought them with her or she would have made arrangements for them to be looked after. No, gentlemen, if she was not faced with an overwhelming emergency, I believe Mrs Persson was lured down here and then made a prisoner.'

'By Zenith?'

'Possibly.'

'If not by Zenith, then by whom?'

'By Hitler. Or one of his people.' Begg placed his foot firmly upon the road which led away into the darkness. There seemed nothing below them but other roads, on which those tiny wayfarers came and went.

'How do you know she came this way, old man?' Taffy Sinclair wished to know.

'I have only instinct, Taffy. An instinct honed, I might say, by a lifetime spent travelling between the worlds.'

From somewhere, still unseen, came the booming of that unearthly balance.

THE FIFTH CHAPTER:
AN UNEXPECTED NEWCOMER

With the familiar world far behind them, Begg and his fellow detectives were by now crossing a long, sinuous causeway from which gleamed a faint silvery light.

'What surprises me,' said Lapointe, is why so few people have reported finding this entrance to the moonbeam roads.'

'I suspect because it is not always open,' Begg suggested. 'If Mrs Persson came this way but was abducted, perhaps she opened the gate but had no time to close it. My guess is that Hitler's men, with whom she was clearly involved in some way, had scumbled on the road and bribed Caron, who had already sold them arms, with those filthy photographs. No doubt they also bribed M. Caron to let them know when she next planned to use his shop. Your men said they saw others enter the shop and not re-emerge, eh?'

'Three of them. Isn't it possible Mrs Persson unwittingly led them here?'

'Impossible to say, Lapointe. I am hoping that mystery will shortly be solved!'

'But how do you know we are even on the right road?'

Then Begg pointed downward. Stretching ahead of them the others now detected the faintest of pale traces, almost like ghostly drops of blood.

'What is it?' Lapointe wanted to know.

'I believe those frauds of mystics like to call it ectoplasm,' said Begg, 'but I prefer to think of it as the traces left by every human soul as it passes through the world – or, in this case, between them. Only those "old souls" like Mrs Persson, who has moved for so long between one plane and another that she has developed a form of longevity we might even call immortality, leave such clear traces.' His smile was grim. 'We are still on her trail.'

Only when he looked back did Taffy Sinclair see, not unexpectedly, similar glowing traces running behind them. And he knew for certain who had left them.

After a further passage of time, when the booming of that ghostly balance seemed somewhat closer, Sinclair realised they had left the moonbeam roads and were again passing through a more earthly sequence of vaulted chambers. Again the electric lamp was in Begg's left hand. Again his right hand gripped his service revolver. Was it his imagination, the Home Office pathologist asked himself, or was there something almost familiar about the smell of the air? Pine trees? Impossible.

'Where are we?' enquired Lapointe, still in a whisper.

'If I am not mistaken, my old friend,' answered the Englishman, 'we are somewhere in the Bavarian mountains. Probably near a place called

Berchtesgaden. Either that, or my nose deceives me!'

'So we were right!' Bardot exclaimed. 'Mrs Persson is working for the German insurgents!'

'That, Inspector Bardot,' responded Begg, 'remains to be discovered.'

Soon the ground began to slope upward and they heard the sound of voices, almost drowning that of the mysterious balance. They were unmistakeably speaking German and the loudest of them had a distinct Austrian accent.

Sir Seaton doused his lamp. But he did not return his revolver to his pocket.

The unseen Austrian's voice rose with excitement. 'Victory is in our grasp, my friends. Almost our entire army is passing through the Eagle Gate as we speak, to assemble in the Great Siegfried Cavern, awaiting our signal. Those degenerate fools thought they had defeated us, reduced us to a mere rabble. But they reckoned without our heritage, the ancient Nordic secrets locked deep within our Bavarian homeland. The Hollow Earth theory has been proven a scientific fact. You have done well, Frau Persson, by voluntarily showing us this road. We should have been sad if you were to become the subject of the next set of pictures sold in Paris by Herr Caron. By next Saturday the course of history will be changed forever. We shall strike a blow against the Jewish race from which it will never recover. If you continue to co-operate, you shall witness my becoming world leader, master of time and space. You will make a fitting consort. We shall rule the universe together!'

They heard only a murmured reply. But the Austrian, evidently Colonel Hitler, continued his monologue unchecked. He hardly understood the nature of his own situation, so blinded was he by petty dreams of power and banal notions of his own superiority. A typical megalomaniac. Yet why on earth would a woman of Una Persson's intelligence and integrity lend herself to such evil folly?

Using the ancient columns as cover, the four crept closer. Now, in a circle of light, they could make out the figures of a short fat man, a squat military type with a hideously disfigured face, another with gaunt, almost skeletal features, a black medical boot. To one side of these stood a tall, lugubrious-looking individual and another man of medium height with a lock of greasy hair falling over one eye and a short, dark Charlie Chaplin moustache. They recognised them at once from the 'Wanted' posters. Here was the entire upper hierarchy of the Hitler insurgents. Now all four detectives drew their revolvers and advanced. This was their chance to capture all the leaders of the German insurgency at once.

Mrs Persson, seated at ease on a chair to one side of the main group, was the first to notice them.

'Raise your hands!' Begg barked in German, motioning with his Webley. 'You are all under arrest.'

'Thunder and lightning!' The tall man, whom they recognised as Captain Hess, one of Hitler's closest co-conspirators, made a movement to his belt. But Lapointe crossed quickly and placed his hand on the man's arm.

Colonel Hitler glowered, his tiny blue eyes points of almost insane range. 'How did you—?'

'Cross from one plane of the multiverse to another? The same way Mrs Persson did. Indeed, she led us to you . . .'

'But only a few of us knew the secret!' Herman Goering, the fat Nazi, looked rapidly from face to face. 'Zenith swore—'

'So Zenith is in league with you!' Lapointe looked almost disappointed. 'Well, he will be arrested in good time.'

'But I am surprised, Mrs Persson, that you should associate yourself with such scum. Enemies of all that is civilised . . .' Begg shook his head.

Una Persson stood up. Her beautiful face was a mask of coldness and her eyes showed no expression. 'Ah, Sir Seaton.' Her voice mocked him. 'So you are, like so many of your kind, the sole arbiter of what is civilised.'

'Englishman, *we* are the ones who will save everything valuable in civilisation!' The gaunt man with the medical boot was Herr Goebbels, the journalist. 'There would be no civilisation if there were no Germany. No music, no art, no poetry. All that is best in your own country is the creation of the Nordic soul. And that threatens you, from without and within, is also Jewish. By saving Europe from the Jews, we shall establish a new Golden Age across our Continent. Even the Slavs will welcome this renaissance and willingly join in. Soon we shall be able to manipulate the very stuff of creation.'

Unthinkingly, a furious Taffy Sinclair took a step closer to the crazed creature. 'I find you unconvincing, Colonel Hitler. How would you establish this new civilisation by blowing up innocents and throwing the whole of our world into turmoil?'

The hideously scarred soldier, Captain Erich Röhm, laughed in Sinclair's face. 'Only through blood and iron will Europe be cleansed. I am a soldier. I know only the art of battle. But even I understand how the Jews continue to corrupt political and cultural life! Martin Luther warned us. So, too, have a succession of popes and bishops. Not only do Jews refuse the true Messiah, they wish to wipe all trace of Jesus Christ from the world! Once the warriors of Europe rose up to save Christendom from destruction. Now we rise again to mount our great crusade against the sons of Shem. By working against us, gentlemen, you are making a terrible mistake. Join us! The Holy Grail itself will soon be in our hands. He who holds the Grail controls the Balance and therefore the universe itself!'

144

'You are as mad as I understood you to be, Messieurs.' Lapointe drew a set of handcuffs from his overcoat pocket and advanced towards the glowering Hitler. 'Now, if you will kindly—'

And then a shot rang out from the shadows and the revolver went spinning from Lapointe's grasp. Another shot and Bardot clutched his right shoulder. Blood began to seep through his fingers.

'Drop your weapons!' came a cold commanding voice. 'Drop them or you shall all die immediately.'

And strolling out into the circle of light came a tall, stiff-backed man wearing a black domino obscuring the upper half of his face. He was dressed in perfect evening clothes. In his right hand was a smoking 9mm Sabatini automatic.

Begg recognised him immediately. 'So it was true,' he murmured. 'I have been guilty of under-estimating you, *mein Herr*. I knew that if Monsieur Zenith was not helping this gang, it had to be someone as knowledgeable in the ways of the multiverse.'

The newcomer's thin lips formed a mocking smile of triumph. 'You had thought me defeated, Sir Seaton, in the matter of the Corsican Collar. Then your life was saved by my old enemy, your cousin, who calls himself Zenith. But you knew I would return to continue with my quest.'

Lowering his revolver, Begg turned at once to Colonel Hitler. 'Believe me, if you think to link your interests with this creature's you are mistaken. He will betray you as he has betrayed

145

every other man, woman or spirit whom he has persuaded to act in his interest. You might know him by another name, but I can tell you his real identity, for he is the master of lies. His name is Johannes Klosterheim. Some believe him a fallen angel expelled from Hell itself. I do know that he was once a member of the Society of Jesus, before he was expelled not only from that order, but excommunicated by the Pope himself.'

'*Klosterheim*!' Captain Goering's plum features shook with amusement. 'What nonsense! This is Herr Johan Cornelius. You would have us believe that we have linked our fortunes with a figure from folklore – the infamous Gaynor the Damned!'

'As he is called in the opera,' said Begg quietly, 'but Wagner took certain liberties with the old legends, as before him did Milton.'

Even Lapointe, Sinclair and the pale, wounded Bardor looked at him as if he were mad. All knew the stories from the opera, if not from their schoolbooks. The enemy of Parsifal, who had sought the Grail and found it, only to be cursed with eternal damnation, to wander the earth until the end of time for the crime of attempting to drink Christ's very blood.

'Drop your weapons, gentlemen, or this time I shoot your colleague in his heart and not his shoulder,' was Klosterheim's icy response.

And now the Nazi colonel himself was staring a little nervously at the masked man, as if wondering whether any bargain he might have made with him could possibly any longer be to his advantage.

Then Mrs Persson stepped out of the circle and went to join Klosterheim, standing close beside him, making it clear she was the fiend's ally.

'It's said that promise of the Grail's power will corrupt even the noblest of human creatures,' declared Begg. 'Had I realised exactly what we were up against, my friends, I promise I would never have led you here! This will be forever on my conscience.'

'Fear not, Sir Seaton,' came Klosterheim's hollow, terrible voice. 'You will not have to suffer for very much longer. Meanwhile, I shall be obliged if you will drop your weapons at your feet.'

And as their revolvers clattered down, he uttered a mirthless laugh which echoed on and on through the vaulted chambers and chilled the blood of all who heard it.

THE SIXTH CHAPTER: THE ULTIMATE POWER

Begg felt physically sick as he stood with his hands raised, watching the Nazi gangster gloat over his reversal. He had underestimated not only Hitler and Company but everyone he had opposed. He had been foolish to assume that he alone, save for Mrs Persson and Monsieur Zenith, knew the secret of the moonbeam roads. He had wanted too badly to trust that pair. Cursing himself for not considering his old enemy Klosterheim's ambitions, he refused to believe he might have been forgiven for thinking him dead. Klosterheim was generally considered by almost everyone to have met his end in Mirenburg a decade or more earlier. Not that Begg himself had been there to witness the evil eternal's demise, but it had been none other than Zenith who had given him the information.

From his earliest appearance as a Satanic angel expelled from Hell in the myths and legends of the seventeenth century, Klosterheim had been said to die more than once. But his antipathy to Begg's family – or at least the German side of the family, the von Beks – was well known. He had survived one apparent death after another through the years, remaining alive for two things only – to kill all who carried the blood of his old enemy, Ulrich von Bek, and to lay his hands upon the Holy Grail and thus control, in his understanding, the very nature of reality. Yet here he was in alliance with Una Persson, Countess von Bek!

More than once Begg had narrowly escaped terrible death at the hands of this near-immortal and now, it seemed, there was no hope of escape at all.

Klosterheim's sunken sockets hid eyes which burned within like the unquenched flames of Hell. He pocketed his revolver while the triumphant Nazis trained their own weapons on the detectives. Then the masked man bent and placed his thin lips upon those of Mrs Persson. Begg was astonished. Klosterheim had never shown warmth, let alone passion, for another, least of all a woman. And Mrs Persson smiled admiringly back at the deathless devil with whom she had cast her lot. Colonel Hitler meanwhile glowered jealously, clearly furious that the woman had collaborated with him because Klosterheim had instructed her to do so. Noting all these ramifications, Begg now believed himself thoroughly outwitted. Was it possible that Zenith also allied himself with his old rival?

'I cannot believe this of you, Mrs Persson!' exclaimed Taffy, still shocked and clearly unable to accept this turn of events. Like all his colleagues save the wounded Bardot, his hands were now firmly tied behind him by Herr Hess. It was just possible that a tear gleamed in his eye. 'How can any decent Englishwoman possibly ally herself with such riff-raff?'

'Oh, I think you'll find it's quite commonly done, Mr Sinclair.' Mrs Persson seemed almost drunk as she leaned against the gaunt skeleton who was not only her ally but apparently also her paramour, even her master. 'We women are silly creatures, eh, thoroughly addicted to powerful men! There's a larger interest here, as I'm sure you'll appreciate. Very few of us are privileged to know one of Satan's own angels . . .'

But Sinclair, his mouth set in a hard, disapproving line, was unable to answer.

149

Now the Nazis began to push their captives back towards the moonbeam roads.

'We await only Count Zenith,' chuckled Captain Goering. 'And our plan will be complete. On Saturday, the *Hindenburg* brings from America the Jewish Palestinian deputation to Munich. They intend to discuss an obscenity with Comrade von Hugenberg, chairman of the Munich Supreme Soviet – the establishment of a new Jewish state in the Bavarian lake district! Can you imagine a worse insult to the Christian community? But it will never take place. Our man Zenith will introduce a bomb on board while the *Hindenburg* refuels overnight at the Eiffel Tower in Paris. He will take the Star of Judea in exchange. That is the priceless emerald which the Jews intend to use as down payment on the land they buy from the treacherous Bavarian soviet. The *Hindenburg* will blow up. The French will be blamed for their sabotage and a wedge will be driven between the various allies. Jews, Frenchmen and Bavarian communists will all he implicated by the British and Americans. Chaos will ensue. Meanwhile, we will be ready, as soon as news of the *Hindenburg*'s destruction comes through, to announce a new National Socialist Bavarian state. But the Freikorps will already be through the Eagle Gate and crossing the moonbeam roads into the Arcades of the Opéra, a stone's throw from the Arc de Triomphe. We shall announce our victory there. Our guns will by that time command the whole of Paris.

Germans will rise to our victorious standard and this time the British and French will find it impossible to subdue us. For Paris will already be hostage to our cannon!'

'But this is madness!' gasped Lapointe. 'All you will succeed in doing is harming hundreds of innocent people. You will be defeated again. Your logic is entirely flawed, Captain Goering.'

'Nonsense. You are addressing the cream of the Nazi elite!' put in Herr Goebbels. 'Our plan is flawless!'

'Has Herr Klosterheim talked you into this?' asked Bardot, through gritted teeth. His wound had, for the moment, stopped bleeding. He assured his friends that he had only sustained a flesh wound. Slowly the group had come to a halt at the very edge of the silvery road through the multiverse.

'We have perfected this plan together with Herr Klosterheim's involvement,' said Hess, his strange eyes shifting from one to the other. 'By Sunday Europe will have accepted the reality of a new Germany. We already know that many Frenchmen as well as English aristocrats will flock to our standard!'

'Klosterheim uses you for his own purposes,' said Begg quietly. 'He has beguiled you, as he has beguiled so many others. He has no interest in reviving Nazi Germany or, indeed, doing anything but gaining control of the Cosmic Balance. Mrs Persson, you know this to be true!'

'I have no reason to disbelieve him, Sir Seaton.' With a low laugh the adventuress turned away.

Now again came the rhythmic booming as of some great drum. Most of them shivered as they heard it, standing at the beginning of the moon-beam roads. Motioning again with their pistols, the Nazis forced Begg and Co. to move ahead. By the second, the noise of the great regulator came closer. And the vision of the multiverse grew more vivid, the roads more colourful and complex.

The detectives gasped. Below, above, on every side of them, the distance was filled with glowing silvery roads, twisting in all directions and forming an extraordinary labyrinth. On this spiderweb of pathways, unconscious of the drama being played between the Nazis and their enemies, travellers walked between a million and more realities.

'Where are they going, Begg?' murmured Dr Sinclair.

Begg's own face was alive with wonderment. 'I had heard of this . . . Sinclair, old friend, these people are walking the moonbeam roads between the worlds. Simply – walking across the multiverse!'

Klosterheim read the bewilderment in Taffy's eyes. 'Do not fear, doctor. You will soon have the whole of eternity to contemplate this puzzle. Now – move on. There are still more wonders to greet you . . .'

Bardot groaned, evidently believing himself feverish. He was the only one of the prisoners not to be bound. His arm hung limp at his side and his right hand staunched the blood from his wounded shoulder. He seemed dazed, unable to accept the actuality of these events. He looked up through the swirling, scintillating colour which filled the great ether, the shimmering lines of light cutting between them, the distant figures, the immense beauty of it all. Then he looked back at the grotesquely grinning uniformed men training their Lugers on the captured detectives. Behind them, removing the black diamond mask he affected, Klosterheim stood stock still. He had wrapped his great cloak around him, as if against a chill, though the temperature was moderate. From within the head the cold eyes shifted from face to face, offering no expression, no sense of any humanity.

To Begg's certain knowledge, the former priest was virtually indestructible. Like Zenith, like Mrs Persson herself, he was an eternal, one of those whose longevity was considerably greater than that of an ordinary human being. He was accustomed to life in the semi-finite. Some said they sustained their long lives by dreaming a thousand years for every day of their ordinary existence and that what we witnessed were dream projections, not the actual person. That most of them lived forever was, in Begg's opinion, debatable. Yet those who had encountered Klosterheim over the centuries came to believe that he had truly been one of Satan's favourite accomplices, until the time when Satan himself sought reconciliation with their former

153

lord. Then Klosterheim had turned against Satan, too. As he perceived it, he had been betrayed by the two mightiest masters in his universe. For all his well-hidden spirituality, Begg was not a man to accept supersition or supernatural explanation, but he could almost believe the stories as he stared back at Klosterheim. Begg's own face was expressionless as he considered ways and means of turning the tables on their captors.

Step by remorseless step they moved along the opaque, silvery causeway towards that sonorous booming until at last the road ended abruptly, upon the edge of the void, its silver falling away like mist. For the first time a smile crossed Klosterheim's thin, bloodless lips. And he looked down.

Begg was the first to follow his gaze.

The detective's first instinct was to step back. He stifled a sound. There, immediately below them, its blade pointing down into the dancing, obscuring mist, he made out the shape of a gigantic black sword fashioned to resemble a balance, with a cup depending from either arm. Within the metal of the black blade scarlet characters writhed and twisted while the cups moved slowly, gleaming like jewelled gold. It was as if they measured the weight of the world's pain. Multicoloured strands of ectoplasm swirled from the cups and Begg knew in his soul that he did indeed look upon the legendary Cosmic Balance, which regulated the entire multiverse, weighing

Law and Chaos, good and evil, truth and false-hood, life and death, love and hate, maintaining the equilibrium and therefore the existence of all created matter.

In spite of the booming voice of the swaying arm, Klosterheim's cold tones could be heard clearly. 'If the multiverse has a centre, then this can be said to be it. I have sought it for many years and across many universes. And you, gentlemen, will have the privilege of seeing it before you die. Indeed,' and now he chuckled to himself, 'you will always see it before you die . . .'

Now it was Lapointe's turn to speak. 'You are a dangerous fool, M'sieu Klosterheim, if you believe you can control that symbol of eternal justice. Only God Almighty has any way of altering the scales maintaining the balance between Law and Chaos. What you see is doubtless only one manifestation of the Cosmic Balance. Can you *control* a symbol?'

'Perhaps not,' came the sweet, calm voice of Mrs Persson. She had turned up the collar of her long, military coat. Framed by her helmet of dark hair, her beautiful, pale, oval face shone with the reflected light of the great scale. Her indigo eyes were sardonic. 'But the one who gives power to the symbol can sometimes control what it controls . . .'

Lapointe turned away from her with an expression of disgust.

Hitler, Hess, Goering, Rohm and Goebbels had crowded to the edge of the road to stare down at the great balance. 'All we need now is to set into that hilt the Star of Judea,' said the Nazi colonel.

'Which you will not receive until next Saturday as I understand it,' said Begg, genuinely puzzled. 'Tomorrow is that?'

Hitler became suddenly alert. He turned questioning eyes to Klosterheim.

'I brought you here, where Time has no end and no beginning, merely to show you why and for what you will die,' declared Klosterheim. 'A small offering to the Gods of Chaos who will soon be serving my cause.'

'And what is the chief price you pay for their compliance?' Begg enquired coolly. 'The souls of four mortals could hardly be enough.'

'Oh, they are scarcely ordinary mortals. Their crimes have resonated across the entire multiverse. Their souls have far greater weight than yours, Sir Seaton, certainly in that respect. Yet will the Balance accept them? We still await the one who brings us the Star of Judea. The *Hindenburg* docked an hour ago by his time and now stands ready at Eiffel's great mooring mast.' Klosterheim's cold voice was almost amused. 'With that great and ancient jewel, I will make my true offering and in return shall have control of the Balance.'

'How could a mere jewel – any jewel – have value here?' demanded Dr Sinclair, his eyes half-mad with what they had seen.

'The Star of Judea is of immense value to the Lords of Chaos, Taffy,' murmured Begg. 'They'll reward any being who brings it to them. It will even seem to give that being control of the Cosmic Balance. Meanwhile . . .' He noted an opportunity and gestured, drawing the Nazis' attention away from his friends . . .

Suddenly, a revolver appeared in Bardot's left hand. Begg had anticipated this and deliberately distracted their enemies, giving Bardot time to act. The Frenchman's eyes were a mixture of contempt and pain. 'You poor, unimaginative brutes could not imagine one of us owning a second weapon. Throw up your hands and drop your guns, gentlemen.'

The startled Germans swung round, staring into the barrel of Bardot's serviceable Hachette .38. They looked from him to Klosterheim to Mrs Persson. Only the woman found some amusement in this reversal. Yet she did not move, either to comply or to resist.

At Bardot's demand, Captain Hess drew his elaborate, ornamental dagger from the scabbard at his belt and cut the ropes binding the metatemporal detectives. His deep-set eyes were dreamy, as if he believed himself the victim of an hallucination. Constantly his gaze returned to the great scintillating scales moving gently in constant balance, their movement continuing to create the deep booming, like the heartbeat of the multiverse.

Klosterheim snarled. 'How do you think you can defeat my plans now, merely by turning the tables on my servants?' And then, without warning, he rushed at Hess, pushing the startled Nazi to the edge of the moonbeam road. Before the detectives could reach him, he shoved again and this time Hess's arms flailed as he fought to keep his balance. He reached towards Klosterheim, yelling something unintelligible, and then he fell backwards.

They watched him drop, spinning and waving his awkward arms, like a scarecrow, falling, falling down towards the Balance, passing the swaying beam until he disappeared in the pulsing light coming up from one of the cups. They heard him scream, a high-pitched and terrible noise, and then he had been swallowed into the light which flared suddenly scarlet.

Klosterheim stepped to the edge and watched with an air of satisfaction. 'A sign of my good faith, I hope.'

Colonel Hitler swore in German. 'You killed him. You killed my closest friend!'

Klosterheim shrugged. 'It's disputable that he's actually dead, but my master needs blood and souls.' He shrugged then. 'The Grail—'

'That thing is not the Grail!' growled Röhm. 'There cannot be two grails!'

Now Klosterheim smiled. 'Not in your mythology, perhaps. But one cup holds the stuff of Chaos, the other holds the stuff of Law. That is what regulates the multiverse. That is why they are in constant conflict.'

Still cursing, the Nazi colonel reached down and picked up his fallen Luger. In one movement he pointed and pulled the trigger, firing shot after shot into the mocking figure. Again came that cold, humourless chuckle. Klosterheim spread his arms and looked down at his unwounded body. 'I am not so easily killed, Colonel Hitler. How can you take away the soul of a man who has no soul?'

Still Una Persson did not move. It was as if she were waiting, perhaps to watch the opposed groups destroy one another. Still that enigmatic amusement filled her indigo eyes.

Only when Röhm retrieved his own automatic pistol and pointed it at her did she frown. Begg was sure, eternal though she might be, that she was not invulnerable.

'*Arioch! Arioch! Aid me now!*' called Klosterheim in that strange voice which seemed to deaden the air it filled.

THE SEVENTH CHAPTER: OLD SOULS

Begg acted. He knew he could not kill Klosterheim easily, but the Nazis would soon return their attention to the detectives. He raised his Webley and, taking careful aim, shot Röhm between the eyes. The captain's expression changed from anger to surprise. And then he, too, lost his balance and fell, his body spinning downwards to stop suddenly, as if in the grip of some powerful magnetic force which held him spreadeagled and screaming silently in space above the Balance.

Another shot. And this time it was Lapointe who sent Captain Goering into the void, to hang in the air immediately above the cup which held the weight of Chaos.

'No!' cried Una Persson suddenly. 'No! Don't kill them! Not yet! You don't know what you're doing. There's a plan—'

But Begg had no choice, for the malevolent club-footed Goebbels screamed something about betrayal and turned his gun on her. The Webley's bullet found its target in Goebbels' heart and another Nazi went down, whirling and shrieking, to come to a sudden halt just before he was swallowed by the cup which now boiled with smoky scarlet and black.

'You fool, Sir Seaton!' cried Mrs Persson. 'No more shooting, I beg you. Don't you realise you're aiding Klosterheim? Their souls are already pledged to Chaos. They are the blood sacrifice they intended to make of you. One last action and he can use them to destroy everything. Everything!'

Begg was confused. He kept his Webley levelled at the remaining Nazi, the slavering, terrified Hitler, who whispered in his lisping Austrian: 'She's right. Nothing but harm will come from killing me.'

'Then get on your knees and keep your hands above your head,' snapped Begg. Slowly, every part of his body trembling, Hitler obeyed. Taffy Sinclair knew his old friend well enough to understand that Begg accepted that he had, inadvertently, done Klosterheim's work. The beat of the balance changed subtly. Now it was as if they heard distant wildfire, like the crackling and snapping of burning timber.

Una Persson came to stand beside Begg. He stepped backward as if she threatened him, but instead her expression was one of mixed anger and fear. 'I did not believe you could follow me,' she said. 'Oh, Seaton, your courage is now likely to lose us the fight – even perhaps destroy the multiverse! Do you understand what this means?'

And still the massive, sword-like balance, its cups swaying and groaning, continued to beat and pulse and the light around its hilt was like a golden halo surrounding metal of a blackness greater than the void. From somewhere below, Begg thought he heard the murmur of distant laughter.

Klosterheim's voice joined in that laughter. It was the bleakest, most desolate sound Sir Seaton Begg had ever heard. He lowered his gun, looking helplessly from Mrs Persson, to Klosterheim, to the kneeling, gibbering Hitler and to his friends.

'Oh, by Jupiter!' he whispered as realisation dawned. 'Oh, my good Lord! What have I done?'

The booming of the great balance had now taken on a different, arrhythmic note. Under its deep, masculine voice, Begg thought he could hear the thin screams of the Nazis. The gulf surrounding the not-dead men apparently boiled with blood and black smoke.

'We would have mastered creation and moulded it in our desired image until the end of time,' wept Hitler. Begg did not care that he now lowered his hands and buried his face in them. 'Klosterheim! That was what you promised me!'

'Like you, my friend, I have made many promises in my long career.' Klosterheim's toneless voice betrayed no emotion. 'And like you, Colonel Hitler, I have broken many promises. I helped you and your followers because it suited me. Now you have failed me. It no longer suits me. Your actions brought my enemies to me and we have reached this pass. Only the blood and souls of your colleagues will compensate for your clumsiness.' He turned to the metatemporal detective. 'My master has his initial sacrifices, thanks to you, Sir Seaton. Now he will come to my aid, as he said be would . . .'

Begg could not disguise his own self-disgust. He was about to speak when a new voice, light and mocking, sounded from out of the scarlet mist behind them. He recognised the voice at once.

'Oh, do not count on Lord Arioch turning up just yet, Herr Klosterheim.' The newcomer's tone held mockery, amusement, a kind of courage which could belong, Begg knew, only to one man. He looked in surprise back down the road which had brought them here. Strolling towards them, swinging his cane, for all the world as if he were still the insouciant *flâneur* of the Arcades de l'Opéra, wearing full evening dress, including a silk-lined cape and a silk hat, which emphasised the bone whiteness of his skin, the glittering crimson of his eyes, was Monsieur Zenith. 'Good evening, gentlemen.' He lifted his top hat. 'Mrs Persson. This is not quite the scene I imagined I would find. Where, for instance, are Herr Hitler's friends?'

'I fear they have become at least a potential blood-offering to whatever demon of Chaos Johannes Klosterheim obeys,' replied Begg in chastened tones. 'I believe I have made the greatest mistake of my life. Can it possibly be reversed, cousin?'

Still the elegant *boulevardier*, Zenith paused and selected one of his opium cigarettes from his slender, silver case. He lit it with an equally elegant silver Dunhill. 'I must be truthful with you. Sir Seaton. I am not sure. Theoretically, if Chaos or Law achieves total ascendancy, then Time stops. Like those fellows down there, we shall be frozen forever at the moment before out deaths. Scarcely a palatable fate.'

'Indeed.' Begg looked about him and then down again at the great balance below. 'What is this gem they said you'd steal?'

'It is already stolen.' Zenith smiled almost to himself 'That is what brought me here. I possessed it before the ship ever left Jerusalem. Their perception of time remains, as ever, very crude. The gem emits both light and vibrations and acts as a kind of compass. Madame Persson understood this. It was what we discussed before the situation grew less controllable. My object remains the Da Vinci in the Louvre, which I expected to possess by now. They have absolutely no right to it, you know. I had not reckoned, however, on Herr Klosterheim's involvement. The rules of this game seem significantly changed. I had underestimated its nature. Madame Persson suggested . . .'

'I regret that I misled you a little, old friend.' Mrs Persson still stood close to the expressionless Klosterheim. 'Self-interest demands a fresh strategy. A new reality.'

'The Nazis continue to be useful,' said Klosterheim. 'Whether their souls go to Chaos or their bodies serve my cause, it matters not. Like all women, Mrs Persson understands where her loyalties are best placed.'

'Great heavens, man! Does life have no value to you?' Taffy Sinclair broke away from his fellow investigators and strode towards the cadaverous creature. 'How on earth can you allow such infamy?'

Klosterheim's dreadful laughter whispered into the void. 'You speak to one who has defied both God and Lucifer and now stands ready to control the nature of reality itself. I am not the first to try. But I shall be the first to succeed.'

'Such confidence is reassuring in these uncertain times.' Zenith seemed almost amused. 'I envy you, Herr Klosterheim. When do you expect my lord Arioch?'

'He will come imminently. He promised.' Klosterheim turned those hollow eyes on the albino. 'He shares my impatience and my ambition.'

'Some would say he is already with us.' Monsieur Zenith motioned with his sword stick. Klosterheim's eyes followed it, as if he thought Zenith pointed out the powerful Chaos Lord. He saw nothing but the Balance below and four bodies suspended above one of the cups, an instant from being absorbed into the cause of Entropy.

Behind Begg. Commissaire Lapointe was forcing Hitler to his feet and handcuffing him. 'It is my duty, gentlemen, to get this fellow back to the authorities in Berlin. As to the rest of the matter, I fear it is far beyond my competence. So if you will permit me . . .' He began to push the whimpering insurgent colonel ahead of him, followed by his wounded assistant, whose expression was one of regret and embarrassment. 'Duty demands,' murmured Bardot.

'Of course,' agreed Begg. 'I have no objection. Were the situation a little less complicated, I would be with you. Can you find your own way back?'

'I hope so. With good fortune, we will meet again in Paris very shortly.'

'You may count on it, Commissaire.' Monsieur Zenith bowed and again raised his hat. 'I will take the most conscientious care of your colleague.'

Herr Klosterheim however would have none of this. 'I cannot permit any of you to leave. Not now. Your souls are the price of my success.' When Bardot's pistol was again turned to aim at his chest he let out a laugh that was almost humorous. 'Oh, fire away, my dear policeman. Have you any idea how many times I have been killed by the likes of you? Your lives are mine, just as those others belong to me. They are already promised to my patron . . .'

'My dear Klosterheim,' drawled Zenith, 'are you truly so ignorant of the change in your situation that you believe you can threaten these good officers and stop them performing their duty? I believe the clinical term for your condition is 'denial'. You no longer possess any power to speak of.' And, smiling, he pressed a silver stud in his ebony cane and swiftly withdrew the slender blade.

Sinclair had expected to see polished silver steel. He gasped as instead he saw that the sword in Zenith's hand was actually darker than the ebony which had contained it and along its slim, vibrating length writhed bloody scarlet characters, the runes of some long-forgotten lexicon. He turned, questioning Begg, and to his astonishment he saw his colleague laughing, the Webley held so loosely in his hand it threatened to fall into the void.

'Aha!' exclaimed Begg, almost in delight. 'Here is your sought-for demonic aid, my dear Klosterheim! What a jest! What a jest!' And he stepped back as his cousin advanced, the thrumming blade, which seemed to cry with its own voice, held before him, advancing on Klosterheim who looked from Mrs Persson to Zenith, to the sword, and was bewildered at last.

'Mrs Persson, you assured me . . .'

'I told you that the black broadsword you call Stormbringer was no longer in Monsieur Zenith's possession. I said nothing of any other blade, bearing similar characteristics, which he finds convenient to carry in a more modern form under a different name.' The English adventuress was grinning like a lioness who had just made a kill. 'You must know, Herr Klosterheim, that just as the wielder of the sword takes many guises, so does the sword itself. And even that creature which inhabits the sword has more than one identity!'

Now she stepped aside as Klosterheim began to back away from the advancing albino. 'I shall not be threatened, Monsieur! Arioch! Lord Arioch of the Seven Darks! Aid me, I beg thee. Arioch, thou promised me . . .'

'Lord Arioch's promises are of a practical and volatile nature, also,' declared Zenith, the slender sword still pointed at Klosterheim's throat. 'It surprises me that you did not consider this when laying out your equation for this particular adventure. There are only a few for whose blood and souls he has no appetite at all.'

'But you forget, monsieur. That blade and your master feed on souls as well as blood.' Klosterheim's smile was bitterly sardonic. '*Nein?*' With a quavering laugh, somehow even more disgusting than any previous expression he had given, he folded his arms and challenged Zenith to stab him.

If anything, the albino's smile chilled the onlookers' blood more than the other eternal's laughter. Without hesitation, Monsieur Zenith stepped forward in an elegant fencer's movement and his delicate black blade took Klosterheim in the throat.

For a second the ex-priest continued to laugh and then his eyes widened. He clutched at himself, at the shivering blade. He gasped. He groaned. He staggered backwards towards the very edge of the moonbeam road and hung there, swaying, as blood bubbled from the wound Zenith had made. '*Nein!*' he said again, this time without any form of irony, only with the most appalling fear. '*Nein!*'

He realised suddenly where he stood and made an attempt to regain his balance, but it was too late. His deep-set eyes burned with terror, lighting that cadaverous head with an unholy fire. Begg and the others could not tell what emotion they witnessed, but they would agree that it was emotion.

'How can this be?' Klosterheim spoke in the old High German of his youth. 'How—?'

'You forgot, Herr Klosterheim.' With a lithe, sudden movement Zenith resheathed the black blade. 'My sword is capable of conferring souls as well as stealing them.' He stepped forward again and his hand was light on Klosterheim's chest as he tipped him, gently, off into the void above the pulsing Balance. 'And only a creature with a human soul, no matter how corrupt, can enjoy that moment of forever, poised between eternity and oblivion, which comes with the end of everything. Meanwhile, I send you to consider that thought for as long as you shall last. Which, of course, shall be until the end of Time.'

And then Klosterheim was falling backwards screaming, to join those others who hung in the void, like flies in a web, conscious and frozen in the instant before their deaths.

Monsieur Zenith turned with a bow. Reaching out, he kissed Mrs Persson's hand. 'Well played, madam. Our plan was almost foiled by these good-hearted fellows.' He inclined his head towards Begg and Sinclair.

'You two had planned all this?' Sinclair found himself torn between rage and relief. 'All of it?'

'Most of it,' declared Mrs Persson, advancing towards the famous pathologist. 'Really, Doctor Sinclair, we had no intention of deceiving you or your colleagues. Neither did I expect to be detained by them, so very likely you saved my life by arriving when you did. From then on I thought it the best strategy to pretend to ally myself with Klosterheim, at least until Monsieur Zenith made his somewhat belated appearance. We really did not know you would have either the powers of deduction or the sheer courage to reach this place. Then, when you did turn up, I for one was rather baffled. It seemed that everything Monsieur Zenith and myself had worked out was threatened.' She drew a deep breath. 'Happily, as you see—'

'Klosterheim, for all his evil, did not deserve such a fate,' declared Begg gravely. 'And neither did those others.'

'Oh, I assure you, dear cousin, they do indeed deserve everything.' Zenith looked down into the void to where the great Balance still swayed. 'And this affair is probably not yet over, though your part is certainly done.' Then, with a casual movement of his wrist, he threw his swordstick after the man on whom he had just conferred life and a kind of death at the same moment, and turned to guide the two men back in the direction from which they had come. 'Quickly. The thing that is my sword is not so easily defeated in its ambitions.'

Begg hesitated, demurring, and Zenith's face became a mask of urgency. 'Hurry, man! Hurry! If you value your soul!'

From somewhere below there now sounded a voice more terrifying than anything they had yet heard and, blossoming upwards, they saw a huge, bloody black cloud rising, rising like a wave which, instinctively, Begg knew must soon engulf them. The noise grew until it deafened them, causing bile to rise in their throats, and at last Begg obeyed his cousin. Grabbing Dr Sinclair's arm, he turned and ran, Mrs Persson and Zenith the Albino immediately behind him.

The moonbeam road quivered and trembled beneath their feet, as if they experienced a powerful earthquake. Still they ran, knowing that not only their lives but their eternal souls must be the price of any further hesitation . . .

. . . Until suddenly a deep calm settled over them and a silvery whiteness had sprung up, forming a kind of wall, and they were once again in the catacombs they had left behind for what seemed millennia.

Monsieur Zenith straightened his silk hat on his head. 'I shall miss that cane,' he said. 'But I know the exact place I can buy another in the Galerie du Baromètre. Come, Mrs Persson, gentlemen. Shall we return to the Arcades de l'Opéra? I think we have a rather extraordinary adventure to celebrate.'

EPILOGUE

His shoulder thoroughly bandaged, Bardot was the last to join the four men and one woman who shared an outside table at L'Albertine the following day. He was received with a great sense of celebration as the hero of the hour. 'Without you, my dear Bardot, we should perhaps even now be enjoying the fate of our Nazi antagonists. As it is, the arrest of Colonel Hitler took the wind out of the Freikorps insurgents, who were indeed massing to enter the tunnel to take them directly into Paris. The *Hindenburg* made a successful mooring at the Eiffel Tower and spent a tranquil night there. The Star of Judea was returned. Even now negotiations to found a new Jewish homeland in Bavaria are proceeding and it is fully expected the exodus to Southern Germany will begin some time towards the end of next year!' Seaton Begg clapped his French colleague on his good shoulder and ordered him an Armagnac.

The autumn sun was rising high in a golden sky and the great fountain in the centre of the arcade was falling in dark blue and green sheets against the verdigris, marble and tile of the statuary. There was a tranquil, leisurely quality to the day which Begg agreed he had not experienced for some time. It was as if the atmosphere were created by the capture of Hitler and his men.

'Illusion though it might be, my friends,' murmured Commissaire Lapointe, 'it seems to me as if our world is about to embark upon a new era of peace and prosperity. Call me superstitious, if you will, but I believe in our defeat of the Nazi gang and their subsequent fate, we achieved something. Do you follow my meaning, Sir Seaton?'

Begg permitted himself a small smile. 'We can hope you are right, my dear commissioner. But you are of another opinion, I think, Taffy.'

Dr Sinclair did his best to make light of his own

thoughts. 'It was that Balance,' he said. 'Something was going on down there which terrified me. And the manner of Klosterheim's death – well, I still have difficulty sleeping when I think about it.' He glanced almost shyly at Monsieur Zenith, who leaned back, taking a long puff on his Afghan cigarette.

'I am sorry you were forced to witness that, Dr Sinclair. If I had had any other choice, of course I would not have done what I had to do. But Klosterheim was the force behind Hitler and his men. He has lived for a very long time. Some will tell you he counselled Martin Luther. Others say he was the angel who stood with Duke Arioch at Lucifer's right hand during the great war in Heaven. He had no soul. That is what gave him such confidence. Having no soul, he was almost impossible to destroy. By conferring a soul upon him, I could kill him. Or, at least, I hope I killed him . . .'

'But I think what is concerning my old friend Sinclair,' interrupted Bardot, 'is a very important question.'

'Which is?' Zenith seemed genuinely puzzled.

'Taffy and I have both wondered about it,' put in Begg, leaning forward to address his cousin. 'Our question would be – where did that soul come from? Whose did you use? You can surely see why we would be wondering . . .'

'Aha!' Monsieur Zenith turned, laughing, to Mrs Persson. She clearly knew the answer. She leaned down and petted her two Orientals, who lay, perfectly behaved, at her feet. 'I think I will leave that to you, Mrs Persson.'

The exquisitely beautiful adventuress straightened up and reached for her glass of absinthe. 'It was the last soul the sword drank. It has been many years, if I am not mistaken, since you have unsheathed that particular weapon, Monsieur Zenith?'

'Oh, many. I suppose, my friends, I will have to let you into a secret I have kept for rather a long time. While I have in the course of the past two thousand years sired children and indeed founded a dynasty which is familiar to anyone who knows the history of the province of Wäldenstein and her capital Mirenburg, I am not truly of this world or indeed this universe. It is fair to say that I have, in the way some of you will know to be possible, been dreaming, as it were, myself. I have another body, as solid as this one, which as I speak lies on a 'dream couch' in a city more ancient than the world itself.' He paused almost in sympathy as he observed their expressions.

'The civilisation to which I belong is neither truly human nor truly of this universe. Its rulers are men and women who are capable of manipulating the forces of nature and, if you like, super-nature to serve their own ends. They are sometimes, in this world, called sorcerers. How they learn their sorcery is by making use of their dream couches, sleeping sometimes for thousands of years while they live other lives. In those other lives they learn all kinds of arcane wisdom. Upon waking, they forget most of the lives they have 'dreamed' save for the skills of sorcery, which they employ to rule the world of which their land is the imperial centre. I am one of those aristocrats. The island where I dwell is known, as far as I can pronounce it in your language, as Melnibone. We are not natives of that world, either, but were driven to inhabit it during a terrible upheaval in our history which ultimately turned us from peaceful beings into the cruel rulers of a planet.

'The demonic archangel upon whom Klosterheim called to aid him is our own patron Lord of Chaos. His name is Arioch. Both your Bible and the poet Milton mention him. On occasions, he inhabits that black blade you saw me use. On other occasions, the sword contains the souls of those its wielder has killed. Some part of those souls are transferred to whoever uses the blade. Other parts go to placate Arioch. When Satan attempted, hundreds of years ago, on this plane – or one very much like it – to be reconciled with God, neither Klosterheim nor Arioch accepted this and have, across many planes of the multiverse, sought not only the destruction of God himself, but also of Satan – or whatever manifestations of those forces exist here.'

'You have still not explained whose soul Klosterheim's body drank,' pointed out Sinclair.

'Why, the last soul it took,' said Monsieur Zenith in some surprise. 'I thought that is what you understood.'

'And whose was that—?'

Monsieur Zenith had risen swiftly and elegantly and was kissing Mrs Persson's hand, moving towards the shelf where he had placed his silk hat and gloves. 'You must forgive me. I have some unfinished business at a nearby art gallery.'

Almost instinctively, Commissaire Lapointe rose as if to apprehend him but then sat down again suddenly.

Sir Seaton Begg, with dawning comprehension, laid his hand on his old friend's arm, but Taffy Sinclair was insistent. 'Whose, Monsieur Zenith? Whose?'

Monsieur Zenith slipped gracefully from the table and seemed to disappear, merging with the sunlit spray of the fountain.

'Whose?' Sinclair turned baffled to look at Mrs Persson, who had taken her two cats into her lap and was stroking them gently. 'Do you know?'

She inclined her head and looked questioningly, intimately at Sir Seaton Begg, whose nod was scarcely perceptible.

'It was his own, of course,' she said.

NEW MYSTERIES OF PARIS

BARRY GIFFORD

I was recently told a story that was so stupid, so melancholy, and so moving: a man comes into a hotel one day and asks to rent a room. He is shown up to number 35. As he comes down a few minutes later and leaves the key at the desk, he says: 'Excuse me, I have no memory at all. If you please, each time I come in, I'll tell you my name: Monsieur Delouit. And each time you'll tell me the number of my room.' 'Very well, Monsieur.' Soon afterwards, he returns, and as he passes the desk says: 'Monsieur Delouit.' 'Number 35 Monsieur.' 'Thank you.' A minute later, a man. extra ordinarily upset, his clothes covered with mud. bleeding, his face almost not a face at all, appears at the desk. 'Monsieur Delouit.' 'What do you mean, Monsieur Delouit? Don't try to put one over on us! Monsieur Delouir has just gone upstairs!' 'I'm sorry, it's me . . . I've just fallen out of the window. What's the number of my room please?'

André Breton, *Nadja*

Nadja was taken to a madhouse in 1928. Some place in the French countryside where ordinary people, those fortunate enough to have escaped scrutiny, who have avoided so far in their lives being similarly judged and sentenced and dismissed from the greater society, will not be reminded of their own failings by the screams of the outcast.

It is reasonable to suppose that by that time there could not be much difference for Nadja between the inside of a sanatorium and the outside – but Nadja was here, she left something of herself. Certainly she's dead by now, buried in a field behind an insane asylum, cats screwing on her grave.

The day she threatened to jump from the window of her room in the Hotel Sphinx on the boulevard Magenta I should have known she was not a fake. Who can tell the genuine mad from the fake? Nadja could. She was always pointing them out to me. In a café she'd whisper, 'Look at her. Biting her nails. Pretending to be waiting for someone. She's a fake. Her lovers disappear.' 'But how can you tell,' I'd ask. 'Look at my eyes,' Nadja would say. 'Can you see the way they are lit from behind? I'm dangerous. To be avoided.'

Who was Nadja? What was the significance of Nadja in my life? Why does she return, a constant, though I've neither seen nor heard of or from her in fifty years?

I saw a woman in a marketplace in a Mexican city, Merida, perhaps, in the Yucatan, twenty years ago or so. She resembled Nadja, or what she might have looked like, according to my idea of Nadja had she still been alive, let alone an inhabitant of a jungle town in Mexico. I followed her as she moved from stand to stand, inspecting the fruits, dresses, beads, kitchen knives, crucifixes. Was this a woman or a phantom? Her grey hair was worn long and chick and fell across her face so that her features were indistinct, shadowed. Nadja had been blonde, with the short, curled haircut of the day, a brief nose, sharp black hawk's eyes, a long mouth with slender lips, purple, that grinned in one corner only. This hag in the marketplace was fat, toothless, I would say, judging by the line of her jaw, dark-skinned. Nadja had been white as the full moon of February over Venice, almost emaciated, seldom are, with a full mouth of teeth, crooked but strong. She was capable of cracking open with ease in one swift bite a stalk of Haitian sugarcane.

How could I imagine this hideous, crumbling jungle creature to he Nadja? Some feeling made me follow until, crossing a busy street, I lost sight of her. I panicked and looked around wildly. She was gone and I was forced to suppress a great scream of pain. Unused to this severe sort of anxiety, I battled to control my emotions, there in the midst of a crowd of Indians.

It was what Nadja had meant when she stuck

her tongue into my ear as we rode in a cab along the boulevard Raspail. As quickly as she'd done it she withdrew to the opposite corner of the seat and said, staring blankly ahead, 'To me nothing is more terrifying than the curse of self-fulfilment.'

What did Nadja do before we met? I asked her many times and mostly she would avoid answering by laughing and kissing me, adjusting my tie, or brushing my lapels. She did tell me she was born in Belgium, near Ghent, and that her father raised flowers. She went to the local school, a convent, and moved to Paris when she was seventeen. She met a man, unidentified, got married, gave birth to a daughter, who promptly died of pneumonia. Those were facts, according to Nadja. The man was gone soon after the daughter.

Other than that there was little Nadja would admit. None of it was important, she said. 'Not to you!' She instructed me to invent her story, it was all the same, unrelated to today. 'Who is the hero of a film that has at its centre a peacock flying through and landing in the snow?' Nadja asks, licking my chin as if she were here.

I must recall how and why I became involved with Nadja. I was walking along the rue Vaugirard, preparing to turn into the Luxembourg, when I saw a woman standing in front of a butcher's shop, desperately examining the contents of her purse. I say desperately because there were lines of great consternation on her face, as if she had misplaced and was frantically searching for the ticket that would allow her to claim a side of beef she'd pawned or left to be laundered. The weather was foul, it was early November and it was raining. The air was ugly, full of wood smoke and water, black, brown and grey. The woman, who was Nadja, was a disconcerting sight, her hair matted, stockings torn, coat soaked. I approached her immediately and asked if I might be of service.

'This is an evil afternoon,' she said. She looked at me. 'Can you buy me a drink? There are ravens everywhere now. Even in the shops, in the road. The government is full of them, as you no doubt are already aware. What would a government be without its ravens?' She stared at me with horrible yellow eyes. There was no possibility of refusal. 'Of course,' I said, and Nadja smiled, a sweet genuine smile, and gently took my arm.

Nadja had a harelip. Have I mentioned that? Or had been born with a harelip. She'd had it fixed, but that was the reason for her lopsided grin that added so inexplicably to Nadja's desirability.

She disliked being thought of as foolish, though she often sought to contribute to the common good by committing foolish acts, such as disrobing in the Louvre in front of the *Mona Lisa*. For that 'act of valour', as Nadja referred to it, she spent several days in jail, not having the money to pay the fine for being a public nuisance.

Following the incident at the Louvre, Nadja made a similar gesture of liberation on the avenue d'Iena near the German Club. The Germans, she claimed, would not have her arrested; instead, Nadja said, they would pretend to ignore her. Then came the affair at the Trocadéro where Nadja disrobed and poured a bucket of red paint over her head. Neither time was she detained. The *Mona Lisa* episode had made her famous for the moment and her exploits of this order were no longer effective. Trocadéro was Nadja's final mention in the newspapers. After that hers was a presence of secrets.

Nadja had a habit of laughing at the wrong moment. Someone would be in the midst of telling a story, approaching a crucial point, and Nadja would begin to laugh, softly at first, then gradually increase the level of laughter to a kind of shrill cry, shocking all those present and of course preventing the narrator from finishing his tale. The phenomenon would not occur always, but often enough so that I would be on edge whenever we were in the company of others. Several times I was forced to escort Nadja out of the room until she regained her self-control.

The unpredictable laughter was not her only social aberration. Nadja refused to be photographed. True, photographs of Nadja do exist, but they were taken surreptitously, without her knowledge; usually when she was drunk.

Contrary to what most of my acquaintances thought at the time, Nadja was the least mysterious person I have ever met. Everything about her was obvious. Her motives were plain, she desired love, sanity, colour – all healthy pursuits. Failure on any one count can hardly be held against Nadja. Disgrace, after all, is merely a manifestation of value. The price of anything is always set in advance. Nadja made me see this. Truth is perhaps more horrible than anyone would dare admit.

She was standing there in the dream, the gun still in her hand pointing down at the body, when the cops broke in. It was Nadja with a Barbara Stanwyck hairdo in a black robe, a silk one with gold brocade on the wide lapels. 'I shot him in the face,' she said, 'and he tumbled like laundry down a chute.' Those were her exact words. They were fresh in my mind when I woke up. The name of the movie was *Riffraff*, that much I could remember. But it wasn't real, it was a dream, right? I hadn't seen Nadja in four years, and I knew who the man on the floor had to be.

One morning Nadja awoke and could not see out of her right eye. She sent a *pneu* asking me to meet her at the Café des Oiseaux that afternoon. 'It's awful and wonderful,' Nadja said as soon as

I sat down at her table. 'There is a cloud in my eye, floating across the centre.'

'Is it any particular colour?' I asked.

'Red,' said Nadja. 'Like a veil of blood.'

'Perhaps it is blood,' I said. 'Have you made arrangements to see a doctor?'

'Doctors can only destory,' Nadja said. 'Have you a cigarette?'

I gave her one, lit it and watched her blow out the smoke.

'Usually cigarette smoke is blue,' she said. 'Mixed with the red it's actually quite beautiful, like two ghost ships passing through one another on the rolling sea.'

I asked Nadja what she intended to do about this problem.

'Nothing.' she said. 'So I have one normal eye and one very interesting eye. The left shall be the practical side, the ordinary eye, useful and necessary. The right shall be the dream side, the indefinable, the exquisite and ungraspable. The right eye is my entrance to a drifting, unstable world ruled by colour and magic. Nothing is absolute there, it is a true wilderness. Covered by this thin red veil realities are made bearable by their vagueness.'

I suggested to Nadja that the presence of blood in her eye, if indeed that was what it was, might be a sign of a more serious condition, a remark that caused her to explode with laughter.

★   ★   ★

Who was Madame Sacco? Unlike Madame Blavatsky no religion was founded in her name, and also unlike the Russian she was not a charlatan. Her real name was Paulette Tanguy. born in Belleville. She set up shop as Mme Sacco on the rue des Usiness several months after the death of her third husband, an Italian, whose name I've forgotten, though I do not believe it was Sacco. In any case, he was seldom mentioned, and neither was she very forthcoming regarding his two predecessors. As to how Mme Sacco acquired her gift of clairvoyance, I never knew. She was never mistaken about me and I trusted her completely.

Mme Sacco knew of Nadja's existence prior to my ever mentioning her. When Mme Sacco told me about my pre-occupation with a woman named 'Hélène', I was necessarily astonished. Only a day before Nadja had said to me, seemingly apropos of nothing, 'I am Hélène.' These women were already connected! My reputation in certain circles for naivety was apparently not altogether undeserved.

They did not, however, get along well. Nadja distrusted clairvoyants – 'seers' she called them, rudely. 'Even if they know what they're talking about,' Nadja said, 'even if their predictions are accurate, what right have they to inform?'

Mme Sacco sensed immediately Nadja's hostility, and her performance in Nadja's presence was subdued. 'There is a great deal I could tell you about this woman,' Mme Sacco said after Nadja had departed, 'but she is opposed to it and therefore I cannot pursue her. I do know,' and here Mme Sacco smiled, 'that she is dishonest, she feigns madness and is a danger to you.'

'Do you mean,' I asked, 'that Nadja is sane? That she intends to harm me?'

'Oh no,' Mme Sacco said, smiling even more handsomely than before, 'she is genuinely deranged. Her pretending is the way she fools herself. As to harm, consider what you already do to yourself. This Nadja is a brief disruption in your life.'

Walking away from Mme Sacco's I heard laughter coming from above me. I looked up and saw a boy sitting on a windowsill, playing with a live monkey. It's me, I thought. I am the monkey.

Nadja, why is it so difficult to remember exactly what you looked like? Your precise words escape me also. My recreations are passable but not accurate. You made me examine my actions, forced me to consider possibilities other than the obvious. I am desperate now for the absolute taste of you.

I am in my studio at one minute past four o'clock in the afternoon, listening to the traffic pass in the street below my open windows. The sky is solidly grey with perhaps a stripe of white. I am embarrassed by my eagerness for night, the darkness, which I never used to be.

One evening in Père-Lachaise, as we strolled among the graves, you began to sing – some children's song, I believe – and I was horrified. I dared not mention the fact to you, knowing you would ridicule my timidity; but I could not suppress the unholy feeling I derived from your merrily singing in the cemetery. Virtually everything you did disturbed, upset, surprised me. And yet I suffer.

Wherever Nadja is must be a better place than this, especially for her. I prefer to imagine Nadja in paradise, satisfied at last with the circumstances of her existence. She could never be happy in conventional life, better than she is allowed the latitude of feeling beyond desire. That her behaviour was considered hizarre, her appearance unsightly, and she found herself rejected on her own terms, could not have given Nadja much hope for even an acceptable afterlife.

I recall the time Nadja decided she would be an artist, a painter. She borrowed money from me for materials and did not leave her room at the Hotel Sphinx for several days. At the end of her siege Nadja emerged with one painting, which she showed to me at the Dôme. It was a self-portrait, *Nadja Among the Carnivores*, she called it. In the painting Nadja was depicted nude, walking in a street surrounded by ghoulish figures: huge goblins with beaks, monstrous dark shapes, devils with pitchforks, deformed crones, a conglomeration of hideous Bosch-like characters. The style was, as one might imagine, crude, the technique primitive. One could not, however, deny its power, the unsettling effect of the painting.

I told Nadja that I was impressed by the force

of her work, and that I would gladly purchase the painting from her. She refused my offer. 'It is not for sale,' she said. 'Now that you've seen it, I can destroy it.' I begged her not to, but at that moment she began tearing the canvas apart, shredding it into strips. 'Now,' Nadja said, smiling, 'I have been an artist. You are my witness. I never have to prove myself again.'

My feeling about Nadja is ultimately one of sadness, loss, but not without a certain degree of satisfaction in having kept faithful to my perception of her intentions. I do not pretend to have understood Nadja, though I remain to verify her existence.

As we were walking together along the Quai de l'Heure Bleue on a November afternoon, Nadja stopped and pointed to the river. 'November is the first of the Suicide Months. Look there, in the middle of the Seine, I am drowning and boats pass oblivious to my distress.'

Here in the fading afternoon light, the world spinning senselessly as always, besieged by despair and unreasonable notions, I recall Nadja's succinct admonition, 'Prepare.'

ETHNIC CLEANSING

DOMINIQUE MANOTTI

DAY I

'Twenty thousand now,' says the fat, greasy-haired man in a cheap brown suit, his forehead and upper lip covered in perspiration. He repeats: 'Twenty thousand now,' as if to convince himself of the amount, and taps his desk drawer. 'Cash. And twenty thousand when the job's done, if it all goes well, no discussion. Again, cash.' Breaks out into a fresh sweat. I'm handing over forty thousand euros to a guy whose name I don't even know. He mops his forehead with the cuff of his brown suit jacket, which is nice and absorbent, as if he does it all the time. It's come to this . . . This or fleeing abroad. This and fleeing abroad?

The guy standing in front of him – athletic body, well-groomed, shaved head, smooth, tanned, tight black T-shirt, black jeans, black leather boots, not far off forty, from the slight slackening of the skin and the stomach – wordlessly extends an open hand across the desk. The fat man hesitates for a moment, opens the drawer and tosses an envelope onto the desk. The other guy picks it up, counts the notes in no hurry, and slips them into his underpants, under his jeans, pulling in his stomach.

'How long?'

'A week, max.'

'Fine.'

He automatically hitches up his jeans and leaves. Does his sums as he goes down the stairs (avoid lifts, potential hazard). Forty thousand, not exactly a fortune. But I'm not getting any younger . . . Besides, it's not the riskiest job. That's why it's worth it, don't want to stick my neck out, or share. Not bad. He's back in the street. Little wink at the copper plate by the entrance to the building. Alfred Poupon Property Agent, Staircase A, 3rd floor, left. Old Poupon was sweating, he recked of fear. Not used to this type of operation. Is that a good thing for me or dangerous?

Hidden behind a third-floor window, Alfred Poupon watches the man walk off down the street with the wad of notes in his underpants. He turns the corner, calm and assured. That's it, he's gone.

End of a suffocatingly muggy August day. Zé leaves Paris at the wheel of his white, five-year-old, all-purpose Clio. He turns off the périphérique onto a very wide main road alongside a chaotic sprawl of showy office blocks. This new business district is the big city's latest growth spurt. At this hour, and in the middle of August, it's completely deserted, quite sinister. Zé cruises slowly. He's approaching the A86 motorway which is becoming the second Paris orbital, spots the slip road, turns onto it, goes even slower. The target's there, set back from the road below him, a few metres from the security barrier. Zé's on the alert, eyes sharp, neurons buzzing: take it all in at a glance, clock everything, don't risk a second drive-by. An isolated five-storey building of dirty, greyish brick, with a long crack running diagonally from window to window. All the openings, which must have been bricked up once, are now gaping. Behind the building, a huge overgrown waste ground dotted with loose stones, apparently empty, sloping down to a canal where there's little activity.

But the building in the middle of this wilderness is teeming with life. At ground level, on the strip of beaten earth between the façade and the motorway slip road, there's a whole crowd of black men in jellabas or brightly coloured shirts coming and going amid the dust – squatting, sitting on wooden packing cases, standing around, chatting, playing cards and doing business. An old man in a long, immaculately white robe sitting motionless on a chair against the wall, face upturned, eyes closed, seems to be drinking in the light of the orange sunset which makes his face glow.

Through the cracks in the wall, glimpses of a central wooden staircase, women in flowing boubous busy around makeshift fires surrounded by hordes of children jostling and running. The upper floors look very animated too. Zé thinks he catches a whiff of the familiar smell of groundnuts and spices simmering. That's the real thrill of the chase, when the hunter feels this close to his prey. Get a grip. Professional. Loads of squatters, all looking alike. No hope of passing unnoticed with your white mug, even with a deep tan. He pulls out onto the motorway and accelerates.

DAY 2

In a midnight-blue tracksuit, Zé jogs along the former towpath beside the canal. A few ware-houses, silos and barges line the quay. Not a soul. He draws level with the Africans' squat. A fence, broken in several places. Still nobody about. He pulls his tracksuit hood over his shaved head and slips through to the waste ground. A series of stony humps and dips overgrown with brambles, like a field of ruins dominated by the grey brick building, obscured at the bottom by brambles. From this side, everything looks dead. The ground- and first-floor windows are still bricked up with concrete breeze blocks and on the upper floors only a few small holes have been made here and there. Clearly the squatters are wary of the waste ground and are trying to keep it out.

Zé moves slowly and noiselessly, camouflaged by the undergrowth, and comes across a whole network of paths and hidey-holes dug into the ground, protected by cardboard, planks, and sometimes carpeting. You can bet that after dark, this sort of wild garden, so close to the dormitory suburbs, will be teeming with people. Zé looks for a hole that appears to be empty and finds one on an area of high ground near the motorway from which he can watch the building. He clears some space for himself with a few flat stones, wedges himself in and waits. The building looks deserted. In the late afternoon, Zé distinctly hears the noise of people flocking back to the squat and going about their usual business. In the openings of the façade he's watching, he sees lights flickering. Then darkness falls and the waste ground comes alive. Life rises up from the canal, floats above the ground, as if immaterial. Rustling, whispering, half-glimpsed flames. Zé hopes he's not in the path of the main tide of people and focuses on the façade. Sniff out any clandestine contacts between the squat and the waste ground. That's his way in. He lights a joint, to blend in, and pulls his hood down over his eyes.

As the night's very dark, for a few hours he concentrates on the sounds so as to chart the comings and goings, and thinks he's identified more intense activity under the brambles at the farthest corner of the building. He doesn't budge. He waits. Around 4 a.m., life begins to flow back towards the canal and dissolves into the night by osmosis.

Zé uncurls himself, dives under the brambles closest to the building and finds a clear path running its entire length. At ground level, the five bricked-up basement windows must open into the cellars. Zé stops in front of the fifth one, bricked up like the others, and prods the breeze blocks. Finding they're loose, he pulls a knife from his pocket and inserts the blade between the rubble stones. They're a snug fit, but not cemented in. Zé moves away quickly, and hides in a dip in the ground, keeping still again. Take time to think. I've found the front door. No doubt I'm sharing it with dealers I know nothing about. So I don't know what I might find behind it. Don't want to know. Too great a risk of being seen. Come back tomorrow, properly equipped, and give it a go, blind.

Around 5.30, the lights begin to come on again in the squat. Between the dealers leaving and the squatters waking, I have got a good half hour to act undisturbed. That's plenty. Zé too makes his way back to the canal.

DAY 3

Back to the waste ground, same time, same clothes, to find the same hole and wait there. The routine, in other words. Zé's brought an old rucksack, crammed full, and a sleeping bag. The hours tick by. Nothing out of the ordinary. Only, around midnight, a kid who's already well out of it and really wants to hang out with 'a grown-up' and 'possibly more'. Zé frightens him off with a few curses in Serbo-Croat and the kid doesn't insist.

194

4.20 a.m. Zé gets up, walks quickly over to the fifth basement window. Crouching in front of it, from his rucksack he pulls a pair of rubber gloves, a balaclava and night-vision goggles, which he puts on. He inserts a flat hook between the breeze blocks and loosens them just like that, throws his rucksack through the window and drops down into the cellar. First surprise, he hits the ground sooner than expected. A huge underfloor space rather than a cellar. Barely room to stand up. Senses a presence in a corner: a horizontal shape beginning to sit up. In two strides, Zé's on top of him, pinning him to the floor. He knocks him out with a punch to the chin. He finishes him off with a stone picked up from the ground. Quick, find the trap door leading up to the ground floor.

Torch. Some kind of flimsy wooden partition gives way to his touch. Piles of rubbish. Towards the centre of the building, a few wooden cases full of wire jewellery, wooden statuettes and leather belts, street hawkers' wares no doubt, wonderfully flammable material. And the trap door. A gentle push: it yields easily; glance around, I'm just under the main staircase.

The wooden staircase. Perfect. Zé lets the trap door close, hurriedly goes over to the body, drags it under the trap door, piles up the planks from the partition, the boxes full of stuff, the guy's sleeping bag, syringe, needle, tourniquet, spoon, cotton wool, bottle of water and even a dose of smack: do the job properly. Sprinkles several litres of methylated spirits over the whole lot. Then takes a spirit stove out of his rucksack, lights it, throws it onto the sleeping bag and opens the trap door. The fire catches immediately. Zé picks up his rucksack, runs to the window, clambers up into the open air with no difficulty. He walks quickly down to the canal without looking back. He must get as far away as he can before the fire spreads to the upper floors. As he walks, he stuffs the balaclava, gloves and goggles into his rucksack, reaches the towpath and breaks into a run, like an early-morning jogger. He watches the building out of the corner of his eye. Judging by the façade, nothing's happening. The fire hasn't caught, did it burn itself out in the cellar? Not enough meths? He carries on jogging, keeping up the same pace. Just as the outline of the building vanishes behind the carcass of an abandoned cement silo, he hears a rising scream. Don't turn around. Hot flush. That's it, you did it. They chucked you out of their place, you chuck them out of yours. Nice work.

He keeps on running. A kilometre further on, the rucksack will sink to the bottom of the canal, in two kilometres, he'll be back in his Clio and will drive straight down to Marseille. Tomorrow, he'll be out of the country. The fire engulfs the cellar, a magnificent blaze sucked towards the stairwell, which grows scorchingly hot before the staircase bursts into flames in several places, crackling. The dangling naked electric wires catch fire and give off a smell of burning rubber which masks that of the corpse being slowly burned to cinders. Wreaths of grey and black smoke billow from the ground floor, spread over the motorway, rise to the roof. Men abruptly roused emerge to see what's going on just as the first flight of stairs collapses in a shower of sparks. Screams. In a few seconds, the alarm's raised and the whole building resounds with panic-filled shouts, jostling, stampeding. The fire spreads to the upper storeys – there's little to hinder it, the doors have been ripped off and the curtains replacing them catch fire at the slightest gust. The women and children gather by the windows at either end of the building, the men try to halt the progress of the flames by blocking any opening with everything they can get their hands on; it's a ludicrous battle which only feeds the flames. Gas stoves explode here and there. Women jump out of first-floor windows clutching their children. Others on the fourth and fifth floors fling bundles of clothes out of the windows, hover over the void, scream for help. The distraught squatters scatter onto the motorway slip road where traffic is at a standstill.

The fire brigade arrives, sirens wailing, three fire engines, just as the roof over the staircase collapses. They extend their ladders, evacuate the inhabitants, attack the flames. Four more engines arrive. Then the police show up. Two police stations have been mobilised, plus a brigade of riot police. The area is cordoned off. Nobody's allowed near. Not onlookers, friends or family. Orders are clear: avoid any demonstration of support for the victims, no breaches of the peace. All the uninjured squatters are herded into big buses: immediate removal to a municipal sports centre placed at the disposal of the disaster victims. The dead are taken to the morgues in ambulances and the burned and the wounded to various hospitals, as and when the fire-fighters are able to drag them out of the blaze. Some people manage to slip through the police cordon and run off across the waste ground.

By 6 a.m., in the building where the fire's still smouldering, only a few bodies are left, along with the fire-fighters still battling the flames and drowning what's left of the squat under gallons of water. According to the police bulletin, 123 people were living in this squat, seven are dead and fifteen others injured, three of whom are critical; 101 people are in the municipal sports centre where identity checks are being carried out. The plan is to escort any illegal immigrants to the border and rehouse those whose papers are in order. The investigation should establish whether the fire is of criminal or accidental origin.

TWO YEARS LATER

A twelve-storey steel and glass structure hugs the curve of the A86 motorway slip road, which has been concreted over and where at this very moment a garden is being laid out. The façade overlooking the canal has reflective glass echoing the changing hues of the weather, blue sky, clouds, storms, in an arresting mirror effect. A vast paved esplanade stretches down to the canal. In the centre is a circular, white stone fountain with geometric sculptures. On either side, a row of lime trees in front of two multilevel apartment blocks. Terraced gardens that will soon be verdant slope down to the canal. An old-fashioned bandstand has been installed on the quayside, which has been turned into a promenade.

It's summer, the weather's very hot, the whole complex is still empty, a few finishing touches yet to be added. The Bâtimo construction company is holding a party to celebrate the completion of the works before the August holidays. White marquees have been set up along the canal and a throng of men in dark suits and a few women in light dresses are crowded around the buffers piled with refreshments and champagne. Entrepreneurs and politicians big and small, of all persuasions, mingle and rub shoulders.

When the mayor arrived, flanked by his deputy, he was a little tense. The tragedy that took place here two years ago is on everyone's mind, he was thinking. Granted, the police investigation concluded it was an accident following a fight between dealers who had broken into the basement of the squat. But eight dead . . . Granted, the city council rehoused all the legal immigrants. But not locally, not together, a long way from Paris . . . and the illegal immigrants were deported before they'd had time to recover. Granted, some immigrant support organisations were invited to this inauguration of the new canal district'. But only those with close ties to the mayor's office. What if the others, the ones the police repressed with some brutality during the fire and afterwards, were to decide to come and spoil the party . . . Then he relaxes a little more with each glass of champagne. And whisky. After all, the fire, the dead, you're probably the only one still thinking about it. Too sensitive . . .

Marchal, the CEO of Bâtimo, has invited Louvois, the big boss of the construction group that bears his name and which owns Bâtimo. The big boss hasn't come, but he's sent his son. And Marchal is blowing his own trumpet.

'With this scheme completed, we'll be pitching to the mayor and the regional authorities for the renovation of the entire canal area. We're the experts in mixed business and residential developments. This is the way forward.'

The mayor, who's perked up, glass in hand, explains to the Paris and regional authorities: 'We need to change the image of social housing. There's a high demand for quality social housing here. Among out council employees alone . . .'

Louvois junior gazes after a tubby man in a navy blue suit, panting and sweating profusely, who's drinking too much, steering between groups, always on his own. A man who looks completely out of place. He leans towards Marchal. 'Who's that guy? Do you know him?'

'Yes. Alfred Poupon, a property agent. He's got an extraordinary nose for sniffing out new sites. He's the one who discovered this one, under the most difficult circumstances.' A pause. 'The old buildings were occupied, and the mayor wouldn't hear of expulsions, of course.' A fresh silence, no questions. 'He made a lot of money from the deal, but he's a sad case. Everything he makes, he loses on the horses.'

Translation © Lulu Norman and Ros Schwartz

L'AMÉRICAINE

MAXIM JAKUBOWSKI

Cornelia took the RER from Roissy-Charles de Gaulle. A taxi would have been easier and more relaxed after the seven-hour plane journey, but she knew she had to remain as anonymous as possible. Cab drivers have a bad habit of remembering tall, lanky blondes, particularly so those who did not wish to engage in needless conversation and reveal whether it was their first time in Paris or was she coming here on holiday?

Because she knew there were countless CCTV cameras sprinkled across the airport and the train terminal, she had quickly changed outfits in a somewhat insalubrious toilet shortly after picking up her suitcase from the luggage carousel, and by the time she walked on to the RER train, she now had a grey scarf obscuring her blonde curls and wore a different outfit altogether from the flight. It was far from foolproof, but at least would serve its purpose in muddying the waters in the eventuality of a later, thorough investigation.

The commuters on the train to Paris looked grey and tired, wage slaves on their mindless journey to work or elsewhere. A couple of teenage Arab kids listening to rap – or was it hip hop – on their iPods glanced at her repeatedly, but her indifference soon got the better of them and she wasn't bothered until the Luxembourg Gardens stop where she got off.

She had booked herself into a small hotel there on the Internet the previous day. She checked herself in under the false name on her spare passport, a Canadian one she'd seldom used before. She took a shower and relaxed before taking the lift to the lobby around lunch hour, and noticed someone new had taken over at the registration desk from the young woman who'd earlier checked her in. She calmly walked back to her room and stuffed some clothes into a tote bag and went down to the lobby again and left the hotel. Fifteen minutes later, she registered at another hotel, near the place de l'Odéon, this time under her real name. This booking she'd made by phone from New York a week or so before. She was now the proud tenant of two separate hotel rooms under two separate names and nationalities. Both rooms were noisy and looked out onto busy streets, but that was Paris, and anyway she wasn't here for a spot of tourism. This was work. She settled in the new room, took a nap, and just before the evening walked out and took a cab to the place de l'Opéra. There was a thin jiffy bag waiting for her at the American Express Poste Restante. Here, she retrieved the key she had purchased back in

Brooklyn Beach from a Russian connection she occasionally used. She then caught another taxi to the Gare du Nord, where she located the left luggage locker which the key opened. The package was anonymous and not too bulky. She picked up a copy of *Libération* and casually wrapped it around the bundle she had just retrieved from the locker and walked down the train station stairs to the Métro and took the Porte d'Orléans line back to Odéon. In the room, she unwrapped the package and weighed the Sig Sauer in her hand. Her favourite gun. Perfect.

The Italian girl had always preferred older men. Some of her friends and other fellow students at La Sapienza, Rome's university, had always kidded her she had something of a father fixation, and indeed her relationship with her gastroenterologist dad was prickly to say the least, seesawing between devotion and simmering anger. At any rate, he also spoiled her badly.

But boys her age seemed so clumsy and un-interesting, coarse, superficial, so sadly predictable, and she found herself recoiling instinctively from their tentative touches all too often. Not that she knew what exactly she wanted herself.

Whenever asked about her plans for the future, she would answer in jest (or maybe not) that she planned to marry an ambassador and have lots of babies. When Peppino – the name she would use for her much older, foreign lover so as to make him difficult for her parents to identify – quizzed her about this, she would add that the ambassador would also be a black man, a big man in both size and personality. Peppino would smile silently in response, betraying his own personal fears and prejudices, only to point out that she'd be wasting so many opportunities by becoming merely a wife. After all, this was a young woman who by the age of twenty-two had a degree in comparative literature, spoke five languages, and would surely make a hell of a journalist or foreign correspondent one day.

Her affair with the man she and her friends affectionately called Peppino had lasted just over a year and he had been the first man she had fucked. To her amazement, he had become not just a lover but her professor of sex; unimaginably tender, crudely transgressive, and it was the first time she had come across a guy who understood her so well that their contact when apart became almost telepathic. However, he was also more than twice her age, lived in another country and happened to be married, which sharpened her longing and her jealousy to breaking point. The affair had proven both beautiful and traumatic, but eventually the enforced separation from Peppino could not be assuaged any longer by telephone calls, frantic emails and mere words. For her sanity, she was obliged to break up with him, even though she loved him. She had a life to live, adventures to experience; he had already lived his life, hadn't he? Now was her time. The decision was a painful one and he naturally took it badly. Not that her state of mind was much better, racked by doubts, heartache and regrets by the thousands as both Peppino and she could not help recalling the days and nights together, the shocking intimacy they had experienced, the pleasure and complicity, the joy and the darkness. Sleepless nights and silent unhappiness followed in her wake and she agreed to visit a girlfriend from her Erasmus months in Lisbon who lived in Paris – ironically, a city he had always wanted to take her to.

It was a wet spring and the thin rain peppered the Latin Quarter pavements with a coating of grey melancholy. Flora had gone to her grandparents' house in the country and left the Italian girl on her own for a few days. Initially, she had looked forward to the prospect but now felt herself particularly lonely. When she was not busy exploring the city with her friend, memories just kept on flooding back.

She was sitting reading a book at the terrace of Les Deux Magots, sipping a coffee, half-watching the world pass by – women who walked elegantly, young men who looked cute but would surely prove dull in real life she thought – when she heard the seductive voice of the bad man over her shoulder.

'That's a quite wonderful book, Mademoiselle,' he said. 'I envy you the experience of reading it for the first time. Truly.'

Giuly looked up at him. He looked older. How could he not be?

Cornelia much preferred ignorance. A job was a job and it was better not to have to know any of the often murky reasons when she was given an assignment.

Had the target stolen from another party, swindled, lied, killed, betrayed? It was not important.

Cornelia knew she had a cold heart. It made her work easier, not that she sought excuses. She would kill both innocent and guilty parties with the same set of mind. It was not hers to reason why.

She had been given a thin dossier on her Paris mark, a half-dozen pages of random information about his haunts and habits and a couple of photographs. A manila folder she had slipped between her folded black cashmere sweaters in her travelling suitcase, to which she had added a few torn-out pages from the financial pages of the *New York Times* and a section on international investment from the *Wall Street Journal* to muddy the waters in the event of an unlikely snap examination of her belongings by customs at either JFK or Roissy. He was a man in his late forties, good-looking in a rugged sort of way which appealed to some women, she knew. Tallish, hair greying at the temples in subdued and elegant manner. She studied one of the photographs, and noted the ice-green eyes, and a steely inner determination behind the crooked smile. A dangerous man. A bad man.

But they all have weaknesses, and it appeared his was women. It usually was. Cornelia sighed. Kept on reading the information sheet she had been provided with, made notes. Finally, she booted up her laptop and went online to hunt down the *clubs échangistes* her prey was known to frequent on a regular basis. They appeared to be located all over the city, but the main ones appeared to be in the Marais and close to the Louvre. She wrote down the particulars of Au Pluriel, Le Château des Lys, Les Chandelles and Chris et Manu, and studied the respective websites. She'd been to a couple of similar 'swing' clubs back in the States, both privately and for work reasons. She'd found them somewhat sordid. Maybe the Parisian ones would prove classier, but she had her doubts. Cornelia had no qualms about public sex, let alone exhibitionism – after all she had stripped for a living some years earlier and greatly enjoyed the sensation – but still found that sex was an essentially private communion. But then she'd always had an uneasy relationship and perception of sex, and at a push would confess to decidedly mixed feelings about it.

Would sex in Paris, sex and Paris prove any different, she wondered?

She rose from the bed where she had spread out the pages and photos, switched off the metal grey laptop and walked pensively to the hotel room's small, poky bathroom. She pulled off her T-shirt and slipped off her white cotton panties and looked at herself in the full-length mirror.

And shed a tear.

The bad man had no problem seducing the young Italian woman. He had experience and a deceptive elegance. Anyway, she was on the rebound from her Peppino and a vulnerable prey. Had her first lover not warned her that no man would ever love her, touch her with as much tenderness as he? And had she not known in her heart that he was right? But falling into the arms of the Frenchman was easy, a way of moving on, she reckoned. She knew all he really wanted to do was fuck her, use her and that was good enough for now for Giuly. She was lost and the excesses of sex were as good a way of burying the past and the hurt. This new man would not love her; he was just another adventure along the road. So why not? This was Paris, wasn't it? And spring would soon turn into summer and she just couldn't bear the thought of returning to Rome and resuming her PhD studies and being subsidised by her father.

She rang home and informed her parents she would be staying on in Paris for a few more months. There were protests and fiery arguments, but she was used to manipulating them. She was old enough by now, she told them, to do what she wanted with her life.

'Respect me, and my needs,' she said. Not for the first time.

'Do you need money?' her father asked.

'No, I've found a job, helping out in a book-shop,' she lied.

The Frenchman – he said he was a busi-nessman, something in export/import – ordered her to move in with him and Giuly accepted. She couldn't stay on at Flora's without revealing her new relationship.

At first, it was nice to sleep at night in bed with another person, a man. Feeling the warmth of the other's body, waking up to a naked body next to her own. And to feel herself filled to the brim when he made love to her. To again experience a man's cock growing inside her as it ploughed her, stretched her. To take a penis, savour its hard-ening inside her mouth, to hear a man moan above her as he came, shuddered, shouted out obscen-ities or religious adjectives, and experience the heat waves coursing from cunt to heart to brain. Of course, it reminded her of Peppino. But then again, it was different. No fish face at the moment of climax with this new man, just a detached air of satisfaction, almost cruelty as he often took her to the brink and retreated, playing with her senses, enjoying her like an object.

Day times, he would often leave her early in the morning and go about his work while Giuly would explore Paris, fancy-free, absorbing the essence of the city in her long, lanky stride. For the first time in ages, she felt like a gypsy again, like the young teenager who would live on the streets of Rome and even enjoy sleepless nights wandering from alleys to coffee shops with a cohort of friends or even alone, drinking in life with no care in the world. In Belleville, she discovered a patisserie with sickly-sweet Middle-Eastern delicacies, near Censier-Daubenton she made an acquaintance with a young dope dealer who furnished her with cheap weed, which she would take care never to smoke at the man's apartment off the quai de Grenelle. As with Peppino, she knew older guys secretly disapproved of her getting high, as if pretending they had never been young themselves. Neither did they appreciate The Clash, she'd found out . . . He would leave her money when he left her behind but she was frugal and never used it all not asked for more.

And at night, after her aimless, carefree wanderings, he would treat her to fancy restaurants – she'd cooked for him a few times at the flat but he was not too keen on pasta or tomato sauce or seemingly Italian food – and then bring her back to the apartment where he would fuck her. Harder and harder. As she offered no resistance and her passiveness increased, the bad man went further. One night, he tied her hands. Giuly allowed him.

Soon, he was encouraged to test her limits.

She knew it was all going in the wrong direction and she should resist his growing attempts at domination. But the thought of leaving this strange new life in Paris and returning to Rome would feel like an admission of defeat, an acknowledgement

211

that she should not have broken up with Peppino, and broken his heart into a thousand pieces, as she clearly knew she had. Maybe this was a form of penance, a way of punishing herself? She just didn't know any longer. Had she really ever known?

One dark evening, after he'd tied her hands to the bedpost and, somehow, her ankles, he'd taken her by surprise and, despite her mild protests, had resolutely shaven away her thick thatch of wild, curling jet-black pubic hair and left her quite bald, like a child, which not only brought back bitter-sweet memories of her younger years but also a deep sense of shame at the fact she'd always insisted Peppino should not even trim her.

The next day, the Frenchman used his belt on her arse cheeks and marked her badly.

Sitting watching a film that afternoon in a small art house by the Odéon was painful, as Giuly kept on fidgeting in her seat to find a position that did not remind her of the previous evening's punishment. Her period pains had also begun, as bad as ever; she'd once been told they'd only go away after she'd had her first child.

That night, the bad man wanted to fuck her as usual and she pointed out that her period had begun. He became angry. He would have been quite furious had she actually revealed that she had once allowed Peppino to make love to her on such a day and the blood communion they had shared was still one of her most exquisitely shocking and treasured memories. He brutally stripped her, tied her hands behind her back and pushed her down on the floor, onto her stomach and sharply penetrated her arsehole, spitting onto his cock and her opening for necessary lubrication. She screamed in pain and he gagged her with her own panties and continued relentlessly to invest her. Giuly recalled how she had once assured Peppino as they spooned in bed one night how she would never agree to anal sex with him or anyone. Another promise betrayed, she knew. She grew familiar with the pain. She had never thought it would be so easy to break with her past.

Later, as she lay there motionless, the bad man said: 'Next week, I shall continue your education. I'm taking you to a club and I want to watch you being fucked by a stranger, my sweet Italian girl.'

Giuly could say nothing. When he left the apartment, he retrieved her set of keys from her handbag and locked her in. They were on the fifth floor and she had no way out. Giuly sighed.

It was a night full of stars and the Seine quivered with a thousand lights.

The taxi had dropped Cornelia around the corner of Les Chandelles. She looked out for a decent-looking café and sat herself at a table overlooking the street, where she would be highly visible to all passers-by. This was one of those rare occasions when she had lipstick on, a scarlet stain across her thin lips. She wore an opaque white silk shirt and was, as ever, braless. Her short black skirt high-lighted her endless pale legs. She'd ruffled her hair, blonde Medusa curls like a forest; and slowly sipped a glass of Sancerre, a paper-back edition of John Irving's *A Widow for One Year* sitting broken-spined on the ceramic top next to the wine carafe.

The bait was set. A lonesome American woman on a Friday night in Paris, just some steps away from a notorious *club échangiste*. L' Américaine. She'd found out earlier, through judicious tipping and a hint of further largesse of another nature, from the club's doorman, that her target was planning to attend the club later this evening. The entrance fee for single women was advantageous but she felt she would attract less attention if she were part of a couple. She'd gathered on the grapevine that lone men would often congregate here in search of a partner before moving on to the club.

She'd been told right and within an hour, she'd been twice offered an escort into the premises. She hadn't even needed to uncross her legs and reveal her lack of underwear. The first guy was too sleazy for her liking, and altogether too conde-scending in the way he spoke to her in the slow, enunciating manner some Frenchmen automatic-ally do with foreigners. She quietly gave him the brush-off. He did not protest unduly. The second candidate was more suitable, a middle-aged busi-nessman with a well-cut suit and half-decent aftershave. He even sent her over a glass of champagne before actually accosting her. Much too old, of course, but then there was something about Paris and older men with younger women. The water, the air, whatever!

They agreed that once inside she would have no obligation to either stay with him or fuck him, at any rate initially. Maybe later, if neither came across someone more suitable. He readily acquiesced. Cornelia knew she was good arm candy, tall and distinctive, a beautiful woman with a style all her own, and an unnervingly visible mix of brains and provocation. She'd worked hard on that aspect of her appearance.

Despite its upmarket reputation, Les Chandelles was much as she expected. Tasteful in a vulgar but chic way; too many muted lights, drapes and parquet flooring, dark corners or *coins calins* as they were coyly described on the club's website, semi-opulent staircases leading to private rooms and a strange overall smell of sex, cheap perfume and a touch of discreet disinfectant not unlike those American sex-shop cabins or the tawdry rooms set aside for private lap dances in some of the joints she had once navigated through.

She spent some time at the bar with her escort and enjoyed further champagne, and allowed him to show her some of the nooks and crannies of the swing club, which he appeared to be a regular at. Now she knew the lie of the land. She offered to dance with him.

'Not my scene,' he churlishly protested.

'It warms me up,' she pointed out. He nodded in appreciation.

'Just go ahead,' he said. 'Maybe we can meet up later, if you want?'

'Yes,' Cornelia said.

From the dance floor, she would have a perfect vantage point to observe new arrivals as they passed on their way to more intimate areas of the club. She moved languorously to a Leonard Cohen tune and marked her area between a few embracing couples. She'd always enjoyed dancing, it had made the stripping bearable. Cornelia closed her eyes, carried along by the soft music. Occasionally, a hand would gently tap her on the shoulder, an invitation to join a man, a woman or more often a couple in a more private location, but each time she turned the offer down with an amiable smile. No one insisted, obeying the club's basic protocols.

Amongst the French songs she had not previously known, Cornelia had already delicately shimmied to recognisable tunes by Luna, Strays Don't Sleep and Nick Cave when she noticed the new couple settling down at the bar.

The girl couldn't have been older than twenty-five with a jungle of thick dark curls falling to her shoulders and a gawky, slightly unfeminine walk. Her back was bare, pale skin on full display emerging from a thin knitted top, and she wore a

216

white skirt that fell all the way to her ankles, through which one could spy her long legs and a round arse just that little bit bigger than she would no doubt have wished to have, an imperfection that actually made her quite stunning. With deep brown eyes and a gypsy-like, wild demeanour, she reminded Cornelia of a child still to fully mature. She wore dark black shoes with heels, which she visibly didn't need, as she was almost as tall as Cornelia. A sad sensuality poured out from every inch of her as she followed her companion's instructions and settled on a high stool at the bar. The man ordered without asking the young girl what she wanted. Her eyes darted across the room, looking at the other patrons of the club, Judging them, weighing them. It was evidently her first time here.

Cornelia adjusted her gaze.

The man squiring the exotic young woman was him, her target. The bad man. Her information had proved correct. As she watched the couple, Cornelia blanked out the music.

Less than an hour later, she had made acquaintance with them and suggested to her new friends they could move on to a more private space. Throughout their conversation, the Italian girl had been mostly silent, leaving her older companion to ask all the questions and flirt quite openly and suggestively with the splendid American blonde seemingly in search of local thrills. At first, the man appeared hesitant, as if the visit to Les Chandelles had been planned differently.

'I've never been with a woman before,' the Italian girl complained to the man.

'Would you rather I looked for a negro to fuck you here and now with an audience watching?' he said to her.

'No,' she whispered.

'So, we all agree,' he concluded, getting up and gallantly taking Cornelia's hand. 'Anyway, you can do most of the watching as I intend to enjoy the company of our new American friend to its fullest extent. You can watch and learn; I do find you somewhat passive and unimaginative, my dear young Italian gypsy. See how a real woman fucks.'

Giuly lowered her eyes and stood up to follow them.

Once they had located an empty room on the next floor, Cornelia briefly excused herself and insisted she had to walk back to the cloakroom to get something from the handbag she had left there as well as picking up some clean towels, which their forthcoming activities would no doubt require.

'Ah, Americans, always keen on hygiene,' the bad man said and broadly smiled. 'We'll be waiting for you,' he added, indicating to his young companion to start undressing.

'I'll leave my clothes too,' Cornelia said. turning round. 'Don't want to get them crumpled, do we?'

'Perfect,' the man said, turning his attention to Giuly's slight, pale, uncovered breasts and sharply twisting her nipples while she was still in the process of slipping out of her long white skirt. There were red marks on her butt cheeks.

When Cornelia returned a few minutes later, the bad man was stripped from the waist down and the Italian girl was sucking him off while his fingers held her hair tight and her head forcibly pressed against his groin, even though his thrusts were making her choke. He turned his own head towards Cornelia, a blonde apparition, now naked and holding a bunch of towels under her left arm.

'Beautiful,' he said, and released his pressure on Giuly's head. 'Truly regal,' he observed, his eyes running up and down Cornelia's body. 'I like very much,' he added. His attention now centred on her groin. 'A tattoo? There? Pretty! What is it?'

Cornelia approached the couple. The man withdrew his cock from the Italian girl's mouth, allowing her to breathe better, and put a proprietary hand on Cornelia's left breast and then squinted, taking a closer look at her depilated pubic area and the small tattoo she sported there.

'A gun? Interesting,' he said.

'Sig Sauer,' Cornelia said.

There was a brief look of concern on his face, but then he relaxed briefly and nodded towards the American woman, indicating she should replace Giuly and service his still jutting cock. Cornelia quietly asked Giuly to move away from the man so that she might take over her position. The Italian girl stumbled backwards to the bed. Cornelia kneeled. As her mouth approached his

219

groin, she pulled out the gun she had kept hidden under the white towels, placed it upwards against his chin and pressed the trigger.

The silencer muffled most of the sound and Giuly's cry of surprise proved louder than the actual shot which blew the lid of his head off, moving through his mouth and through to his brain in a portion of a second. He fell to the ground, Cornelia cushioning his collapse with her outstretched arm.

'Jesus,' Giuly said.

And looked questioningly at Cornelia who now stood with her legs firmly apart, the weapon still in her hand, a naked angel of death.

'He was a bad man.' Cornelia said.

'I know,' the Italian girl said. 'But . . .'

'It was just a job, nothing personal,' Cornelia said.

'So . . .'

'Shhhh . . .' said Cornelia. 'Get your clothes.'

The young Italian girl stood there, as if nailed to the floor, every inch of her body revealed. Cornelia couldn't avoid examining her.

'You're very pretty,' she said.

'You too,' the other replied, red-faced.

Cornelia folded the gun back inside the towels. 'Normally, I would have killed you too,' she said. 'As a rule, I must leave no witnesses. But I'm not big on killing women. Just dress, go and forget him. I don't know how well you knew him – I suspect it wasn't long. Find a younger man. Live. Be happy. And . . .'

'What?'

'Forget me, forget what I look like. You don't know me, you've never known me.'

Giuly nodded her agreement as she pulled the knitted top she had worn earlier over her head, disturbing the thousand thick dark curls. The other woman was in no rush to dress, comfortable in her white nudity. Her body was also pale, but a different sort of pallor. Giuly couldn't quite work out the nature of the difference.

Cornelia watched her hurriedly dress.

'Go back to Rome. This never happened. It's just Paris, Giuly. Another place.'

Back in the street, Giuly initially felt disorientated. It had all happened so quickly. She was surprised to see that she wasn't as shocked as she should have been. It was just something that had happened. An adventure. Her first adventure since Peppino. Under her breath, she whispered his real name. The Paris night did not answer.

She checked her bag; she had enough money for a small hotel room for the night. Tomorrow, she would take the train back to Rome.

The Louvre was lit up as she walked towards the Seine, and into a harbour of darkness. At her fourth attempt, Giuly found a cheap hotel on the rue Monsieur le Prince. The room was on the fourth floor and she could barely fit into the lift. Later, she went out and had a crêpe with sugar and Grand Marnier from an all-night kiosk near the junction between the rue de l'Odéon and the boulevard Saint Germain. People were queuing outside the nearby cinemas, people mostly of her own age, no older men here. She walked towards Notre-Dame and wasted time in a bookshop, idly leafing through the new books on display. She would have dearly liked to have a coffee, but no Latin Quarter bookshops also served coffee, unlike her favourite haunt, Feltrinelli's in Rome, where she had spent much of her teenage years. But she knew that if she walked into a café and took a table alone, someone would eventually try a pick-up line and disturb her, and tonight she felt no need for further conversation. So she finally went back to her small room and slept soundly. A night without nightmares or memories.

The man in the Police du Territoire uniform handed her passport back to Cornelia. 'I hope you enjoyed your stay, Mademoiselle?'

L'Américaine candidly smiled back at him as she made her way into the departure lounge at the airport. 'Absolutely,' she said.

NOCTURNE LE JEUDI

To Patrice Correr

SCOTT PHILLIPS

For over two years the English bookseller has lived in a former maid's room on the top floor of an old building on the rue Yves Toudic in the tenth arrondissement of Paris. Day and night he hears through the walls shouting matches of impressive vulgarity and ferocity; the adversaries are a mother and daughter, aged about eighty and fifty respectively. For some months after moving in he was rather afraid of these hideous creatures nesting at the end of the hallway, until the day he realised that they were the same pair of old ladies he'd met a dozen or more times on the stairs. During these encounters the old dears flash him sweet charming smiles and their voices – hoarse and masculine behind closed doors – take on in public a honeyed, almost childish tone. The daughter, slightly handicapped in a manner that remains unclear to him, squints and limps and dresses like a nun. Once they've disappeared into their apartment the screaming fits start up again with as much hateful fury as ever, those sweet voices deepened and amplified: 'Get up you lazy cunt,' the mother barks, 'I want my dinner.'

'Fuck off, ass pirate,' the daughter answers.

Before moving in here he'd never heard a woman called an ass pirate before; now it's his daily lot. Normally it's the daughter who calls her mother this; the older woman prefers the term 'whore'.

Tonight he thinks he heard the curt sound of a fist against flesh, which bothers him; not knowing which woman is the aggressor this time, he decides to go out. In any case he would have had to leave for dinner, since as usual he has nothing to eat in his room. He almost never slept in it in the days when he had a girlfriend; since she showed him the door six weeks ago – six weeks! – he feels the need to get out in the evenings in order not to submit to depression. He grabs a book at random before opening the door, then double-bolts it behind him.

In the corridor he runs into a young man leaving the toilet, so wasted he has to lean on the wall to remain upright. He wonders if this isn't the owner of the burnt, twisted spoon he found on the sink the other day.

'Evening.'

The young man gives him a benevolent smile, shrugs, manages to burble an incoherent response before heading in a leisurely way down the stairs, leaning heavily on the rail. The English bookseller waits until the other has had the time to get to the ground floor before descending himself.

The café on the street corner, as most of its business comes from students in the morning and at noon, is closed evenings; and without thinking about it he chooses its rival across the street where he takes a bar stool, orders a beer and starts reading.

After a second beer and a ham-and-cheese sandwich he shudders at the unpleasant sensation of a hand on his shoulder. Looking over his shoulder he finds at his back a neighbour from the fifth floor, a retired pharmacist whose name he can't recall.

'Buy you a round, young man?'

'Sure,' says the Englishman, wishing to remain alone but unwilling to hurt his neighbour's feelings.

The pharmacist, still standing, orders two draughts and grabs the book without asking his permission. 'It's in English? What's it about?'

'The death of John F. Kennedy, it's sort of a rehash of all the theories about who was behind the assassination.'

'Oh? And who was that, do you think?'

'The author of the book thinks it was probably the New Orleans mafia.'

'Wrong,' says the pharmacist with a dry smile, shaking his head.

'Oh, well,' says the Englishman, with no desire to pursue it further.

'Who profited from it?'

'I don't know . . . Khruschev, Castro . . . ?'

The pharmacist closes his eyes, as if patiently addressing a small child. 'The Jews, naturally.'

'Oh,' says the younger man, whose stomach has just started hurting. He has no desire to despise his neighbour, who, pain in the ass though he may be, is alone in the world; he has let it drop that neither his ex-wife nor his daughter nor his grandchildren have any contact with him any more. 'Is that so?'

'You don't believe me? John Kennedy was going to give the Arabs back the land they got stolen away from them in '47. The Jews didn't have any choice. It was the Mossad that did it.'

The bookseller swallows the rest of his beer in a swig, stands up looking at his watch and feigning surprise. 'Shit, I'm meeting someone at the Bastille in fifteen minutes, I've got to get going. Thanks for the beer, the next round's on me.'

'I've got my car outside, I'm free at the moment, you want me to drop you?'

Holy fucking God no. 'That's nice of you, I think the Métro's quicker this time of day.'

Aware of the pharmacist's eyes on his back, he leaves, crosses the street and walks to the place de la République, where he stops in front of the Métro entrance. Having nothing planned for the evening, and anxious to avoid the nauseating prospect of an evening listening to the neighbours, he decides to see a movie at the Bastille after all.

The film is a piece of shit, an English love-and-war story; he stays seated until the end anyway, reading the credits along with a few other disillusioned, compulsive film buffs. When the lights go back up he sneaks into the screening room next door where another film is fifteen minutes under way. That's all right, it's the third time he's seen it and he knows the opening by heart.

In fact the first time he saw it, six weeks ago, he was with the girlfriend, a fact that occurs to him towards the end of the film. It's an American comedy, just the kind of thing she hated, and though it would be wrong to attribute the breakup to his insistence on seeing the movie, it was nonetheless the day after that she gave him the sad news that she was leaving him. At the time he'd felt no sadness, just a vague sense of humili-ation – obviously he would have preferred to be the one doing the leaving – and irritation, since replacing her would not be easy.

Now he feels shadowed by deep depression, and for the umpteenth time since the breakup he misses her. He's tired of jerking off, and his efforts to meet other women have come to nothing. Add to that the fact that his bookstore – where the ex-girlfriend in question still works – trudges forward day by day on an inevitable march towards the mortification of bankruptcy. He wonders at what point he will give up and go back to England, finds the prospect sickmaking.

Outside the air is cool, though not bad for the season. He stops off in a beer bar with a Belgian monastery theme where they know him. Without waiting for his order the waiter brings him half a litre of Abbey beer; he relaxes, begins to read again.

At a quarter to midnight, having read fifty pages and drunk a litre and a half of Trippel, and having got up three times for a piss, he leaves the bar and crosses the place de la Bastille. He ends up standing before an art cinema that runs *Dr Strangelove* every night at midnight; it seems to him, drunk as he is, to be the only film in the world that could improve his outlook on life.

As expected, he leaves the cinema with his spirits considerably lifted. Anxious to read a few more pages before sleep he stops in a café on the place and orders half a litre of Munich beer. When it comes he drinks it as though it were his first of the night and not the tenth and then, warmed and happy, orders another.

The boulevard Beaumarchais is nearly deserted when he starts walking it around two-thirty in the morning. He doesn't give a shit about the girl or the bookstore or Paris. If he has to go back to England, *tant* fucking *pis*.

When he first hears the woman's cries, he doesn't identify them as such and doesn't turn to look. When they continue, overlaid by others, male and full of rage, he looks across the boulevard to see a struggle between a man and a woman, the former attempting to forcibly drag the latter towards the front door of a nearby building.

The woman is young and, like her assailant, of

Asian origin. Her struggles against his efforts to drag her are frenzied, and he understands that she's in a panic, begging for help in a language he can't understand or even identify.

While the bookseller, stopped in his tracks, continues to watch, the woman continues to scream and her attacker continues to drag her towards the doorway. They're both Japanese – Korean, perhaps? – and he decides they must be a couple, that this is a mere domestic dispute and therefore none of his affair.

He continues on his way home.

The young woman's cries follow him up the boulevard, mixed with those of her enraged attacker, and the sounds of the occasional automobile passing at that hour of the morning. It must have been a couple having a spat, he tells himself, none of his business. They were probably drunk, both of them, and he knows better than to place himself between a man and a woman in the middle of a fight, especially when they're drunk. And if that's not the case then surely some passerby will note her distress and stop to rescue her . . .

As he reaches the boulevard des Filles du Calvaire, he realises that he no longer hears the woman's voice; in fact he hears almost nothing. It's the quietest moment he's experienced since the day he arrived in Paris.

Now he's stricken with an unexpected panic; how could he bear the knowledge that an innocent had suffered for his lack of courage? He turns on his heel and starts running at top speed towards the Bastille. Despite the dissipation of the last few weeks he's in good physical shape, and he is rather proud of the fact that he's running so fast without losing his breath. He crosses the boulevard and when he finally makes it to the spot where the struggle took place he sees no one. The night is calm, the door to the building closed, and no witness is present to tell the fate of the unhappy couple. He pushes the door without managing to open it, tries to ring the bell, knocks as hard as he can, but fails to awaken the building's concierge, if it has one. He's not even sure that this was where he was dragging her. In any case there are no more screams, no visual or auditory trace of the fight.

After a minute he gives up, takes up once more his slow ascent of the boulevard Beaumarchais towards his empty room, feeling not quite as nauseated as he will tomorrow morning.

DEUS EX MACHINA

A Short Story about Hope

SPARKLE HAYTER

Going through a rough time in a happy and beautiful place like Paris puts one's misery in sharp relief. The more luminous and prosperous Paris looks, the more Shay feels excluded from it. Her self-pity steadily darkens that winter despite her earnest efforts to make her dismal state of affairs romantic, invoking the spirits of great writers forged by poverty and depression. After all, while Hemingway was poor, he found a moveable feast. Orwell, down and out in Paris, scratching with bugs from old grey mattresses in flop hotels, sick from the stench of sulphur burned to try to keep the insects down, found in it all the brilliance to become a great writer. Then there was the composer Virgil Thomson, an intimate of Gertrude Stein and Miss Toklas, who once said, glibly, that he preferred to be poor in Paris rather than in America because 'I'd rather starve in a place with good food'.

Shay tries to be buoyed by that philosophy but now she wonders if it isn't better to starve in a

231

place with bad food, where the warm gusts of air and laughter escaping through restaurant doors on cold winter nights are scented with less delicious flavours and don't remind her how long it has been since she's been able to afford even a medium-rare *bavette* in Béarnaise sauce with *frites* and a glass of beer, under ten euros in most joints in her neighbourhood. And besides, those who found inspiration and the seeds of prosperity in hard times were usually iconoclastic geniuses. She isn't sure any more she has even the spark to genius, that she can justify coming here. It had all been done, hadn't it? Every inch of this city, every quirk of the culture, had been covered long before she arrived, right down to the joys of the classic French *pissoir* which Henry Miller spoke about with such eloquence and affection. Most of them were gone now, the ornately decorated circular tin urinals, little green kiosks, open at the top and bottom so you could see the legs and heads of those using them, exchange a friendly wave or have a neighbourly chat. It would be hard to update that – the new version was an oblong booth made of corrugated fibreglass in dull beige or brown. It cost 40 cents to use it, and you had a limited amount of time in the closed, modular bathroom before it flushed itself with water and cleaning chemicals. She'd heard about someone who lingered too long in one and drowned.

During this time, she develops a terror that this is how she'll die, not in a public toilet per se, but in some ironic, comic or embarrassing way, which will stick in people's minds so everything she has done before will be blotted out by it. Instead of 'award-winning graduate of the Iowa Writers' Workshop and performance artist Shay Rutherford dies' or even, 'artist of some renown in certain circles dies during performance', she'll be remembered as the woman killed by the cork of the bottle of champagne she was opening to celebrate some long-awaited good news, or run over by a truck full of monkeys bound for the zoo, the driver later revealed to be a long-lost cousin, or by a car full of clowns in civilian clothes on their way to a wedding, or simply remembered as the woman killed while walking down the street by the last *Titanic* survivor who falls out of a window while watering her peacock tulips and, miraculously, survives yet again thanks to Shay's broken body cushioning her fall.

Aware of her awesome ability to make her fears come true, she gets the idea that she should control her own death by killing herself. At this point, she is without hope, and this plan gives her a certain discipline and purpose. A project. She used to be much better at making her dreams come true – for example, her dream of living one day in Paris brought her to Paris. Now the fears rule, hard as she tries to keep them at bay. All the mistakes, the triumphs, have taught her nothing useful. She has experience now, and is hidebound by it, unable to move in any direction, lacking the same energy and daring she once had to challenge the maze, too prone to analysis – 'what worked, what didn't work, how did I do it before', at the cost of all spontaneity. If experience was wisdom, it was greatly overrated.

The suicide note is the first thing that grabs her in ages, and she writes the initial draft in a frenzy, feeling unshackled from her fears, temporarily. But unfortunately, the fears kick in again as she edits and she can't stop rewriting the note. Is she being too honest or too obtuse, too easy on herself or too hard? On others? Will people understand why she'd rather die than admit failure and go home? Will they lament the waste of a young talent, or her wasting their time and that of other people by trying to be an artist all these years? After all, what did she have to show for all these years in school and in Paris except a couple of lit mag publications and one article on French words that look like English words but mean completely different things that was printed on page seventeen of a free newspaper for Anglos? She imagines her death notices will read like her rejection slips: 'over-dramatic', 'not much there to interest us', 'belaboured ending'.

Soon, she begins fictionalising here and there to make it a better read, and before long, the note isn't about her any more, but about a man named Harry Waller, who sits down one day and loads a gun with bullets, placing it carefully by the side of a typewriter where he proceeds to write his farewell – the story of a life gone wrong, the love and opportunities lost, the heartbreak that he feels physically, a genuine pain in his heart whenever he thinks of his sad, bad and mad moments, as if these regrets reside in his heart like shards of glass. As he approaches the end of his ten-page suicide note, he suffers a sudden coronary, and instinctively picks up the phone and calls 911. Alas, by the time paramedics arrive, he is dead.

Afterwards, she reads it and decides it is good, not just good but *redemptively* good. Faith is restored. She spends precious euros at an internet café emailing it to magazines who take electronic submissions and on postage sending it to those that do not. Then she waits, living on street *crêpes* and water and the certainty that she has turned a corner and the future is wide open. Not only is it a great short story, she thinks, but it would make a great independent film, the note framing Harry Waller's wild woolly life as an international oil rig salesman, which was much funnier and more interesting than her life.

But it turns out the editors don't agree it is great, or even agree with each other about why it is not. 'Too long', says one. 'Too short and undeveloped', says another. 'Very funny but not right for us'. 'Failed to see the humour', and so on.

That day she receives the last rejection slip for 'A Short Story about Hope'. She hasn't eaten in two and a half days and is more than two months behind on the rent, phone and EDF. The man who runs the Manhattan School for Business English in Paris, where she was working black, refuses to pay her the 1,500 euros he owes her. He knows that she can't do anything about it without revealing her *sans papiers* status and getting kicked out of France. She wasn't angry when he fired her – she hated the job and the students, who seemed to think she could do all the work in getting them to understand English. pumping them full of useful English words and phrases while they did nothing, sitting by slack-jawed and dull-eyed like force-fed geese. But she is angry that he won't pay her what she is owed.

Having been through the gamut of 'black' jobs, off the books, which are few, badly paid and usually menial, there remains prostitution and begging – never! – and thievery, which she considers. Back in college, she used to pick pockets as a party trick. There'd be some meaty and easy pickings in some of the tourist areas, like place du Tertre where the crowds jostle with sidewalk artists, who advertise their skills with portraits of celebrities that are at the same time more flattering and less interesting than the originals. But she could only do it if she knew her victim was a greedy despoiler of planet Earth and its people, and that would require an unrealistic amount of research. Otherwise, she was liable to pick someone who looked the part, some big-spending German with a big belly, and worry later he was just an innocent tourist, maybe here for a last vacation before he begins the cancer surgery to remove the watermelon-sized tumour in his stomach. So thievery is out. There are no options other than starve in Paris or find her way back to her home town in Wisconsin to work in the chese-flavoured foods factory or the Walmart, like her sister Tiff who has sacrificed everything to stay home to look after her mother, who is suffering from some mysterious undiagnosed ailment that keeps her in bed most of the day watching game shows and screaming at CNN.

No, the bottom line is she'd rather die in Paris, she thinks.

But now she feels incapable of writing even a suicide note.

When Anna calls from Oslo, Shay is wondering where her next meal will come from. Literally, she is thinking this when the phone rings, and she hears Anna's invitation – she has a one-night stopover in Paris, and would Shay join her and some Norwegian friends for dinner that night, her treat?

There seems to be a bit of magic left in her world.

But no money left. The biggest problem now is that the restaurant they are meeting at, Hotel du Nord by Canal St Marttin in the tenth, is way the hell across the city from her apartment near Convention. It is too far to walk in bad shoes, in bad weather – it is a record a breaking winter – too far to walk even in good shoes in good weather, and all she has in her pocket is a used Métro ticket with a smeared date stamp. It has already saved her a couple of tickets for 'stealing trains' – not paying the fare, in other words. If the cops stopped her at one of their random underground check stops, she just showed the old ticket and babbled in English and they waved her through.

You couldn't jump the turnstiles any more, not since they'd all been replaced with electronic turnstiles and six-foot gates. But you could still sneak through if you went right behind someone with a ticket, so close you were touching. It helped if the station was crowded. The trick was picking out someone who wouldn't mind and wouldn't rat you out, or someone so preoccupied they wouldn't notice – people on cellphones, with small children, too many bags, or muttering to themselves. She slips through by helping an African woman struggling with her two tired, dead-weight children. There is no check stop, so she is able to get off without any problem at Jacques Bonsergent and walk the four blocks to Hotel du Nord.

The windows of Hotel du Nord are frosted, it's so cold outside, but the warm, amber lighting glows through. The cold follows her inside and clings to her like an aura, which makes the maitre d' shiver when he approaches her. Anna is already there with a male pilot, Peter, and two other, flight attendants for her airline – a gay man, Baard, and another woman, Liv. While waiting for Shay, they've already polished off a couple of bottles of wine, so it's a pretty happy group. Shay gets into the mood, sharing some of her favourite stories about Anna back during Anna's modelling days in New York, when they had both been twenty-something and beautiful, invited everywhere. There was that night at Elaine's, a book party for some friend of Anna's. They'd brushed shoulders with Arthur Miller and Robert Altman, and Jerry Stiller had introduced them to Matt Dillon. Or the night Shay had turned off her phone to write, hearing Anna's message too late, 'I'm hanging out with Mick Jagger and Carly Simon at Whiskey. Where are you? Come down.' There were parties with free food and drinks almost every night, and too many nights dancing after hours at Splash with gay boys. Anna still parties occasionally with glamorous people, but not exclusively – obviously, or Shay, long past glamorous with her two pairs of jeans and three shirts, all fraying, would not be here.

Exuberantly joining the many wine toasts, snapping photos of the happy group, Shay is now the picture of gaiety, enjoying herself for the first time in she doesn't know how long.

Just before midnight, Shay announces she has to leave if she is going to catch the last Métro home and Anna says, 'No, stay. You can take a taxi.' Then she slips a bill to Shay under the table when the others are distracted by cellphones or off in the bathroom. Fifty euros. Too much! Shay whispers.

Anna insists, and Shay puts the bill in her purse. It is a godsend. If traffic flow is good, she can get home for under twenty, and have enough left over to eat for a week. Maybe in that week she would have The Idea, the one she would write that would save her. In any event, she won't starve.

After dinner, she walks the Norwegians back to their hotel – it is 2 a.m. and they have an early call the next morning so they all kiss and say goodbye to Shay. She looks for a taxi, but the streets are full of people who have missed the last Métro, and the lines at the taxi stations are ridiculously long. So Shay walks further, looking for a street where she might find a free cab without competition. Occupied taxis whiz past her. When she sights a rare free one on the horizon, people pop out of nowhere to grab it from under her. At one point, this means a handful of late-partying Chinese tourists whose bus has broken down near Folies Bergère, all of them in bright red scarves and hats so they'll be easy to find in a crowd. Even the infrequent Noctabuses that roll by are so jammed she can't get on.

Clapping her gloved hands to keep them warm, her collar up and scarf around it to keep out the cold, she walks on, wondering if she might freeze to death before she finds transportation, and what her obits might say in that case, a drunk and bankrupt American found frozen stiff in a taxi-hailing posture? Would her life mean anything then, other than as a martyr for the late-night Métro service movement?

Then, on a little street off Sebastopol, a car pulls up beside her, and the driver rolls down a window. Before he can say anything, she says, 'Are you free?'

He nods, and she jumps in, calculating that her miserable, bone-chilling walk has saved her five euros at least. With this, she can treat herself to a pouch of tobacco, which will aid the creative processes in untold ways. After a few minutes in the cab, she realises that the driver hasn't turned his meter on, which will save her a few more euros – life is going her way again. Traffic is light and signals are turning green as far as the eye can see.

After a few blocks, though, she feels guilty about cheating a working man, and mentions the meter. He clacks it on. It's then she notices he is taking a strange route to get to Convention, heading east instead of south and west. She suggests a faster route. He ignores her. She sees his eyes in the rear-view mirror. They are shiny and red, the pupils dilated. He has no driver ID for her to see. The doors are auto-locked.

'I've changed my mind,' she says. 'You can let me off here.'

He keeps driving. He looks like a smallish man, like many men here not much bigger than she is. His hair is brown and greying. But she cannot see his face or get a clear image of what he looks like.

Vaguely, she remembers a story about a young woman in England who was picked up by a fake cabbie, raped and killed, her body left in a mattress factory dumpster in Shropshire. She remembers it only vaguely because it was in French, and she read it in a detective magazine while waiting at a doctor's office, preoccupied as usual by her own problems. Now it has happened to her and this will be her obit: 'American in Paris slain in grisly rape-murder', a dripping blood-red headline in a pulpy barbershop magazine.

He turns south. They cross the river to the Left Bank, over a bridge whose name she doesn't know.

There is a button to unlock the back passenger side on the door beside her, but she will have to wait for a red light, then move fast in order to escape. Tonight, of all nights, they are hitting all the green lights in a seamless journey to hell.

'You are American,' he says, in English, with barely an accent.

She says nothing. He wants to make small talk?

'You are frightened.'

She says, 'Please let me out. I just want to go home.'

'You love to scare people. How does it feel?'

'I don't like scaring anyone. If you're talking about Bush, didn't vote for him, I despise him. Can you let me out here?'

'You think it started with Bush? They're all gangsters. And I know gangsters. What's your price?'

He believes I'm a hooker, she thinks, and says, 'I'm a writer.'

'Are you? What's your price?'

242

Now she's sure he's crazy, and she tries to reach into her handbag for her cellphone. She has no credit on her phone, but maybe she can bluff the guy. She thinks of what she'll say, 'Yeah, I found him. You still tracking me? So you know where we are?'

Before she can, he stops and because of her search for her phone she's distracted from her original goal to unlock her doors and escape. She's a moment too late. He relocks her doors with his lock, which overrides hers, and then he sticks a gun in her face.

'Give me your purse,' he says.

She's stunned to see a gun in her face, in Paris. She's never seen a gun before here, except in the movies or on the news. Only the cops and the gangsters have guns here. In her peripheral vision, she sees that they are near the Mitterrand library on the south-east side of the river, a deserted area at night, with lots of lit-up skyscrapers and no people. Even if she could scream, nobody would hear her. She gives him her purse and asks, meekly, 'What are you going to do with me?'

He doesn't answer. She sees his eyes in the rear-view mirror and thinks he is smiling.

'You can let me out. I can't identify you. I've barely seen your face.'

He doesn't respond to that. 'I have committed the perfect crime,' he says.

'It's hardly perfect. The owner of this cab is sure to notice it's gone—'

'He won't miss the car for a while. I staked out this cab for a long time. That was a perfect crime too, but not the one I'm talking about. It's a night for perfect crimes, and I am on a roll. Earlier tonight, I robbed a robber and killed a killer.'

He's an admitted killer and she is going to die . . .

'Don't you want to know?' he asks.

'Know what?'

'How I committed the perfect crime?'

'Sure.'

'What constitutes the perfect crime? Motive, means, opportunity?'

'An iron-clad alibi,' she says.

'I have all that. You see, the people who would look for me are dead in what appears to be an accident, a gas leak that has filled the house with fumes and exploded, killing everyone. The house was well sealed for the winter. The gas could not escape. There were pilot lights on the stove and the furnace, and a light bulb that had started to short-circuit in the basement. Everyone drank a great deal tonight and went to bed around eleven. I saw the explosion from a hill overlooking the house, and then I drove away. It's been on the radio.'

'Murder made to look like an accident, OK. But what's your iron-clad alibi?'

'I wasn't there when the victims were killed. I'm not here now. I'm in Monaco. There's a paper trail there, a hotel reservation, meals ordered in, a priest with secrets who will say he and I enjoyed a long conversation. Of course, I was never meant to be in Monaco. That was just my cover. I was meant to be on my way to Central Africa, delivering a bribe to a general there. I have delivered the money elsewhere.'

For forty-five years, since he was a kid, he had worked for a man he refers to as the 'Big Man'. The Big Man was a 'facilitator', someone who would do the dirty jobs legitimate companies and countries would not. If a bribe was needed to keep an oil company drilling in a third world country after a coup, the man would make it happen. If an inconvenient person threatened to make trouble, the Big Man made sure the person disappeared. Of course, the Big Man never touched the money or the bodies himself. The cabbie did that, travelling on false passports and under false identities, never who or where he was supposed to be.

He tells her the Big Man got his start at the hands of his father, who did similar work in North Africa when it was still French and colonial, making contacts that spanned the continent. The cabbie, in turn, had followed his own father into employment with the Big Man before they all returned to France. He had been stripped of his identity at an early age and groomed to be invisible, effective, and completely beholden to his masters.

He has a powerful need to impress her, she realises, to be the Big Man, to be recognised after years of anonymity. In the moment, she can't figure out how to exploit this to her advantage. Should she flatter him, be sympathetic, or be mildly disdainful? She's never been good at this.

The driver babbles on. He first hatched the plan because he was getting tired of all the travelling, not to mention the danger. There was a dispute with another lieutenant in the Big Man's organisation, and the Big Man himself was putting more and more distance between them – not that he minded. He now hated the Big Man. Everything he did, the way he spoke, the way he walked, the way he ate, mouth open, talking, crumbs spraying around him, was annoying. He began to feel like he was losing position, and that this might lead to his own 'disappearance'. So he went with the flow, caused no trouble, plotting, looking for his chance.

She doesn't believe a word of it now. He's crazy, or full of shit, she thinks, until he starts going into detail. There's a poison he liked to use – ricin, because it's lethal in small doses, easily obtainable and virtually untraceable. Sometimes he had to shoot men, though, and contrary to what you see in the movies, a silencer doesn't completely silence a gun. But if you put a condom over the barrel before you shoot, that absorbs the remaining sound—

As he talks, her terror grows. Around her neck, her scarf seems to tighten on its own. It would be too easy to strangle her like this, so when he is looking at the road, she slowly pulls it off, inch

246

by inch, into her pocket, where she feels her digital camera.

He tells her about specific victims and dates and places, and she is able to piece this together with news stories she's read. Now she believes him.

'I have killed people whose deaths nobody will want to investigate. It would shine too much light into too many dark corners. I have made it look like an accident. I have stolen money nobody knows exists, except for people who cannot admit to it. I'm not even here. It's perfect.'

They are outside the city now. She is his next perfect crime.

Or maybe not. When she sees him pull into the Bois de Vincennes and into a dark wooded area, she turns her camera on in her pocket. The battery was low when she left the Hotel du Nord, but she is sure she can get one good flash out of it.

As soon as he parks, she flashes the rear-view mirror, temporarily blinding the man, then throws her scarf over his neck, pulls it tight with every ounce of strength she has. At her wrist, the camera swings on its strap.

The attack catches him by surprise and this gives her a moment to consolidate her strength, tightening the scarf more and twisting it to stop his gurgled attempts to scream. He struggles, jerks his body forward and sideways, trying to turn around. Then he tries to aim the gun over his shoulder at her, while reaching for the scarf with his free hand. She manoeuvres her arm in front of the gun and is able to knock it away from her head. He loses his grip on the gun and drops it. She holds on. Her leather gloves give her a good grip. He goes limp.

But she doesn't let go. She holds on until she is sure that be is, at the very least, unconscious. She unlocks her door, then manually unlocks his and gets out. She takes the bullets out of the gun, puts them under his seat and the empty gun in his pocket. She grabs her purse and pops the trunk, dragging his body out and along the ground to the back, where she slumps his torso into the trunk before heaving his legs in. Carefully, she removes her scarf from the neck of the man, without checking to see if he is dead or not. She doesn't care to know. She only checks that she has all her things and no blood on her.

When she is about to close the trunk, her eye catches on the faint glint of shiny leather. It is a valise, wedged under the man's foot next to a spare can of petrol. She carefully opens the petrol and pours it on the body and the back seat of the car, thinking this might fuck with any DNA evidence, though she doesn't know how. Does it even matter? There have probably been a hundred people through this cab in the last week and, anyway, nobody knows she is here. She is 'black' in France and there is no reason to suspect her of involvement in this, part of a larger crime that cannot be investigated.

The valise is locked, so she takes it with her,

closes the trunk, and begins walking. Later, she will jimmy the lock open, find the valise full of cash, and count it – 100,000 euros in small, nonsequential bills.

For now, she heads towards the Château de Vincennes Metro station. It's almost 5 a.m. She feels great. It has occurred to her that b) she may have committed the perfect crime and b) she now has the whole 50 euros and no cab fare to pay. 'Picked up the wrong girl,' she thinks. 'Fucked with the wrong girl. Your perfect crime, my ass.'

The first Métro comes within the hour and she vanishes into the crowd of bleary-eyed morning commuters, looking, with her valise, just like one of them.

HEATWAVE

DOMINIQUE SYLVAIN

Lieutenant Blaise Reyer walked into his office and felt like turning round and walking straight out again. Three offensively colourful guys were clustered in front of his desk. They were wearing cyclists' helmets, hallucinogenic jerseys and skin-tight cycling shorts, and were all talking at once. Who to, Reyer wondered, since I'm not there? That morning. Reyer had shaved his head, but not his beard. He'd had nightmares all night and looked more than ever like a former KGB apparatchik who'd gone into some dodgy business. He skirted four gleaming bicycles, parked casually in the corridor, slipped between the merry cyclists and found, brazenly sitting in his chair, his number one enemy of the moment, the excessively young and excessively polite Lieutenant Zaraoui.

'Am I seeing things or are you taking over my job, Khaled?'

'Morning Blaise, the chief wants us to work as partners on this case.

'And as you weren't in yet . . .'

As partners. But I don't want to pattner

anybody, thought Reyer, regaining possession of his chair and his desk.

'What case? The Tour de France stick-up?'

The multicoloured trio looked at Reyer as if he were speaking Martian. The lieutenant took the opportunity to study them. One was tall and fair-haired, another tall and dark-haired, the other short and dark. They were all approaching forty, but not a hint of paunch. Reyer instinctively pulled in his stomach and looked at the ID cards laid out before him. Mathieu Grémond, the tall fair-haired guy, Philippe Lancel, the tall dark one, and Paul Perroux, the runt. Addresses scattered between Bastille and République.

'Guillaume Garnier, these gentlemen's friend, has just suffered a heart attack,' explained Zaraoui. 'A stone's throw from here. In place Léon Blum.'

'Because of the heatwave,' added Perroux, the short, dark guy.

'This gentleman's probably right,' adds Zaraoui. 'But there was an anonymous phone call. A woman rang twenty minutes ago. To say that Garnier had been murdered.'

Reyer pinched the bridge of his nose; that helped him keep his cool. At the same time, he acknowledged that procedures were likely to be a bit hit or miss. Paris was suffocating in a crazy heatwave, the disastrous football World Cup defeat was still festering in people's minds like an open wound, the Tour de France favourites had been disqualified for failing a dope test, and three clowns prancing around in poofter pants had been getting up the nose of the police force since dawn.

'How did he die?'

'He collapsed while we were taking a break. We'd stopped at Café Mirage for a drink, our bikes were parked nearby . . .'

'What were you doing in a baking hot Paris when you could have been riding down quiet country lanes?'

'The Tour de France arrives tomorrow, Inspector,' replied Grémond, the tall fair-haired one.

'I'm aware of that. So?'

'We wanted to party all weekend, soak up the atmosphere.'

'Too bad,' retorted Reyer. 'Where's the body?'

'At the forensic lab in place Mazas,' answered Zaraoui. 'But It'll take ages. Nearby all the pathologists are on holiday.'

Reyer wiped a hand over his face, suppressing a superhuman urge to give the three jokers a mammorth clout – Zaraoui too, while he was at it. He'd left home on the verge of imploding. By 6 a.m. the thenmometer was already announcing 29°C, the radio massacres and tsunamis, and his ex-wife a demand for money. She'd phoned early to be sure of cornering him to talk about their daughter who was off 'to the States with her boyfriend and needed cash'. The boyfriend in question was a little jerk, with parents to match. And on top of all that, he had to team up on a ridiculous case that would have been done and dusted if some hysterical woman with a cock-and-bull story hadn't got Zaraoui all agitated.

Reyer felt an attack coming on and made for the toilets, He splashed cold water on his face and the back of his neck and attempted a few breathing exercises, visualising a pure sky over an emerald sea, a method advocated by Marthe Morgeval, his new shrink. A girl with a velvety voice and sensational breasts. Reyer pictured himself with his nose buried in those silky, pneumatic torpedoes and managed to stem the tide of words rushing into his mind.

'It's going to be a tough day,' he said to the mirror, on which a cycling enthusiast had plastered a Floyd Landis sticker.

An hour later, Reyer and Zaraoui went up to the ticket window of the Josephine Baker swimming pool and asked to speak to the manager. He confirmed that Guillaume Garnier had spent his last evening swimming lengths in the company of his three friends.

'At a quarter to midnight, I had to ask them to leave. Otherwise they'd have spent the night here. Their wives sat waiting for them, sipping cocktails. Mind you, it was very nice.'

'I'm sure it was,' said Zaraoui with a smile.

Another habit that annoyed Reyer. Why smile when you're a cop? This wasn't a fucking cocktail party at Paris town hall.

'I expect you'll want to talk to Perroux and Lancel's wives,' added the manager.

'Do they sleep here?'

'Natasha Perroux and Beatrice Lancel are life-guards. They're on duty today. Last night they were off, but they still kept their husbands company.'

Reyer had an urge to take off his shoes and socks and go to question Natasha and Beatrice bare-foot, by the side of the pool. The manager preferred to call them into his office.

'Grémond's single. So was Garnier,' Zaraoui thought it useful to mention as they waited for the wives.

'So what?'

'Garnier was a good-looking guy.'

'What do they do with themselves apart from cycling and taking dips?'

'They're reps for the same sportswear manu-facturer.'

Reyer told himself that this case was far too sporty for a torrid July day. He'd wandered over to the bay window and was admiring the girls in swimsuits. Suddenly he froze, then got a grip on himself. Marthe was lying on a blue mat. She was wearing a white bikini that made her more seduct-ive than ever. And chatting to a hulk who was lingeringly rubbing cream into her bronzed shoulders.

Natasha and Beatrice seemed upset by Garnier's death. Natasha was a fine specimen but Beatrice had the eyes and voice of a little girl that must make some men want to protect her. Personally,

Reyer would rather apply a mammoth slap. They both agreed that Garnier was a live wire.

'He could never sit still,' added Natasha.

'Do you know if he had any enemies!' asked Zaraoui. The question didn't inspire the girls. Zaraomi moved on to the anonymous phone call, and Reyer took the opportunity to slip away. He showed his police ID to the girl in the changing room and demanded a pair of swimming trunks, a towel and an electronic locker wristband. He changed and ventured among the tanned bodies. Marthe was still lying on her stomach and Hulk was chatting to the small of her back. To see his shrink's face. Reyer had to get into the water. He swam two lengths and got out of the pool. The girl in the white bikini wasn't Marthe.

When he returned to the office, the manager was back, and Zaraoui and the two girls were exchanging platitudes. All four noticed Reyer's wet hair, but nobody said anything.

'You didn't go for a dip, did you?' asked Zaraoui once they were back outside on quai Panhard et Levassor.

'You think I'd skive off when I'm on duty?'

Zaraoui shrugged.

'The girls are stunning, especially Beatrice,' he went on. 'Yes, but I can't see them bumping off a cyclist . . .'

Reyer watched Zaraoui out of the corner of his eye. The young lieutenant was no more inane or disagreeable than any other, but his drawback was that he existed. That was his biggest flaw. Reyer wished he could take the Métro to Marthe the shrink's place, bury his face between her breasts and fall asleep there for a century or two. But three little bicycles were beginning to do laps between his ears. That's what was so awful about being a cop. You always ended up seeing evil everywhere. You always ended up getting interested.

'Perhaps he was on something,' continued Zaraoui.

'He wasn't competing in the fucking Tour de France, as far as I know! Have to wait till the lab guys feel like going back to work. Meanwhile, we'll have to rely on hunches and legwork.'

Zaraoui merely raised an eyebrow. The complicated thing about him, apart from the fact of him, thought Reyer, is that side of him that's smooth as a saddle, reliable as a well-oiled chain, straightforward as handlebars. Because, despite all of it, you want to give him a mammoth clout every five minutes. Reyer was about to get into the unmarked car just as three excitable characters drew up and parked on the pavement. Too late, Reyer spotted the TV camera, the mic covered in mammoth hair (mammoths were cropping up everywhere, this was getting worrying), and the *France* 2 logo. Zaraoui stepped in calmly. Reyer turned his back on the TV crew and lost himself in the blue-grey of the Seine, concentrating hard on the seagulls' cries. He pictured himself floating towards Le Havre, in a little old tub, with Marthe.

256

She was lying on deck in a white bikini, and he was rubbing cream into her back . . . 'Blaise! Hey, Blaise!'

Reyer turned in the direction of Zaraoui's voice. The journalists had evaporated into the thick air; all that was left were a few ozone fumes, and for once, Reyer was happy to breathe them.

'They gone?'

'Yes, to the swimming pool.'

'They interview you?'

'I was concise and natural. I talked without telling them anything. If you must know.'

'They were pretty well informed.'

'Apparently.'

Zaraoui looked as though he'd swallowed a piece of rotten fish. Reyer stared at him until his resistance broke.

'Actually, the chief wants us to move fast because he had a phone call from the TV people. This morning. He thinks the media were tipped off by the same mystery woman.'

'And you forgot to tell me?'

'I didn't have time.'

Mostly you were afraid I'd go off and partner myself. Because the chief's afraid I'll flip my lid, live on TV. And as we're the only ones he can lay his hands on, seeing as everyone else is spreading their toes in the sun, he asked you to keep an eye on me. Reyer considered giving his colleague a mammoth wallop but decided to take a deep breath instead. Zaraoui found a map of Paris in the car and located a few strategic points. They decided to start with Sportitude, the company where the three merry cyclists worked.

Sportitude, what a name, thought Reyer as Zaraoui parked on a pedestrian crossing. Sounds like vicissitude, turpitude, solitude. Sport Attitude would have been more appealing. Reyer made an effort to put his words away in a drawer in his mind. Those creatures were terrifying, ready to take off from your neurons and land on your stomach, ready to leap off again from your flabby bits in glutinous gangs bent on entering your ducts and crawling up them until they reached . . .

'Blaise! Hey, old man, you OK?'

Call me old man again and you'll get a mammoth fist in the face, kid, thought Reyer, giving his partner a look filled with loathing. The young lieutenant smiled at him. Reyer sighed, then stepped inside Sportitude. The place was inhabited by an army of dummies in cute little outfits. There was only one warm-blooded creature in the place: a girl with glasses. Reyer made a beeline for her, and she recoiled slightly. He showed his ID, the triumphant figure of the Republic intimidated the girl, even made the colour drain from her cheeks. As he felt no desire to question her, Reyer signalled to Zaraoui to act alone. The girl knew the merry cyclists, they were nice guys, she didn't know anything about their private lives. And she looked uneasy. This little goose is sitting on a secret, thought Reyer before spotting a door with a sign saying Service Personnel Only. He walked over to it, heard the girl protest, flung open the door and came upon two youngsters smoking a spliff. He dealt them both a mammoth cuff around the ears.

'POLICE!'

'What the hell . . . ?' yelped the one who'd been knocked furthest.

Zaraoui raced over. He apologised for his colleague's 'overreaction'.

'Go to the police and press charges. Feel free,' said Reyer. 'My chief smokes spliffs in his office too. The whole force smokes dope. We have the occasional Ecstasy rave, too. Right, joke's over. Talk to me about Garnier and his trio of funny friends.'

After a hiatus, the youths regained their wits and their dignity and talked. He wasn't sure how reliable their information was. The youngest one stated that Garnier had no enemies at work and 'put more energy into cycling than working his ass off'. The other kid thought there was a married woman in Garnier's life, but he'd never personally seen a husband complaining. The three merry cyclists seemed to get on very well.

'Did Garnier ever join you for a smoke?' asked Reyer.

'No, he was a very healthy guy.'

Reyer walked out without a word. Zaraoui had to run to catch up with him. He found him sitting in the car, staring into space.

'I thought inspiration had struck.'

Inspiration had struck. Nice, Zaraoui's turn of phrase.

'With me, the only things that strike are my fists.'

'That's what I wanted to talk to you about, Blaise . . .'

'Made me feel great . . .'

Zaraoui's mobile rang, interrupting them. Reyer gathered the lieutenant was talking to his mother about a lost key. Funny, these kids who take personal calls while on duty. Zaraoui ended the call and started to apologise.

'Actually, yes, inspiration did strike,' Reyer cut him short. 'You're going to call the swimming pool and ask to speak to Beatrice and Natasha. We need to identify the anonymous voice . . .'

Zaraoui called directory inquiries to obtain the number and did as Reyer had asked. He ended the call and looked embarrassed.

'Sorry, but I can't remember. I don't have a musical ear.'

'You're useless, full stop.'

Zaraoui was about to open his mouth but thought better of it. He switched on the ignition and pulled away.

'We're going to the café,' said Reyer.

'I know.'

The two men let an awkward silence set in. Reyer could feel bad vibes exuding from Zaraoui's body. Had he finally managed to annoy Mr Butter-wouldn't-melt-in-my-mouth?

'You're angry, Blaise,' said Zaraoui. 'But that's perfectly natural. Basically, to achieve ataraxy, you have to control your emotions. You're not ready for that, you're too passionate.'

'Ataraxy. Shit. Where did you dig that up?'

'I studied philosophy. But as a guy can't make a living from philosophy, and I wanted to be in the real world, I joined the police. I put myself in the firing line.'

Reyer nearly pinched himself to make sure an evil spirit hadn't abducted him to some parallel universe. A North-African philosopher landing in the police force. Who's on the wrong planet. Shit.

'But what the fuck are you doing as a cop? Can't you see the force is bent, the plebs and the people hate us and the politicos keep us on a tight rein. No need to put yourself in the firing line for that. And you can't make a living as a cop either.'

'Maybe not, but you can act day to day.'

'Zaraoui, you don't believe what you're saying.'

'Oh yes I do.'

They parked in front of Café Mirage and exchanged hesitant glances before getting out of the car. Reyer leant on the copper bar. A relic from the 1950s. A TV hummed on a high shelf, giving the latest on the Tour de France. The customers were heatedly predicting the winner. To wind up his partner, Reyer ordered a glass of champagne.

'Have a drink with me? Just to put yourself in the firing line.'

Zaraoui ignored him and ordered a coffee. Reyer pointed to the barman, signifying that once again he'd leave Zaraoui to do the questioning. The barman hadn't forgotten his recent tragedy. Four cyclists on the terrace, he serves them four diabolos, one collapses – dead. He brought down the table and the drinks in his fall. People were talking about the quality of the lemonade and the clientele. Could an ill-intentioned person have slipped something nasty into Garnier's glass.' The barman didn't think so. He hadn't spotted any odd-looking customers. And besides, most people were avidly watching the sports coverage on the TV. Reyer asked him for his ID and made a note of his name and address. He downed his champagne in two gulps and went out to make a call. He ran into Lieutenant Corinne Moutin and asked her to check whether the barman had a record. He spied what he was looking for on the other side of the square.

He walked into the Pluie de Mots bookstore, strode over to the assistant and flashed his ID.

'I need to check something in a dictionary.'

'I'd have lent you one even if you hadn't been a cop,' replied the assistant with a half smile.

He pointed to a shelf. Reyer opted for the illustrated Larousse and looked up 'ataraxy'. The definition made him raise one eyebrow, then the other: 'a state of freedom from emotional disturbance and anxiety; tranquillity'. He dumped the dictionary on top of a pile of *The Da Vinci*

Code. Moutin called as he was walking back across the square.

Zaraoui was leaning against the car bonnet, arms folded, his expression neutral. A state of freedom from emotional disturbance and anxiety, thought Reyer. Then he thought of Marthe's hands. Her slender fingers covered in silver rings. Reyer had never seen so many rings on such tiny hands. Marthe knew some awesome words too. Words she had no need to control. They did everything she asked, without jumping about all over the place. Reyer got into the car and waited for Zaraoui to slide behind the wheel.

'The barman's clean,' he said. 'Moutin just called me.'

Zaraoui headed towards Bastille and rue du Faubourg Saint-Antoine. He parked in front of the driveway of a furniture shop. Reyer gazed blankly at the window. A guy came out and offered him a sofa at a special discount. Reyer thrust the bust of the Republic under his nose and then followed Zaraoul into the courtyard of the Étoile d'Or. They stepped into a haven of greenery. There was a mass of container plants and also trees planted in the ground, Virginia creeper, clematis, honeysuckle.

'For a guy with no ambition, he didn't do too badly,' remarked Reyer.

Garnier had lived in a two-room ground-floor apartment, probably a renovated workshop. A woman with short, dark hair was sitting on the

263

steps waiting. She looked as if she had her head in the clouds, but soon realised they were policemen.

'Nothing's happened to Guillaume, has it?'

It was Zaraoui who broke the bad news. She started to cry. Reyer bit his lip. He hated seeing people cry. He didn't like seeing them roar with laughter either. Fact was, he didn't like emotional excesses of any kind, he felt they were viruses with the power to infect you and turn you into a limp rag. In an effort to control himself, he peered through the window into the deceased's home. Clean, tidy, well furnished, at least if you like pretentious modern furniture. He left Zaraoui to calm the girl down and went to sniff around the courtyard. Nothing ugly there. The din of the traffic was no more than a purr. To think some people could treat themselves to peace and quiet bang in the centre of Paris. Reyer thought fleetingly of his two-room apartment in the crummiest block in rue de Montreuil. Above a supermarket. Ugly but practical. You can't complain the whole time. He assessed the situation. The girl had stopped blubbing. She was chatting, Zaraoui by her side.

'Trapezius, infraspinous, masseter, gastroenemius, semi-tendinous, brachioradialis, sartorius, he knew them all. I was impressed by that. And he was funny too.'

Zaraoui turned to Reyer and explained that the young woman was a masseuse who lived in the same apartment block as Garnier. He pointed to a copper plate half hidden by the Virginia creeper. 'Clara and Alexandre Lorieux, physiotherapists'.

'I found out later he'd only begun studying medicine to please his father. Then he droped out of uni and got a job with Sportitude. But he hadn't forgotten the names of the muscles, tendons, bones and joints, articulations, the . . .'

This girl's going to spill over with words, thought Reyer, swallowing his saliva. And they're going to infect me. Perhaps I should give her a mammoth slap, start her crying again. Tears aren't so had. Luckily. Zaraoui interrupted her verbal diarrhoea.

'How long had you been his mistress?'

'Two years. We'd decided to tell my husband. You see, I've travelled a lot with Alexandre, from India to Yemen, from Thailand to Mexico, from Burma . . .'

For pity's sake, cut it short, girl, because otherwise that mammoth thrashing will be inevitable and the consequences incalculable. Reyer's eye was drawn to the courtyard entrance. The TV crew had turned up.

'. . . from Burkina Faso to Komodo Island. But to be honest, I travelled further with Guillaume just staying put in Paris.'

'We're going up,' commanded Reyer.

They pushed Clara towards the staircase. It was a communal area, but the Lorieux had generously decided to share their travels with their neighbours; the walls of the narrow staircase were plastered with photos of a trip to India. The apartment wasn't exactly spacious, crammed with potted plants, and the exotic photos continued over the pastel walls. Reyer concluded that Clara's husband needed to feel he was somewhere else even when he was there. He had probably never heard of ataraxy, he thought, wandering over to the window. The TV crew were pestering a neighbour. The sound engineer was waving his mammoth-hair-covered mic above his head; his hair was tousled as if he'd just got out of bed. Which he probably had. It was all right for some, living in apartments surrounded by greenery and pretty flowers and doing nothing much with their mornings.

Meanwhile, Clara had started wittering on again. Reyer tried to catch Zaraoui's attention to convey that it would be better to focus on Clara's voice, rather than listen to her rabbiting. But Zaraoui was absorbed in her gibberish. He didn't miss a single word as it cascaded out of the physio onto the rug, Reyer watched the words hounce off the walls, windows and ceilings like transparent jelly creatures. Jelly that could go on bouncing ad infinitum with no need of an energy source. Reyer rushed off to find the bathroom to carry out his vital cold-water ablutions and his little breathing routine. He was amazed to find a shrub the size of a man filling almost the entire bathroom, its branches spreading into the tub. He pictured himself on a beach with Marche. She was wearing nothing but a sari and was emerging from the

266

water smiling. The pink fabric embroidered with gold thread hugged every single one of her curves. Reyer heard the entryphone buzzer and went back to the sitting room.

'Don't answer, it's the TV people,' Zaraoui told Clara.

The girl had finished jabbering. Reyer said to himself that a woman so desperate to talk was capable of making anonymous phone calls. It would be right up her street. He went over to the entryphone.

'If you don't confess, I'm going to answer it!' he barked. 'The TV lot will rake over every aspect of your life. Then you can say goodbye to your business, you'll have to practise elsewhere. Bye-bye green oasis in the middle of Paris.'

'But I didn't kill Guillaume. I loved him!'

'That's not what I'm talking about. I mean the anonymous phone call. If that dishevelled-looking guy has just given your name to the muck-rakers, it's because he knew you were sleeping with Garnier. The whole building probably knows. And your physio husband too.'

Flashes of inspiration were a lot more interesting than the aftermath, so Reyer let Zaraoui add the finishing touches. He searched the bar, found a bottle of rum and took a few swigs from the bottle. He spotted the telephone, dialled Marthe's number and listened to the message on her answering machine, so professional but so electrifying. This shrink would have no chance in the anonymous phone call business; there was no mistaking her siren voice. He hung up, wiped his damp hand on his shirt and pricked up his ears. Zaraoui was painstakingly preparing the ground. Clara had seen Garnier collapse on the café terrace. For the simple reason that she'd been nearby. Garnier had told her he'd be taking a break at Café Mirage during the morning. He liked playing that kind of game. Arranging to meet her in places he went to with his mates. Exchanging secret looks. She'd been sitting on the terrace, she'd seen him raise his glass to his lips and collapse before he'd even drunk a drop.

'Why do you think it's murder?' asked Zaraoui.

'This morning, Guillaume took his bike out of the garage and left it in the courtyard for a minute while he popped back upstairs to phone me. He always took his water bottle filled with an energy drink.'

'Phone you, why?'

'Just to tell me he loved me . . .'

That set off the waterworks again. Clara wept, sobbed. Reyer let her cry, then asked, between hiccups, where the husband was. 'I don't know.'

'The water bottle on the bike. Where's the bike?'

'Probably at the station,' replied Zaraoui. 'Garnier's friends parked it in the corridor with theirs. You don't leave expensive machines like that out on the street.'

Reyer called the station. They kept him hanging on. A duty officer said he'd find out about the bike. And informed him it had gone. Reyer asked to speak to his chief. The chief passed the matter on to his team. The chief's secretary eventually remembered a tall, thin, fair-haired man. He'd calmly walked out with the bike, it hadn't occurred to her that he might be stealing it. The description matched that of Alexandre Lorieux. Reyer took another swig of rum and reflected on the situation. The number of cyclists in Paris was at its peak during the Tour de France. Might as well try to find a minuscule needle in a colossal haystack. He watched the muck-rakers through the window. They'd let the dishevelled guy go and were hassling another guy. A tall, fair-haired man, the beanpole type, standing beside a bicycle. Looking distraught. Reyer raced down the stairs, bottle of rum in hand. He wielded it like a sabre to threaten the journalists, then sent it flying over the ancient cobblestones. The cameraman filmed him. The sound engineer swung his mammoth-hair device in his direction. Reyer gave the journalist a pithecanthropine clout, grabbed Clara's husband's arm and marched him up the stairs, pronto. The physio wouldn't let go of the bike. Getting up the stairs was a struggle.

Lorieux admitted he'd poisoned Garnier with a shrub brought back from India which was flourishing in his bathroom. It was a magic tree that killed and left no trace. Thousands of Indian wives had found that out to their cost when their husbands had tired of them.

That evening, Reyer hammered on a familiar door in the Canal Saint-Martin district. She opened the door, calm, smiling, wearing a simple tight-fitting T-shirt and a ridiculous little pair of trousers which were too short. He explained that he'd solved a case in a matter of hours but his chief had suspended him all the same for assaulting a bunch of journalists. He needed an emergency consultation. He knew it was 9.46 p.m., but anxiety was quick to spread over ravaged terrain.

'I'm an ataraxic cop,' said Reyer sitting down facing Marthe.

That's a good opener, he thought. With words like that, I might just interest her, surprise her. A surprised woman is always a good thing. After all, that poor sod Garnier managed to surprise little Clara with muscle names. Gastroenemius is over the top, biceps femoris, I'm losing it, you're my Achilles heel, my trapezius balance, my brachioradialis muscles want to enfold you, my pectorals marry you . . .

'Sorry?' said Marthe in her melodious voice.

Be still my words, whoa, whoa, slow down my horses running before the cart, it's to her I must offer you, to her alone, and to her body that could help me so much . . .

'An ataraxic cop. From ataraxy, tranquillity of the soul. But not just any tranquillity, Marthe. Absolute tranquillity.'

ELLE ET MOI: LE SACRIFICE

JAKE LAMAR

S. has changed her hairstyle. It happened during the rentrée. Before, her chestnut brown mane had hung loosely, girlishly, about shoulder-length. Now she wears it quite short, swept away from her forehead, with a little upward flip at the bottom. It has an early 1960s look about it, this hairdo – and it accentuates her long, porcelain throat. She is no more and no less beautiful to me than before. In fact, S. is not really beautiful at all. But there is a great beauty about her, as Georges Guétary once said of Leslie Caron.

Anyway, I am devoted to her whatever she does with her hair. Because we are meant to be together. I know this. I'm serious: I *know* it. Like you know you're you when you look in the mirror. I look at S. and know what our destiny is. And she looks right through me.

Maman mocks me, tells me I have no chance. I hadn't told her my concept of destiny with S. All I said was that I thought S. could be interested in me. Someday.

'That's your medication talking,' Maman sneered.

'Do you really think she'd be interested in a mental case?'

This is what Maman always says when she wants to hurt me. But I know I am not a mental case. I was a troubled young man, yes. But I'm OK now. I am completely lucid. And Maman knows I'm not crazy. She wouldn't call me a mental case if she thought I really was still sick. She says it now just to humiliate me, to rub my nose in the stinking shit of my past.

Besides, Maman doesn't want me to have any women in my life. She wants me all to herself. She always has. Maybe that was my problem, eh? I'd like to have this all out with her, hold the mirror up to Maman. But I never do. I will, though. Someday. When I can afford my own apartment.

Maman and I live together in the same dreary flat in a characterless street in the fifteenth arrondissement. This is the apartment in which I grew up, the only home I have ever known; the apartment in which my father died, four years ago, back when I was a mental case, living in a hospital among other mental cases. Every once in a while, Maman tries to make me feel responsible, as if my psychiatric condition caused Papa's heart attack. But she dare not harass me too much about that. Because we both know the truth. Maman always said this place was too small for three people. She lived alone with Papa during my first two years in the hospital. She lived completely alone, after my father's death, for two years. She has now lived alone with me for two years and she definitely prefers me to utter solitude, as well as to Papa. She always preferred me to Papa. Would always rather touch me than touch Papa.

But we don't talk about that.

I need to get my own place, some place where S. and I could be alone. Maman is wrong. I plan to tell S. everything about my past. And I am certain she will understand. She wouldn't coddle me, wouldn't excuse the errors of my youth. She would be firm yet compassionate. Who knows? It might even make me more interesting to her. Hey, I'm not just a twenty-four-year-old computer geek. I'm a twenty-four-year-old computer geek who spent four years in a mental hospital! I'm sure S. would begin to see my time in there the way I do. Some young people spend four years at university. Some spend four years in the military. I spent those formative years of eighteen to twenty-two in a nuthouse. This was my sentimental education.

The guys at work needle me for what they call my 'crush' on S. Not that I talk to them about it. Not really. But I have occasionally spoken about her to my colleagues, four computer geeks who — except for the fact that none of them ever spent four years in a mental hospital — are pretty much just like me. They don't know I was hospitalised. They just think I spent four years jerking off, watching TV, reading sci-fi novels, surfing the Internet and playing video games while collecting unemployment hand-outs and sponging off my parents. That's what a couple of them did for four years after high school. For me to think I might have a chance with S. (yes, it must be obvious, even without my explicitly stating it) I'm conveying to my colleagues that I consider myself somehow superior to them. So they must relent-lessly take the piss out of me, try to cut me down to their size. Of course, I do consider myself super-ior to them. I don't tell them that. Just as I don't tell them that it is my destiny to be with S. Not a 'crush'. Destiny.

My colleagues suffer from a common form of self-disgust. After all, we're just five losers working in a computer repair service centre. We make very little money. We know we're smart but it's not like any of us got into one of the *grandes écoles*. We're neither handsome nor charming. How dare I consider myself superior to any of them? Especially in terms of attractiveness to any woman, let alone a woman like S. My four colleagues and I, it must be said, are able to occupy a level field of sexual conquest. This is another source of their feelings of intra-office egalitarianism. We have all partaken of the Nerd Girl.

Ombline, the Nerd Girl, works in Accounting at the computer repair service centre. She is the female version of the five of us 'technical consultants'. Smart but unsuccessful, not especially appealing to the eyes. She's a bit overweight, a bit pimply. A little older than us computer geeks, maybe twenty-seven or twenty-eight. Still wears her slightly oily, slightly dandruffed mousy brown hair in juvenile pigtails. But Ombline, the Nerd Girl as my colleagues call her, is the seductress of the computer repair service centre. Even though she still lives with her parents, in a drab concrete slab of an apartment building in the downscale nineteenth arrondissement.

I learned Ombline's modus operandi just as my four colleagues had before me. Ombline invites you out to dinner. She gets quite drunk and demonstrably horny. She invites you to her apartment. You quickly greet her aged parents, who are always sitting in front of the TV, looking just barely alive. You repair to Ombline's bedroom. She puts on some loud music – usually the Rolling Stones, circa 1971. You have hurried, almost furtive sex, only half or three-quarters undressed. It's like you're both sixteen and worried that her parents might burst in at any second. Ombline comes quickly, easily, even faster than you. After some awkward post-coital fondling she tells you you have to leave. You say goodbye to the parents who are still sitting in the living room, clinging feebly to life, in front of the TV.

Over the past two years, Ombline the Nerd Girl has regularly fucked the technical staff in a sort of five-man rotation, one man at a time, three to four weeks between each man. So there is no jealousy.

No sense of competition even, since none of us believes that Ombline is worth fighting for. And she seems perfectly happy with the situation.

Naturally, I haven't told Maman about Ombline. I don't know what Maman thinks about my sex life. She asks no questions. But then I got careless. I mentioned, rather subtly, I thought, my feelings for S. I could understand why Maman would get upset. It was, after all, my – how to describe it? . . . *too intense* – attraction to a young girl that got me sent to a mental hospital for four years.

But we don't talk about that young girl.

What, I begin to wonder, is Maman's game? On the one hand, she seems worried that I might confront S. with my feelings. On the other hand, Maman taunts me, seems to be trying to goad me into doing just that – confronting S.

And what would happen if I did? Would S. understand the intensity of my conviction? My utter certainty that we are destined to be joined together forever? I would have to explain to S. that these are rather recent feelings. Though I had admired her for many years, thinking of her, talking about her from time to time with my fellow inmates during the four years I spent in the hospital, it is only in the past few months that this idea of mine, this idea of our shared destiny, has blossomed into an article of absolute faith.

I know that if I did express all this to S., she would be taken aback. Probably be slow to embrace my point of view. It would take time for the idea to grow on her. She is, after all, a wise and mature woman, some years my elder. And she already has a man in her life. As far as I can see, she is trapped in an unhappy marriage. Though, of course, you can't even call what they have a marriage, can you?

'Send her an email,' Maman says. 'Tell her everything you feel. I know you. You'll be more honest typing this all into a computer than you would ever be speaking to her face to face.'

'I don't even know her email address,' I protest.

'I'm sure it's very easy to find,' Maman retorts.

It's my turn with the Nerd Girl. Lying on Ombline's bed, in her adolescent's bedroom – still decorated with Noir Desir posters from 1994 – each of us three-quarters undressed, sticky and sated, we say nothing for a long time. We're listening to Mick Jagger warble 'Wild Horses' at high volume.

'What would you think about starting a serious relationship with me?' Ombline asks as the song fades out and silence fills the room. Well, not total silence. I can hear the sound of the TV coming from the living room. Ombline's aged parents are watching an old episode of *Navarro*.

I tell Ombline I cannot commit to her. She is not upset. She tells me she likes me best of all the technical consultants and she wants me to be her one and only lover and I) since I know she has the pick of the crop, and 2) since I know I'm not going to get any easier or better sex anywhere else, and 3) since I know that, someday, I am going to want to get married and have children, I might as well face reality and decide that, yes, I want to commit to her.

That's when I tell Ombline about my feelings for S. Perhaps, I go into too much detail, explaining my whole conviction of destiny. Ombline tells me that I'm sick. She tells me I should be put back in the hospital (until that moment, I never knew she had known I'd been hospitalised). She tells me to get out of her bedroom or she'll call the police.

I dress hurriedly, scurry through the living room, barely say goodbye to Ombline's decrepit parents, hunched before the flickering TV screen.

I catch the Métro back down to the fifteenth. And while Maman sleeps in the next room, I write the email to S. I put it all down. Everything I feel. In 2,222 words. I find her address easily. Just as Maman knew I would. I send the message at 02.22. Two has always been my lucky number.

I will not tell you what I wrote to S. It is too intimate. It is between S. and me. At least, that is how I wanted it to be.

I barely sleep. In the morning, over breakfast, I tell Maman about the message I have sent.

Maman takes a bite of her croissant, chews contemplatively, then says, her voice thick with scorn, 'She'll never answer.'

'Salut, Jean-Hugues,' an unfamiliar, deep male voice says.

I am sitting in a corner booth in a café near my house, reading a Norman Spinrad sci-fi novel. It is late on a Saturday morning, early November – unusually, bitingly, cold for this time of year in Paris. I look up, expecting, of course, to see someone I know. Not one of my computer geek colleagues. I know their whiny voices too well. I brace myself for the sight of one of my old acquaintances from high school, someone who has recognised me as the troubled boy from their class, despite the fact that I have grown a thick beard, as a kind of disguise, since getting out of the hospital two years ago.

But as I look up, I see before me, in the smoky air of the café, two men I have never met before. They are practically identical, maybe forty years old, the two of them sporting shaved heads. Not cleanly shaved: each large, finely shaped skull bears a thin layer of greyish stubble. Both men wear black leather jackets and black pants. You might take them for a homosexual couple. But there is nothing remotely delicate about their appearance. If they are fags, they are tough, violent fags.

'Do I know you?' I ask, stupidly, since I am sure that I do not.

'No,' one of the stubbleheads says as they both sit down at my table. 'But we know you.'

From this moment on, everything has a strange, dreamy feel about it. One of the stubblehead twins talks, the other never says a word.

279

He just glares menacingly at me. The talking stubblehead tells me that they have read the email I sent to S. last week. They know that I was in a mental hospital. If I send another message to S., if I try to contact her in any way, they will make sure that I will be put back in the hospital. Or worse. I could very well be put in prison – for a very long time.

'Think about how that would hurt your mother,' he adds.

I think about it. I couldn't care less. But I say nothing.

I assume these guys are part of the most private, inner security team that S. has. I cannot help but feel flattered by their attention.

The guy who has done all the talking asks if I understand what he has just said to me. I say yes. The stubblehead twins rise, tell me one more time to stay away from S.

Just as they are turning to leave, I blurt out the question: 'Has she read my email?'

They both smirk at me. The talkative stubblehead nods, then says: 'Do you really think she'd be interested in a guy who looks like a garden dwarf?'

Then they walk away, chuckling.

I take this, the entire encounter, as a challenge.

Over the next nine or ten hours, everything happens in a kind of dreamy haze. I wonder why the stubbleheaded goons only decided to confront me today, nearly a full week after I sent my email to S. It must be because she is making an appearance in a *grande halle des expositions* in my very arrondissement this Saturday night.

That is the immediate, specific reason for the goons showing up to try to intimidate me.

The larger reason is that they want to stop me from really making myself known to S., to confronting her face to face. Hell, for all I know, S. might have read my email and found me a fascinating young man, someone she would actually like to meet. Probably it was her husband – sorry, the man in her life, the father of her four children, who has never bothered to marry her – who sent the goons to try to intimidate me. He's scared. Terrified that I will steal his woman from him. That she will see me, our eyes will meet, and she will experience a total *coup de foudre*– love at first sight.

This all seems so clear to me Saturday afternoon. I must make myself known to S. I must confront her. Face to face. Tonight. At the convention centre. I know the back exit, where all the featured guests, all the celebrities, leave the grand hall. I will be waiting there tonight. I will make myself known to S.

There is only one huge problem. The men who would thwart me now know my face. 'A garden dwarf' they called me!

That Saturday afternoon, I stand before the bathroom mirror, scrutinising the image before me. Yes, it's true I have let my hair grow long, my beard is a bit bushy and unkempt. And, I see it for the first time, my nose is rather bulbous. A shocking moment of self-recognition. I *do* resemble a garden dwarf.

If I am to confront S. face to face I must make my face unrecognisable to the stubbleheaded security men. Standing before the bathroom mirror, I take in hand my dead father's electric razor. I shave away my whiskers. I then apply the buzzing razor to my shock of head hair. By the time I'm finished, I look not unlike the stubblehead twins themselves.

This way, I should blend easily into the crowd outside the grand hall. Even the security men will not recognise me, for I will look so much like-one of them, so little like a garden dwarf. But S. will see me for who I am. The moment our eyes meet, she will realise that I am her salvation.

'Aren't you staying for dinner?' Maman asks absentmindedly, not even looking at me, as I walk through the living room, wearing my winter coat on this cold November night. Then, just as I am about to pass her, she glances up, sees me with a clean-shaven face, a head of ultra-short stubbly hair. 'Jean-Hugues!' Maman shrieks.

I do not pause to explain or to comfort her. I just keep walking, right out the front door.

*   *   *

S. was smiling at me. I am sure of it. S. looked directly into my eyes. And she was smiling. Right at me. Her destiny.

I am, for these last few moments before my eternal notoriety, just another face in the crowd. I stand with all the other ordinary citizens behind the police barricades that have been set up outside the back exit of the grand hall. Suddenly, the building's metal doors swing open. A squad of scowling security agents streams out, clearing a path, scanning the crowd with menace in their eyes. I see the stubblehead twins. And I see that they do not see me, do not recognise my face in the crowd.

Then I see S., hurrying out of the building. The very sight of her, in the flesh, takes my breath away.

It occurs to me, at that moment, that some public figures are akin to human sacrifices. Think of JFK, Martin Luther King, John Lennon. Considering that last name, it occurs to me how odd it is that the human sacrifices moved from being politicians and religious leaders to popular celebrities.

But, no matter: Lee Harvey Oswald, James Earl Ray, Mark David Chapman: the names of the men who carried out the sacrifices will be forever linked with those of the luminaries they slaughtered. Is it not the same glory?

A mere second after I first see S., I spot the man

across from me, on the opposite side of the police barricade. He is an older man, maybe fifty. He wears steel-rimmed glasses and a black baseball cap. I see the deranged look in his eyes. And I think: do I look like that?

I can understand, on some profound but, for me, unknowable level, how one might love S. and, at the same time, want to destroy her. But that is not me. I cannot allow this madman in the cap and glasses to possess the glory of the assassin.

Three seconds have passed since S. emerged from the metal doors at the back exit of the grand hall. She strides confidently into the cold night air. She is absolutely radiant, her smile a beacon, her eyes glowing, her new hairdo bouncing as she walks down the column of admirers. The chant erupts: 'Say-GO! Say-GO! Say-GO! Say-GO!'

She is approaching me, quite quickly now. I catch a glimpse of the stubblehead twins, one on each side of the aisle formed by the police barricades. One of them, the talkative stubblehead, looks directly at me. I quickly look away and spot, across the lane carved out by metal barriers, the man in the black baseball cap and steel-rimmed glasses. He is reaching into his jacket pocket. I see the gun emerge in his hand.

'Ségolène!' I scream.

Her name explodes from my mouth, involuntarily-That is when she turns and looks straight into my eyes. She is no more than six feet away. And she is smiling at me. She *knows* me. I am sure of it.

All is instinct now. I see the man in the cap and glasses extending his arm, pointing the gun at the presidential candidate's head.

Surely, you have heard those stories about people being gripped by a superhuman strength, an instinct beyond the realm of actual physical capacity, triggered by an immediate crisis. The mother who lifts a car off a child trapped beneath its weight, that is the classic example.

I don't know if what I instinctively do fits in the same category. But I leap over the police barricade and lunge in front of Ségolène. The gun fires. Just as Ségolène's smiling face passes out of my vision, I am nearly blinded by the flash of the pistol. I feel the burning sensation in the centre of my forehead. It is indescribable, the pain of hot metal blasting through bone and into the brain.

As I lie on the ground, flat on my back, several actions register at once. The talkative stubblehead pulls out his gun, fires and kills the man who wanted to shoot Ségolène Royal but shot me instead. Deafening screams. Everyone, it seems, is screaming. Except for the candidate, who is quickly surrounded and whisked away. To safety. People are gathering around me. I hear screams and questions. People screaming questions: What happened? Did he do it? Who is he?

As the blood pours into my eyes and I feel life slipping away, exactly like wakefulness slipping away as you fall asleep – only a trillion times more powerful, the sensation – I think only of S. She was smiling at me. I am sure of it. She looked directly into my eyes. And she was smiling. Right at me. Her destiny.

FACILIS DESCENSUS AVERNO

JIM NISBET

Bruce inherited a bunch of paper from his mother's father.

After he'd shaken off the good-fuck/bad-fuck couplings of Mr Leather World, whose year of ascendancy Bruce had never precisely determined – and, since M. Cuir du Monde dyed the pelt favoured by *Pediculosus capitis* and depilated all the rest, including that of his legs, pubis, armpits, and back (which might otherwise have been positively ursine), and his neediness, which exceeded even that of Regis Capone, a minor (no pun intended) soap opera star Bruce had dated for a while, occluded all the other factual topics, leaving little room for age determination, although his birthday was very important, etc. – Bruce found himself at the end of a bindle of cocaine with nothing better to do, at four o'clock in the morning, even in New York City, maybe especially in New York City, than to break out and study his legacy.

By the time the sun was well up that July morning, everything had changed.

By the end of the week he'd opened a brokerage account and sold off half his grandfather's gas leases which, though depreciated over their various lifetimes, left him with approximately the same value in cash as remained in the leases, which, though he'd never before shown the slightest talent or inclination for financial manipulations, arcane ones least of all, he fed straight into a diversified portfolio projected to earn him nine per cent per annum, excepting $40,000 in cash which, however, would itself earn four per cent in the brokerage checking account, so long as he maintained a minimum balance, leaving gas leases sufficient to yield some $5,000 a month for the foreseeable future.

Bruce had always perceived his as a charmed life. While everybody around him was dropping like flies in the eighties, for example, and though he visited the Rude Dude Bathhouse (not six blocks from The Trucks) weekly, he had emerged unscathed. He told people it was genetic, he told people it was because he didn't eat right, he told people it was because he was careful: he told himself that his was a charmed existence.

The half-million inheritance, out of the blue from a man he barely knew, served to confirm this de factor analysis.

That, and he judged the men he allowed himself to sleep with by their Facial Index. To wit:

$$F1 = \frac{\text{length of face}}{\text{width of face}} \times 100$$

as measured in an anterior/posterior vertical plane bisecting the sagital crest through the occiput, and, trust Bruce, it's much more interesting than a man's score on the Scholastic Aptitude Test. The less acute the angle, the wilder the sex, or, as Bruce could also put it, copping W.C. Handy's line from *St Louis Blues*, the blacker the berry, the sweeter the juice. Hence the truth of Virgil's dictum, *facils descensus Averno*, the descent to hell is easy – especially if you know the way. Remind me to look up Averno, he would say to whatever bar bait in whatever bait bar he was quoting Virgil, as he dissolved into peals of the histrionic laughter he'd learned from Regis Capone, who in his heyday had the most un-acute facial index to be seen on network television.

In English, one man in one bar, out of the hundreds of men he'd met in dozens of bars, had once helpfully pointed out to him, it's Avernus.

Bruce didn't go home and look it up. Are you kidding? He just never went to that bar again.

Cast in the glare of all that money, the Village suddenly looked tawdry, When he pointed this out to some guy in some bar the guy said, if you think this is tawdry, you should visit the Castro District in San Francisco, where they have bars that cater to big fuzzy guys who want to hook up with little sleek ones, and vice versa.

That's disgusting, Bruce said, scrolling through his cellphone directory for his travel agent's number. Everybody else books online, but, since Bruce could afford it, he preferred to pay others to do the grunt work. After all, what's money for?

His acquaintance was right about San Francisco. Bruce was back in a week. He ran into his friend almost immediately.

They're called bears and otters.

I beg your pardon?

That's what they call them.

Oh, please, the man said, as he palpated his ascot. Do you think I was born yesterday?

Still, the Village looked tawdry.

OK, Bruce thought, there's only one answer to this problem.

Paris.

He'd taken plenty of French in school, and had lived a semester in Bordeaux. He'd read all of Genet of course, worked at the obscurities of Villon and Baudelaire and Verlaine and Rimbaud, perused and found boring Pagnol, plunged back into the existentialists and whatnot, but found himself gravitating towards the English of William Burroughs, Hubert Selby, Jr, John Rechy, Dennis Cooper and Bruce Benderson, writers prejudiced towards an edgy milieu, more towards his taste in the daring and the experimental – and, in short, unapologetically queer. This was before he quit reading novels altogether. Whether or not such work would hold up until such time as he troubled to reread them, Bruce simply didn't care, for he could always stick with pornography.

He traded apartments with a French couple who wanted to spend a school year, nine months, in New York City. An agency handled the details, he didn't even have to meet the people. And why should Bruce have told them that since his was a rent-controlled apartment he'd tenanted for seven years he paid only $275 a month for it? What business was it of theirs? Value is value. Location location location.

He found himself in the ninth arrondissement on a fifth floor – sixth by gringo accounting, and since there was no elevator, he was counting. A plus of the staircase was its age, which must have been 200 years. Each tread had been dished by hundreds of thousands of footfalls and the banister was a continuous piece of naturally finished French oak that whipped up the six floors with nothing less than a magnificent sinuosity. The apartment's entire north wall consisted of a pitch of wire-glass lites, waist-high up to the six-metre ceiling, through which he could see the zweible-based spires of Sacré-Coeur high atop the butte of Montmartre, and he readily became accustomed to hearing the legendary 19-ton Savoyarde, whenever they chose to ring it. There was a working fireplace, with a quintal of cordwood in the cave which was *eight* flights down, and the concierge kept the wooden staircase so thoroughly waxed that the first time Bruce ventured down into the stone vaults of the cave in his stocking feet was the last time. He busted his tailbone not once but twice on those slick treads; his feet shot out from under him as if they had encountered black ice.

The very first piece of rough trade – he said his name was Étienne – he brought home with him immediately put the value of the apartment at 3,000 euros per month, and stole, of all things, a pair of books. Pretty tony rough trade, Bruce was thinking, maybe two weeks later, when he noticed them missing. But that was until he figured out from careful comparison with the inventory manifest, that the nicked items could only have been a two-volume edition of *Anti-Justine, ou, les Délicieux d'Amour dans Les Nuits de Paris*, by Restif de la Bretonne. Though less than perfect, they were valued at 750 euros. and Bruce was entirely responsible for this value – along with that of everything else in the apartment. He himself fervently hoped that his French tenants in New York would manage to lose or misplace damn near everything in his apartment, which he had absurdly overvalued in his own manifest. Still, why the stupid breeders had left such valuable items in plain sight seemed beyond reason. How irresponsible could they be?

He told himself to calm down. At the present differential between their rent and his:

(2,000 euros * 1.2758 $/euro) – $250 – $750 – (agency commission = 10% = 200 euros @ 1.2758 =) $255.16 = $1,296.45.

Therefore, at the end of only one month and despite this one fuckup, Bruce would still be way ahead of the game.

See? A charmed existence.

From then on, however, Bruce took them to a hotel in Pigalle.

And despite this almost nightly additional expense he remained ahead of the game.

He liked Pigalle. Pigalle reminded him of Bruce Benderson's novel *The United Nations of Times Square*. Not that he had read it. But he had his own version of Times Square and, in the same airy rooms of Bruce's mind, Bruce Benderson was known as 'the other Bruce'. He was charmed by the fact that he and that distinguished author shared a given name. People will always, some guy in some bar had once observed to him, elicit the slightest pretext to hold in common with a celebrity, no matter how minor. The pretext? Bruce had asked. The celebrity, had come the reply.

Bruce soon discovered that, in a narrow, cobbled, unlit, dead-end street, parallel to and just down the hill from the rue des Abbesses, he could get anything he wanted. The menu was varied, the prices were right, and most of the talent was Arab or North African or both. All he had to do was take care to distinguish them from the transvestites. But that was pretty easy. The transvestites had their own bar, for one thing, from which they sallied to work and to which they repaired between tricks. For another, the transvestites seemed to be maintaining and upholding a tradition of the *zaftig* in prostitution, of a buxom, wide-hipped, red-lipped, frilled-décolletage and altogether blowsy ideal of womanhood that had to have gone out of fashion, even among horny and naïve GIs, shortly after World War Two.

No matter. The Arab boys, most of them from Morocco, were slim-hipped, full-lipped, tall, and mean. Of these *Apaches sauvages*, Bruce aimed to count his coup.

By and by the concierge of the hotel, a cheap narrow affair that leaned over an alley perpendicular to the cobbled one, across the street from a bar/hotel of heterosexual assignation such as, too, seemed to be a relic of another era, a place where you'd go to fuck a woman who reminded you of your mother, got to know him. This individual had determined Bruce's purpose right away, of course. He rented Bruce a room at an hourly rate equivalent to a whole night's stay in any nearby hostel. Bruce didn't care. Bruce was ramping up.

Soon enough, he'd more or less forgotten whatever other reasons he'd told himself he'd come to Paris. Museums, food, history, the language, whatever, Bruce was having none of it. He didn't have the time. Much as he'd been in New York, he became a creature of the night. After only six weeks he had solid connects for cocaine, heroin, hashish, and amyl nitrate. While he was all too familiar with each of these substances, he was also chary of them. The idea was to accommodate the tastes of his dates. No trick he was willing to engage, however, as it turned out, wanted anything to do with any of them. Himself, Bruce sipped Côtes du Rhône with his *steak pavé*, pastis before supper, beer for refreshment in between. After all meals were over, during the night, which was the dark part of the morning to ordinary people, he would take only calvados, and that sparingly. Of debauchery, as it is usually defined, only sex interested him.

Soon enough he was hitting the hotel two and even three times a night, each time with a different date. Upon reflection, it reminded him of the old days. Although, of course, in the old days, when he was young and good looking and everything was free, sex, especially, was free. Upon reflection – for Bruce was not incapable of reflection, far from it; Bruce deployed most of his waking hours in such manner as to distract or fragment reflection – he realised he had never dated older men, ever, in the old days.

Now, of course, and he tittered inwardly, it would be quite a chore to find men older than himself sufficiently sub-decrepit to date at all; downright onerous.

Akhmed was a looker. His facial index was straight off Easter Island, a thick-lipped mask of brooding menace. Bruce had run across him more than once and subsequently found himself seeking him out. Akhmed was one of those rough types Bruce favoured. Akhmed's delusional system went so far as to include the old prison adage, *I pitch but I don't catch*. Like that kid who killed Pasolini. In other words, Akhmed could do all kinds of weird things to Bruce, but Bruce couldn't so much as discuss Akhmed's giving Bruce a blowjob. No matter. Bruce could scare up a good-faith sissy any old time. Akhmed shaved maybe once in two weeks, so, after their every meeting, one or another of Bruce's shoulders prickled from the abrasion for a day or two. Never did Bruce's face prickle. Think of the 'Were you in the Army?' '*Oui, La Légion Étrangère.*' 'No kissing.' '*Bon – ptui!*' scene in Fassbinder's film of Genet's *Querelle de Brest*. Finding aloe vera at the sign of the green cross turned out to be not so much trouble as he thought it might have been. Akhmed rarely bathed, either. And he didn't like to talk. But he liked it that Bruce bathed. And he tolerated that Bruce liked to talk. Both traits were distinctively American, so far as Akhmed was concerned.

That's typically American, Akhmed said off-handedly one night, as he watched Bruce ablute over the bidet. Clean at home, filthy abroad.

What's that supposed to mean? What's the matter with a little personal hygiene? Akhmed deigned no reply. Bruce might have suggested to Akhmed that he might himself consider periodic upgrades to his personal hygiene, but, the truth was, Bruce liked him just the way he was. Visit the planet, was Bruce's credo, but don't disturb the fauna.

Still, he couldn't see what Akhmed's problem was with cleanliness.

Forget it, Akhmed said, and he settled his black-eyed gaze upon the faux Degas screwed to the wall at the foot of the bed. I'm hungry. You ready to go?

They had fallen into a routine of a meal after the hotel room. These repasts were uncomfortable, for Akhmed didn't want to talk and Bruce did. Bruce wanted to know where Akhmed was from, what his mother was like, how many brothers and sisters, their circumstances, how much and what kind of education, and so forth, but very little information was forthcoming. Akhmed was only there to eat, and he was there to eat only because Bruce would pick up the cheque.

Once Bruce pointed out a couscous place and suggested they eat there. *Non,* was all Akhmed said. Instead, they stuck strictly to French bistros and cafés more or less south of Pigalle and, Bruce presumed, resolutely out of whatever neighbourhood Akhmed called his own, which, by hints Bruce detected here and there, was within walking distance of Barbès-Rochechouart.

One night as they lay in bed *entre'acte,* Bruce having paid in advance for a double play, as Bruce prattled on about how most people in New York had an overdeveloped sense of style, Akhmed blew a plume of smoke at the ceiling and abruptly said, In many countries in the middle east and about a third of those in Africa, I could sell you to the Islamists and they would drill holes in your knees.

As Bruce was somewhat taken aback by this turn in the nonversation, as a witty friend used to term the appropriately uneven match of social skills, he simply asked why.

Because you're American, Akhmed said, as if staring the obvious.

No, Bruce said, why would you sell me? And, despite himself, the construction *sell me* sent a shiver up his spine, a shiver unexpected, licentious, and unexplored.

Akhmed, who seldom deigned to look Bruce directly in the eye, did so now, and he did so out of frank incredulity. For the money.

And now another unexpected sensation shimmied up Bruce's spine like a fun-loving *singe* after a *banane flambée au rhum*: Sold for money. Not ideology. Money. OK. Got it. But in the here and now what it means is that all this terrific sex we've been having tonight, and for any number of nights over the past four months, means nothing to this guy. I'm hurt, Bruce said sarcastically, but to himself. Mordacity as a defence mechanism. The root is to bite, but the one bitten is oneself. Because, quite irrationally, be was hurt. A little bit, anyway. But beneath that he liked it. *Les Délicieux d'Amour dans Les Nuits de Paris*, indeed. He liked it.

And what would you do with the money, he asked.

Akhmed shrugged. Same thing I do with all my money.

Which is?

I send it home to my mother.

All of your money?

All of my money.

Admirable. A Confucian would call that *filial piety*.

Whatever a Confucian is, Akhmed glowered, is not me.

Mostly a lost value, in my society anyway, Bruce concluded lamely.

Akhmed's silent expression reflected only a sour disinterest.

Bruce snuggled up and traced Akhmed's lower rib with a forefinger. And you don't send the least tithing cent to your local mosque? he asked playfully.

The side of Akhmed's hand clipped Bruce above the ear, catching his head between it and Akhmed's chest, the musculature of which Akhmed had the reflexive foresight to tense, thus inducing a temporary tinnitus in both of Bruce's ears.

Cocksucker, Bruce said reflexively, though he said it in French. He didn't mean it that way, in the way that Akhmed thought he meant it. Bruce meant to say *mangeur de bite!* merely as an exclamatory remark, an expostulation of marvel over the abrupt change in the course of events. But Akhmed thought Bruce was calling Akhmed an eater of dick which, even in ordinary circumstances, would have represented a breach of protocol – another word the French may have invented, which thought caused Bruce to giggle incontinently.

Under the circumstances, Akhmed beat the shit out of Bruce. Beat him well and thoroughly, all the while saying to himself, Akhmed, you are a fool. It's his western way. He's an idiot. He has no idea who you are. All you're doing is thrashing your meal ticket. And cross-rationalising: he insulted me. I pitch but I don't catch. I've had it with this *suceur*, all he does is insult me. When he wakes up, maybe he will have learned his lesson.

Indeed, Bruce lost consciousness long before Akhmed finished with him. So that Bruce took no pleasure when, at the end, having set aside everything of Bruce's that could possibly have any value, including his clothes, Akhmed fucked him again. Fucked him hard. Fucked him so hard that it was all that Akhmed could do to refrain from finishing the job, i.e., killing the fuckee. For he hated himself at the last moment of pleasure, because it was pleasure, and for that pleasure, he hated himself.

Finally, pretty worn out, he rolled Bruce's senseless and pasty white old man's bag of bones, some of them broken, off the bed onto the floor, doubled the dive-hotel pillow between his back and the wall, and smoked himself a cigarette. His hands were trembling. Strictly adrenalin, but he saw it as a weakness for which he blamed the old man and gave him a kick.

But, after only a few drags, Akhmed became too introspective to relax. What he had done, what had happened, was complex. The rigidity of the discipline he applied to his prostitution, to his money, to the whole of his circumstances, as altogether illegal as they were altogether modest, here in this thousand-year-old city of extreme decadence, of lights everywhere and of people from all over the world, a city which allowed him to live in a way that he could never live almost anywhere else . . . did not apply so easily to the emotions coursing through him. He felt himself a one-man colonial uprising. He would never feel himself up to the stature of a warrior of God. Yet God must have something to do with it, else why do fools such as this Bruce cross his path? He'd never had a French client who wanted to ask him about his mother. Never had a French customer who cared what he did with his money or his rime away from work. Nobody had even so much as asked him what part of Morocco he was from; to them, it seemed to him, Morocco was a sort of child's alphabet block lost among similar blocks, indistinguishable, one from the other, in a pile called 'Africa'.

Meanwhile, the very freedom against which he and others like him railed was the very freedom which enabled him to pursue the almighty euro according to his lights. To wit: his mother had thought for years that Akhmed was teaching Berber as a second language at L'Ecole de Science Polytechnique, a position modest enough, but secure and respectable, which enabled her to live in a paid-for house.

At least, that's what he let her let him think that she thought.

With a grunt of frustration he stubbed out his cigarette on one of Bruce's exposed butt cheeks and threw the end at the bidet. The tang of burnt flesh suffused the room with unexpected vigour. A memory fleeted across Akhmed's mind, and he frowned. He looked down on the unconscious Bruce with the scowl of an annoyed and very handsome Easter Island deity. The American's hands were small, like his eyes and his dick. His paunch, despite a gym membership, was pronounced. Akhmed half-consciously compared the flatness of his own abdomen by touch. I could kill this guy. He looked at Bruce. Maybe I already have.

He didn't bother to check.

Outside in the hall, which was really just a landing not one metre wide, a man and a woman trudged up the staircase, breathing hard between snatches of conversation. Footfalls passed by the door and the couple worked their way up to the next *étage*. The couple's desultory remarks diminished. A door opened and then closed. Silence returned to the hotel. Out of the little window adjacent to the bed, several floors down via an airshaft, along the narrow alley to its mouth, a feeble klaxon marked the slow progress of a police Peugeot threading through traffic on the boulevard Clichy. On the way to some place else.

No, Akhmed thought. I cannot blame this man for my life.

He took a bird bath at the sink and soaped his split knuckles. It felt good. Then he gathered Bruce's effects and decamped.

That felt good, too. Akhmed had pulled off a bigger job than normal, and felt like thereby he'd improved on his circumstances. Which he had. Bruce's wallet, cellphone, watch, the opal ring, the credit cards, but especially the passport, brought Akhmed some thirty-five hundred euros.

He took the money and went home to his mother for a while.

It felt good, when he considered how this largesse had come about; which, soon enough, was never.

It took six weeks for the bruises to revert through purple, blue and yellow to the natural sallowness of Bruce's skin, better than two months for the two broken ribs to heal and for his piss to stop going pink except every once in a while, and even longer for the lousy French dentist to grind the posts and take the mould and design and build and fit and finally install a bridge for the two lower front teeth that had been knocked out. The guy didn't even wear latex gloves, for chrissakes, while he had his hands in Bruce's mouth, and he reeked of cigarettes. What the hell, Bruce wryly reflected, maybe it had become his destiny to have to pay for any kind of dirty behaviour, getting old isn't for sissies, and the dentist had to take his hands out so Bruce could laugh without choking on mirth.

No matter the time, however, for it took him the better part of three months to gather up a new passport and replacement credit cards – forget the keys to the French couple's apartment, which for some reason Akhmed had stolen too, even though he had no idea where Bruce lived. You think you can pay two bucks for a lousy key in Paris, like you can in the States? Forget it, mon vieux. It turns out that a French key, some of the designs of which are hundreds of years old, can easily cost a hundred euros. Some have to be hand-forged, for chrissakes. Losing your keys in Paris is a very big deal, very expensive. Dealing with a Parisian locksmith is very much like dealing with a hair-dresser: they're artists!

But that inconvenience, too, passed, and in the course of these things Bruce learned a lot about the French language, the French people, Paris, bureaucracy, and keys. He learned that a kidney is *un rein*. He learned that there are as many French words for keys as there are Eskimo words for ice. He already knew that a civil servant is called a *fonctionnaire*, but he discovered that, whereas such a beast is held in almost universal contempt, the true example of it is a proud creature, able to perform miracles on a whim. Not only that, but many of them are queer, they have parties and disposable income and houses in the country and, moreover, some of them know Paris like, surprise surprise, like Bruce knows lower Manhattan, inside and out.

In other words, by the time four or five months had passed, a whole new world had opened up. And before Bruce knew it, it was nearly time for him to go back to New York.

He had learned a lot in his stay in Paris. He retained a certain satisfaction. He had begun to run with a tonier crowd, too, much like the various crowds he'd occasionally run with in New York, which consisted for the most part of *boursiers*, for example, men who worked in the stock exchange; and bankers, other government officials, real estate agents, and so forth. Professionals.

But what he hadn't learned always lingered in the back of his mind. The polite doings of his new friends could be amusing. They enjoyed a cocktail and could talk – boy, could they talk. They knew wine and France and food. They knew contemporary culture, they knew a great deal about America, they knew a great deal about the long, complicated history of France.

Bruce noticed that his new friends smoothly, adroitly, and almost certainly avoided topics like

Vietnam, Algiers, Congo, the Middle East, and the hegemony of American consumerism. Finally, one night, one man among them who, though not uncivilised, nurtured some obvious antipathy towards him, drank enough to express loudly and clearly and in so many words that the reason nobody talked to Bruce about certain topics was that Americans don't know fuck-all about the rest of the world, and for the very simplest of reasons, which is that Americans don't care fuck-all about the rest of the world, because they only care about themselves, and, pay attention, forty per cent of American high-school students can't find their own fucking country on a fucking globe.

Bruce took umbrage. He suddenly found himself in the very uncomfortable position of defending not only himself, but his patrimony. Which was ridiculous. Why was it ridiculous? Because, in fact, as his arguments unravelled, his antagonist – hesitant at first, for he didn't want to make a scene, but, sensing that Bruce's entire political acts consisted of little more than know-nothing bluster – proved himself devastatingly correct. Bruce didn't know anything about the rest of the world. He supposed he'd allowed himself to lose track of the names of the President of Israel, for example, not to mention that of the leader of the Palestinians, forget Syria, even though the titular head of Syria had been there his entire adult life, and never mind the name of a single other so-called foreign leader. Bruce kept his head to the extent that he managed not to blurt out that he'd stopped voting ages ago, mainly so he would never be called for jury duty, but the fact of it stuck in the forefront of his mind and stayed there, hindering his wit to the extent that he could name no more than two out of three personalities prominent upon the political landscape of France itself, not even a woman conspicuous among French leaders friendly to the idiotic foreign policies of the United States, despite the great cost to her domestic popularity.

Finally, as much as the average French fairy with a drink in his hand appreciates a good political debate, the atmosphere at the party began to sag under the imbalance of the argument. *Cela suffit, Alain. Alors,* the man's friends began to say to him, back off, let's have a drink. And yeah, Bruce found himself saying, in English, I didn't come here to talk about politics, I came here to get laid.

A silence fell over the room. Bruce realised, too late, what he already well knew, that not only did damn near everybody in the room speak more English than he spoke French, but he had just lost the argument all over again.

Bonne chance! somebody observed, not too quietly, and a few too many people laughed a little too loudly and altogether genuinely.

No loss, Bruce told himself, struggling for composure, in the lift down to the street, alone except for a little lady in a sweater with a dog likewise, I never liked any of those besuited fucks anyway.

Though it was the last week of his scheduled tenure, Bruce paid but little mind to the details of his departure. The plane reservation had been secured at the beginning of the trip. Physically, he'd left but little impression on the apartment. He hadn't burned five sticks of wood from the quintal.

Increasingly, however, as the day approached, something nagged at him. He knew what it was. He'd been putting it off, why or how or when he hadn't bothered or been able to discern, but suddenly, with three days to go, his mind was made up.

He went to the ATM in the little triangular place and withdrew five hundred euros.

He took a late supper – it was long past dark – in the deserted bistro opposite the teller machine, drinking an entire carafe of Côtes du Rhône with his *pommes frites* and *steak pavé*, and only varied the routine by calling for a pricey *bas armagnac* with his coffee afterwards. *Vogue Homme*, an element of his habitude, remained face down beyond his place setting, unperused.

At half past midnight he headed up the rue de la Tour d'Auvergne. And did Bruce notice the five-gallon wooden molar hanging, brown roots and all, barely two metres above the sidewalk, marking a long-shuttered bar called La Dent Creuse, The Hollow Tooth, the French equivalent, as goes capacity for drink, of the hollow wooden leg? He did not. Just up the block, at rue des Martyrs, he took a right. All the shops were closed. Traffic was light.

At Pigalle, things were different. The never-moving neon wings of the Moulin Rouge loomed scarlet over a thronging abundance of tourists of sex and otherwise, as well as hustlers and pick-pockets and every sort of prostitute and dope dealer, as well as people like himself, on the way to some place else, more or less.

He took the alley past the hotel, up to the dead-end street. At the foot of the steps, which lead up to the rue des Abbesses, he took a left. The shadows were there. They rippled on the cobbles. The sound of high heels receded down the curve at the far end of the street. It had been nearly five months.

Akhmed was there.

So was Bruce.

They each had something, one for the other.

LA SHAMPOUINEUSE

JEROME CHARYN

I.

He lived in a honeycomb, a prison with wallpaper and a panoramic view. He could have climbed right into the graves of Maupassant and Maria Montez from his balcony window. But Calvin Morse wasn't supposed to climb. He wasn't supposed to walk or fly or leave his honeycomb. He was an accountant on the lam from federal prosecutors and a little gang of mob bankers and lawyers.

Until last week he worked for a factory that made faucets – faucets of silvered chrome – that went into every building put up by Joshua Lightning's own construction company. Lightning & Lightning was a kind of corporate octopus, but Calvin had been the full-time accountant for its largest affiliate, Lightning Faucets & Chrome. How could he have guessed that the ingenious way he cooked Joshua's books would be copied by Lightning & Lightning's other accountants, and that federal prosecutors would consider him the brains behind the whole octopus?

If he hadn't gone to Columbia with Josh, roomed with him for three years, he would have been disposed of, dumped into a truck, and become part of lower Manhattan's landfill. But Josh had pleaded Cal's case with the mob bankers, had convinced them that he could hide Cal, keep him out of harm's way. Josh would have preferred that he disappear into Bolivia or Brazil, where gringo prosecutors would never find him, but Paris had always been Cal's dreamland, ever since he read Baudelaire and Maupassant at Columbia.

He'd gone to work for Josh's dad right out of college, had to attend accounting school at night, and slave for Lightning Faucets & Chrome – he'd been married and divorced, had one daughter at Amherst and a second daughter at Yale, and all his vacations up until now had been packaged retreats that Lightning & Lightning put together and paid for: the Bahamas, Cape Cod, the Hemingway country of Key West.

Cal had five million in a retirement account, held at Lightning & Lightning's own private bank, but he was having a crisis long before federal prosecutors swooped down on Lightning's books, which were almost like fairy tales with elaborate fictional plots. He couldn't bear his accumulations of money. His daughters went to Joshua for their tuition, not to Cal. He'd always been absent, even while he was at Faucets & Chrome. He was a walking, talking filament of fire, a hot wire that could create or swallow up a whole column of numbers and categories – he was like a musical instrument that had learned to play itself. In fact, his only pleasure had come from his manoeuvrings with a sea of lines on a ledger book. He'd never been in dove, and his connection to his daughters was so ambiguous and remote that it too was at the point of disappearing.

But there was a touch of eccentricity to Cal – his passion for Paris, a city he had only seen once in a mad weekend whirl when he accompanied Joshua to a convention of faucet makers at some *palais* in the middle of nowhere – he'd barely had time for a pilgrimage to Baudelaire's grave, a hike in Montparnasse, a visit to the Dingo, where Hemingway had first met Scott Fitzgerald. Yet that weekend had sculpted Cal, defined him in some essential way – and his dream, or delirium, was to escape Lightning Faucets and live in that city of desire he knew so little about.

And now he hid in a luxurious apartment with a bird's-eye view of Maupassant. He hadn't realised that his flat on the rue Boulard would be just another tomb. Joshua had commanded him never to venture into the street – not even after midnight. All his meals were prepared by the concierge, a Portuguese woman who also dusted the apartment and did his laundry. He had 180 channels he could watch on a plasma screen that covered an entire wall. A call girl visited him on Tuesdays, a ravishing *métisse* with green eyes and mocha skin. Her name was Mélodie. She was a *figurante* at some theatre company in the provinces, could recite Molièere and Shakespeare, and talk to Cal about books until he was blue in the face. The sexual splendour she offered was beyond the realm of what he might have imagined, and yet something gnawed at him. Mélodie could deliver all the mechanics of love, even camaraderie and companionship, but it felt like the dress rehearsal for a play that Cal would never be in.

He had a suspicion that Mélodie might be spying on him, and he wondered if she was Joshua's own mulatto mistress. She knew things about Cal she ought not to have known, that he was a fanatic about fantasy baseball, had used his command of statistics to invent his own baseball league, where Babe Ruth could bat against Sandy Koufax, and Joe DiMaggio could duel with Willie Mays in centrefield – Cal's artistic trick was to merge time and space in his fantasy league, as if the whole history of baseball could collapse into one titanic season. He'd 'cooked' baseball with the same imaginative leap in which he'd cooked Lightning's books.

And so he would lie with Mélodie on his coverlet, the cemetery outside his window like some burning woods, and even as she devoured him with her green eyes, he couldn't wait until she left. But when he tried to stop seeing her, Josh suddenly appeared with a split of champagne.

'I don't believe in Mélodie Montesquieu,' Cal sang while he sipped. 'She belongs in fantasy baseball. She could play shortstop without her clothes. She'd win every game.'

'Don't knock the kid,' Joshua said. 'She visits you as a personal favour to me. Our people worry, worry that you'll crack. That you'll wander into some hole that belongs to the feds. Uncle Sam could haul your ass right back to the States.'

'And Mélodie writes reports and convinces your money-men that I'm more valuable to you alive than dead.'

'That's the equation – in a nutshell.'

2.

Josh had left him some mad money – a thousand euros, in case there was a sudden call from Lightning's lawyers to vacate the rue Boulard and hide somewhere else. He sat on the euros like a squirrel, slept with Mélodie, promised himself he would see a tiny piece of Paris before he died.

He had to deflect the concierge, who was Josh's own gatekeeper. He went down the back stairs, entered a garden with its own glass gazebo, climbed a wall that led him onto the rue Daguerre, a market street that emboldened Cal, made him feel that he'd discovered a little paradise of cafés and stalls and shoppers clutching little baskets composed entirely of string.

How much of a sin could it be to stroll among the shoppers, sit at a café like some hidden king of fantasy baseball? But he couldn't take the chance. Suppose the concierge saw him on one of her own shopping sprees? So he climbed back over the wall to his tomb above the cemetery. And after a few days he went on a second outing, to the cemetery itself, where he found Maupassant and Maria Monte: among graves that were scattered like broken teeth.

Montez was a sultry Technicolor queen of the 1940s who starred in a series of flicks about the harem girls and thieves of a Baghdad that rose up ludicrously on Hollywood's back lots. What he loved about Montez was her long silences even when she was asked to play Scheherazade. She could barely mouth a single line of dialogue – she belonged in fantasy baseball rather than Baghdad of the back lots. Perhaps he could remake Montez into a manager of some fantasy team. He had discovered her years ago in a late-night festival of B-movies, her face all aflame, her lipstick as red as lacquered blood, and Montez had remained with him, like a ghost at the very edge of sleep.

And then he saw her – not in the cemetery, but in a salon on the rue Daguerre, after Cal had decided to have his hair cut. The hairdresser herself couldn't intrigue him; it was the shampoo girl, Marie, who wore lipstick and nail polish right out of the *Arabian Nights*. She looked at Cal with her own Arabian eyes, and he muttered 'Maria Montez'.

He had a kindergarten command of French, but it didn't seem to matter with Marie. She sat

him down in her private throne where she sham-
pooed customers' hair, put a huge plastic napkin
over his shirt, clutched him around the ears, and
drew his head back into the hollow of a sink.

She rinsed his hair, poured shampoo on his
crown, and rubbed the shampoo into his scalp
with the palms of her hands. Then there was a
curious surprise – the shampoo girl began to
massage his scalp with her ten fingers, like ten
little animals with their own moist mouths. Cal
had never considered until that moment how alive
his scalp was in all its bumpy terrain.

He never wanted to leave Marie's throne. He
couldn't have told you how long she had massaged
his scalp, and when she rinsed his hair, Cal
suddenly felt his own strange isolation – he was
more connected to a shampoo girl and her ten
fingers than he had ever been to his wife, his
mistresses, his daughters, and Josh.

3.

He didn't have to get his hair cut each time; he
could simply have a shampooing with the *fille*, as
everybody called her – the salon's own little girl
who would never graduate, never grow up into a
full-fledged hairdresser. The other girls in the
salon poked fun at Cal, this perverse little
American who looked like a hobo; his cuffs were
frayed, his trousers wrinkled, his shoes beginning
to unravel. He was Marie's one and only 'fiance',

offering her his own head of hair like some wild flower that had to be rinsed and stroked.

They did have a conversation of sorts, but they could just as well have been the inmates of a madhouse with its own elemental language of long silences. She called him 'Monsieur', and he discovered with a series of groping questions that she lived in one of Paris' poorest *banlieues* with her parents and three older brothers. She herself had hardly gone to school, but would rather wash men's hair than scrub kitchen floors or bathe the bodies of old people in some sanatorium.

It was hard for Cal to manoeuvre while he sat on Marie's throne, but she did agree to meet with him one afternoon during her lunch hour. They bought sandwiches at a bistro on the rue Daguerre and smuggled them into the cemetery.

He couldn't explain his affection for Marie. They had little to talk about. The rigid rules and laws of fantasy baseball would have baffled her, and she'd never heard of Baudelaire. And while he blabbered in her ear, sang to her about the mysteries of Maria Montez, she scratched the side of his face – gently, gently – with a polished fingernail; it was the most erotic gesture he had ever experienced. They kissed for twenty minutes right on the Allée Transversale, in front of tourists with their little guidebooks to all the notable graves, and Cal could hear his own heart pound like some maddening earthquake.

She laughed and wiped the lipstick off his mouth, and led him back by hand to her salon.

She had never once pronounced his name. He fumbled against her – could he ride home with her on the Métro?

'*Non, chéri.*'

She called him darling but wouldn't pronounce his name. She did promise to meet him for another stroll in the cemetery. But when he returned to Marie's salon the very next afternoon, three sombre men were waiting for him. They looked like taller, harder replicas of Marie, each with a pencil-thin moustache. He searched inside the window – Marie wasn't near her throne.

The three men kicked him like a dog and left Cal lying on the rue Daguerre. The concierge had to bring him back to his apartment. She washed his face with a little rag. She'd lived in London for a year, and could admonish him in his own language.

'Monsieur has been a bad boy,' she said. 'Monsieur is not supposed to kiss *la shampouineuse.*'

Cal loved the sound of it – *shampouineuse*.

He was crazy about the *shampouineuse* of the rue Daguerre. But how would he ever find her again? She disappeared from the salon, and none of the hairdressers would offer him a clue. And then Mélodie Montesquieu stopped visiting him on Tuesdays, stopped visiting him at all; she was his courier to the world outside his little tomb.

Lightning & Lightning had decided to shut him down. He'd have to flee, but where could he go? He called American Express – his account had been frozen. He called his bank collect – his new balance was one dollar and twenty-six cents. And all the codes to his retirement accounts had been changed. He was locked out of his own past, like some mechanical monster without a persona.

He rode in a cab to the American Express offices on the rue Scribe with the possibility that his passport might get him a line of credit or some cash. But men with razored moustaches lurked about, reminding him of Marie's brothers, and he couldn't get near any of the managers.

Mélodie awaited him when he returned to his tomb on the rue Boulard. She sat smoking a cigarette that filled his bedroom with a foul odour and nearly burnt his nostrils. But she didn't bask on his bed like some Delilah without her clothes.

'This is your apartment, isn't it?' he asked.

'Mine and Josh's. I'm married, and this is where we meet.'

'Your name isn't Mélodie, and you're not an actress.'

'I'm a housewife who does tricks on the side. My name is none of your business.' Her green eyes grew bolder as his grew opaque, and she apologised for her bluntness. 'I'm sorry, Cal. Mélodie is the name I use with all my tricks.'

'He means to kill me,' Cal said.

'It's not that simple. Let's just say he's decided to abandon you. And you'll have to fish around on your own.'

'Fish with what? I had five million I can't touch. I—'

'He thinks you should run to Morocco.'

'Why Morocco?' he sang in his own sad voice.

'Because it's easy to get lost.'

Lightning & Lightning would kill him as soon as he landed, hire someone to tear Cal limb from limb.

'I'm staying right here,' he told her.

'Darling, your little *shampouineuse* can't save you. She can hardly save herself. Her brothers heat her black and blue.'

'And who tipped them off?'

'I did,' she said with her own kind of truculence. 'You weren't supposed to leave the building – darling, wasn't I enough?'

'You're Josh's girl.'

'Ah,' she said, her big toe riding up his trouser leg. 'Wouldn't you like a freebie, Cal?'

'No.'

4.

He was running out of euros. Perhaps they were hoping to starve him to death. They toyed with Cal, left souvenirs on his dining-room table while he slept. An old *Photoplay* magazine with Maria Montez on the cover – it must have cost a fortune, a collector's item from the forties, with a note attached. Keep away from cemeteries, Cal. You won't survive your next trip.

But he did rush into the Montparnasse cemetery, hoping he might find Marie, even in some spectral form, floating above the tilted tomb of Maupassant. Instead, he found Melodie Montesquieu in the company of two suspicious men – assassins he assumed, handpicked for the job. They could borrow a shovel from some gravedigger and bury Cal next to Maria Montez.

He nosed past Mélodie and the two men, saw the mayhem in their eyes, and left the Montpamasse cemetery. He had a gelato at an ice-cream parlour on the rue Daguerre, bought an orange that he peeled with his fingers. But a shiver travelled up his spine when he saw Mélodie and the two men enter his own building on the rue Boulard. They would wait for Cal behind the door, massacre him with Mélodie's kitchen knives.

Cal had lost his lair, and he'd have to loop across Paris like some grey wolf. He went to the Dingo, sat on its cramped seats, but he couldn't conjure up the ghost of Scott Fitzgerald with his first or second glass of Sancerre. He checked into a fleabag hotel on the rue d'Odessa – the young people flocking in the little square outside his window hypnotised Cal with their swaying bodies, and he watched them for hours.

But the grey wolf had to return to the one street that mattered to him – the rue Daguerre. He promised himself that he wouldn't look into the window of Marie's salon, but he did look. And the *shampouineuse* was at her station, the little throne that her customers sat in while she washed their hair.

Marie had welts under her eyes, bruises printed on her face. The bell attached to the door clacked as Cal entered the salon. The hairdressers were not happy to see him. Still, Cal sat down on Marie's throne. She clipped the plastic bib to his collar, but would not offer Cal the simplest sign of recognition. The *shampouineuse* was like a machine with bruised eyes.

'Monsieur,' she said, gripping him by the cars and pulling his head back into the basin. The first drop of shampoo excited him. His scalp burned with a liquid fire. Then her hands caressed the soft pit of skin that covered his crown. He blinked, his head rising above the basin for a moment – Mélodie and her two assassins stood outside the window. But Cal no longer cared. His head sank back into the basin. He would rupture time with his own implacable logic. All he had to do was convince the *shampouineuse* never to take her fingers out of his hair.

GUY GEORGES' FINAL CRIME

ROMAIN SLOCOMBE

At work, in the design department, in the corridors and the canteen too, it was all the women were talking about. The RTL announcer had been first to broadcast the news, at 7 a.m. on that Thursday 26th March 1998. And the other radio stations soon swung into action.

> After long months of investigations, the police have finally named France's most wanted man, the serial killer of east Paris. His name is Guy Georges. Thousands of copies of his photograph have been circulated to the police; every officer has been issued with one. A manhunt has been launched, his arrest is now only a matter of hours . . .

Julie Coray, sitting at a table at the back of the *Reader's Digest* magazine canteen in Bagneux, a southern suburb of Paris, raises her glass of mineral water and smiles at her colleagues: 'At last I'll be able to go home in peace tonight. It's been horrific, especially on the nights we're going to press: my road's really badly lit and when you come out of the Métro around midnight or one in the morning, I can't tell you how awful it is . . .'

'Where d'you live, Julie?' asked Farida, the new editorial assistant.

'Between Denfert and Gaîté. Rue Cels, next to Montparnasse cemetery . . . In the fourteenth.'

Sylvie Mariani, the picture editor, shrugged her shoulders: 'You weren't in much danger, anyway: that's outside the killer's stamping ground. The guy only operated around Bastille . . .'

Slightly miffed, Julie cut herself a piece of ham and mushroom pie, muttering: 'Yeah, but still . . .'

Farida, in her guttural Maghrebi accent, came to her rescue: 'Well, I'd like to see you do it, Sylvie . . . You're married and you go home early to feed your kids. But for four months women have been scared stiff, I swear, at night it's terrifying. You let yourself into your building looking over your shoulder in case some guy with a knife's about to jump you and force you to go up with him . . . Bastille or anywhere else, it's the same, I don't see the difference. Once you've been raped and murdered, you've been raped and murdered. It's too late to put up your hand and say "Hey, mister, that's cheating, this isn't your patch!"'

Farida had a point and her colleagues all giggled, Sylvie included. They could laugh, now that the nightmare was over. A nightmare for Paris's female population that had been going on since the end of November, with the discovery – by her own father – of Estelle Magd's body, raped, her throat slit, in her home. After years of bewildering judicial negligence and bureaucratic incompetence, the police had finally made the link between different cases that had strange similarities. Examining magistrates working on rape and murder cases that bore the hallmark of the same sexual criminal had agreed to share the evidence in their possession. Now DNA test results were being compared in public and private laboratories all over France. Mainstream newspapers and magazines had got hold of the story, at the risk of unleashing a panic: a bloodthirsty wolf, a psychopathic killer – he was North African, Egyptian to be precise, they said (on account of a footprint discovered in a pool of blood, the second toe longer than the big toe) – was terrorising Paris, slitting the throats of lone, pretty young women in car parks or in their homes. A steady stream of suspects were questioned but to no avail, photos on file of thousands of offenders were shown to the only survivor who'd been able to get a good look at the killer, but in vain. Photofits of the olive-skinned man followed, none of them reliable. Gossip and fanciful accusations threatened to jam the switchboard of the Paris murder squad headquarters, women trembled with fear, and gallant men saw their colleagues of the supposedly weaker sex all the way home at night . . .

And twenty-four-year-old Julie Coray, a striking brunette from Rennes who'd recently arrived in Paris, landing this rather well-paid job as graphic designer for the French edition of Reader's Digest Select Editions, would shudder every evening as she inserted her key in the lock of her small studio flat, on the top floor of a dilapidated building on rue Cels.

From the neighbouring desk, Robert Flageul – usually in charge of rewriting dramatic first-hand accounts and other 'human interest stories' that the review pre-digested each month with the aim of bringing tears to pensioners' eyes – cut in, addressing the picture editor: 'Plus you had it all wrong, Sylvie. 'The beast of Bastille', 'the east Paris killer', it's all just tabloid cliché, I shouldn't have to tell you that. The first crime attributed to this Guy Georges was Pascale Escarfail, the humanities student, murdered on the 24th of January '91 in her flat in the fourteenth arrondissement, on rue Delambre, just round the corner from Julie, which is a long way from Bastille, and more south than east. And other times he rampaged through the thirteenth, the tenth, the nineteenth . . . His turf seems pretty vast to me. Not to mention the assaults he must have committed before they'd made the link with him . . .'

Back in design, Julie Coray saw that her boss, the magazine's art director, wasn't yet back from his lunch with an illustrator at the Japanese restaurant next to the motorway, below the RER station.

Knowing Gilles – a cigar-smoker and something of a foodie, too – he wouldn't return before 3 p.m., so she had time to make a call before carrying on with the layout. Julie rang the mobile number of Claire, her best friend, a Breton like her. Claire Le Flohic was in her sixth year of medicine and was doing her internship at Cochin Hospital.

She answered after the fourth ring. 'Oh, it's you? Your name didn't come up . . . You're lucky I answered, I was about to reject the call, I'm on duty till tonight.'

'I'm calling from the land line, at the magazine. Did you hear the news?'

The young intern answered in a voice quivering with excitement: 'You bet! In fact, I wasn't allowed to tell anyone but I'd known for two days they were going to get him. My cousin's working at the Nantes lab that found the killer's DNA. They'd been on the case for weeks, they compared it manually with 3,500 specimens before they found it. Suddenly there it was, just like that, bingo! They couldn't believe their eyes! Amazing . . . !'

Twenty-four years old like Julie, Claire was a true-crime fan and passionate about forensic medicine, which she intended to specialise in. She was already pestering the professor to let her attend autopsies in criminal cases – in theory, off limits to trainees – during which Claire impressed him with her knowledge of heparic temperature, rigor mortis and dermabrasions, as well as marks from blows and wounds. The case of the 'east Paris killer' literally fascinated her, and Claire was convinced that she herself resembled one of the psychopath's victims, found raped and murdered in an underground car park on boulevard Reuilly in January 1994: Catherine Rocher, a pretty, twenty-seven-year-old marketing assistant. 'A tall girl with long brown hair, well mine's more chestnut and *very* long, but we both have a straight nose, a long smiling face and we're full of life! The killer goes for that kind of girl. If I were a psychological profiler, I'd infer that he'd been very unhappy when he was young, his parents probably knocked him about, he had a difficult childhood, is unemployed, has already done time for rape or assault, he lives in a squat, maybe prostitutes himself and is ashamed of it. He's angry with the whole world and especially when he sees a beautiful girl go by, looking happy, he can't help it, he's compelled to follow her home, tie her up and rape her . . . And afterwards, he slashes her, aiming for the neck. There was blood all over the fl—'

Julie shuddered in disgust, thinking her friend a bit twisted for revelling in such macabre details. It was as if, from fantasising about this series of sexual murders, she'd begun to imagine herself as one of the victims, and got a kick out of it. 'You're right, I'm a real perv,' Claire laughed.

'Well anyway,' Julie interrupted her, 'it's finally over . . . We can breathe . . .'

Through the bay window, she watched the light play on the buds of the trees on boulevard Louis Pasteur. It was a beautiful spring afternoon. This weekend, she'd go for a walk in the Bois de Boulogne, or the Luxembourg Gardens, or treat herself to a movie with Claire . . .

'Don't you believe it, darling!' The medical student's tone turned menacing. 'Nothing's over till he's arrested! Right now the cops only have his name and his photo . . . And even if they catch him and he gets life without remission, he'll be out after twenty years, you'll see, if he doesn't escape earlier! And then, when he's out, he'll start again. I've really studied his case: this 'Guy Georges', since now we know his name, is incurable. He's not a madman, more an intelligent thug. He looks normal, maybe even likeable, it's just he can't resist, it's in his past or his genes, *he has to kill*. Once a month if possible. He's dodged the police so often he thinks he's invincible. And at those moments, the wretched girl in front of him, tied up, weak and terrified, is just an object, not a human being. An object of rape and then murder.'

'Claire, please stop . . .'

The intern chuckled. 'OK, I'm stopping, you poor thing. But nothing's over, you'll see. He knows he's a marked man, he could get even more dangerous, take a girl hostage, I don't know . . . So you still have to be extra careful going home tonight, OK?'

Julie rolled her eyes and pulled a face.

'All right, all right. And if I'm too scared when I come out of the station, I'll call you to come and escort me to rue Cels, OK?'

The two friends burst out laughing, blew each other kisses down the phone and ended the call at the same time.

The afternoon went by like a dream. Concentrating on the Mac screen, on her photos, titles and fonts, and files to be sent to the printer, Julie wasn't aware of time passing. It was the end of March, the days were growing longer, but eventually the light faded ... At 7 p.m., Gilles stood up, put on his raincoat and waved goodbye to his assistant. 'Right, see you tomorrow, Julie. I'll leave you to finish off the cover. Send it to Magnus, wait for his approval, then you can go home.'

'But . . .'

'Don't worry, you'll be fine. See you then, bye!'

Magnus Laksson, a Finn who'd settled in the US, supervised the art direction for all the international editions. His trenchant opinions, utter lack of diplomacy, and ultra-conservative view of what *Reader's Digest* should be in America and elsewhere, made him the *bête noire* of art directors working under him. Julie sent him the mockup of the cover accompanied by a few polite phrases in her approximate English and waited for the verdict, which, with the time difference (Laksson had no doubt gone for lunch), only arrived on her screen at 10.30 p.m., French time.

The Finn *hated* the cover.

The response, in two laconic, brutal sentences, reminded Gilles and Julie that the cover should never allude visually to the issue's central theme but must be kept to some neutral and soothing image – and demanded a new one before the end of the day.

Julie didn't dare disturb Gilles at home so, valiant Breton that she was, she laboured over a new version of the cover which took until twenty-five past midnight, sent it to the US and shut down her computer. If she stayed to wait for the American reaction, she'd miss the last train home from Bagneux. And she didn't have enough money on her for a taxi to Montparnasse at the night rate, which was at least sixty francs. Julie ran down the empty corridors, her coat under her arm, to the foyer where the North African night watchman, deep in a sports paper, nodded at her vaguely. She raced down the front steps and set off across a deserted Bagneux, in the glow of the streetlights, into an icy wind she hadn't expected. Anticipating going home much earlier, Julie had even put on a miniskirt today, something she hadn't dared do in four months, terrified by the possibility of a nocturnal encounter with the Ripper. But the morning news had reassured her on that score . . .

Her heels clicked on the tarmac, she ran through the labyrinth of narrow streets, lined with peaceful small pensioners' houses, as far as the main road which she crossed, defying the red pedestrian signal, between two cars hurtling at well over 50 miles an hour which honked warnings at her. The train indicator board in the empty station showed the Paris train was at the platform.

'Oh no,' Julie groaned, inserting her season ticket into the machine.

The 'doors closing' signal sounded as she reached the platform. She ran as if her life depended on it, leapt between the sliding doors, forcing her way through, and she was inside, panicky and breathless, frantically tugging at the handle of her bag which was wedged between the strips of rubber, as the train pulled away.

The few passengers in the compartment stared at her briefly before falling back into the apathy of exhausted workers or depressed night owls. She flopped onto a seat, her heart thudding, and watched vaguely as the suburban lights and bare station platforms slipped past. Ravenous (she hadn't eaten since midday), sleepy, her head nodding, she nearly dozed off and missed her stop. Denfert-Rochereau. She jumped up and just made it through the hissing doors.

Because she'd got on at the end of the train, Julie, walking along the platform towards the exit, came first to the narrow staircase that led directly to the square, in the former railway station converted to a regional express station. Which would mean having to cross the vast Denfert-Rochereau traffic intersection in the wind and cold

. . . Julie opted for the next exit, which connected to the Métro, lines 4 and 6, and would bring her out of the station as close to her home as possible, with only rue Froidevaux to walk up to rue Cels.

In the bowels of the empty station, she used her ticket again to exit the row of ticket barriers and turned, following signs to the Porte d'Orléans line. It was a complicated network of corridors but the young provincial woman was becoming familiar with it. At the next intersection she had to turn left, then sharp right towards the escalator. It was in this last corridor that she saw him.

Julie considered herself good at remembering faces, and she'd studied the photofit of the 'east Paris killer' in the media many times. The only difference was that the man had grown a thin moustache. Everything else matched the description given by the survivor. In his thirties, tall, athletic-looking, lithe, the dark skin of a North African. Closely cropped hair, practically shaved. Their eyes met just as he drew level with her. For that fraction of a second, Julie detected the glimmer of interest in the man's eyes, saw the quick, sidelong glance at her slender legs below her miniskirt. She hurried on, short of breath, looking down, her expression as neutral as possible. Her heart was pounding wildly. What an appalling coincidence, what terrifying bad luck . . . Just as long as he didn't turn round now and follow her! Julie didn't dare look over her shoulder. She let her shaky body be carried by the escalator, praying she'd find an RATP employee still at the ticket window. It was almost one in the morning. The last trains had probably all left. She pushed the heavy glass door and saw with annoyance that the ticket office was closed, the blind was down, the lights out. Now she only had to walk up the last flight of steps to the square, where the wind was gusting hard and clouds scudded across the sky, revealing glimpses of a perfectly round, wan moon. It illuminated the powerful musculature of the Denfert Lion, which watched over the middle of the square in bronze impassivity.

On the other side of avenue General Leclerc, one of the severe twin buildings of the former 'Barrière d'Enfer' tollgate housed the entrance to the sinister Catacombs – the place where, in 1785, the Prefect Lenoir dumped millions of skeletons, hauling them from the charnel house of the Innocents in macabre cartloads and filling the air of Les Halles with a foul stench. Julie turned left, walked past the gate to the little park and reached the corner of rue Froidevaux, just before the taxi rank where one solitary vehicle was waiting. After crossing the road, attempting to look natural, she half turned round.

The olive-skinned man was there, standing at the top of the station steps, lighting a cigarette and looking to left and right. He saw the trembling young woman't silhouette and, putting away his lighter, strode deliverately in the direction Julie had taken.

She nearly fainted. He'd spotted her. Singled her out as his next victim. At this stage of the game, he had nothing left to lose. Wanted by every police force, accused of six or seven rapes and murders; what difference would one more or less make to the sentence he'd get? Guy Georges wanted to experience the pleasure of a terrified, pretty young woman one last time, thrust his penis into her and then his blade, before ending his life behind bars. The full moon was beckoning, arousing his powerful killer instincts . . . Julie, after hesitating and deciding not to get into the taxi, feverishly repeated to herself Claire's words of advice, as she scurried beneath the trees which were bending in the wind: '*If you notice you're being followed, never go straight home. Go and sit in a public place, a café, wait for the guy to realise he's been seen and give up.*' In front of her, rue Froidevaux, the quickest way to rue Cels, stretched out along the cemetery walls. Ill-lit, gloomy, completely deserted. A real death-trap, an invitation to murder . . .

Julie was beginning to understand what the prostitutes of Whitechapel must have felt, wandering anxiously in the fog, straining to her the footsteps of Jack the Ripper. Changing her route, she turned left into rue Boulard, then walked up rue Daguerre. The shops were all closed, but still, she'd be nearer her building, where she was hoping to see, two streets before hers. La Bélière, a night bistro, usually open at this late hour.

A quick sideways glance told her that the man

in denim, whose cigarette made a red dot in the shadows, had also turned into rue Daguerre.

Further up the narrow street, she saw, far away like a safe haven, a reassuring port in the storm, La Bélière, its lights blazing. Walking faster, Julie pulled her mobile from her bag, pressed 'contacts' and then 'call' as soon as Claire's name appeared. Her friend absolutely *had* to come to meet her in the café. Cochin Hospital, like Claire's flat, very close to her work, was only fifteen minutes away on foot. The killer, who only attacked lone women, would give up and go away if he saw them together.

'Hi, this is Claire Le Flohic's phone. I can't speak to you right now, but leave me a short message and I . . .'

Putting the phone away, Julie pushed open the door of the smoky bistro. There were hardly any customers.

'We're about to close, miss,' warned the owner, who was drying glasses behind his bar.

Julie clasped her hands: 'Please, just a coffee,' she begged. 'I'm meeting a friend, she won't be long.'

She sat down at a table towards the back, near a window. Took out her mobile again and toyed with it. Her coffee was brought, along with the till receipt. She paid immediately. Just as the waitress left her table, Julie saw the olive-skinned man enter, sit on a bar stool near the door and order a drink. Julie looked down at the steaming coffee, the bill, her hand quivering over her mobile. Then she pressed 'call' again.

The voicemail message again. She listened to the end this time and when it was her turn to speak, after the beep, whispered into the phone: 'Claire, it's Julie. Listen . . . Call me back as soon as you get this, it's urgent. You have to come and meet me, I'm in La Bélière on rue Daguerre. I don't dare go home, I don't know what to do. Claire, I'm scared . . .'

She ended the call, making sure to keep the mobile on. Minutes went by. Julie gulped her coffee. It was still scalding, and very strong. At the bar, Guy Georges was chatting with the owner, a glass of beer in his hand. 'What a moron that man is,' Julie said to herself. 'Can't he see the guy looks exactly like the photofit? He could at least make a discreet call to the police . . . But hey, he's a man, what does he care, he can't understand the terror Parisian women have been living with for four months . . .'

Claire's voice came back to her, telling the story – which she seemed to delight in – of the attack endured by Elisabeth O, the only victim kept prisoner by the killer to have come out alive . . .

The girl was going home late, after spending the evening with friends . . . She arrives at the entrance to her building, punches in the door code . . . crosses a courtyard, goes through a second door and up the stairs . . . On the first floor, where her flat is, she hears the entrance door to

337

the building slam shut. Then, hurried steps on the staircase, and a shadow jumps on her . . . The attacker puts a knife to her throat and she hears a hoarse voice say: 'Don't shout, don't move. Open your door.' Terrified, Elisabeth obeys. The door closes behind them, the guy immediately tries to reassure her: 'If you behave yourself, you won't get hurt. I'm on the run. I just need to sleep here for a few hours. I'll be off in the morning.' The flat was a duplex, with the bedroom on the lower level. They go down together . . . He'll have to tie up his prisoner, Guy Georges apologises, so he can sleep . . . He lets her smoke a last cigarette, then starts to bind her wrists, chatting all the while. Despite his North African appearance, he has no accent. She asks his name. He answers: 'Eric'. 'You don't look like an Eric,' she observes. Irritated, he growls: 'Just call me Flo.' Then he takes off his shoes, settles down as if he really does want to sleep. It's completely dark in the bedroom, but a light's still on in the hall . . . The killer gets irritated again, and goes to switch it off. In the meantime, Elisabeth, who's surreptitiously managed to free her hands, opens the window and jumps into the yard, running off down the street . . .

Julie, who was spinning out her coffee while she recalled Claire's story, looked up. Surprise: the man was no longer at the bar, the owner was alone, wiping it down. The man had left. Julie couldn't believe it. The killer had lost heart, seeing her talking on her mobile and clearly waiting for someone. Yes, of course . . . And anyway, she now acknowledged, maybe it wasn't Guy Georges after all . . . Her imagination was playing tricks on her . . . A photofit isn't necessarily faithful . . . If it was really true to life, the cops would have caught him ages ago . . .

The other customers were getting up to go.

'This time, we're closing, young lady!' the owner called as he locked his till.

Julie was back outside in the icy wind, nervously inspecting both sides of the road. The customers were laughing as they walked away, the bistro's metal shutter crashed down with a painful grating sound. She pulled on her gloves, shivering. Steam formed in front of her mouth. Giving up on Claire, Julie turned right, walking back up the road towards her building. She passed the picture framer's, the accordion shop, and turned right at the corner of the bakery Le Moulin de la Vierge. Julie was now in rue Fermat, practically on her doorstep.

Crossing the road in front of the traffic wardens' station, all closed up of course, she realised she was completely alone. No sounds of voices or steps. The area was desolate. She need only stop at 5 rue Cels, press in her door code, push open the door, slip under the porch and cross the courtyard to the staircase. Which she did as quickly as possible. She only had two floors to go when she heard the outer door slam shut. She should have heard it a little earlier. Then rapid steps on the staircase.

Her heart beating so hard she thought it was going to burst, Julie ran up to the fourth floor, the last, charging into the narrow corridor of the attic rooms. The fluid, quick steps were coming up the stairs, closer and closer. She grabbed the keys from her bag, trembling, had trouble inserting the right key in the lock. The second the door was finally open, a shape rushed at her and shoved her roughly inside. Julie stumbled, with a squeal. The door slammed.

'Don't shout. Don't move.'

Some groping around, then the man found the switch. Light shone from the ceiling, revealing the North African man in his jean jacket. Julie opened her mouth, tried to scream (*The ones who got away*, Claire repeated, *were the ones who screamed their heads off. The man ran for it . . .*), but couldn't. No sound came out.

'Don't be afraid,' Guy Georges declared. 'I don't mean you any harm. I just need a roof for the night, that's all. I'll be off early in the morning.'

She nodded, her eyes filled with tears.

'You see, when I saw you in the Métro, I fell for you straight away. I need help, you're beautiful, you look kind. I'm homeless, my landlord threw me out because I'm three months behind with the rent . . .'

340

Julie went on nodding her head, sniffing.

'Don't cry. Take off your coat.'

She obeyed, still trembling. Threw the coat over the corner of the sofa that she and Claire had gone to buy last week, at Ikea.

He sat on a chair, lit a cigarette.

Julie stammered: 'What . . . What's your name?'

'Florent. My mother's French, my father's Algerian.'

Her heart sank. Florent . . . Flo. Doubt was no longer possible. The name he'd given Elisabeth before she escaped. She was in the presence of Guy Georges. The *prisoner* of Guy Georges. The Beast of Bastille . . .

Now she knew what was in store. Claire had told her enough times:

> He ties the girl up, trying to reassure her. Then he takes out a knife and rips her clothes. His usual method is to slice the bra between the cups. That's his serial killer 'signature'. Then he slashes her knickers, on the side. He tells the girl to suck him, then he rapes her. Finally, he starts stabbing, violently, going for the neck . . .

Since she couldn't scream, Julie attempted to soften him up.

Seem friendly. Human. That way, maybe . . .

The ones who were nice to him, who did whatever he said – like Catherine Rocher who gave him her credit card, with the pin number – it was no use. They're all dead.

'Would . . . Would you like a coffee?'
Guy Georges smiled. 'Good idea.'
Shaking, Julie went to the kitchen area. She took out an aluminium saucepan, turned on the tap, poured in cold water. Lit the gas (she broke four matches before managing to light one). Then, standing on tiptoe, she took the packet of coffee from the cupboard.
'Do you want a hand?'
'N-no thank you.'

My forensic medicine professor performed the autopsies on three of the victims. He told me that to reach the vertebrae, having gone through the throat, required tremendous strength . . .

Or a tremendous hatred of women. Of women, or the whole world . . .
Julie struggled to open the filter and put it in the plastic cone over the coffee pot. Poured ground coffee into the filter. Poured in double the amount before she realised.
'What do you do?' asked Guy Georges, behind her.
'G-graphic designer for a magazine . . . You?'

'I was working in a Japanese restaurant, washing up . . . But I got sick of it, I didn't go back and they fired me. Can I help with the cups?'

She moved aside.

'No, stay there . . . Please.'

In Julie's handbag, the phone began to ring. Beating her to it, Guy Georges fell on the bag, opened it, found the mobile, pressed the red button. The ring tone broke off. He put the phone in the top pocket of his jean jacket.

'You can call your friends back tomorrow,' he smiled. 'After I've gone . . .'

The water was boiling in the pan. Julie turned off the gas, poured the water onto the coffee. She took two cups and two saucers from the kitchen cabinet and two spoons from the drawer. She turned back to the centre of the tiny studio flat and, making the spoon quiver, put a cup and a saucer on the coffee table, in front of the sofa.

What would he use to tie her up?

Usually, he finds shoelaces in the flat. And he brings his own gaffer tape . . .

The coffee had almost finished filtering. Julie threw the filter into the sink and picked up the pot of black, boiling liquid.

Which pocket was he hiding the gaffer tape in? And the knife? And when would he say 'I'm sorry, but I'm going to have to tie you up and gag you for the night'?

After the coffee?

Guy Georges, still with his reassuring smile (but his eyes were cold), raised his cup towards her, holding the edge of the saucer. Julie flung the contents of the coffee pot straight into his face.

He let out a howl. Leapt up from the chair, which toppled over behind him. He lurched forward, his face dripping with black streaks and his skin visibly reddening. He walked forward, hands out in front of him. His big killer's hands . . .

Julie turned back to the cooker, grabbed the enormous iron frying pan given her by Grandma Coray, who lived on the Brittany coast.

And brought it down, with all the strength she possessed, on the Bastille killer's shaved head. Again and again. A red mist passed before her eyes. The man had fallen to his knees, and uttered a groan between every thud of metal to his skull.

By the time Julie Coray had recovered her wits, Guy Georges was no longer moving. A large pool of blood was seeping across the carpet, mixed with the spatterings of coffee.

Julie went to vomit in the sink. Nor having eaten, all she brought up was a little bitter bile. Wiping her mouth and face with a cloth, she went back to the lifeless body.

A wallet was sticking out of the front pocket of the killer's jeans.

Overcoming her revulsion, Julie tried to find a pulse on the man's right wrist. Nothing. She placed her fingers on the carotid artery. Nothing there either. Finally, she decided to pull out the wallet, and opened it.

She found an identity card in the name of Florent Chétoui, born 22 September 1967 in Blida (Algeria). And a pay slip from the restaurant Delices d'Osaka, rue de la Croix-Nivert, Paris 15, with a short letter of dismissal.

Julie's mobile began to ring again. In the front pocket of Florent Chétoui's jacket. Fighting waves of nausea, the young woman turned the inert body over and retrieved the phone. Big blisters were swelling the face, turning it a purplish red.

'Julie? You OK?'

Claire.

'Yes, well . . . I'm OK. I think . . .'

'It didn't sound like it. Your message, on my voicemail . . .'

'Yes, I'm OK . . . Better.'

'Did you see, they got him, huh?'

'What? Got who?'

'Guy Georges of course! Didn't you listen to the news? Two cops recognised him and caught him, softly softly, early in the afternoon. He was coming out of Blanche Métro station, went into a Monoprix . . . They cornered him by the perfume counter,' she chuckled.

'. . .'

'Apparently he didn't struggle or anything . . .'

Stepping over the body, Julie rushed to the TV, pressed the button. She caught the start of the late-night news on TFI. First the presenter's voice, then his smiling face:

> . . . freely confessed to the murders of Pascale E, in 1991, and Magali S, in 1997. Police are continuing to question him. According to the police, Guy Georges is not North African but mixed race, Afro-European, and only vaguely resembled the two photofits . . .

Julie had another urge to vomit. She turned down the volume and picked up the mobile again.

What were they talking about, when she had a man's body in her attic studio in the fourteenth arrondissement? A man she'd just killed, thinking she was acting in self-defence . . .

Was that Guy Georges' fault, or Julie Coray's?

It was all unbelievably unfair.

She had to think hard before calling the police.

Tomorrow, it was Julie Coray who'd be front page news. Unless . . .

Maybe Claire had the answer.

Dear Claire.

Breton women are strong. They help each other out. If Claire was coming from Cochin, she could borrow a dissection saw from there . . . Julie eyed the roll of 30-litre bin liners in the open kitchen cabinet, under the sink.

'Claire . . .'

'Yes . . .'

'I've got a *big* favour to ask you . . . If you could come now . . .'

A sigh.

'Oh, you poor thing . . . I called you because I turned my phone on again and got your message. I couldn't sleep, they've stuffed me with painkillers . . . I'm in Cochin, with a long-leg cylinder cast . . .'

'A what?'

'A long-leg cylinder cast. The kind that goes all the way up your leg from the foot to the top of the thigh. I got hit by a taxi crossing the road outside the hospital, just after we spoke, ar midday today . . . D'you realise, I'm in hospital *in my own department*! It's a pain . . . In plaster for two months! I'm sorry, but I think you'll have to cope on your own like a big girl . . .'

Letting the phone fall to her side, Julie Coray straightened up, dazed, and stared at the corpse for a long time. The broken skull, the dented frying pan, the overturned cup and saucer, the coffee pot she'd thrown, smashed to smithereens, the puddle of red, glistening blood with black swirls, reflecting the light bulb on the ceiling. Then her eyes turned back to the TV where the TFI newscaster opened his arms before passing to the next topic. Julie turned up the sound.

. . . that's all we can say for the moment on what's been today's main news story. Guy Georges will never commit another crime. The spectre no longer haunts Paris, women are safe again and can look forward to the future with a smile!

Putting the mobile back to her ear, Julie wished her friend goodnight and a speedy recovery, promised to visit her in hospital very soon, ended the call, left the TV on for background noise – and pulled from the cupboard a plastic sheet, a broom, a bucket and a floor cloth.

On rue Cels, like everywhere else in the capital, the bin men came every day. Tomorrow morning, Julie would phone *Reader's Digest* to tell them she had a cold.

Then she'd go to a DIY store to buy a metal saw.

Translation © Lulu Norman and Ros Schwartz

UN BON REPAS DO IT COMMENCER PAR LA FAIM . . .

STELLA DUFFY

The journey from London to Paris is easy. Too easy. I need more time, to think, prepare, get ready. Security, supposed to be so important now, these days, ways, places, is lax to the point of ease. I love it, welcome the apparent case. I believe in fate, in those big red buses lined up to knock us over, in your number being up, the calling in of one's very own pleasure boat. I do not believe that taking off our shoes at airports will save us. I show my ticket and my passport, walk through to the train, and get off at the Gare du Nord. Too easy. Too fast.

Less than three hours after leaving London I walk straight into a picket line. It seems the French staff are less fond of the lax security than I. Or perhaps they just don't like the non-essential immigrants they say Eurostar is employing. I accept the badly copied leaflet thrust into my hand and put it in my pocket. *Bienvenue en France.*

I can't face the Métro. Not yet, this early, it is not yet mid-morning. In real life I would choose to be asleep, safe in bed – not always achieved, but it would be my choice. I like my Métro in the afternoon and evening, a warm ride that promises a drink at the other end, a meal maybe, lights. In the morning it is too full of workers and students, those interminable French students, segueing from *lycée* to university with no change of clothes between. Ten years of the same manners, same behaviour day in day out, week after week of congregating in loud groups on footpaths where they smoke and laugh, and then suddenly they're in the world and somehow those ugly duckling student girls are born again as impossibly elegant Parisiennes, fine and tidy and so very boring in their classic outfits. French and Italian women, groomed to identical perfection and not an original outfit among them. So much more interesting naked. Round the picket line, out into the street. Road works, illegal taxi drivers offering their insane prices to American tourists doing London (theatre), Paris (art), Rome (Pope). The Grand Tour as dictated by the History Channel.

I cross the street in front of the station, head down, heading down towards the river. There is something about traversing a map from north to south that feels like going downhill, even without the gentle slope from here to the water. Where I'm headed it certainly feels like going downhill. I don't want to look at this city, not now. I see gutters running with water, Paris prides itself on clean streets, on washing every morning, a whore's lick of running cold to sluice out the detritus. Two young women with their hands held out sit at the edge of businessmen's feet, rattling coins in McDonalds cups. I try to pass but their insistence holds me, I say I don't speak French, they beg again in English. I insist I don't speak that either, they offer German, Italian and Spanish. I have no more words in which to plead either ignorance or parsimony, I scavenge in three pockets before giving them a dollar. It's my only defence against their European polyglossary.

Still too early. Still too soon.

Paris is small. The centre of Paris I mean. Like every other city with a stage-set centre, there are all those very many suburbs, the ones Gigi never saw, where cars burn and mothers weep and it is not heaven accepting gratitude for little girls. It is not heaven I am thanking now. I continue my walking meditation, past innumerable Vietnamese restaurants, and countless small patisseries where *pain au chocolat* and croissants dry slowly on the plates of high glass counters, and bars serve beers to Antipodean travellers who really cannot believe this city and call home to tell loved ones readying for bed about the pleasures of a beer in a café at ten in the morning. That glass pyramid can wait, this is art, this is the life.

It is a life. Another one.

There are no secrets. This isn't that kind of story. Nothing to work out. I can explain everything, will explain everything. But not yet. There are things to do and it must be done in order and the thing is, the thing is, we always had lunch first. She and I. She said it was proper, correct. That French thing, their reverence for food, an attitude the rest of the world outwardly respects and secretly despises. It's just food for God's sake, why must they make such a fuss? The linen the glass the crockery the menu the waiters with their insistence on pouring and placing and setting and getting it all right. Pattern, form, nothing deviating, nothing turning away, nothing new. Like the groomed women and the elegant men and the clean, clipped lapdogs. Nothing to surprise. So perhaps more than a reverence for just food, a reverence for reverence, reverence for form. Female form, polite form, good form, true to form. Formidable. Hah. Polyglot that.

(So strange. I can walk down the street, give money to a beggar, I can make a play on word form. I am able to buy a train ticket, sit in a bar, order wine and slowly drink the glass as if nothing has happened, as if life just goes on. Even when I know how very abruptly it can stop.)

So. Lunch. Dinner. From the Old French disner, original meaning: breakfast, then lunch, now dinner. Because any attempt to dine, at whatever time of day, will of course break the fast that has gone before, whatever time period that fast encapsulated, night, morning or afternoon. Whenever I broke my fast with her, for her, she insisted we dine first.

Some time ago I spent a weekend with friends in London. At their apartment, their flat, my

352

London friends talk about words. The English are very good at discussing words, it lessens their power, words as landmines, easily triggered, makes them readable, understandable. Stable. My friends discussed lunch or dinner, dinner or tea. If the difference were a north/south divide or a class construct. In London they talk about north and south of the river, here it is left and right. The faux-bohemian sinister and the smooth, the near, the adroit. I prefer north and south, it's harder to get lost. Apparently they've found her. Marie-Claude. Found her body. It's why I'm here.

When I tear my eyes from the gutters and the beggars and the street corners designed to frame a new picture with every stone edge, I look to high chimneys. I am not keen to see shop doors and windows, avenues and vistas, not yet. There is something I need to see first. One thing. I can manage right up and far down, to the far sides, I have the opposite of tunnel vision. There is graffiti, very high, on tall chimneys and cracked walls where one building has been leaning too long on another. This is not what they mean when they talk about a proper view, a scene in every Parisian glance, but it's diverting enough. I am eager to be diverted. I take a left turn and a right one and another left, still closer to the river, nearer the water, but a narrow road uphill now, heading east, there are more people on the street, or less space for them to walk, they touch me sometimes, their clothes, coats, swinging arms. I do not want to be touched, not like this anyway, not dressed, covered, hidden. It will all be open soon.

These side streets, those to the left and the right, east and west, are not so pretty as the views the tourists adore. She and I sat together once, in the restaurant, and listened to an old Australian couple discuss the difference between London and Paris. The woman said Paris was so much prettier, the French had done very well not to put the ugly modern beside the old beautiful. Her husband agreed. And then he said, in a tone calculated to reach the walls of stone, that the French had capitulated during the war. That is why their city was not bombed, why Paris was prettier than London. Though he agreed, the weather was better too, which helped no end. The afternoon progressed, the Australian man drank more wine, and he went on to eat every course the waiters placed before him. I cannot begin to think how much of the waiters' saliva he must also have enjoyed.

The street I find myself in now is not that pretty. It is poor and messy. Here they sell kebabs and Turkish slippers and cigarettes, and the bread in these shops was not freshly baked on the premises first thing this morning, and the fruit has not been raised lovingly in a farmer's field with only sunshine and rain to help it on its way, there are no artisans here. But this is Paris too, regardless of how few tourists see these sights. Marie-Claude showed me these streets, brought me here to explain that there were worlds where no one cared

354

if the Pyramid was appropriate or not, that the walls around Rodin's garden were too high for locals to climb, that even one euro for a good, fresh, warm croissant is too much for too many. She insisted she knew these streets well and they knew her and that what I read as amused tolerance in the faces of the half-strangers she greeted was friendship and acceptance to her. It may well have been. She is not here now for me to compare the look in her eyes against theirs and I do not have the courage to lock eyes with these men. These shopkeepers are all men. I have thought about this many times. Where are the women shopkeepers? Can they really all be at home with so many children and so much housework and such a lot to do that they do not want to run their own family business, stand alongside their loved one, work hand in hand? Or perhaps they do not have the skill to sell all this stuff? These lighters and batteries that will die in a day. These shoes made by God knows how many small children in how many village factories. Perhaps it is simply that women are better with fruit and vegetables, the items that were once, more recently, living. Maybe this is why the women run market stalls while their husbands and sons and fathers run shops. Or perhaps the women are afraid of bricks and mortar, always ready to pick up their goods and run.

She did not like to run, Marie-Claude, said it made her too hot, sticky. Sticky was not good.

Cool and calm and smooth and tidy and groomed and perfect. These things were good, right, correct. To be that way, held in, neat, arranged, arrayed, that was appropriate, proper. *Propre*. Which is clean. And it is also own, as in one's own. Thing, possession, person. One word, two meanings. So many ambiguous words. Yes. No. The things that can be read into any phrase. And accent makes a difference of course, culture, upbringing. We often fail to understand those we grew up with, our brothers and sisters, mistaking their yes for no, truth for lies, despair for hope. How much harder to understand total strangers, when they stand at shop doors, form a picket line, love you, leave you, cheat, lie, misbehave.

It was the drugs of course. It always is. She simply couldn't say no, *non, nyet, nein, ne*. That's what I hate about all those heroin chic films – one of the many things I hate about all those heroin chic films – how they always make the users look so dirty. Messy. Unkempt. She, as I have explained, was the opposite. Our media, those stupid cop shows and the angry young men films made by angrier (but so much duller, and often older than they admit) young men, has convinced us that the drugs make you ugly, your hair lank, eyes glazed, skin grey. Which could not be further from the truth in her case, her metabolism loved it, thrived on it. Yes, she might not have been able to keep going at this rate for more than another decade, she'd have had to slow down eventually, but careful, planned use, clean equipment and good veins, hungry lungs, open mouth, eager nose – her body loved it all. Loved all her body. I did. He did. They did. She did. We did. Maybe you did. I don't know, it doesn't matter, this is my side of the story. Yes. Yes. In my own time, taking your time to explain. I apologise, I know you value your time . . .

I do not mean explain as in excuse. I mean as in reason. There are always reasons.

There was the habit of course, the way ex-smokers regret the loss of a packet to open, cellophane to rip off, mouth to hold, match to strike. I know she liked the accoutrements, the little bit of this and little bit of that, the choice of vein, the pick of needles – in her job she had the pick of needles – the choice of drug too of course. For up or down or round and round.

Here it is. He was her husband, is her husband, and I her lover. Then he found out, talked to me, told me some of her other truths, and now she is dead. That's why I'm here, to help with the confirmation. She is drowned, was drowned, has been drowned. Which makes sense. She adored her bath, Marie-Claude, sadistic marquise in soothing warm. The bathroom was her shrine. It was the right place to do it, to stop, in the shrine to herself and her form and her desire. Always her desire. Not for her the current vogue for minimalist white, cool and plain. She chose the palest pale apricots and soft barely-there peaches and tiniest hints of warm flesh to tint her warm room, the warmer shades coloured her own skin tones better. Only very tiny babies look good in white, she once said, it suits their newborn blue, the veins that are not yet filled out with warm blood, blue and white and the clean absence of colour suit only a learner heart, lungs in practice. The rest of us need warmth on our skin, colour in our light. Cold winter mornings were her hardest time. Although that must have been hard too, the night last week, a warm evening and her face held under the water, nose and grasping mouth under the water, until her lungs exploded and she breathed a mermaid's breath just once.

There is a plan here. I have followed it to the letter. His letter.

I go to her restaurant, our restaurant, their restaurant. I ask for her table. The waiter, clearly a part-timer, one I have not seen before, raises an eyebrow, the maître d'. just turning from seating a couple of regulars, sees me, hurries over. Pushes the foolish young man aside, takes both my hands in his, takes my jacket, takes my arm, takes me. He is so very sorry. I must be tired. Here, here is my seat, here is her table, there are tears in his eyes. They will feed me he says, it will be their pleasure, they are so sorry. I expect they are. She was here almost every day. Not always with me. Of course the staff here are sorry.

I eat my meal. Three courses. I do not need to order, the patron himself tells the waiter to say that this is his recommendation, I agree. The patron does not come to speak with me, not yet, not now. He has work to do. and so do I. And anyway, he and I should not be seen together, not yet. Wine. Water. Coffee. Armagnac. She thought it was very foreign of me to ask for a liqueur with my coffee. The kind of thing only tourists or old ladies might do. Apparently it was inelegant, childish. I did it despite her disapproval. I do it to spite her now, despite her now.

A classic French meal, in a classic Paris restaurant. Sun shining through the mottled glass windows, lead light yellow and green and red. A businessman dines alone across from me. He too has three courses and wine and coffee, and will go to the office after his three-hour break and work steadily until dark. A wealthy tourist couple argue over the menu, which is entirely in French, it makes no concession to their cash, demands they rack their misspent youth for lost words. To my right a young couple, run from their work for half an hour here and an hour in bed, then back to run the world. To my left a middle-aged gay couple and their sleeping dog. This is civilised Paris, the dog is as welcome as the homosexuals. Everyone should eat well, taste is all. I could sit here all afternoon and stare around me. I could never go to my next appointment. I have no choice. It is fortunate that the young man who places the burning plate in front of me with a low 'attention Madame' annoys me, draws me back to this place, this time, to what happens next. He annoys me in two ways. One, as he too clearly stated, I am Madame, not Mademoiselle. He could have been kinder, generosity is always welcome. Two, I didn't think it was just the plate he was suggesting needed care. This I understand as well. Those that fed her knew her. There are many things of which I must be careful.

They are well-trained though, these young men. Young men only of course, no waitresses, the food too precious to be tainted by women's hands. These are the best. There is the waiter who, hearing a lighter fail to strike three times across the room, arrives with another lighter, working correctly. The customer wishes to light his own cigar and the waiter leaves it beside him. Two minutes later, cigar lit and smoking, the customer continues to strike again and again at his own lighter, striking against hope, the failure of his own tool still a problem despite the waiter's speedy solution to the immediate problem. And where any normal person might laugh at the man, or think him a bloated fool, too occupied in his missing flame to pay attention to his charming dinner companion, she who sits bored and irritated by his attention to pointless detail, the waiter senses the man's distress as well as the woman's slow fury, takes away the offending lighter, there is fuel in the kitchen he says, and returns just moments later, the fresh flame a bright torch to lead him on.

I love these windows, in summer they slide back to tables on the street, in winter they hold back, with their coloured glass, the worst of the grey. Today they keep me in warmth, for now. Cheese. Time is passing. Time is near. I feel it, waiting, demanding. I wonder if she felt it, if she knew her time was near. I doubt it. She had such an exquisite sense for food, for wine, for sex, for fabric – a perfect cut, an ideal line. But very little awareness at all of the kind of day-to-day passing of time that most of us understand once we have left youth behind, once we are Madame not Mademoiselle. One of the perfectly trained young men takes a short stout knife and digs me out a crumbling chunk of Roquefort. It is not what I asked for. I did not ask. In his wisdom he decided this was the correct coda to my meal. It is perfect, both creamy and crystalline, aggressive in my mouth. I also requested goat's cheese. His disdain is too well trained to show a customer of my long standing. In contrast to the Roquefort it is a smooth bland paste. The young man is right, it is no doubt wrong to eat the two together, yet, in my mouth, where they belong, the blend is perfect. The one all flavour and bite, the other a queen of texture, of touch. Marie-Claude and I were no doubt wrong together, actually perfect. No doubt perfect, actually wrong.

Through the hatch at the back of the room, I watch the only black man in the building. Daoud has spent the past hour washing dishes, will give hours yet. Sweat falls in a constant drip from his face to the scalding greasy water, his bare hands plunge repetitively, constant action, disregarded heat, all movement, all moment. I am fond of Daoud, my French is poor, his English non-existent, we have smiled to each other through his hatch, during a hundred or more lunches. I have always thanked him too, for his work. Marie-Claude said that in Algeria he had his own restaurant. She dismissed it though, said the food could not be of any standard. I am not especially fond of North African food myself, often find it cloying, heavy. But Daoud is a generous man and, much as I suspect he found her non-recognition easier to bear than my typical foreign civility to all, he did not repel my need to patronise, to charm. Today he has not once looked towards me. He must know I am here, but he has not offered me a glance. In the time-honoured tradition of silent servants and slaves everywhere, I assume he knows what was done. Or maybe he's just pissed off I haven't been here for so long. I doubt many of the customers here feel enough white liberal guilt to specifically insist that some of the tip must be shared with the dishwasher. I wonder which annoys him more? My need to expiate the colonialist's guilt with ten-euro notes or my part in the death of his boss's wife? Fortunately I do not speak his languages. He will never be able to tell me.

Near the end of the service the man himself comes out from the kitchen, the patron. A big man, with the haircut he fell in love with at the age of eighteen and hasn't cared to change for forty years, his broad body held into the black shirt and trousers beneath the stained apron, not a traditionally good-looking man by any means, but his food is beautiful. His staff must have told him I was here the moment I entered the building, but he has waited until after the meal, as always, to come and be among his guests. He walks the room, greeting customers and friends as if they were all alike. He does not come to my table, to me at her table. I understand. This is a public place, he must be careful. We must be careful.

I drain the last of my armagnac, an oil slick of golden liquid clinging to the side of the glass. I am tempted to run my finger in the residue, lick it up. I don't. I pay my bill, leave the room, I have an appointment near the river.

I leave the restaurant in the quiet street with no river view, full of food and wine and apprehension. I enjoyed the meal, it was always good to eat there, but as so often, on leaving, I wonder if a meal in an elegant room with subdued lighting and quiet conversation can ever be as ripe or delicious as the proverbial chunk of bread and lump of cheese in the fresh air with a river view? Certainly it is not that much more expensive, the river view comes at such a cost these days, every modern city in the world having finally realised the pleasure of water and priced their dirty old riverside or waterfront or sea wall or boardwalk accordingly. In the old days, when rivers were full of filth and traffic and we could not control their tides, the choice for those who could afford it was to look away from the water, to turn the backs of their buildings to it. In time though, roads became our dirty passageways and now the water is the view of choice. It is the place where people stand, gazing out and down, demanding explanation from a flow that has existed long before us and will, global warming notwithstanding, continue. The river will always continue, no matter what gets in its way. Which is how I come, at the appointed time, in the correct place, with due formality and careful ceremony, to be staring down at the bloated body of my lover.

The Seine was not made for death, there has been the occasional broken princess at its side, but by and large Parisians have done well to keep their bloodied and often headless corpses firmly in the squares, on dry land – not easy when the square is an island – but they've done pretty well. The polite man in a white coat is telling me they pulled her from the river just over a day ago, then brought her here. She had no bag, no wallet, no phone, no identifying tags. She had my name and number, written small, folded smaller, in the discreet gold charm on her discreet gold bracelet. My French is schoolgirl French at the best of times, good for menus and directions and, once, for flirting with young soldiers in New Caledonia, drunken conversations with Spanish relations where French is our only common language – confronted with Marie-Claude's bloated body and seaweed hair, the best I could do was stutter no, *non, encore non,* and eventually *oui, c'est elle –* Marie-Claude.

After that came a long time of asking questions, her home, her details, her family. I suggested they call her husband, he'd know these answers. I gave them her home number, a junior was sent to call, returned saying there was no reply. Well, no, he was probably still at work. Why did she carry my number on her? I didn't know. I didn't know she did. Were we good friends? Yes we are. Were. Were we lovers? Yes. We had been. A long time ago. When did I last see her? It has been a month, I was due to visit next week. We both have lives of our own, we did not see each other all that often. Just enough. They said they would probably have more questions for me later, there were certain things they didn't understand. I expect one of them was that the water in her lungs was not the same as the water in the river. I didn't suggest this though, if they hadn't figured it out yet, they would in time. They asked me for my passport and requested I didn't leave the city. I told them I understood. I would be as helpful as I possibly could. I cried. Both in truth and for effect. I was – am – sad for her. They were very grateful for my help. And I think they believed me, it's always hard to be sure of the truth in translation.

More than four hours had passed by the time I left. I assumed they'd have someone follow me, if only to make sure I didn't jump in the river as well. She didn't jump, they must know that. I walked a long time by the water and it was cold and damp, but that felt right. I had expected her to look bad, to look dead. I hadn't thought about her being ugly, dirty, unsuited to the place. Marie-Claude could never have been suited to that place. The light was far too white. Eventually, when I had walked far enough and long enough I found a bar and began to drink. I drank to my good health and her had death. I drank to a night in Paris when I came here with a girlfriend and left with a drunken Glaswegian squaddie. I drank to the birthday lunch I ate once in a half-broken mausoleum in Père-Lachaise, wet and alone and angry. I drank to the day I showed my mother Paris, she who never thought she'd visit the city of light and found it pretty, but wanting. She could not abide tourists, and I did not know what else to show her, not then. I did not know Paris so well then, did not have Marie-Claude's desire to guide me. I drank to him, the husband, how good he had been, how useful, how loving, how lovely. What a good husband and what a good lover. And I drank to her and to me.

Late that night, very late, I have no idea exactly how late, I was not looking at watches or clocks, paying attention to opening hours or closing, I took a taxi to a hotel I remembered from many years ago, a hotel that had nothing to do with her or with me. I leaned against the door and rang the bell until a furious night porter let me in and I bribed him with a fifty-euro note to give me a bed for the night. The young woman who had been shadowing me since I left the mortuary waited on the other side of the road until I was shown to a room, drunkenly closed my curtains and, half an hour later, turned off my light. She waited an extra fifteen minutes to be sure, and then trod wearily home. I expect she thought police work might be more fun.

And now I am sober. I am no actress, I admit that, but it is easy to persuade a young woman watching at a distance of twenty feet that grief is drunkenness, lust is love, despair merely an absence of hope.

I arrange my bag, collect my things. I was in this hotel last week, left a case with the friendly night porter. He is a better actor than his work record would show. I thought he really was angry when he answered the door. Or perhaps it was just a way for him to demand the fifty I gave him instead of the twenty we had agreed. Either way, he has done as requested. It is all here. The case with my new clothes and the wig, glasses and keys. The keys to her apartment, our apartment, the home in which I loved Marie-Claude. Our Paris home. I had thought it special and separate. I did not know there were two other keys she also kept as well as the one home she shared with her husband, other apartments she maintained. She was very good at it, the hiding, the lies. Me too. I get changed as quickly as I can, leave the front door looking like a different woman. Even if the watcher has stayed longer than I believe she has, she will not see me now.

Those people complaining at the Gare du Nord are right, it is easy to get in and out of the country. It is easy not to have your passport checked on leaving Britain when you journey to Bilbao in a friend of a friend's yacht. When you arrive in a tiny seaside village early in the morning where no one cares where you've come from, as long as you are prepared to spend money. It is simple to take one train to Barcelona and then another through to Toulouse and buy a car and drive to Paris to meet your lover's furious husband. I don't suppose, however, that entirely white group of protestors at the Gare du Nord were complaining about the travel plans of someone like me. A woman growing older becomes more and more anonymous. A wig with more grey than brunette, makeup carelessly applied, dull clothes that don't quite fit, plain and low-heeled shoes – the mask of a middle-aged mother is not a difficult disguise and the vanity pangs when passing a mirrored shop front are a price well worth paying for the gift of near-invisibility in the eyes of the young men who man the passport and customs desks.

I hurry away. To a place he has told me of. We meet there in secret, in case he too is being watched. We burn her diaries. I do this as myself, wig and false clothes removed. The light of the small fire keeps me warm, as does his skin. We are careful. It is too good to spoil, this being together. When the work is done, her words burned, he turns to the little case he brought with him, takes out a picnic of bread and cheese and wine, and we toast each other. Our very good fortune to have found each other. And we thank her, for the introduction. In an hour it will be time for me to hurry back to the hotel, hide this other me, he will need to get to the markets, to carry on, as a good widower, and a better restaurateur, in dependable grief.

It began six months ago. He called and asked me to come. So I did. He made the travel arrangements, explained what he had decided needed to happen. We met at the restaurant, late, when only Daoud was still there, hosing down the floor, sluicing away bread and blood and grease so the kitchen would be clean for the morning. Daoud was surprised to see me and, I quickly understood, disappointed. His boss shouted at him for staying so late, taking so long, told him to fuck off, there were plenty of other illegal immigrants hungry for work. I said I did not know that Daoud was illegal, the patron did not either, not for sure, but the way his employee ran from the building suggested he had made the right guess.

We had a drink. One then another. He explained how he found out, the confrontation, the confession.

First she told him about us and then, horrible and painful, for me to listen to, and – so he said – for him to explain, about the other lover. And the other. Her one husband and her three lovers. A third drink. There is a peculiar sadness in finding yourself one of many, we are human, we search for the tiny spark of difference. I was the only woman in her selection of lovers, for that I was grateful, a little.

Her latest conquest was a young man, totally besotted, telling all and sundry apparently, not aware of the rules of engagement, the tradition that his attitude ought to have been quiet and careful. The husband was worried for his wife. Worried that other people would realise what she'd been doing, uncover her lies. That they too would see her for the beautiful whore she was. I said I did not think her a whore, he said, we were the ones who paid for her charms. In kind, in love, in our constant waiting for her to return. It was not a financial transaction, but a debt paid was still a debt paid. I began to see his point of view.

I had known about her drug habits, had thought them part of her charm really, a hint of access to a world I had never understood, touching the glamour of oblivion when I touched her. He told me it was worse than that, the new young man fed her habits, enjoyed them with her. He said it was becoming a problem, she only saw me once a month, she was able to make her use look as tidy as I believed it was, but in truth, she was further gone than I realised. Further away than I realised.

He fed me that first night. After all the talking and the tears, took me out to the kitchen and fed me. A mouthful of this, half a slice of that. A little more wine, another bite, a sip again, bread, cheese, water, wine, meat, bread, wine, wine, wine, him. Fed me himself. I think now I must have known that would happen. I must have walked into the meeting that night and seen him and known we would fuck. Perhaps I had always known, right back when she first took me to the restaurant and ordered my meal for me and made my choices and fed me his food and paraded me in front of his staff. I was complicit in their married games from the beginning and maybe it was inevitable I would switch sides. Certainly it did not feel as if I made a choice that night. He fed me well, I fucked him well, we were both sick with jealousy and love for her. He was a good lover though, as was she. I am not a French woman, either classic or modern. I do not take an absurdly inflated interest in grooming or diet or accessories – she did, we were her accessories – I am, though, inordinately interested in passion. Food and passion. He was skilled in both. Both take careful preparation, he was well planned.

He became my lover, she continued as my lover. She continued with her other lovers. She became increasingly indiscreet as the fervour for her young man increased. As I explained, she did not look like the classic televisual drug addict, the more she played with the young man though, the more he enjoyed her illicit largesse, the wider her mouth, spilling secrets. Eventually her husband decided the time had come. *Aux grands maux les grands remèdes*. Cliché is so French.

I would come to visit her, tell her I knew about her young lover. We would arrange to meet him. There would be a scene, somewhere public. I would force from her confession of their desire. Then I would reveal I also knew of the other lover. Daoud, the washer of filthy dishes in her husband's kitchen. She would deny, fight, shout, and finally, worn down by my heartbreak, agree. Admit. Admit in front of the young man, who would not be sober or clean, who would vow to do something about it. And when her body was found, a day or a week later, the mark of suspicion would be ready on his brow.

It was complicated, uncertain, not at all possible to guarantee what would happen. And yet, in the hotel room bed, in his wide arms, with his food in my belly and his kiss in my mouth, I was persuaded it could all work out. If not exactly as planned, then at least go some of the way towards making the potential true. All we really needed was for her to admit and for him to become angry.

I suppose I could have said no. At any time really, I could have taken my jealousy and fury home with me, travelled away from that city and never seen her again, left them to their desire and bitterness and passion. But I agreed with him, it wasn't fair, she wasn't fair. One understands the role of spouse, or of mistress, either of these makes sense. And a spouse knows there is the chance to be cuckolded, a mistress understands she is not first. But a third lover? A fourth? He was right. She was taking the piss. And besides, after just a short while, I quite liked the idea of having him to myself. He was – is – a very attractive man. If not conventionally so. But then I am not, unlike so many Frenchwomen, a lover of convention.

And it appears the plans of her husband, my lover-chef, have worked. I dressed in the disguise he chose for me, travelled as another woman, hid in this city and drowned another woman. Now she is dead and she is not beautiful, the drowned are not beautiful. I have been here a week. First the police came to speak to Daoud, but he had an alibi, he was washing dishes. Plenty of people saw him doing so. The husband had an alibi – he was working, in the kitchen, talking to his customers, creating art from raw ingredients, feeding the discerning masses. The young man did not have an alibi. He was sitting at home that night, alone, shooting up with the heroin substitute she brought him from her office, using the syringe she brought him from her office. Her husband told the police about her lovers, her drug habits, her hidden life. He did not tell the police how we parcelled her up in restaurant waste bags and carried her to his van, more often used for transporting sides of beef and mutton, and we took her to the river and we let her fall. So much is hidden under cover of darkness. And London has more CCTV cameras than any other city in Europe. But not Paris, those ugly cameras spoil the view. I told the police about our relationship. They were surprisingly ready to believe a respected medical professional could behave in such a manner, for them, the addition of lust to substance multiplied readily into disaster. It made it simple too, for them to understand the jealousy of her young lover, his head swimming, his hands holding her beneath the water. Crime passionel is no longer a defence of course, but I trust his time in prison may help him with his addiction problems. *Tout est bien qui finit bien.*

I did not have an alibi. But then I was not in France. My passport proves it, the strong security both our countries now pride themselves on proves it. There may have been a middle-aged woman in a grey wig and ill-fitting clothes at some point. She may have been in France, in Paris, but she was not noticed.

I miss her, of course, though not too much, I suspect we were nearing the end of our time anyway, everything has its time. And I have my new lover now, he who feeds me so well. Too well almost. It is lucky my own husband and children demand so much energy at home, keeping me busy, I might get fat otherwise. Family is so important, isn't it?